IN SEARCH OF
SPICE

D1333821

REX SUMNER

Published in June 2015 by

MyVoice Publishing
www.myvoicepublishing.co.uk

ISBN 978-1-909359-26-0

Note: this is a work of fiction. No characters are based on actual
people, alive or dead; policies and actions of countries and
governments depicted bear no relation to actual historical fact.
Customs of various people are from the authors imagination and
have no bearing on actual customs of any people.

Contents

Acknowledgements

I would like to give particular thanks to my wonderful team of readers who have provided valuable reaction to this book. Without you guys this work would be very different. I have thanked particular contributions by naming a character after you, although their disgusting habits and interesting behaviour bear no relation to your own.

I would also like to thank the many authors, too many to list, whom I have enjoyed over the years, and whose work has of course influenced my own.

Particular thanks to my sons who were the first to read the manuscript and influence the early direction of the book, and to my long suffering wife who has delighted in my enthusiasm and encouraged me to write for decades.

I must emphasize that you should not expect to find any of the customs described in this book anywhere in the world. Yes, I have borrowed liberally from many cultures but adapted the customs to suit my world. You may rightly recognise Fijian customs, however the Fijians are a very modest people, unlike the Vituans.

The interesting custom from Malacca, while being historical fact in our world, is unlikely to persist to this day. The custom of the Sung to carry a number of courtesans with them is directly borrowed from historical Chinese accounts. Personally, I think it was a much more civilised approach to meeting new people than the Western one of overbearing force.

I am not a swordsman, Asmara would run me through in a moment. While I know some terms, specialist moves like the Heron Strike are entirely my imagination, not designed for imitation.

Welcome to Harrhein and please enjoy a world vibrant in its differences.

Rex Sumner
Kuala Lumpur 2015

Harrhein

Over the past five hundred years, the kings of Harrhein consolidated the kingdom by conquest, bringing Fearaigh and Galicia into the country.

Coillearnacha stayed separate, with another race, Elves, occupying the western shores. An uneasy truce prevails, with frequent raids from both sides of the border.

No one knows what happens in the far north. Expeditions founder on the enmity of native peoples.

To the east lie the islands and peninsulas of the warlike Spakka, who delight in raiding Harrhein and capture every ship they can, while in every other direction lies limitless ocean.

To break free, the people of Harrhein need to make a deep sea vessel and sail over the edge of the world.

Extracted from the Royal Records in Praesidium

Part of the Charter for raising the Queen Rose, the list of those brave and adventurous souls who underwrote the cost of the expedition.

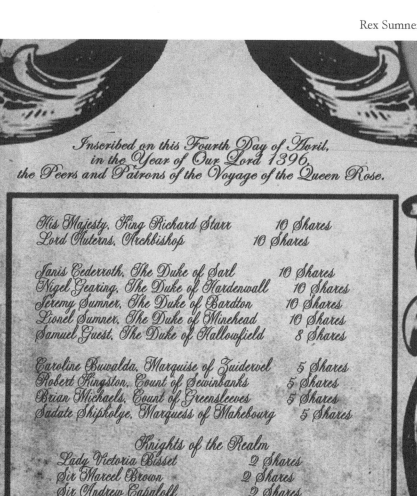

Inscribed on this Fourth Day of Avril,
in the Year of Our Lord 1396,
the Peers and Patrons of the Voyage of the Queen Rose.

His Majesty, King Richard Starr	10 Shares
Lord Auterns, Archbishop	10 Shares
Janis Cederroth, The Duke of Sarl	10 Shares
Nigel Gearing, The Duke of Hardenwall	10 Shares
Jeremy Sumner, The Duke of Bardton	10 Shares
Lionel Sumner, The Duke of Minehead	10 Shares
Samuel Guest, The Duke of Hallowfield	8 Shares
Caroline Buwalda, Marquise of Zuidervel	5 Shares
Robert Kingston, Count of Sewinbanks	5 Shares
Brian Michaels, Count of Greensleeves	5 Shares
Sadate Shipkolye, Marquess of Mahebourg	5 Shares

Knights of the Realm

Lady Victoria Bisset	2 Shares
Sir Marcel Brown	2 Shares
Sir Andrew Capaloff	2 Shares
Sir Robert Carter	2 Shares
Sir Andreas Esbech	2 Shares
Sir Peter Finnis	2 Shares
Sir Samuel Gearing	2 Shares
Sir Kell Martin	2 Shares
Sir Austin Merritt	2 Shares
Lady Alexandra Myers	2 Shares
Sir Adrian Newton	2 Shares
Sir Ronald Strachan	2 Shares
Sir Andrew Wallas	2 Shares

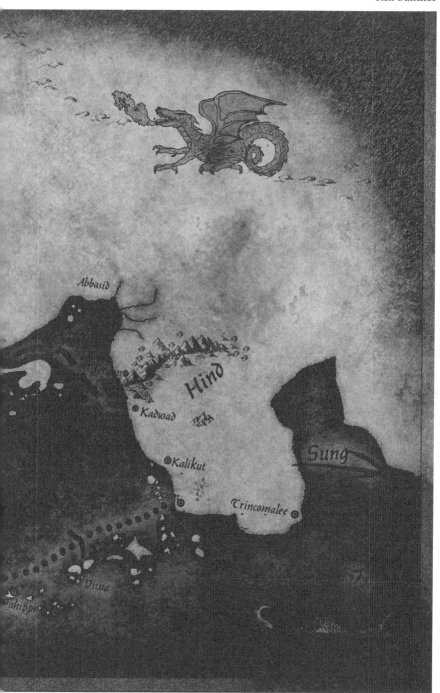

Treason

A tall austere man walked through the doorway from the inn and spoke to the booth's sole occupant. "Hello Victor. Have you picked the Champion yet?"

The elderly man turned from his seat in the gallery overlooking the fighting court and smiled.

"Oliver! Oliver Bouvier! What a surprise, and just in time, my wine glass is empty and the bottle is gone. The Navarre red is excellent. As to the blades, well I think we are going to see some unusual upsets today."

Oliver turned and gestured to a serving girl. "A bottle of Navarre red, if you please." He seated himself beside Victor, easing his spare frame into the seat and looked with disapproval into the salle. "A cryptic clue as always. What have you seen?"

"There's a girl come through the qualifying, don't know who she is but her craftsmanship is awesome. She has been going through her opponents like chaff, and one opponent even resigned rather than face her. She is fighting next, up against a professional from Lansbridge, her first real test. Here she comes now."

A girl strode out of the fighters tunnel into the courtyard, tall and elegant, moving lithely like a panther. She was slim and willowy, with broad, muscled shoulders, a little heavier on the right. She wore the leather and chain mail armour of a bladesman, plus a mask over her eyes, enough to obscure recognition. Bright, dark red hair was visible under her hauberk and a beautiful rapier grew out of her hand as if it was permanent.

"A beauty, and young, I reckon. Who is she?"

"No idea, but she has been damn well taught. Strong too, see how tall she is. Only girl to make it through qualifying."

A buzz went through the crowd and a cheer arose from the open area below

"What's that they are calling her? Russet? And Red Rattna? That awful barbarian queen who bathes in her victims' blood? Don't we know her real name and background?"

"No, she's a mystery entrant. She has red hair and a quick blade, that's enough for the crowds. See, she wears a small mask, as is her right. It is clear she is a Noble's daughter who has worked with an expert bladesman. She uses a rapier very well, going through all the parries fluidly and automatically. In one of the bouts she met a compound attack by a simple displacement combined with an envelopment and took him."

"I have no idea what you said."

"Ah, Oliver, if you are going to watch fencing, you should learn the terms."

"I don't care about the terms or fencing, I only came to speak with you. Disgraceful they let a girl compete."

"I think like everyone else you hope to see a little blood, and I am sure even a puritan like you would enjoy a girl's blood even more."

"Or a lot. Even better. Damn Papists, happy to see them all die. Not sure if the crowd want to see the girl's blood or see her shed others blood." He mused this last, looking around at the crowd and stroking his prominent nose.

"Well, I think they will be disappointed. She's a clean fighter; she hits the marks perfectly and never takes a risk. At least not yet. She may have to at this level. Just look at Morten. You can see he won't give her an inch."

The fighters were ready, toeing the line and raising their swords in salute. Morten had a longsword. He held it with both hands, his left hand cupped around the pommel. The referee called the start and the jury stooped to watch for hits. Morten came forward carefully and made a small feint, which Russet ignored. He gave a beat to her blade and stepped back in surprise at the speed of the counter-beat. His eyes narrowed and he lunged into the tiny, high opening presented, then desperately tried to bring the sword down in a parry as she slipped his blade, ducked to the floor and sliced up at his hand by the wrist, raising a fountain of 'blood'; actually red ink in small sachets strapped to each bladesman's body. The referee's whistle went abruptly and both players stopped.

"Damn! She's good," said Victor. "She won it with that. Very, very clever and she played for it perfectly."

"What? Over? Why, she barely touched him."

The crowd was murmuring, unsure what had happened, though a canny few were making their way to the bookmakers, strategically placed near the lanes leading into the crowded square.

"Tendons" said Victor with a smile. "That sachet marks the tendon, either he fences now with his left hand or he retires. Morten will retire, he can't fence left handed. Not at this standard."

"But, but it was just a touch!"

"It doesn't take much to slice open a tendon, that's why it is protected. It takes one hell of an accurate blademaster to make that shot - she had a tiny, tiny area to hit, the crease which allows the wrist to turn, which was moving damn fast but she hit it."

The referee examined Morten's wrist, but Morten only had eyes for the girl, with a stunned smile on his face. His voice carried.

"I misjudged you, ma'am. I congratulate you on your win, quite brilliant. You totally foxed me. May I have the honour of knowing my victor's name?"

The girl smiled. "Thank you, sir, for your kind words. I fear for now I must keep my identity secret a little longer, you will understand later. Good fortune." Her voice was low and melodious, but it carried clearly round the sale.

The referee spoke quietly to Morten, who responded firmly, "I do."

The referee turned to the crowd. "A tendon shot wins the bout for the Mystery Entrant. Morten retires, declining to fence on with his left."

The crowd did not erupt. They muttered, as they felt a little cheated at not seeing more of her. The lucky ones nodded their heads and headed off to the bookies to collect their winnings. The mutterings increased, a little angry, but deflated when the rough crowd outside the Upturned Oxcart pub began to cheer and shout, waving their beer pots.

"Well done Russet!"

"The Red Rattna strikes again!"

"Fastest win for the Red Rapier!"

"Gives us a kiss for luck!"

At this last, the girl smiled and blew kisses to them, causing the noise to double.

"Umph," said Victor, "she is very young. She should stay focused - her next match is against the Champion - she needs to be ready for him, he is superb, highly skilled. Come Oliver, I shall let you buy me lunch and another bottle of this excellent red and I shall explain what happened."

"Never mind, I don't need to know." Oliver was impatient. He looked around. They were in a private booth of the Drunken Courtier, a public house; the veranda overlooked the raised fighting dais, with the door open so the waiters and waitresses could see them. "Is this place secure?"

"Of course it is," Victor glared at him. "I have more to lose, consorting with the likes of you. I don't want anyone seeing you, let alone hearing what we talk about."

"Very well." Oliver didn't look convinced. "So, what is the latest news?"

"All in good time. So impatient, it is not polite to discuss business till after we have eaten."

"I pay you enough not to have to put up with your foibles." Oliver hated Victor for his upper class smoothness, but masked the hatred behind impatient anger.

"Nonsense. And I am going to need more; I have to keep up my position in society. You must follow the customs or you will stand out, and the waiter may report it. He will think it deuced odd if we are talking business over food." Victor waved at the waitress through the doorway. She nodded and moved off.

Victor leaned forward. "I spoke yesterday with a friend from Westport. He tells me you can forget Fearaigh."

"I did not expect anything else. They do not love us."

"They don't care much for your ways, they prefer the old religions, trade with the Elves and they love the Starrs. Half the army is from Fearaigh."

"Tell me something I don't know, and show me the money is not wasted." Oliver's eyes gleamed in his pale face.

As Victor started to speak, a young man pushed his way into the room. "Hello, gentle sirs, my name is Andy. Can I help you with your order?"

"Excellent!" Beamed Victor. "You can indeed. First we need another bottle of the Navarre, then tell me the menu. Who is the chef today?"

"Mrs Jenks has the oven today, sir; she recommends the pheasant pie, or the steak and oyster pie. Otherwise I could do you some nice wood pigeons, or there is some ham, and I think if I hurry I can rustle up a lamprey, as it's you, sir."

"Lamprey? Mrs Jenks? Really, ah yes that would be wonderful - I shall have it with a couple of pigeons, they go well together and Mrs Jenks cooks them superbly. The Navarre will complement the pigeon beautifully. Will you share with me, my friend?" he asked Oliver.

"Thank you, no, that would be far too rich for me. Some light chicken broth, bread and a bit of cheese." Oliver tried to smile, which was scary.

"Certainly, gentle sirs," nodded Andy, "it will be about half of the hour, if that is acceptable?" He minced out and they heard him snap at the serving girl to bring the wine.

"Count Rotherstone is on everyone's lips," murmured Victor, wiping his mouth on a napkin with precise care. "He is considered the leader of the revolutionary cadre, even though he does nothing overtly. Raphael is not taken seriously, though a significant number of invitations are arriving for him."

"Invitations? So what? Be serious, man!" Oliver stared at him.

Victor sighed. "Prince Raphael is single. The increases in invitations are coming from mothers of unmarried girls. They are hedging their bets, offering their daughters in the hope of catching a king. The increase means many of the upper classes think there is a chance he may inherit. A good chance."

"Ah, I see." Oliver was actually impressed by the subtlety, but took care to hide that. "How many are converting to the true religion?"

"That I cannot know, it is not widely talked about and very private. But there has been a sea-change in outlook. It is no longer derided, but talked about as just another religion. As you know, most of them care little for religion in any form, so this is a good sign." Victor smiled and sipped his wine, building suspense before he delivered the good news. "The merchant boys are successful as officers. It is agreed to allow many more of them to join, and their competence allows the nobility to move their sons to the City Guard rather than fighting regiments." He sneered. "The weaker, diluted nobility, of course. They don't want to fight the barbarians on the northern border, or meet Spakka raids in the east. They are happy to let your lads do that for them, and the rate of retirement is up hugely."

"Very good," Oliver was pleased. He placed a large purse on the table, which vanished into Victor's pouch. "And the Palace Guard?"

"Oh, no problem there. I lunched with the adjutant three days ago and on my advice he is taking on a cadre of not just officers, but guardsmen as well. You will own it within a few years. Worth an extra purse, I fancy!" He watched greedily as Oliver reluctantly placed a smaller purse on the table.

"What is the King's attitude to the new parliament? Has it changed?"

"Not really. He's not convinced they can do anything worthwhile, and isn't paying much attention to them. The Princess is a different matter. She's been bending his ear about it and I understand she is now forbidden to talk about parliament at meals. I believe she is spending time listening to them in session?"

"Yes, she does. I don't think she likes me very much." Oliver smiled with satisfaction.

Victor took a larger sip of wine, to stop himself commenting on the princess's exemplary taste.

Oliver did not think he would get much more from the old courtier, and decided to leave. Excellent news on the officers, which would speed the process, and even better news on the guard. He thought briefly of his own commission, sitting in his pocket, and wondered when he would take it up. The king would not like to find out members of parliament were officers in the new army they were raising.

The daughter was an issue. She would work out the possibilities, and they needed to debate some sensitive issues in the coming weeks. He decided to bring forward the plan to remove her and install Raphael. He stood abruptly, seeing Victor's raised eyebrow at his silence, and threw a coin on the table. "That's for lunch. I shall meet with you again in a month's time. Get a table at the archery tournament, I shall find you." He pulled on his cloak and left.

Victor sighed with pleasure and ruminated on the ills of life that had destroyed his investments and forced him into taking the puritan coin. To say nothing of the wretched boy who had sucked him into this mess in the first place. Still, he could see the way the wind was blowing and it would be important to come out on the right side.

It was the last bout of the day and had stretched to half an hour, the longest bout so far. The Champion, Ariston, was moving easily, but giving the Red Queen huge respect. Both players were level on 11 points - 12 was the victory target. They had been on 11 for the last ten minutes, an unprecedented time with no score.

Ariston was a well-muscled man in his late twenties, approaching six foot tall, balanced and moving well. He was still smiling as he fought, but his grey eyes showed his care, watching the girl like a cat, riveted on her face. The sweat rolled down his face and his shirt was stained dark. Most was sweat but a few minor sachets had burst.

The girl was laughing. Not all the time, but you could see the joy on her face as she moved lightly and easily, matching Ariston"s every move. This did not bother Ariston; you could see he loved every moment of the challenge. The crowd was hushed. This was a bout such as you were lucky to see once in five years, and to see two blade masters enjoying each other's skill was unusual to say the least. Once Ariston had skidded on a flower thrown from the crowd, and the Red Queen had backed up and let him recover.

Victor's face wreathed in smiles as he watched with reverence. He had a crowd of his friends on his veranda with him now.

Ariston launched an attack in the high line, arm raised, forcing the parried response higher and higher, to the full extension of the girl's reach. In a moment, it would be too high and he would overcome her as he pushed her off balance. A trick he would not have tried had he not sensed her tiring. She went from the high quarte parry, flowing smoothly into a derobement, trapping and forcing his blade outwards as she went forward and leapt impossibly high into the air, pushing his blade well out of line. The forward movement and the jump prevented him from disengaging and he started to back-pedal.

The girl's blade disengaged, her foot came up high to replace it and continued pushing his blade out of the way and then her rapier arced back towards his eye.

The crowd sighed, and Victor breathed, "The Heron Strike! That I should live to see it."

At the very peak of her leap, her rapier swept down to his face and Ariston literally saw death. Somehow, she stopped the stab a fraction from the eye, and alighted with a small, victorious smile, her point resting on his cheek. Ariston relaxed and with care brought his sword back to the en garde position, almost touching her arm in the process. He swung the sword round in the loser's salute.

The arena erupted with shouts and screams, people throwing all sorts into the salle. Mainly flowers, some jewellery, even fruit.

The referee went into a huddle with the four men of the jury, rapidly joined by the tournament director.

Ariston went to one knee, and spoke quietly so only the girl could hear. "My thanks, my Lady, for the finest fight I have been privileged to enjoy. It has been an honour to cross blades with you, and I know you will win this tournament."

"You are too kind, good sir. I cannot tell you the pleasure it has given me. I had quite forgotten the tournament, to be honest."

They grinned at each other in mutual respect. The referee called for quiet, repeatedly, until the noise fell. The tournament director stepped up and the crowd stilled, uncertain. This was not expected.

"We have a little difficulty here. The Strike of the Heron may be a winning blow in a real fight, but in tournament the eyes are sacrosanct and use of the foot in this manner is illegal. By making this attack, the mystery entrant has struck a foul blow. Although the Champion has ceded defeat, we cannot accept it. The score remains 11 each and the mystery entrant must be disqualified."

At first, there was a stunned silence. The crowd started to hiss and rise. Before it could reach any volume, the girl stepped forward and stood beside the tournament director, who was looking decidedly nervous.

"Good people of Praesidium, listen to me. I accept the director's decision. He is correct, my actions were outside the rules of the tournament and I apologise I was carried away by the bout and performed an illegal move. It is only right I concede defeat to a very worthy Champion."

The crowd clearly disagreed with her.

She held up her hand for silence, and slowly got it. Behind her mask, her green eyes flashed. "I have made my decision. It is the right one. You will accept it, for now I shall reveal who I am and you will realise that once you know, I cannot carry on."

That got the crowd's attention, sure enough and they fell silent as she raised a hand to the half mask that covered her eyes and the top of her face. She ripped it off and shock rippled round the crowd. A small, square, determined chin and the flashing eyes dominated and enlivened a plain face, high cheekbones and famous nose. The tournament director, the jury, the referee and Ariston dropped to their knees, the Champion with a huge grin on his face.

"Arise," she smiled at him.

"Your Highness, we are well served by our future Queen, both in your martial abilities and your wisdom."

"Regrettably I am unable to continue tomorrow, for my father does not know I am here. I intended to step back today, whatever the outcome and hoped to sneak back to the Palace without his knowledge. I fear that is no longer an option."

Ariston extended his arm. "May I have the honour of escorting you to your changing quarters, Highness?"

She smiled, placed her hand delicately and lightly on his forearm and they walked off the salle to a standing ovation.

Victor turned to his friends. "That was quite incredible. I think we need a barrel of wine, never mind a bottle. Ha! I had a feeling it was the Princess."

"You say that now. I didn't see you rushing to the bookies for a bet." Francis was a fellow aficionado and a long time crony.

"That might have been injudicious to say the least. I believe there was quite a lot of money laid on her being Red Rattna's granddaughter. There was no money on her being our own Royalty."

"I should think not. Who would have guessed that pretty girl could do that?"

"Anyone in the army, for a start. She caused quite a stir when she served on the frontier." Adrian was a recently retired soldier.

"The Princess? She fought in the army? You're joking." All the others looked at him in astonishment.

"Indeed I am not, but your response just shows how out of touch you are here in the capital. We've always had a fighting monarchy here in Harrhein, although the women try to turn the nobility into stuffed cockerels."

"Well, if you say so. Anyway, that winning strike. It was impressive, to be sure, but why is the Heron Strike so special? It looked spectacular, why isn't it done more frequently?" Bruno did not understand fencing, or fighting. But was a keen follower of the elder men and their largesse.

"Hah! Looks are deceptive." Victor was delighted for the opportunity to explain. "Usually when you get so high, you open up your body to your opponent who will always get his blade back and skewer you with ease. You have no defence. But she was cunning in a way no man could be. Incredible elasticity of body, she leapt high to keep his blade in contact with her own and how she got her foot up there, I don't know. Once she got her foot on his blade, he couldn't get back to take advantage as she went on the attack. Mind you, doubt anyone over the age of twenty could get their foot up that high."

Count Rotherstone sat at his desk reading a report on the peccadilloes of a baron he planned to subvert. A hesitant knock on the door revealed his secretary, a young priest called Thomas who was terrified of him.

"Ah, three messages have come in, sir," stammered Thomas, as those cold grey eyes looked down that long nose at him. He always thought the Count looked like a grey heron, about to strike and skewer him, "Two from the brothel in Piccadilly and one from the Candler."

"Read me the Candler's message." The Count returned his gaze to the report.

"Yes, sir." Thomas looked down at the message. "A gentleman came into the shop and purchased two ash black candles." The Count looked up sharply, and Thomas jumped. "He commented that the kitten was causing trouble again and it was time to drown her." Thomas looked blankly at the message. "That's all there is, sir."

"It is sufficient," breathed Count Rotherstone. "Put the messages on the desk and leave. Ask Bessin to attend me."

Princess Asmara Starr relaxed in her bath, smiling and wincing a little as her hand maid worked on her scratches and pulled muscles. The door opened and a girl slipped in, coming up and sitting by the bath. The princess looked at her and raised a sculpted eyebrow.

"Asmara, trouble. You must leave. There is to be an assassination attempt on you tonight, and it is serious enough that I don't think you can avoid it."

The Princess sat up. "Call Belkin, I need to talk to him. Enough, Sophie, get the towels. Luce, who's behind it?" No fuss, the Princess went from luxuriating to business in seconds, her mind rapidly scanning through her options.

"Well, it is supposed to be your cousin, Raphael."

"He's a dolt and a coward."

"I already told Belkin to come; I knew you would want to speak to him. Told him it was urgent."

"Well done, good thinking. Who's been breathing up Raphael's bottom?"

"You know very well it will be Count Rotherstone. He controls everything Raphael does and with him on the throne he will be the actual king."

Asmara blinked from under the towel. "My father? Is he alright? Is there an attempt on him as well?"

"No, they see you as the danger. With you out of the way, Raphael will have time to ingratiate himself with your father, get named as heir and then they will finish him. But if you stay and fight, it could widen and drag him in."

The door opened and a man came in. He saw the Princess' nakedness and reddened. "I apologise, your Highness, this woman told me to come instantly." He started to turn to leave the room.

"Oh, don't be so silly, Belkin. This is too important to worry about false modesty. This woman is my spymaster, uh, mistress. Tell it all now, Luce."

Belkin ensured he kept his eyes on Luce's face, wondering that she looked vaguely familiar but he could not put a name to her.

Luce grimaced, living her life in the shadows meant she did not want to be known to anyone.

"Rotherstone has given Raphael a Mage, a powerful one. He is bespelling the guards at this moment. It means if they see the

Princess, they will see instead an Elf Crone Witch, and will call for archers and shoot her from a safe distance. That's to ensure you can't escape. At the same time they have a group of killers organised, disguised as elves, which will raid the palace - specifically your room. Your own men will think you part of that party."

"How long will the spell last?" The Princess grasped the plan straight away, wincing at the thought of the guardsmen, whom she loved and with whom she trained at arms, killing her when she knew she would not be able to strike back.

"I don't know, but it could be a week. You cannot hide from your guardsmen for even a day."

"If there is an attack, I need to be with my father, supporting him and helping him. This is a really bad time, I am sure the new parliament is up to something."

Belkin grunted. "You trust this woman?"

"With my life"

"Humph. That's exactly what it is. Very well, crude it may be, but you cannot fight it without a hundred guardsmen, and many will die. Moreover, if they are all bespelled, your most loyal men will kill you. Your father has managed to run the Kingdom perfectly without you for the last twenty years." Asmara scowled at this. "He can sort out the problem much more effectively if he doesn't have to worry about your safety. We must flee to Westport. Fearaigh will be safe."

"No. I will flee, you must stay." Asmara did not like Belkin's words, but she had to accept their truth. She worried that her father needed her and liked to think she was important, so his words hurt. Then glee rose up inside her as her worries about her father diminished. Adventure! She would be out and away from insistent tutors, annoyingly insipid chaperones and dubious dancing masters, free as a bird. No way would she go to Westport. "Go to your rooms and sleep. If they don't see me, they won't be able to do anything. Tomorrow I shall be gone, Luce. So go to Belkin at 10 am. Belkin, request a private audience with the King, tell him what has happened. Introduce him to Luce. Luce, you must in future report to Belkin and the King."

"No, As. Too many people." Luce replied, causing Belkin to look shocked, both at the refusal and the nickname. "I shall report to Belkin, he can tell the King. We will protect him till you return." She looked balefully at Belkin. "You, sir, will need further protection if you are close to the King. I am surprised they didn't think to work out something about you tonight, but Raphael was always sloppy. They may not make the same mistake twice. I suggest you don't see the King for a few days, and ensure he sees you no more than once a month, or you put yourself in danger. The King will understand. He's a smart one. Tell him if you are killed, I shall appear at his bedside with news."

She turned to Asmara, who was nodding. "Now, we must cut your hair and choose your clothes. What will you be?" Belkin noticed she did not ask where she was going and started to ask the question, then thought better of it. The Princess was clearly in complete accord with this strange woman.

"Yes, will shoulder length be enough? I thought to be a mercenary."

"No, you will need it short. Where's that black hair dye? Get a bit of dirt on your face. Keep it there. It will hide your cheekbones and make you look more common. Don't take many clothes, get dirty, change your walk, you know the score, like when we went to Sarumstown."

Belkin started, and wondered if he had an answer to a question which had bugged him for the last year. The Princess had managed to disappear for a whole month before reappearing very content and ignoring the angry instructors and courtiers.

"I need my rapier and bow. The leathers are in the cupboard over there. Sophie, get them, then leave. The less you know the better."

"Mistress, I am coming with you. And I must cut your hair. You will need somebody to look after you. I could be your squire."

"Hah! More likely my dog-robber. I won't have a squire. No, it is too dangerous for you and I will travel too fast. I need to be 100 miles away by dawn and you can barely ride. And you would cut my hair too well. Leave now, take a holiday and visit your parents, give it three months then come back and see Belkin. He will give you a job. Here, take this purse, it will see you through."

Sophie burst into tears, but went and got the clothing, then left, still crying.

Belkin watched her dress, and spoke. "Don't take Farstrider. I know you love him, but everyone knows he is your horse. There is a new grey in the stall three down from him. He's a good horse, take him instead. I will go down now and get rid of the stable boy, then tack him up."

"Wait! Don't take the passageway. Wait a moment while Luce finishes my hair. Luce, take him through the secret ways. I will follow in a moment."

Luce nodded, finished hacking her long hair off and reached for the hair dye. "Belkin, bag up her hair, please. I will dispose of it so nobody knows they should look for a short-haired woman."

She pushed Asmara's head over the bath, rubbed the dye well into her hair. "Let that set while you ride. Find a horse trough in the morning and rinse it." She put the pot in the bag with the hair and rose, turned and grabbed Asmara, hugging her for a moment before turning away and beckoning to Belkin, who swallowed as he saw her tears. He followed her out of the room through a door that opened when she touched something by the fireplace. It was dark in the passageway, but Luce produced a taper from a crevice and led off. She looked back over her shoulder once, "She's like my younger sister. She saved me from the gutter and the whorehouse. I owe her everything. Have no worries, I will do what I can."

She was off, before he could respond and he trailed along as best he could, wondering how she got her information.

Asmara finished pulling on the leathers, retrieved her bow and rapier, pulled out a fat purse and a money belt, slipped them on and followed. Her face was alight with joy, she had worked out where she was going and could not wait. She reminded herself she must look grave and concerned when she said goodbye.

Nobody spoke in the stable, Belkin had not only saddled and tacked the grey, but had chosen a beaten up saddle and old tack, though well oiled. He eased open the door, looked outside, and nodded.

Asmara saluted them , and was through the door, vanishing into the night.

Belkin turned to Luce. "Uh, we forgot to check how she will get in touch with us. So we can tell her when to come back."

Luce allowed a faint smile. "Don't worry about it. She knows how to get in touch with me, and she will contact you if I'm gone. I expect she will send us both a message and another for the King.

We've prepared for this day for the last six months since we got a pipeline into Rotherstone's plans."

She wiped her eyes and was gone.

Fearaigh

Mot raised her head , looking at the trees and her hackles rose. A big, tawny dog with black patches around her eyes, resembling a wolf. Patraigh instinctively pressed his knees to turn his horse and drifted towards the copse at which she stared. He rode along a low ridge overlooking a green valley through which a large cattle herd moved. As he approached the trees, wolves ghosted out to overlook the herd. Pat leant back, unstrapped the short spear from under his leg and squeezed his legs to urge the horse into a gallop, fearing he would be too late.

The lead wolf turned and inspected him, its tongue lolled from one side of its mouth while yellow eyes gleamed, even from the distance. Without thinking, Pat leaned forward and squeezed his legs again, urging the horse to top speed, barely conscious of Mot racing alongside him. The wolves watched him come for a moment, then as one, turned and raced away, vanishing into the birches. He slowed as he came to where they disappeared and Mot cast around. She checked in with her eyes .

"Enough, girl, we've given them a scare," he said, his voice loud enough for the dog to hear.

Pat moved through the trees, his grey eyes intent on the ground, looking for tracks. Nothing. Mot circled ahead, nose down, tail waving. He thought it through. The pack were not scared, they were being wary and they would be hungry. They would come back.

What would they need? They did like that cliff. It was not high, but enough to kill cattle that bolted and they knew it. Easiest way to kill cattle was with gravity, no risk to the wolf and wolves did not take risks. The cliff was still on the far side of the herd, and if the wolves got ahead, they could still bolt them towards it. However, they would be wary now, and would check out the land first. That meant the hill ahead, only place they could go.

Pat squeezed his horse into motion, and cantered towards the hill, Mot following behind. He knew he needed to get there first. He was sixteen years old, a tall, black haired boy who thought he knew it all. He did know animals, better than most, and was elf-taught in the woods.

He learnt a lot about wolves as a child, and lost all fear of them. The bitch was the true leader of the pack, not the dog. He might be the fighter, but he did what she told him, not that Pat could understand or hear her speak but it felt right when he put it that way.

Now, in the autumn, the time the ranchers took the crop of young cattle to market, was the time the young wolves learnt to hunt. The old wolves taught them the easiest ways - and that included chasing herds over cliffs. They also taught them caution, but with some youngsters, they had to learn the hard way. Just like people.

He came up to the top of the hill and reined in, looking down the far slope with a sprinkling of young trees over it, all at an incline with the prevailing wind off the sea. Off to his left he could see the herd snaking out towards the gap in the hills, beyond which the trail led into town and the first farms.

Mot growled, and he saw the first wolf at the same time. It stopped and snarled at him. Pat unclipped his bow from its holster and strung it, pulling a long arrow from the quiver, checking that it was a broadhead. That would stop a wolf, stun it on the head or chest, but needed to be sent on the slant if it was to slip between the ribs for a killing strike.

The wolf watched him for a moment, turned and loped away, unhurried. He saw it in full view heading away from the herd in a direction from which it would be hard to come back and attack. He smiled. The wolf was sending him a message - Pat was too ready and too dangerous. That wolf had seen a bow used before.

He watched as other wolves appeared out of nowhere and followed the leader, and switched his attention to the low bushes. Would the young wolves go too? Or would they itch to find out why the older wolves had given up?

A bush moved, and he smiled. Smoothly, he drew, held the arrow for a moment as he checked the wind was steady, and released. As he watched the flight, he replaced the arrow. It went in a graceful arc off to the left of the bush, caught the wind and swung round to thump through the bush. There came a yelp and a wolf was running, unhurt, untouched, but shocked and startled, away and after the others, joined by three more, all with their tails down.

He grinned, and decided retrieving the arrow would be more trouble than it was worth; he did not want to get off the horse in case another youngster was still waiting.

He sat on his horse, watching the pack disappear. The horse watched as carefully as he did, a lot more concerned than Pat. He waited there until the herd passed the danger point, then galloped down to the rear and set Mot to hurrying up the last of the cattle.

His father came round to him and said, "All clear?"

"Yup. Too late for them to do anything now, they can't get them to the ravine so they'll give up."

His father looked blank for a moment, and said, "The ravine? The cliff? You mean wolves? They drive the cattle to it deliberately?"

Pat stared at him in astonishment. This was his father. Surely he knew?

"Uh, sure dad. They can kill more easily and safely if they drive them over a cliff. They know that - that's why the herds always get hit here."

"Can't be. They're just animals - how would they work it out?" His father dismissed the thought and moved off to the right of the herd, shaking his head.

Mikkel came up beside him, and pulled down the cloth from over his mouth to stop the dust raised by the herd. "Had a mite of trouble, I see."

"No, not really. Why do you say that?"

Mikkel smiled. "You're missing an arrow from your quiver." He pulled up his cloth and swung away to chivvy along a bullock after a clump of tasty grass miraculously untrampled.

Pat reflected his oldest brother might seem slow, but he missed little. He spat dust from his mouth and pulled up his neck cloth.

They came over the rise. His father, with his distinctive white hat, had gone ahead and was talking to men at the yards, still a couple of miles away across the plain. The city of Rikklaw's Port spread out behind it and the ocean gleamed in the distance. He thrilled inside, as the sight of the sea always gripped him, and he stood in the stirrups, seeing sails white against the blue. Mikkel came up beside him.

"Ah, can't wait for a beer. I'm as dry as that last creek after eating this damn dust all week."

Pat grinned at him. Mikkel's fondness for beer explained why their mother banned it at home.

"And now it's time we found you a girl and show you what it's all about." Mikkel went on with a grin.

Pat's face was panic-stricken. Mikkel laughed. His little brother might be wise in the ways of the wild, but the city at night was unknown to him. Girls gave him enough trouble at home.

"Don't worry, laddie. I'll find you a knowing one who will teach you what to do. Mebbe not the first night, though, as you'll be worse for wear on beer."

"I'll be fine, no way am I matching you beer for beer. Just a taste, that's fine for me."

"Ah, that's what they all say. You'll be in there with all of us an' there's a game or two to teach you. Just don't go drinking with strangers - I'll keep an eye on you."

Pat thought gloomily that he would be fine for the first hour, after which his brother would be too pissed to notice anything.

The yards were made of wood, and the entrance was a wide funnel into which the cattle went without fuss, ending up milling about in the large paddock. As Mikkel and Pat shooed the last through the final gate, a couple of men they didn't know pulled a gate round and rammed some poles through it and the wall to hold it secure. Simple and clever, thought Pat, seeing how strongly stakes braced it on both sides.

One of the men saw him looking, and said, "When they panic, they remember which way they came in and they hit it pretty hard. This'll hold 'em, don't you worry."

His father came over to them. "Right lads, good job you've done. Get the horses into the horse paddock, give Rabbie a hand with the spares when he comes in with the wagon and then I have a treat for you."

That got everyone's attention.

"What's that, dad?" asked Selwyn. "Girls?"

"Randy young pup," said his father, swatting him. "No, I've booked rooms at the Herdsman's Inn and the bathroom. There's a hot bath for each of you so You'll smell sweet for the ladies when you go out later. Right now, Sel, you smell like a horse that's been rolling in bullshit."

Shouts of laughter and agreement, and Mikkel pushed Selwyn towards the horse trough. He swayed, but kept his balance and came back with a soppy grin on his face.

"Now, before you all rush off, we'll have a drink at the bar together like civilised folk and I'll give you some coin. I've got an advance from the buyers already, and it's a good one. Seems we're the first intact herd to come through this season and the fattest. All the others had run from wolves a mite and lost weight."

"We have Pat to thank for that," said Mikkel with a glance at Selwyn. "Mayhap he deserves a bonus, dad."

There was a general cheer to this and Pat blushed and mumbled, but nobody could hear over the general noise. He felt his arm grabbed and squeezed and saw his sister Sal smiling at him.

"To be sure," said Dad, "now lets off to the Inn for that bath and we can drink his health."

The Herdsman's Inn was a big place, no longer on the edge of the town which had grown, and the stable no longer had horses in it - they were outside of town. Instead, it was a huge bathing area, with individual tubs beside what had once been a long horse trough, raised into the air. To fill your tub you pulled down a short slab of wood and water cascaded into the tub until you pushed it back up. The tank was on top of the building where the water warmed in the sun.

Pat did not look to see where the water came from, just ripped his clothes off, jumped in and let water cascade over him and into the tub.

"Great idea, Pat." shouted Sal from the next tub as she copied him. "Sel! Get us some soap before you jump in."

"There's a bucket full of it by each tub, Sal," said Mikkel, "But don't tell Selwyn - he'll be gone for half an hour looking for it in the kitchen."

The tubs were big enough so Pat was able to get completely under water, which he did as soon as it was full enough and tried to see how long he could hold his breath. He felt something prod him hard in the stomach and shot up spluttering to see Sal laughing at him.

"Wash your hair properly," she scolded, "and I will check to make sure you don't have lice."

"Aw, give it a rest, Sal! Nobody's got lice." It did not do him any good. She climbed out of her tub and came and checked, lathering his hair up. He did not notice her expression as she went back to her own tub, but Mikkel did. Everyone says goodbye in his or her own way.

In the bar, Pat was the last to arrive except for Sal. His dad grabbed his arm, pushed Mikkel away and said, "I need to talk to you, lad. Let's go over there where we can have some peace."

"No you don't, Dad," said Mikkel. "This is a family matter, we all need to be there and you must wait for Sal. Here, Pat, get this down your throat." He pushed a tankard at Pat, who received it with caution.

"Mikkel, I think I should talk to Pat first." His father stumbled over the words and Pat wondered what was going on. Did his dad want to give him a bonus without the others there?

"In your dreams, Dad. I do most of the work around the ranch anyway, you're just about retired."

His father wattled furiously, blew up like a frog and was about to explode when Mikkel roared with laughter.

"And you're no good with sensitive things. You will say the wrong thing and ruin everything. Pat's a good lad and doesn't deserve that. Wait for Sal, she is the one who should explain."

"What about me? I'm sensitive." cried Selwyn.

"Sensitive like a hog," said Mikkel. "You can listen but say the wrong thing and I'll flatten you. Sal will do the talking, we're there for support."

It was going a bit fast for his father, who was feeling bemused now, not having shared his intentions towards Pat with his other children. Who of course were one step ahead of him. Bemused was nothing to what Pat was feeling. He began to think something momentous was happening and took an incautious swig from the tankard. His spluttering changed the subject. Selwyn hit him on the back, while his father and Mikkel laughed.

"You'll get to like it in no time. Finish that off and I'll get you another."

"Let's not get him pissed straight away," said his father, "we need to have our chat first."

Sal arrived at this moment, dressed in a yellow frock that clung to her curves and revealing a lot more breast than any of the brothers had realised existed, despite having bathed with her half an hour earlier. They all stared, and she smiled with delight, pirouetting for them.

"Well? How do I look?"

"Simply beautiful, my dear. What can I get you to drink?"

"Some wine, please, that light white one they have here that smells of roses."

He moved off to the bar and heard Selwyn hiss behind him, "What are you doing dressed like that? We'll get in a fight for sure, keeping the men off you."

"Don't be an ass, Selwyn," said Mikkel. "She WANTS the men, that's why she is dressed to kill. Shut your mouth, Pat, just because you've never seen her in anything but jeans before doesn't mean she's a boy."

"But her boobs," Pat gestured, "They're so much bigger. I mean, when we're swimming or washing, they're not that big."

"And YOU can stop looking at them right now." Sal glared at him while he looked guilty. "The wonders of clothing, and that's all you need to know. Now move along and give a girl some room."

"Sal, we're just going to go over to that cubicle and talk to Pat. You take the lead, will you; you're really good at this sort of thing."

"Sure, no problem. Has anything been decided?"

"Without you? No chance. Wouldn't let dad talk without you."

"Err, what's going on?" asked Pat. He was feeling more and more left out, and had no idea what to make of his sister's clothing.

Sal took his arm and led him over to the cubicle, the others following with dad at the rear with her wine.

"Pat, you are a very special person. You have skills the like of which none of us has ever heard. You should be a priest or a magician, the way you talk to the animals."

"Umm, I don't talk to them, I just know their habits and what they are going to do."

"Whatever." Sal waved her arm airily and fixed him with a glance. "Nobody else has a clue what you do and it's frightening. Not just that, you know more about treating injuries than anyone else, you can read and write and you are the best archer anyone has ever seen. You seem like a centaur on a horse. Yet you are the only boy of your age without a girlfriend, hell, half of them are married."

"Umm, well there's Fiona..."

"She's not your girlfriend. It takes a lot more than talking occasionally to have a girlfriend. You haven't even danced with her and I bet you've never kissed her."

Pat blushed.

"Do you know why?"

Pat shook his head, mute and without a clue what was happening.

"You are too different. You are too good for Fearaigh. Everyone knows it. What girl wants to get herself pregnant by you and have you disappear?"

Pat blushed again and started to protest, but Sal was not finished.

"Oh, sure, the girls like you, like you a lot. But they know damn well they can't keep you. None of them want to get too close to you because they know they would burn in your flame."

At this, Pat's mouth dropped right open.

"And that's why you are not coming home with us, Pat. You are too good for us and too good for Fearaigh. We love you, and we want the best for you. You need to fulfil your destiny, and that isn't going to happen at home." She leaned forward and kissed his shocked brow. He was speechless.

"Dad, how much money are we going to give him?" She raised an eyebrow.

"Well, I thought we would buy him an apprenticeship. I had thought of officer training, but it seems it costs a lot once you are an officer and we can't afford it."

"But, but, but Mum... and Fiona...and Gary..." stammered Pat. "Officer training? I couldn't be an officer."

"Of course you could. Don't worry about Mum, she wants what is best for you, Gary's the same," Gary was their third brother who stayed at home with a broken leg. "And Fiona is getting married."

"She is?" This was not just Pat, but Mikkel and Selwyn as well, while Connor also seemed surprised.

"Of course, that fellow from Yellow Pond, can't remember his name. Anyway, Pat, is there a craft you want? Join the Priesthood maybe? Or become a soldier?"

Pat was distracted, his mind leaping around and not quite sure what to think about anything, so he answered the questions without thinking.

"Priest would be good, I like the thought of learning so much, but I am too old. You have to join when you are less than seven. And I need the outdoors. I suppose I could be a soldier, but I really would like to go to sea. I felt something special when I saw the sea earlier, and I do want to go and see the ships. Do you think I could work on one?"

At this, Selwyn leaned forward and spoke before a mistrustful Mikkel could stop him.

"I was talking to a fellow down the bar while I was waiting for you lot. He's a sailor, and he was telling me there is a new ship just built, biggest ship ever built, that has just finished her trials and is due to sail next week. They're desperate for crew, because lots of sailors won't go near her, 'cos she is a new type of ship and the Captain is mad, wants to sail over the edge of the world."

"Really?" said Pat. "An explorer? That would be cool! There isn't an edge of the world, Selwyn. Don't be dumb."

"Well, just shows - You're the only person in Fearaigh who would think that. The rest of us think there is and you'll sail over it if you get too close."

"World's round Selwyn. We just don't know what is across the ocean."

"Why doesn't the water fall off the other side then?" asked Mikkel, staring at Pat.

Pat was used to this, it always seemed others failed to notice things or listen when others spoke. Come to that, there were not many others who could read.

"It just doesn't. And the people on the other side probably think the same thing as us."

His dad cut through and brought the subject back. "So, Selwyn, did the sailor say what sort of people they were looking for?"

"Err, no, not that I recall. Shall I go and ask him?"

"Buy him a beer and bring him over."

Selwyn left and Sal turned to Pat.

"Is this really what you want Pat?

He nodded and smiled. "I would love to go to sea. It sounds so exciting, I would be an explorer." All thoughts of home and Fiona had disappeared. His dad breathed a sigh of relief, tinged with disappointment, but smiled back when Mikkel grinned at him, understanding and reading his thoughts. Selwyn came back with the sailor.

"OK folks, this is Mep. He's a fisherman and knows all about the ship."

"Welcome, Mep. I'm Connor and these are my kids, Sal, Mikkel, Patraigh and Selwyn you've met."

Mep grinned and ducked his head, winking at Sal. "Pleasure, folks. So 'oo wanna go t' sea then? Ya is it, youngun?

Pat nodded and smiled back at the affable man, trying to understand his broad accent.

"Have you sailed on big ships?"

"Norra me! I'm an inshore man, don't git out o' sight of land case I can't git back. Make my livin' from the fishin'. Jus' sold a case ta the landlord so ya've a good fish pie or fried fish for supper."

"What do you know about the big ship that is going off to explore the world?"

"The Queen Rose? Lovely lookin' ship she is, bloody huge too, beggin' your pardon ma'am. A carrack, they call hers. They're havin' some trouble fillin' up her crew, so ya'd git a berth, no trouble."

"What sort of job would I get?"

"Well, She's a merchant, see. So she needs all sorts. Sailors, but also sojers though youall is expected to fit. Not that she looks for it, but pirates attack merchant ships alla time, an' ya never know when yore gonna bump inna Spakka ship an' they'll always have a go atcha if'n they can. So they need sojers for dee-fence. Blademen, arrer shooters, pikemen, all sorts. But they also need cooks, chippies, all sorts o' craftsmen 'cos They're gonna live on that ship for ages. I hear they're even takin' animals along so they need a farm boy to shovel shit, beggin' ya pardon, ma'am."

"I'm a range hand, not a farm boy!"

His dad interjected. "Is there some sort of apprenticeship I can buy him to help him on his way? How much money will he need?"

Mep looked at his empty tankard, which Selwyn took wordlessly and headed for the bar.

"Nope, don't give him money. If ya want, ya give the Cap'n some dosh. Dunno how much a share is, but it gives him rights to some o' the profits when they git back. These merchants are a team, see. Nobody gits any pay, they git a share o' the profits when they git back. If ya put money in it, ya git more money at the end o' it. Providing it makes money, o' course. Don't need any money on board, an' ya can ask for some if in a port, but best not. You'll want to go an' get drunk an' chase the skirts when ya git to port, but believe me That's a bad idea. Many a sailorman never cum home again 'cos o' that. Ya can't trust furriners, they do odd things." He fell silent, eyes unsighted as a memory played.

"What do you suggest I do?" asked Pat. "I'm a good archer, and although I can look after animals I would rather learn to be a sailor."

"He's clever too," said his dad, "how does he go about becoming an officer?"

"Waal," said Mep, not knowing the answer. "Becomin' an orficer takes time. Ya don't just becum 'un. Ya works ya way up through the ship. Start off as a hand, young 'un, then learn ya way about the riggin', That's the sails an' masts an' shit, beggin' ya pardon, ma'am. Ya do good, they make ya a bos'n, but ya mest asken the Cap'n if'n ya can figure that navvigashun stuff, that tells ya where the ship is, see. That's the key to bein' an orficer. Me, I can't do that, why this 'un stays where 'e c'n see the land." Mep grinned broadly, and Pat stared at him in amazement, seeing a new life opening up in front of himself, with a picture of shipboard life forming graphic images in his mind. New opportunities were rushing into his imagination in a tidal wave.

"Dad, I've got to do this. Sal, thank you so much. All of you. You are right, I have to go and this is just fantastic. Mep, how do I go about getting a berth?"

"Waal, laddie, ya jist rock up at that ship abaht an hour or two afta dawn. They'll be up. An' ya asken for the mate. He's a verra important man, he is, yessir. He's yer lord gawd almighty for the next year or two. He's the one who decides iffen ya git a job or not. Iffen he ses yeah, and he will, laddie, no trouble 'cos they are short o' hands, then ya tells him ya want to put some dosh in tha ship, an' he'll take ya to the Cap'n to discuss it, so he will."

Mikkel leaned forward at this point. "So why are they so short of 'hands'? Why don't people want to go? Is he a bad Captain?"

"Cap'n Larroche? Nah, 'e's sound as a bell, 'e is. Lovely man, 'e is. Runs taut ship, no trouble aboard, makes money for alla crew. Iffen anyone can go hexplorin', 'e's ya man. But nobodies done it, see. It's a new thing, see, an' lots o' folk liken me, scairt we is. See?"

They did. In the silence Mep drained his tankard and smacked his lips noisily. Pat jumped up.

"Let me get you another one."

"S'arright laddie. Full tank I 'ave. An I gotta talk to me mucker there. 'Bout the fishin' actual, so cummalong an' ya might pick up summin'."

He took Pat off with him, and Selwyn got up to join them, turning as he left and Pat was out of earshot and spoke to Sal.

"Fiona? Getting married? To that prick from Yellow Pong? Is she quite mad?"

"Don't be an ass, Selwyn. Fiona will wait for Pat to come back for the next two years, if not more. But do you think he would have gone if he thought that?"

"But, but, you said all the girls were scared of him because he was so bright and different."

Sal sighed. And sighed again, as she realised that all the men were looking at her in confusion. "Guys, the only reason that Pat is without a girlfriend is because he is too shy to ask them. Plus they are busy fighting as only girls can to ensure than he is never alone with any of them. They all want him more than anyone else because he is mysterious, different and bright. They know he is going to do well for himself and want to latch onto him for the ride. If he had ever gone to one of the dances, they would have fought over him."

Mikkel roared with laughter and slapped his dad on the back. "See? Didn't I tell you she was the one who had to talk to him?"

Connor looked worried. "Ah, that was all well and good while we were around and able to shepherd the wrong 'uns away, but he won't have anyone to do that now. What'll happen if some bitch latches onto him without us to help?"

"Too late for that now, Dad. You can try and extract a promise that he doesn't wed till he can bring her home, but he's not fool enough to do that. Some girl will teach him a lesson or two, and it won't be long now, I reckon. But he'll have to learn how to handle her the hard way. We can't help him anymore. It's called growing up."

Farewells

Pat woke and wondered where he was. He seemed to be lying in a blanket that moved and it came back to him. He was going to sea. He was a sailor. He was an explorer! They were going to find out what was out there beyond the edge of the world, the first people from Harrhein to venture out of sight of land.

His father had brought him aboard yesterday afternoon, and they had been delighted to take him, the mate pleased with his ability as an archer. He was in his hammock, something he had never seen before let alone used. The harsh weave scratched his skin, and he breathed in the smells, identifying them in his mind. Unwashed bodies, normal and ignored. The fascinating new smells of the sea and the tar that was everywhere on the ship. He carefully and gingerly sat up, managed to get his legs over the side and stood up without too much trouble.

Most of the other hammocks seemed occupied, snores and grunts coming quietly from most, but a pair of eyes were smiling at him from the next one. Big green eyes from under a rough black fringe, with a miraculously clear complexion transforming the strong regular features into beauty. He recognised the girl, Sara, who had joined up at the same time as he did.

She copied him and said, "Ha! I was wondering the best way to get out of this thing. I think it is awhile before breakfast, any chance of a wash, do you think?"

Washing had not occurred to Pat, but his bladder was pressing him. "Let's have a look."

They left the wardroom without a sound and went up on deck. They could hear splashing from the seaward side, walked over to some piles of clothing and looked down. There was a raft tied to the side of the ship and a couple of people were washing from it while a man was peeing against the ship. A rope ladder led down to it. Pat started towards the ladder.

"What do you need a ladder for, slowcoach?" cried Sara and he turned to see that she had stripped off her clothes and was running to the side of the ship. "Come on, get a move on." she laughed at him and dived into the water.

Pat gaped. He had never seen anyone dive, let alone from that height. He stripped , but jumped instead of diving.

The water was chill but invigorating and he shook his head vigorously as soon as he came up, feeling the rush of blood and looking around warily for Sara. His limited experience of girls was that ones who talked to him would also likely try to duck his head under the water. She was looking at him with an evaluating eye from a few yards away, taking in his broad shoulders.

"Pat, isn't it? How well do you swim?" she asked.

"Well enough for a plainsman, I guess," he replied with care, becoming even more concerned about her. "I've swum across the Granthel in the mid plains. It's wide there."

"Good," she said. "Let's get some exercise and work up an appetite for breakfast. Swimming is the best, exercises everything. Come on, we can swim out to that island near the harbour mouth and back." And she was off.

Pat was a little startled, he had not thought of swimming as exercise, but he had never had to think of anything as exercise. Life was a constant exercise. However, he was willing and started after her, thinking as he did so he might need the exercise on the ship; there had not been much heavy work yet.

He was barely three quarters of the way back when he saw her standing on the raft, shaking her hair dry. As he climbed out, he heard one of the men say to her, "Breakfast will be in about ten minutes. You're well out of the fo'c'sle, Bos'n will tip the other newbies out of their hammocks. Get to the galley with your plate and mug early. Last ones will do the washing."

"Err, what's the galley?" asked Pat, staring at the sailor. "And the fo ca sel?" The sailor grinned amiably. He was of medium height, stocky and packed with muscle, with long dark hair tied into a pigtail with a bit of string, and big gold hoops in his ears.

"Galley is where the cook gets the food ready. Up forward where the wind blows the smoke away. Fo'c'sle is where you sleep. Really, it's the forecastle, 'cos the ship has a castle at each end, kind of, and the front one is called the fore."

"Why do you call them castles?" asked Sara.

"When pirates have a go at us, you'll see. Cap'n"s had a lot of experience, and the high part of the ship gives you a big hand when they try to get aboard. This is the only place they can get on, and they have to climb up again. We can fill them with arrows from up there, and chop down at them with axes and cutlasses. You'll see some chests at each end, they're full of arrows."

"Doubt they'll fit my bow," said Pat.

"Ah, you're the longbowman?" said the man, looking at him with interest. "I'm Jem, glad to have you aboard. You'll be useful, for sure. Have a word with the mate, show him some of your arrows and he'll get some in before we sail. Anyway, I'm off to get some grub."

Sara and Pat followed him up the ladder, retrieved their clothes and shrugged them on, following him towards the galley. Breakfast was fresh bread with cheese, the bread still steaming. They took it outside and sat on the rail to eat. Pat wolfed his food greedily, savouring the nutty taste of the bread, a very welcome change from the food on the trail. Sara looked unhappy at her plate and ate slowly.

"Want help to finish it?" Pat asked, looking at the half-eaten bread and not noticing her grimace of distaste.

"Go for it," she said, passing it over.

"I love the nuttiness and the chewy bits where the flour wasn't finely ground," he said as he chewed with enthusiasm, missing the look Sara gave him, but her reply was lost as screams came from the fo'c'sle, to the amusement of the sailors eating. A gaggle of the new hands came rushing out followed by a thickset, brawny woman with massive, tattooed forearms. She was red in the face and shouting after them.

"What sort of useless twats have I been landed with this time? Lavata love me, what have I done to offend you?" She cast her eye to the heavens and made a flowing gesture with her right hand. "Its way past dawn and you lot think you can lie about wanking in your hammocks! Get a bloody move on, you'll miss out on breakfast if you hurry it. Ten minutes and I want you lot ready on deck for training."

One of the new crew was foolish enough to stop and ask a question.

"Wash? Wash! You want to know where to wash? In the bloody sea, you dolt!" She got even redder, grabbed the boy by the scruff of the neck and threw him over the side. Pat noticed this was right by the washing platform. He leaned over to Sara and whispered, "Who or what is Lavata?"

"God of the sea. Not heard of him?"

"Err, no. Didn't know there was a god of the sea, thought there was just one god."

The Bos'n kept harrying the new recruits, until she bellowed, "I'm two short. Where are the bilge rats hiding?"

"Sir!" answered Sara smartly. "We've washed and eaten and waiting for orders, sir."

The Bos'n started over towards them. "A bloody soldier. Fat lot of good you're going to be on a ship. I AM NOT A SIR!!!! The Cap'n is Sir. The officers are Sir. You call me Bos'n, understand?"

"Yes Bos'n." Sara answered, poker faced and staring to the front, almost standing to attention.

She glared at Sara for a moment, and went off to collar a bedraggled recruit coming up the rope ladder.

Sara smiled at Pat and said, "She's only pretending, and she's not very good at it. An army bully sergeant would have her for breakfast. She's just trying to get the new lads into sailors as fast as possible. Easier when they're scared of you."

"How come you know so much?" Pat stared at her. He was not used to somebody the same age, let alone a girl, know as much if not more than he did.

"Oh, I've been around. Done some soldiering - interesting she picked it up straight away. Bet she was in the army once. Come on, let's get over to that net. I reckon we'll be climbing that this morning."

Pat looked over, and saw what he had taken for rigging was, in fact, a net leading from the side of the ship up to the first spar.

"Hmmm." he tested some of the rope. "Looks a bit ratty, though. Older than the rest of the rigging. Some of those strands won't bear anyone's weight."

"Umph. Take care, Pat. Likely a trick here."

There was no time for anything else. The Bos'n was harrying everyone over and standing them under the net.

"Right, lads. You want to be sailors, so first thing we need to do is get you up in the rigging. There it is, behind you, get up that rigging quick smart. Climb you wharf rat!" this last screamed at a man who seemed to be about to ask a question.

As one, the recruits turned and started scrambling up the net. Sara raised an eyebrow at Pat, and moved off to the side of the net, grabbing the support rope and used that to go up. Pat ran to the far side, noticing the rope frayed in places throughout the net. As a good cowboy, he knew good rope, and thought Sara had done the right thing so he grabbed the far support rope, which looked sound. He had barely gone two yards up when there was a scream and a crash, and two bodies were lying on the deck grasping bits of rope in their hands. He did not look down, concentrating on finding sound rope and moved up as fast as possible. More cries, as he reached the spar a resounding crash and he looked down as he pulled himself onto the spar and grabbed the next set of rigging.

The entire net had broken in the middle, leaving the supporting ropes and all the recruits were in a mess on the deck except for him and Sara who was grinning at him from the far side of the spar. The Bos'n was screaming at the recruits with a big smile on her face. Pat saw the rigging was now sound rope and a ladder going up to a platform where the next spar joined the mast. He was there in moments, before Sara, who said, "Well done."

The next ladder going up was in reach, so he reached for it and headed up, with Sara behind.

A female sailor went up to the Bos'n, indicated the two at the top, and said, "Me and Nils will take those two now, Bos'n. Natural topsailsmen, they are, we'll have them ready by tomorrow."

The Bos'n looked up at them. "Fine. Make sure they don't try a quick way down till you are sure of them. Don't want them falling from up there. No tricks in front of them, right?"

"Sure boss." She turned to go.

"And don't forget rowing training. They are not excused that."

The woman and another young man swarmed up the ropes and joined Sara and Pat in the crow"s nest, standing on the ropes rather than on the platform.

"Hi guys, I'm Else, this is Nils," said the woman. "We're topsailsmen, and you've just joined us."

"Good show," said Nils, "but now we need to make sure you don't get too confident and do anything stupid. What are your names?"

"I'm Sara, this is Pat. How can you stand on the rope like that? It hurts."

Else laughed. "Your feet will toughen up in no time. I'm glad you two were smart enough to recognise good rope from bad. You know rope?"

"Not really," said Sara, "but I was expecting a trick."

"Uh, I do," said Pat. "I worked on the range with cattle, used a rope a lot. Made my own too."

"Good," said Else. "One of the main things we do is check all the rope every day - and if you don't know rope it's all our lives that are at risk. Rope wears away, just from the wind. We are always replacing it, and greasing it where it rubs. You will see in some places, like there, see, we have wooden beads around the rope to help stop it wearing. We replace the beads too and they usually need lots of grease. Come, we'll do a check now and at the same time we will show you how to walk in the rigging. Sara, you come with me, Pat with Nils."

Captain Larroche stood on the poop deck, the highest deck on the ship. It was at the stern, with only the officers cabins behind it and featured the steering wheel and a view over the entire operating deck of the ship. Sourly, he watched the Bosun hazing the new recruits.

"It's not enough, Brian, but I want to sail on the morning tide."

"I'm sorry, Captain," replied the first mate. "It's been hard. None of the experienced fishermen or coastal sailors will come near us. They don't trust our sailing master, him being foreign. Not that any of them know how to sail a ship like this. Sailors don't like being out of sight of land even less. We are left with the raw recruits. I have been looking for people with balance, woodsmen, country people and the like."

"How are they shaping?"

"Well enough. One pretty boy, sort of, but he's a tough bastard too. Reckons he's the best archer I've ever seen, and says it matter of fact, not boastful at all. Asked him to put an arrow in a barrel for me, and he laughed, said it was too close. Pulled out the biggest damn longbow I have ever seen, marched off a good extra hundred paces and smacked it right in the middle. Another archer, a girl, says she's a mercenary, but too young. High born, I think, running from a forced marriage. A bunch of toughs from the streets of Praesidium. Mixed lot, but we do need the strength. Some farm boys and for some reason half a dozen tavern girls. They're shaping up and will do a job. Fourth Mate will cause trouble and he is poor at his job."

"I know what you think of the Fourth Mate, but he bought a lot of shares. The archers, are they good enough for our pirate plan?"

"Yup. The boy for sure and there is something very tough about the girl. That's them both, up with the topsailsmen."

"Good attitude. What about the toughs?"

"We might have trouble. Mixed bag of pimps, thieves and enforcers. Let's see how your speech goes down. Bosun's got her eye on them. My biggest worry is that fourth mate."

"Bit of a playboy, no harm in that I suppose. Swears he's a sailor, and he has an idea of navigation but his rutter is damn nigh empty. He bought a big share in the trip, though. You worried he will bother the female crew?"

"The way he talks? Too right. I told him if he bothered the girls I would put him in with the Bosun for the night."

The Captain laughed. "Has he seen her yet?"

"Yup. He laughed till I introduced them. She'd been listening and played along well, pinched his arse and promised to carry him off. Frightened the life out of him. But he did say that although he did like the ladies, he had a foolproof plan to make sure he didn't upset any of the crew."

"Did he say what it was?"

"No, just smiled."

"Hmmph. Please God he doesn't fancy the animals. I'd beach him, but we haven't enough investors. Bit short on trade goods despite the crown's backing."

"You always say that sir. It will be enough - where we are going they will fill the ship, and we'll have more than enough for the second trip. If we can find our way back."

"Oh, we will - this priest knows his stuff. Just hope there is still a crown when we get back, not sure that they are aware of the unrest being stirred up by this new parliament."

"No business of ours. We'll still trade, no matter who runs the country."

"Taxes will go up whoever wins." The Captain ended gloomily. "There's the priest arriving now, with his assistant. Get him settled and let's have a look at his charts. Ask the sailing master to attend us as well. Just the soldiers we are waiting for now. They were supposed to be here yesterday, present from the Crown to save us from pirates."

There was a knock on the cabin door and Brian put his head round it. "Crew assembled and ready for you Captain."

"Excellent Brian. I will be right there."

Captain Larroche picked up his hat and walked to the door, placing it on his head as he strode out, automatically ducking under the lintel. He strode to the railing overlooking the main deck where the entire crew assembled, not in any particular order; they were not a military organisation.

He stood for a moment and cast his eye over them. They looked good, he noted, keen and anticipating his words, no signs of unease or fear. His topsailsmen were in the rigging he noted, just the two new recruits with the old hands. He winced. They would need more.

His old crew were noticeable as being older, and most of them married to each other with a few kids sitting cross-legged at their feet. The cook's assistant was nursing her latest babe, he noticed.

"I have called you together to have a few words with you as a crew. You newcomers need to understand how we operate - we are a family, a large extended family and we know each other intimately. We will all profit from this venture, with a division of shares according to our status, but the majority of the money is contained in this ship and its trading goods. It allows us all to live well, as a family. You are now part of this family, though on probation.

"We expect this trip to take about three months. Maybe less, probably more. We could be gone for over a year. During that time, you will get to know us, and we will get to know you. You have been selected to join us not just on your abilities, but on how well we think you will fit in. At the end of the voyage, we trust we shall welcome you all as full family members.

"We don't have punishments like the army or the King's warships. Oh, there are extra duties and the Bosun and her mates will shout at you, but there is no imprisonment or beatings. There is no profit in it. There is only one punishment we enforce."

He paused, and ran his eye over the assembly, who were listening with rapt attention, though he noted the more senior members were looking at the new people, and he picked out those who had the most attention on them.

"We do not tolerate theft, violence or harm to be done to another family member. And when I say violence, I mean spoken violence as well as physical violence, for words can hurt and cut as deeply as any sword. If any of you are found guilty of these offences, you will be beached at the first opportunity. Think on that, because we are going where no Harrheinian has been before, to new lands where you have no idea what life will be like."

He let his eyes sweep over the crowd again, and saw to his satisfaction there were no worried faces.

"You should know this, but I wish to emphasize it again now, because tomorrow we sail, with the tide, and this is your last opportunity to leave us. We bear you no ill will if you cannot abide by our rules, but if you think our laws onerous, do leave us."

Nobody stirred.

A voice lifted up, cutting through the silence. "I think I speak for most of us, Captain, when I say I think your laws are good laws and I for one am happy to abide by them." It was Sara, her voice strong from the rigging, and there was a general nodding of heads from the new recruits and smiles from the older sailors.

"Yeah, Cap'n, proud to be here."

"I'll stick with you as long as I can Captain."

"For life you've got me."

A few more voices rose in assent, and slowly died out. Captain

Larroche smiled at them.

"Well, thank you and I am pleased to hear it. Now remember, being a sailor can be a dangerous thing, I want no stupid heroics putting yourselves and others in danger. If you fall overboard, it is almost impossible to find you and save you, so DON'T! We keep a barrel with a flag on it and a few ropes attached at the back of the boat. When we are sailing, if somebody falls overboard, the barrel goes over the side for them to grab and hang onto and we will try and turn the ship and find you. Get to the barrel if you can, but beware of big fish we call sharks that follow the boat and eat the rubbish we put over the side. They will think you are rubbish too. Topsailsmen, you take especial care. If you fall from high up, we won't bother looking for you because the water is hard and the fall will kill you.

"Now, for a more pleasant thought - where are we going? I am pleased to confirm what I suspect you know - we are going to the fabled spice lands, to Hind and beyond, and this ship allows us to pass out of sight of Spakka pirates and we can bring back the strange and exotic drinks and spices of that fantastic land. We will find out what is true about it and what isn't.

"Some of you have met our new sailing master. His name is Taufik, and he comes from Hind. Shipwrecked here last year by the Spakka, the only survivor of his ship. Sailing ships like the Queen Rose have been used there for many years and he has taught us how to build and sail her. He speaks the languages and will ensure this trip is a success. He knows the dangerous, warlike people, whom we shall avoid, and those keen on trade and friendship.

"Bishop Walters is coming with us. He is a cartographer of great renown, as well as a priest, and has compiled a chart over the years, not just of the lands but also the currents and winds we shall face. From this chart, we know we can sail southeast for a thousand leagues and we shall come to a chain of islands, fire islands that smoke, which stretch for two thousand leagues. So we cannot miss the islands."

The crew realised this was a joke, and laughed quietly, though some were now looking nervous, he realised.

"The islands are inhabited, the larger ones, but by strange people with brown skin and black hair who wear no clothes. They are reputed to be cannibals and warlike, but friendly when they see a show of force. We shall see. The islands make a route we can follow up to Hind where we shall trade.

"In the morning, we shall catch the falling tide to take us out to sea, where God's Breath will take us away down to the tropical islands. We shall be the first men to make this trip and we shall give these islanders a surprise."

There was a resounding cheer from his old crew, to which most of the new crew joined in, a few rather slowly. The sound of pipes broke out and a Bosun's mate stepped forward, playing them. Another Bosun's mate stood beside him and his voice lifted in song as the sound died away to hear his voice.

The pipes blared and the old crew crashed in, showing their pride with the chorus, while the new recruits started to beat time with their feet, trying to pick up the words.

Captain Larroche nodded at the Bosun who made a throat cutting gesture at the piper, who ended his song in a squeal of pipes and bowed theatrically at the crew, who shouted and cheered. Pat felt thrilled and he could feel the energy bouncing off Sara who had a huge grin on her face. The whole crew was lit up.

He heard Sara whisper to Else. "There must be more verses - is that the ship's song?"

"Sure is. Some of them get very rude too. You'll love it, and make sure you learn it. We expect all the newbies to be able to sing in within a week."

Captain Larroche raised his hand and spoke into the almost silence.

"So we sail on the morning tide. Curfew tonight is 2 am and I want you all shipshape and rarin' to go at eight bells. You new crew will have one last afternoon's training, then you have the evening to yourselves and may go ashore. Don't even think about an advance on your pay. Dismissed!"

There was a ragged cheer from the crew, but the Captain did not stay to listen and was gone. The ship buzzed as everyone started talking at once, until the Bosun's harsh cry echoed over their heads.

"Right you landlubbers. This afternoon you will be sorry you came aboard and I don't expect any of you to come back from shore leave. You have half an hour to get some grub down you, then back here on deck at the sound of two bells." She glared at Sara and Pat.

"And don't think you two lah-di-dahs are excused just because you can climb a fucking rope."

Pat and Sara went to the fo'c's'le and found a small teenager standing in the space beside their hammocks holding his own in his hands and trying to work it out.

"Hi," said Sara, "you new? I'm Sara, this is Pat. We're your shipmates."

"Uh, hello, I'm Perryn. How do you get these things up?"

"Simple," said Sara. "You tie one end in that ring and the other in that one."

Pat grabbed one end, tied it up, took the other from Perryn, undid the granny knot and tied a sheepshank.

"He doesn't say much," grinned Sara as Pat blushed, "but he's useful. That's a better knot; best watch how he ties it as you will need to learn knots."

Pat obligingly undid the knot and re-tied it, slowly.

"Thanks," said Perryn. "Umm, what is it for?"

"That's your bed," said Sara cheerfully. "That chest there is yours, you stow your gear in it. Hmmn. Robes? Not much use on a ship. Haven't you got any trousers and shirts?"

"Errr, no - I'm not actually crew, I'm a novice but I asked to bunk with you guys."

Pat looked at him with interest, Sara more critically.

"Been sent out on your quest?" she asked. "What's your skill?"

Perryn looked at her in some surprise. Not many people knew much about the magical aspect of the priesthood. "Yes, it's my quest, I suppose. I am helping Bishop Walters, but he has no magic. Not much vocation for the priesthood either. He's a cartographer. I haven't found my own skill yet."

"Have you got books?" Pat spoke for the first time, a bit eagerly.

Sara and Perryn looked at him in surprise.

"Since when could a farm boy read?" asked Sara scornfully.

"This one can. It's important to learn things."

Perryn looked at him with some respect. "Yes, I have a few. You are welcome to read them." He indicated a sack.

Sara reached in first and pulled out a thick grimoire. "Haileybury's

Analysis of Fire. You're quite advanced."

Perryn stared at her. "You can read too? And you've heard of Haileybury?"

"Yup, read it too, but I can't do magic. Useful to know what you guys can do, though."

Pat had pulled out another book. "This one isn't magic. I know the priest who wrote it."

"What? You know Peronnus?"

"He stayed with us in Fearaigh two years ago."

"That would be just before he wrote this," Perryn said slowly, looking at Pat. "He did say something about a youngster showing him about blood."

"I did take him hunting and showed him a bit," admitted Pat. He realised the others were staring at him and they expected a little more. "You know, where the blood comes from, hearts and stuff."

"Pat," said Sara patiently. She was beginning to understand him after a couple of days. "We don't know. I haven't read this book. Nobody knows what blood is, it's just something that comes out when you cut skin. Most people wouldn't even think about it. Why don't you just accept that and tell us what you know - not everything, just a rough outline, and how you know it."

"Oh. Well, I learnt a lot from the Elves and from talking with hunters, and skinning animals. If you cut up an animal properly, you can see how it works. There are tubes are in the body, they have the blood in them, they go places and sort of disappear. The heart pushes the blood along those tubes. Stop it beating and the blood stops flowing. Every hunter knows that."

Perryn spoke faintly. "So you were the young hunter he spoke about. He had a lot of respect for you. There is a huge argument about this book. The priests don't accept it; lots of people don't believe it."

"Well, they're idiots. Speak to the butchers, they know. Probably the soldiers too."

"Do you mean lots of people know about this?" Perryn asked, still faintly.

"Sure, it's not exactly new stuff. I was shown it when I was six, first time I helped butcher a cow. Way I heard, soldiers are taught where to strike and cut up bodies in their training so they know more."

"But why are the priests not accepting it? They are very upset about this book!" Perryn was getting animated.

Pat shrugged. He was not much interested and was leafing through the book.

"I expect the priests don't like being told anything by somebody who is not a priest," said Sara . "The church is quite hidebound."

"True," said Perryn, thinking of some lectures.

"Perryn, nevermind this," Sara spoke seriously. "Let's concentrate on being sailors. Something tells me we may be the only ones that can read, never mind have this sort of knowledge and it is probably best not to mention it."

"We're topsailsmen," said Pat to Perryn. "Want us to teach you?"

Pat groaned and stared at the hated bit of smooth but heavy oak in his hands. He was not sure how much more of this he could take and he had noticed Sara stop smiling at least half an hour ago. First time, he thought.

They were sitting in a rowboat, called a jolly boat for some strange nautical reason, along with six others, four to a side, each with an oar, and a satisfied, smirking boatswain's mate at the tiller looking at them. All were exhausted, all had blistered hands, some of them had blood smeared on their oars, but finally they were rowing at the same time and the mate had not bellowed at any of them for at least three minutes.

"Right ladies," he cried, "blow me for a cocksucker but I think you landlubbers might even be turning into sailors. Let's see if you can row us back to the Rose, and if you make it with no cock-ups, I'll let you haul me aboard and you can have the rest of the afternoon off."

The energy in the boat surged and all the rowers sat a little straighter.

"Now," said the swain, "Let's see if you remember anything. Larboard, stop oarrrrs - now!" Four oars went level without touching the sea. The boat rapidly turned and the Queen Rose came into the view of the boatswain. "Larboard, prepare to row - row!" The four oars came down into the water in perfect time with the starboard. The boatswain smiled beatifically. The boat shot towards the mother ship, impelled at speed by eight eager oarsmen. "Prepare to ship oars high - ship!" screamed the swain. All eight oars shot upright into the air. "Chainsman, prepare!"

Pat passed his oar to Sara who held it, picked up a long pole with a spike and a hook on it and waited as the boat cruised towards the ship, slowing as it did so. He deftly hooked the chain hanging down the side. This acted as a pivot for the boat to come around and slap gently alongside the ship, bow pointing towards the bow. Pat's muscles rippled as he took the strain under the boatswain's watchful eye, while the others moved not a muscle.

"Right, stow the oars and secure the boat." The boatswain's voice was quieter now, as the crew stowed the oars under the seats and arms reached up to grab the ropes coming down fore and aft from the ship. Each rope split into two and each separate strand ended in hooks, which slipped into rungs on either side of the boat. "Climb aboard, lads and well done. We are the first boat back. Get her up and your liberty starts as soon as she is secure."

The rowers swarmed up the side of the ship using the ropes for their hands and walking up the side as they had learnt. A couple of feet slipped, but regained their hold. Pat secured his boathook and shot up after the boatswain. The rowers had laid hold of the ropes and were pulling them as he reached the deck. The ropes went over a double pulley and the boat rose to the deck in seconds. As soon as it reached deck height, two waiting rowers pulled another rope and swung the yard back over the ship where the boat dropped into a waiting cradle. A canvas tarpaulin went over it and they tied it down.

"Good stuff, lads," cried the swain, "off you go and see you in the morning. Don't get so pissed you spend your first day at sea chucking up in the scuppers."

The rowers all cheered and turned to run towards the fo'c'sle. Big Dan Hemmings cried out, "Don't get pissed, he says! We're not going to have a drop for weeks, so I'm going to get rat-arsed. Hey Pat, where are you and Sara going?"

The assumption irritated Sara, more so when Pat replied, "The Herdsman! Good pub, great beer and good food, and my family will still be there."

"Good shout that," said a little chap with a pointed nose who everybody called Rat to the extent nobody could remember his name. "I've drunk there, great place, barmaids' got tits like the Mountains of the Gods. Let's all go there, good to go together, we're a team."

"No we're not, we're a crew!" Pete crowed. "To the Herdsman!"

"Err," said Sara, who had intended to lie low on board.

"Don't say it, Sara," said Pat. "We're not leaving you behind if I have to tie you up and drag you."

"Oh, alright then. Just spare me the barmaids." Truthfully, she found she was looking forward to it, although she was a bit worried. She had hidden her tracks, surely there wouldn't be a problem.

Paul took a pull on his flagon and looked at the man opposite him. "She's here. I can feel it. I am sure that was her horse she sold - the dealer paid too little for it, so she was in a hurry."

"Could have been anyone. Lots of reasons to get rid of a horse in a hurry, and why come here? Too close and nowhere to go. She will have made for the Elvish court, mark my words. The boys in Bardton will pick up her trail, not us."

"I don't think so - too obvious, the princess is clever. She is likely to be here, and I am damn sure she is going to be on that ship."

"Why? What's the point? It's a death sentence, they'll never come back or if they do, half of them will be dead."

"Don't you believe it. Don't you know the crown is underwriting the trip? And the Church? They expect it to succeed and it will. Just wish we could have got a few more men on board."

"Yeah, Gerry is a useless little shit. I guess that's why he got on board, they turned down half my men. I was sure that somebody like Rafe would get a job."

"He's a vicious killer and a troublemaker."

"Well, they'll need that sort if they get into trouble."

"He'd make sure they did get trouble, and would cause it amongst the crew. Mark my words, that's why they turned down all your men, to stop in-fighting. I would too."

"Hang on, there's Gerry. Gerry! GERRY! Over here. Glenda, another round and one for my friend."

A nervous looking man dressed like a sailor came up to the table and sat down.

"Uh, boss, sorry not to be back before, but this is the first liberty I've had. Last one too, as we sail in the morning."

Paul grunted. "What about the girl?"

"Uh, I think she is aboard. There's this girl, she's damn good and just smarter than everyone else. Right size, but her hair is wrong. It's black and short. Otherwise it would be her. Moves like a fighter and looks a bit like that painting you showed me, except for the hair."

"Hair can be cut and dyed. I need to see her. Has she got liberty as well?"

"Yeah, her group are all going to the Herdsman's Inn, if we cut across to Lime Street, we should see them going up it in a few minutes."

"Right. Let's go and see. Glenda, put them back in the barrel, we'll be back shortly." He jumped up and headed for the door, pushing past the barmaid as she came up with a tray of drinks. She glared at his back, but his companion put a coin in her hand and winked at her before hurrying after him.

A group of about ten sailors were coming up the street, led by Rat who was delivering a running commentary on the area, shops, people and anything else that passed his mind. The others were grinning at him and occasionally adding a comment, with Sara in the middle flanked by Pat and Dan. Perryn brought up the rear looking a little lost and unsure, standing out in his robe.

Paul stiffened and turned away. "It's her for sure. Has she seen me?"

"Nope, carrying on as before, not looking this way at all. You know her?"

"Seen her at court and the training arena. Come on, back to the rooms. Not you, Wilf, you go and round up Rafe and his boys, take them to the Herdsman's and start drinking at the bar. I'll come in with Lance and go to the back. Give us half an hour and start a fight. Lance and I will take her out with that distraction. Got it?"

"Yup, like we got Glanton last year in the Tailings. Simple, I like it." Wilf turned and was gone.

"Uh, what about me Boss? If I come along, my cover will be blown," said Gerry.

"So what?" Paul snapped. "The job will be over. Once she's dead you don't need to be on board. Wait! If they see you with us, they may be suspicious. So go and do what you want, join us at our rooms in the morning."

Gerry slipped away relieved. He did not like Paul and thoughtfully considered his position. He did not like any of his companions, and wondered how a man got into that sort of job in the first place. He sighed. A series of bad decisions, taking the easy way every time. He realised that in his short two days on the ship he had enjoyed himself more than at any time in his life. For a moment, he considered warning his crew-mates, especially Sara, but thought better of it. He was determined to be on the ship in the morning and would never see Paul again.

Rat pushed open the doors and the crew surged into the Herdsman's, which only had a few customers as it was still afternoon. They swarmed up to the bar and started looking at the bottles.

"Rat!" shouted Dan, "I reckon you're a thief, or used to be!" He grinned at Rat's outraged look, especially at the tide of red going over his face. "So you're going to be the bagman. Here's a sov from me. Everyone, give Rat a sov. Rat, you tell us when it's gone and we'll give you another one."

Rat was still spluttering as everyone threw money at him laughing. "First time I've seen you speechless." cried Tom, "How come you've still got two hands?"

"Nah, he's too slow and stupid to be a thief," said Linda, "I reckon he was a wanker looking in windows. EEEEEK!!" She screamed, "a wolf!!!!"

Something furry blurred down the bar and leapt high at them. They scattered, except for Pat, who took Mot right on the chest and fell back laughing to the floor in a shower of saliva as Mot licked and barked for all she was worth.

"So," drawled Sara, "is this the family you said would be drinking in here?" The crew laughed except for Linda who was still having palpitations. "Aren't you going to introduce us?"

Pat grinned. "This is Mot," he said, roughing the dog's neck. "She normally isn't so over the top, but we've been through a lot together and I reckon she knows I am going."

"Why don't you bring her along?" Sara asked. "She could be useful on the ship."

"Doing what?" Dan asked, "keeping the number of cats down?"

"No need for that," said Terri, "you'll see Tom eating those fast enough. But it would be nice to have a ship's dog. Lots of ships have them, don't they?"

"They sure do," said Sara, "extra guard when you are in port. Helpful on shore expeditions. Worth it, I reckon."

"Yeah, well this isn't doing anything for my thirst." Dan complained. "Bartender, gimme a beer - same for all of you?"

"No way," said Terri, "we're not all hulking brutes. You got any nice wines for us girls, sweetie?" She smiled at the bartender. Dan rolled his eyes.

The bartender smiled at her. Not surprisingly, Terri was pretty and a bit too well endowed to do a job in the rigging. "Sure, we have a nice shipment in from Varn. Lovely white wines and we have reds from Westport."

Sara pushed her way forward. "Let's have a look at what you have," she smiled at the bartender who started putting bottles on the bar while Dan grunted and squirmed, though the other boys looked on with interest.

"Ooh!" Terri squealed, "this one looks pretty! Shall we try this one?"

"No," said Sara. "It's thin and sharp and bloody awful, as is most of this stuff. Where's the Chalk Valley whites?" she asked at the bartender, who looked at her with some respect and started to replace the bottles.

"Not often we get girls who know wine in here," he said with a smile. "Here, this is from three years ago. Good year and ideal for the afternoon as a drinking wine."

"Yes, that's perfect." smiled Sara, "we'll take that."

The bartender drew the cork with a faint plop and started to pour the glasses, did a double take and put a small amount in a glass and pushed it to Sara. She tasted it, smiled and said, "Perfect."

"Why did you do that?" Terri asked as the bartender poured the girls glasses and passed them round.

"Often the wine goes bad in the bottle if it hasn't been stored right or moved too much by the carter," replied Sara. "Always check your wine first so you can change the bottle if it's bad. Make sure you remember what each wine you drink tastes like so you can repeat it the next time."

"Yeah, yeah," said Dan. "Never mind the girlie drinks, can we get a beer now?"

"Actually, I want to try the wine," said Pat, "Sara's got me interested and I've never tried wine before."

"Yeah, me too" said Rat, echoed by Tom. Dan looked on with disgust as the boys sipped the wine.

"Wow, that's really good!" Pat exclaimed, "why haven't I found this before?"

"Because it is much too good and expensive for you, darling," said a new voice and a slender arm plucked the glass from his fingers. "Farm boys stick to beer because you drink far too quickly and this would be wasted on you."

"Sal!" Pat cried and hugged her. "We got liberty and came to have a drink with you. Hey guys, this is my sister, Sal. Where is everyone Sal?"

"Oof. Put me down and get yourself a beer. Hi guys, girls. Great taste in wine you have, sister. I'm keeping this glass."

Sara acknowledged her with a nod and a smile, while most of them chorused a greeting and Dan smacked Rat firmly on the side of the head to deflect his gaze upwards.

"So, you are all new crewmen? How do you like it on the ship? What have you learnt?" Sal smiled at them, which caused Rat to drop his beer.

They all started talking at once, showing off their blisters and describing their day while Mot curled herself protectively over Pat's feet. Selwyn came in, shortly followed by Mikkel and Connor. They formed a large group and soon went over to a long table. Food flowed out of the kitchen. When Selwyn started to sing, Sal objected and threw the men off the table to go and make a noise at the other end of the bar while the girls sat and talked.

More people came into the bar, and soon it was full. The girls were at one end of the table while another group were occupying the other half. They were deep in discussion about how to wash hair in seawater without ruining it, when Mikkel wandered over. Sal eyed him suspiciously, fearing he was drunk, but he smiled and stood behind Sara and listened to the conversation.

There was a crash from the far end of the bar, and the girls looked over to see Dan swarming off the floor in furious anger at a laughing stranger, while the others started to pull him back, looking very unhappy with the stranger.

Sal began to stand up when Mikkel whirled and his fist crashed into the face of a man at the table behind them with solid power. The man's eyes rolled up and he fell to the floor, out cold. As he landed, his arm flung forward, dropping a dagger onto the ground. Mikkel swerved to avoid the stab of the man's companion, deflected the blow and started to swing at him. The man put up his arm to deflect the punch and his eyes went wide with surprise as a long arm came under Mikkel's and Sara's knife slid between his ribs.

Mikkel dropped his hands and caught the man, lowering him gently to the floor as his eyes glazed over. He nodded approval at Sara and stood up, bellowing above the noise of the impending fight down the bar.

"CARLSON! GRAB THAT MAN! ATTEMPTED MURDER HERE, HE'S THE DIVERSION!"

The laughing stranger stopped laughing, looked over at Mikkel, frowned and pulled a knife from his belt long enough to be a short sword. The boys around him pulled back while the bouncers, Carlson and his equally huge assistant, slammed the doors shut and barred them, then advanced on Rafe.

Rafe looked at Mikkel again, and dropped his eyes to see the pool of blood around Paul, pivoted, put his arm over his eyes and jumped at the window. And bounced back, the glass cracked but unbroken and the wooden frame still holding. Carlson picked up the stunned man, broke his wrist carefully to dislodge the knife and threw him against the bar.

Carlson looked round. "Did he have any friends?" his voice was high and squeaky, and would have been funny if he was not so menacing.

"He sure does," said Dan, and grabbed a couple of toughs who looked stunned and came forward at his pull.

Sara looked at Mikkel and whispered, "You knew this would happen?"

He grunted. "Saw the way they acted. Heard about him before, political killer. Nasty bit of work."

"Mikkel doesn't miss much," said Sal matter of factly.

"I see," said Sara. "I need to get back to the ship. I can't be questioned."

"I understand," said Mikkel, so only Sara could hear him. "I know who you are, saw you last year. I'll square it with Carlson. Give me your knife, it's mine now. Got another one? Fine. Get the boys together and take them back to the ship. Go with them Sal, take Selwyn. And Sal, leave that boy alone."

Sal glared at him. "I'll see them back to the ship, no worries. What are you going to do with this shit?" She kicked the unconscious Lance.

"Watch him. I need to talk to Carlson." He turned and was off.

"Just what is going on?" Terri's voice was high and frightened, Linda's eyes were huge.

Sara glanced at her. "Old feud from my mercenary days," she said. "Why I didn't really want to come out tonight. I am sorry you were involved."

"Is that man dead? I've never seen a dead man so close."

"Where the hell are you from, sister?" Sal stared at her. "City girl? Don't let it get to you; this scum deserved it and a lot more. Professional killer, right Sara?"

"Yeah, I killed his employer last year and he didn't get paid. There may be more in his band waiting outside." Sara improvised.

"I know." Sal was all efficiency, Sara was impressed, but Linda and Terri were looking scared, especially at this last comment.

Sara called over the buzz of conversation in the bar. "Pat! Dan! Can you come over?"

The boys came over reluctantly, Dan giving one of the men a last kick. They stared at the body on the floor, and the unconscious Lance. Before they could say anything, Carlson's assistant arrived with a girl in tow. He picked up a body under each arm and made off with them, while the girl mopped the blood off the floor and left.

"What..."

Sal interrupted. "Seems Sara has a few enemies and they tried to take her out. That fight with you was a diversion, Dan, so they could kill her. Didn't work out."

"Kill her? You're kidding!" The boys stared at her for a moment.

"We need to get her safely back to the ship and there may be others out there."

The boys looked at her for a moment, and Dan and Pat straightened at the same time.

"No worries," said Dan, "we'll look after her."

"I'll scout ahead," volunteered Rat. He looked at the others and blushed. "I was a thief. Why I am on ship, to change what I am. But I got skills. I'll go over the roofs ahead of you and spot any ambush. You can depend on me."

Sara grabbed his hand and smiled at him. "Thanks Rat." He blushed.

"Leave him alone, He's mine." Sal grinned at her; Rat blushed even more and looked at his shoes. Sal turned to the girls. "Are you going to be alright? Can you get back to the ship without fainting on us?"

This got a reaction. Terri gulped, but Linda glared at her. "We're crew! In this together. Tomorrow we may be fighting pirates and killing them ourselves. We just weren't expecting it here, and it's Terri's hometown. She's not even been drinking in the docks and she's young. But she's strong, aren't you love?"

Terri's eyes hardened and she nodded. "We'll be fine, not only will we not faint on you, but we'll fight beside you if we need to." She pulled her knife from her belt. It was a decent length and well used, but sharp.

Mikkel came up with Connor and Selwyn. "OK folks, time to go. I've squared it all with Carlson, he's going to dispose of the body and sort out the others. We're all coming with you to the ship."

"What'll happen to them?" Sara asked, her face hard.

"Don't ask. Carlson has connections and we've known him for years. They won't trouble you again. Now come on, the back door is open and we're going that way."

Without another word, they filed out through the kitchen into the backyard. Rat squirrelled up the side of an ornate building and was gone from sight with barely a whisper, while Pat slipped ahead, motioning with his hand; Mot crossed the street and ranged ahead.

The others formed a loose bunch and walked down the centre of the street, Mikkel in the lead with Connor and Selwyn at the back, checking behind constantly.

Sara looked at Sal. "You're like a military operation. You seen a lot of trouble?"

"Yup. We run one of the biggest spreads in Fearaigh, and we're always getting raiders coming down from the hills, men, elves, even the odd Dwarven band, though they tend to treat with us first these days."

"Elvish raiders?"

"Renegades. Not part of the main clan, and they need to win their scars. Seems we've developed a bit of a reputation, and they try to hit us at least once every couple of years. They like our horses. Of course the Elf Queen sends a trading caravan once a year."

"I didn't know." Sara frowned.

"Why should you? We look after ourselves and we're proud of it. No mercenaries down our way."

Sara bit back on what she wanted to say, inwardly furious the crown did not know of these raiders into the fiercely independent grasslands. She changed the subject. "Is Pat always the scout? Is he good?"

"Never seen the like. We had a renegade elf we healed after a fight, stayed with us for five years. Said it was because of Pat. When he was just a little thing he used to take him into the woods and teach him about animals and God knows what else. Got him shooting arrows earlier than most, probably why he is so good. Only person I ever saw who could creep up on every animal around. He used to get into trouble when he was small, pinching cubs and the mamas would come after them. Funny though, he would always give them back to the mama and they never hurt him. Seemed like he could talk to them."

The subject of the conversation appeared in the light at the end of the street, nodded briefly at Mikkel and disappeared into the shadows. Mikkel kept them going.

The moon and stars lit the docks almost as clear as daylight, but with plenty of deep shadow. Two sailors appeared and walked up the gangplank, while Pat slid up a stack of bales. He stiffened, seeing movement across the quay on another pile and relaxed as he realised it was Rat.

The main group came up the quay and all went onto the ship. He slipped down and followed them aboard; Mot appeared from nowhere and went across the gangplank without hesitation.

"Hang on a moment, let me check the cabin," he hissed, and slipped to the fo'c'sle. Mot followed him in, her hackles shot up and she raced over to a hammock, growling fiercely. There was a commotion from the hammock, which twisted and a body was thrashing in it, hanging upside down with a face staring into Mot's teeth, whereupon it froze.

Others crowded in behind Pat and somebody lit a lantern, revealing a trickle of liquid coming from the hammock, and an acrid smell.

Dan started to laugh.

"Mot!" Pat said, "to me now. Friend." Mot stopped growling, gave the girl a quick lick and sauntered back to Pat.

"Bet you wish you had come with us for a drink now, Katie." Dan cried, as the tension dissolved.

Mikkel raised an eyebrow to Pat, who nodded.

"Right," he said, "if you folks are all happy and safe, we'll tuck you into your hammocks and get back to some serious drinking. C'mon Dad, you've said your goodbyes, let's get going."

"Not so fast," said Sal, grabbing Rat by the hand as he came in. "These hammocks look loads of fun! Don't you get any privacy?"

"On a ship?" Sara cried, "you must be kidding. You could try right up the rigging though."

Pat was helping Katie out of her hammock and introducing her to Mot, not very successfully, as Mot was trying to help and Katie was still terrified and not sure if she was awake or asleep. Dan helped, less gently and she sprawled on the floor from where Linda pulled her up while Terri hugged Mot and spoke soothingly to Katie.

Outside there was a noise and the sound of horses coming across the quay towards the ship. The gangplank creaked as the first feet stepped on it.

Mikkel stiffened and stepped to the door, Dan and Pat right behind him with Sara slipping in front. There was a group of men coming up the gangplank, slowly and unsurely, clearly not sailors.

In Search of Spice

hadn't been aboard long enough to tell me about the bad boys. No stowaway attempts either, Cap'n."

Brian stepped forward. "Soldiers... - Ah, Pathfinders, if you will follow me I will show you your quarters. We'll settle them first, Mactravis." He nodded at the Lieutenant who dipped his chin, then turned to the soldiers.

"Corporal Strachan, take a detail of three men. Pass your kit to others and take the horses to the local barracks. Get a chitty from the quartermaster, wake somebody up if you have to, but get back here within two hours and get the watch to see you to quarters."

Corporal Strachan sort of saluted, it was a brief gesture at his hat, touched three soldiers, handed his kit bag to another and went down the ramp, sword still out. The soldiers did the same, all without a word. It was impressive, and noticeable that now they were aware of trouble in the vicinity, the gangplank no longer creaked. There was not a sound on the dock either. The other soldiers followed Brian aft, eyeing Connor, Mikkel, Selwyn and Sal who now came forward towards the gangplank.

"Who the hell are you?" Captain Larroche snapped. "Oh, don't tell me, Pat's family? You've got the same far-seeing look."

"Indeed, sir, I am Connor and these are my other kids. Thank you for giving Pat this opportunity."

"Huh? Ah, I think I should be thanking you. Quite a lad you have raised there. Want to get rid of anymore of them?" He eyed the others speculatively.

"Regretfully I rather need them to run the ranch. In truth, we need Pat, but he needs to spread his wings. Now we must go. We have said our farewells earlier, so let us go. Mot, follow!" He turned and started for the gangplank.

Mot sat down at Pat's feet.

Connor reached the bottom of the gangplank, turned and realised only Selwyn and Mikkel were behind him. They looked up to the ship and saw Sal kissing Rat, one hand firmly on his bottom and Pat trying to push Mot to the gangplank.

He touched Mikkel. "Get the dog. SAL! Come, we are going."

Sal released the permanently scarred and gasping Rat, gave a little grin, a wave to Sara, ruffled Pat's hair and sauntered down the gangplank with a whistle to Mot who ignored her. Mikkel went over to Mot, who bared her teeth at him and growled so menacingly he retreated.

Mikkel and Pat stood over the dog, uncertainly, while Mot retreated away from the gangplank, still growling. Captain Larroche watched with interest.

"If that is a sheepdog, you must have bloody big sheep. Devoted to you, is she, Pat?"

"Uh, we've spent a lot of time together, sir. I am sorry, will get her sorted in a minute. She's actually very well trained."

Sara slipped up to the Captain. "They're a team, sir, and a damn good one. Shame to break it up. Could be very useful."

The Captain glanced at her. "Does she eat fish?"

"Huh?" Pat was confused. "Sure, she eats most things."

"Can you train her where to shit?"

"Uh, sure, that's no problem."

"I bet. If I find dogshit on my deck, I'll have you keelhauled. You are now officially in charge of the ship's dog." He turned and stomped to his cabin.

Mikkel grinned, and went down the gangplank to Connor, who did not look too pleased. Mot clearly understood and came back to Pat wagging, and sat at his feet.

The Connorsons went off, with Connor grumbling half-heartedly about his dog.

"I'm pleased she has gone with Pat," said Mikkel. "Help him to remember us and home, stop him being lonely."

"Lonely!" Sal laughed. "With those girls on board that won't last. That Sara girl, the mercenary, seems to have him well in tow. Good for him, I reckon."

"Thought you didn't approve of the girls for him, Sal?" Connor asked.

"This one's different. Got that look in her eyes and she's as capable as him."

Mikkel smiled. "More than that. Pat's going to have an interesting time. That's the missing Princess we've been hearing about, the one that won the fencing championship. Looks like she has picked on Pat as a guard."

"Really? How do you know?"

"Saw her last year when I went to Praesidium. She's cut her hair and dyed it, but the same girl for sure."

Departure

Dan groaned, and applied himself to his bar. He had Pat behind him, and they were pushing the capstan, a big round solid barrel of wood that came off the foredeck mounted on an axle. There were holes in the top into which spars were thrust to form spokes - on each of which a sweating sailor pushed to turn it. A long rope went from it out a good two hundred yards to where a boat had dropped an anchor and they were pulling the rope in. As it came through the thwarts, it went round the capstan twice and down into the fore hold where other sailors coiled it and detached the links. The effect was to winch the ship towards the anchor, the best way of moving the ship in shallow water.

The early morning sun beat down on them from a cloudless sky and they were sweating. The light sparkled and bounced off the choppy sea and they started to feel the motion of the ship. The Queen Rose boasted three masts, the middle one rising almost eighty feet high, with a prominent bowsprit. From the side, she looked a little like the letter U with her high castles front and back, the back one being much larger with the poop deck on it, from where the officers commanded the ship.

They inched her out from the quay and towards the open bay where they could raise their sails. Sara, Else and Nils were in the rigging above them, waving to the crowds who lined the quayside to see them off. Mot lay in the shade of the foresail, which was furled but ready to be pulled into position, just to one side. Every time Pat came round and she could see his face she thumped her tail to encourage him.

A band from the local militia played in between speeches from various people, including the local representative of the Crown and the new Member of Parliament, as the ship inched her way from the dock.

Captain Larroche was resplendent in a dress uniform and great cocked hat on the poop deck, Brian by his side. They stood beside the helmsman who was checking the wind and waves with meticulous care. Taufik and Walters were going over a chart, with Taufik's rutter in front of him. Walters was resplendent in purple robes with a gold cross on the back, while Taufik looked wonderfully exotic, with his dark face beneath a blue turban, and strange trousers that were wider at the bottom then tied in.

Brian bellowed through a speaking trumpet, "Top watch aloft, fore mast!"

A boatswain's mate flicked his rope end at Pat, who relinquished his place to an older sailor and scampered up the rigging. Nils was busy greasing a pulley two thirds of the way up the mast.

"Jib away!" called Brian at a nod from the helmsman, and Mot moved away smartly as three sailors started to pull a rope which went up to Nils' pulley and the triangular sail, a jib, started to rise up and billow in the light winds.

As the wind caught it, the capstan work became easier. The anchor came free and swung up to the ship where two experienced sailors lashed it down. The sailors on the capstan pulled their spars from the sockets, stowed them away and raced to stations on either side of the ship.

"Fore course!" Brian yelled and Pat sprang into action. He was out on the right side of the spar, and pulled the cords that released the sail, allowing it to unfurl. Sara was doing the same on the far side, while Nils was below him pulling it down and lashing it in place. This was the hard part as the wind started to push the sail and Pat punched and kicked the hard canvas to knock the wind out and make it easier for Nils. It took only moments to get the sail set and then he was scurrying up to the topsail to see if that would be required.

Nils spoke below him, "Doubt we'll set the others till we are out of the bay. Too risky if the wind changes with a lot of sail set this close to land."

The Queen Rose was sailing now, moving through the water like a stately swan and Pat heard Mot giving the welcome bark down below, to be answered with a curious chattering. He looked down and, to his amazement, there was a huge fish going backwards on its tail through the water in front of the ship, making this strange noise at Mot, who was barking and wagging her tail furiously. The fish seemed to be laughing at her, and another broke the surface out of the bow wave in a graceful leap.

"Dolphins!" Else cried in delight. "Captain! Lucky ship! The dolphins are with us."

Captain Larroche doffed his hat and waved it at the dolphins and the long time sailors all cheered. You could feel the buzz of confidence and good spirits rising through the ship, while the newcomers stared in amazement.

Nils said to Pat, "Lovely aren't they? We consider them good luck, but they rarely go beside the smaller boats. They like the Queen Rose though. They came with us on some of the trials. Always a good sign when they see us off. Look how many there are."

Indeed, by now there was a whole pod, some playing in the bow wave, but most fascinated by Mot and trying to talk to her.

The Queen Rose cleared the headland and Pat clung on as the deckhands hauled on ropes, the yards swung around and the ship turned on her new course, southeast. The commands roared out and Pat was soon exhausted as they went from mast to mast, setting the huge and heavy sails. Other sailors were up helping now, and the Queen Rose responded, surging forward and causing the water to race past. The dolphins loved it and played at the bow, while Mot held herself up as a figurehead. Pat noticed she was being much more careful now the ship was starting to plunge through the waves and the land had dropped away to a thick line on the horizon.

He was sliding down a rope from the mainmast to the deck when he noticed the fourth mate come out of the poop cabinway below him. The Fourth sauntered up the ladder to the poop deck, a self-satisfied smile on his face, looking like a dandy in fancy clothes that Pat thought with disdain as suitable for court, not a ship.

Pat reached the deck and Mot appeared to check on him. He stooped to pat her. "Like your breakfast, did you girl? Gonna have to get used to fish and biscuits. Better make friends with the cook too." Mot thumped her tail, and then her ears went flat as a piercing scream went off beside them followed by a truly outraged shout.

"WHAT THE FUCKING HELL IS GOING ON?"

He turned and stared; the most stunningly beautiful girl he had ever seen looked furiously around out of brilliant blue and very angry eyes. She had long, golden blonde, artfully curling hair that dropped to her waist, pushed to the side by impossibly large, high and well-revealed breasts. These were bursting out of a blue dress tailored down to a tiny waist, then flaring across wide hips and turning into a froth of white cloth from which extended long slender legs, to dainty feet in little slippers, which were tapping dangerously on the deck.

Pat felt his stomach turn over as he looked into the slanting eyes with high cheekbones and the full red lips, and realised that she was staring at him as if it was his entire fault. He went red and backed away, suddenly absolutely terrified.

Captain Larroche strode forward and looked down from the poop deck. "Suzanne?" he asked uncertainly. "What are you doing on board?"

She looked up at him and bridled. "Who the hell are you? Where's that damn puppy?"

Sara appeared behind Pat and whispered in his ear. "That's Suzanne Delarosa. Supposed to be the most beautiful girl in the country and certainly the highest paid courtesan."

Captain Larroche started slightly, unused to being spoken to in this manner. "I am the Captain of this ship and I would like to know what you are doing on it as a stowaway?"

"Stowaway? STOWAWAY! Do you think I wanted to be on here when you sailed? That damn lying pup said he was the captain and you weren't sailing for a week! Do you think I would have come aboard otherwise?"

The Fourth looked over the rail and smiled. He opened his mouth to speak but Suzanne got in first.

"There you are, you little shit. What the hell are you playing at? Turn this ship around and get me off."

"Unfortunately, madam, that isn't possible," began Captain Larroche.

"Isn't possible? ISN'T POSSIBLE! I'll tell you what isn't possible, me being stuck on this fucking tub for the next year till you come back, if you ever do. Put me back ashore this instant."

The Fourth smiled. "I'll quiet her down sir. Told you I had a plan to keep myself busy and away from the crew." He winked at the

Captain, who gazed at him in astonishment and anger, and started to make his way down the ladder to the deck, a self-satisfied smile on his face.

"So," hissed Suzanne, quietly and viciously, for she has heard his aside. "You planned this. Do you realise that you cannot possibly make enough money in your entire lifetime to pay for a year with me?"

"I am sure we can work something out, my dear." He smiled at her over his shoulder as he came down backwards.

Suzanne's eyes narrowed, she whirled like a dancer, one long leg extending and snapping viciously into a kick as she swung round. Her heel slammed into his groin as he turned and started to jump the last few steps to the deck. The pop of his testicles bursting was a distinct sound over the murmur of the wind in the sails amidst the otherwise total silence across the ship.

The Fourth's mouth opened, but nothing came out. His eyes crossed and he collapsed forward onto his face, breaking his nose on Suzanne's knee on the way down. He bounced off and lay on his back, blood streaming from his nose. There was utter silence as the blood slowed and stopped.

Suzanne looked at him for a moment. Then she looked up at the Captain. "I am aware that striking a ship's officer is an act of mutiny, but I would point out I am not a member of your crew, rather an innocent girl who had been kidnapped. A crime for which you will be held responsible, as Captain, in any court in the land." This last she snapped like a lash.

The Captain realised the truth of this, and went red in anger, not at Suzanne but at his Fourth Officer towards whom he glared. Suzanne noted this and continued, her quick mind racing ahead, searching for the best options.

"I understand you are unable to return me to shore, so I am clearly here for the duration, at neither your, nor my, pleasure. So we must make the best of it. You are short of an officer, so I am prepared to take the position. You will find me a damn good officer - I am extremely well educated and will learn navigation rapidly. I think I have also demonstrated that I can act quickly and effectively to diffuse any problems with the crew, and I can also make myself popular without sleeping with them." She gave a grin. "Besides, I am sure none could afford me. What's my rate of pay?"

Captain Larroche stared at her for a moment. The silence spilled, but the whole ships crew was watching, more appearing by the second.

"Way to go, girl!" Sara called. "He deserved it for that trick."

Suddenly all the girls were clapping, a few of the men too. Most, like Pat, were still in shock - Pat had not closed his mouth since he saw her.

"Hey Cap'n!" Sara called, "we need a female officer; there are enough girls in the crew."

Suzanne winked at Sara, did a miniscule double take, and looked up at the Captain.

"Well," he said, "That's not so easy. We still have a Fourth, though you may have disabled him and -"

"He's dead," Suzanne said without emotion. She nodded to Pat and Sara, the nearest crew, "Check him and then chuck the offal over the side." She glanced up at the Captain. "I know how to fight, Captain, and I just meant to make him ugly but a nose break like that will sometimes drive splinters of bone into the brain."

Pat and Sara went to the Fourth and after a brief touch to the neck, Pat nodded to Sara, happy to let her talk. She looked up at the Captain. "He is dead, sir." She looked appraisingly at Suzanne who was looking as innocent as an angel. Pat grabbed his feet and started to drag him towards the side.

"Belay that," snapped the Captain. "Take the body to the infirmary, have it wrapped in cloth and weighted. We'll bury him tonight - we don't want sharks following the ship." He looked at Suzanne, but she was ahead of him.

"Aye aye, sir!" She looked at Pat. "You heard the Captain. Get on with it, lively now. I will go and change into more suitable attire, sir. You," she said to Sara, "get me a bucket of sea water to wash this damn paint off. I'll be in the Fourth's cabin." And she went back into the cabin way. Sara grinned and went to fill a bucket.

Captain Larroche, left open mouthed as he was trying to find something to say, shut it abruptly, turned from the deck, went back to where Brian was standing, and looked at him. Brian spoke in a low undertone.

"Well, I think that solves a huge problem, sir, and I also think she will be a damn sight better officer than many we could have recruited - certainly better than him."

"I am not happy about setting a precedent of being able to kill my officers for promotion - would think you would be worried about that too. We are not a damn pirate ship."

"Don't worry about it, sir. That's a very, very clever girl. See how quick she worked out what was going on and what her options were? I'll have her report to you when she comes back and you can tell her the rate of pay, and then send her to me for her duties. She'll make a damn fine officer, much better than Reilly. Everyone understood what happened and Reilly wasn't popular."

The Captain looked at him bleakly for a moment, then turned away, and spoke to Lieutenant Mactravis.

"Lieutenant, please ensure you have your most far-sighted men up top, as high as they can get in the rigging. They will find small stands near the top of each mast. Once we are out of sight of land, we are at the most risk from Spakka longships, which sail parallel to the shore looking for our merchant ships. I plan to drive straight through them and off to the south east; they should not be able to touch us, but I don't want to get too close."

"Sir!" said Mactravis laconically, completely unworried by the recent events. "Can I take a couple of your topsailsmen to explain any tricks for far seeing at sea?"

Captain Larroche nodded and went to his cabin. He felt like a drink.

Sara knocked on the door and opened it at the call, lugging in the bucket of seawater.

"Shut the door," said Suzanne, and as soon as it was closed, "What the devil are you doing on this ship, Princess? In disguise too?"

Sara was taken aback. "How did you recognise me?"

Suzanne smiled. "I am often at court with clients - one of my accomplishments is make-up, acting and role play, as they wouldn't want anyone to know who I am. I've been introduced to you in several different disguises."

"Damn," said Sara, "you were Lady Dunmuir, weren't you?"

"Yup, that was a fun evening. You had such a pretty dress. Now, does anyone else on board know who you are?

"No, don't think so. Funnily enough, Pat's brother - Pat is the boy who took the body away - recognised me when he was saying farewell to Pat, but didn't tell anyone. I selected the Captain of Pathfinders and his men, but they don't know me, except for the Sergeant. He won't tell anyone. It needs to stay that way, Suzanne."

"Politics?" Suzanne arched a delicate, chiselled eyebrow. "Don't tell me, let me guess. Not a love affair, I'm sure. Your father is furious with you for doing so well in the blade competition? And you are avoiding his wrath? No? Didn't think so, he would be proud of you, thinks too much of you."

"How do you know that? You haven't...."

"Your father and I have.... history. I loved your mother. She was very special to me."

Sara's eyes narrowed. Suzanne's eyes were suspiciously bright and damp. She was trying to equate the country's leading courtesan, who had 'history' with her father, with a girl who had known her mother and loved her.

"I never understood how you received an invitation to the Autumn Ball. Father wouldn't say a word. I was very suspicious."

"Your father is a dear but I let him down badly, long ago. The Church hates me, once I had too much influence. If they knew we saw each other they would make political trouble for him."

"Saw each other? Political? Just who are you, Suzanne, and why don't I know?"

"I'm just a girl from Galicia who ran into trouble with royalty. Not your father, a Galician bastard. The reason you know nothing about me is I operate a sizeable chunk of your spy network for Luce."

Sara sat down on the bed with a thump and stared at her. Suzanne smiled and went on.

"So, it must have been Rotherstone. The bastard. What did he do?"

"He, he, he set a priest on me, a magician. Persuaded all the guards who saw me that I was an assassin."

"Hmmph. That would have been Bessin. He's a hypnotist rather than a magician, not much difference really. Damn good. That's bad news. No wonder you're in hiding. This is a good place for you in that case. Does Luce know you are here?"

"No, we had several alternatives laid out and she knows this is one of them, but she doesn't know which one I chose."

Suzanne had stripped off her dress while she talked and was now rinsing the make up off her face. She wound her hair into a rope, tied off the end with a little chain with weights on. Sara stared at it.

"Makes a good weapon, unexpected too." She winked again. "Right, while we are on the ship, I shall report directly to you rather than through Luce. What's your name and rank on the ship?"

"Ah, Sara, I'm a topsailsman but my fighting position is archer on the poop."

"OK Sara, I shall ask for you as my personal assistant when you are not on duty. That way we can discuss matters with no interference. I doubt that I can be your boss, though, in the fighting, as I am not much good as an archer. My bouncers get in the way."

She smiled, grabbed a long cloth and started winding it around her chest to keep her breasts under control. She rifled through the Fourth's clothes, selecting a uniform with a surprisingly good fit.

"Hmmph. Needs a bit of needlework, I'll do it later, this will do for now. Pass me that belt. Right, how do I look? Ready to face the music?"

"You look fine, more like an officer than Reilly did. Not sure whether to call you sir or mother!"

"Make it Fourth. Give me a hat and let's see what the Captain has decided."

"Come in," said Captain Larroche heavily, knowing damn well who was at the door. He raised his eyebrows, though, when Sara started to followed Suzanne into the room.

"If you please, Sara, I wish to speak to Suzanne alone," he said icily. Sara jumped and retreated, not having thought it through and wanting to support Suzanne.

The Captain stared at her for a moment. Damn, with the paint washed off she looked like a competent, efficient officer, nothing like the strumpet he expected.

"Madam, we have a mutual problem here. We both equally regret your presence but I cannot afford to either turn back to return you to shore or to provide you with a boat even if you could sail it. We are under a very real threat from Spakka pirates until we are well away from shore, which have never allowed a Harrhein ship to sail away."

Suzanne regarded him levelly, nodding once.

"Nevertheless, you have murdered an officer of this ship and there needs to be a trial."

"The death was an accident. I intended to flatten his nose, that's all. Well, maybe I wanted to cripple his love life as well." Suzanne bristled with suppressed anger. "I've been kidnapped, sir! In any court on the mainland, any presiding lord would find the man guilty and sentence him to death. It may have been by covert means rather than violence, but it was still kidnap and I have no hope of returning home to my life, business and loved ones until the end of this voyage. Further, it is going to damage my business, tarnish my reputation, and worry my loved ones. Captain, I am sure that I don't need to remind you that you are responsible for the actions of your officers, particularly in port, and with Reilly's demise it is you who will be in court if we don't sort this out to the satisfaction of all concerned."

"Are you threatening me, madam?" Captain Larroche's voice dropped low.

"Not at all, sir, but as a good officer I am making sure you are in possession of all the facts before you make a decision."

Unmollified, the Captain glared at her a moment longer. She did not quail.

"And have you considered how we present this to the crew? How are they going to react to this manner of promotion? You realise that this is how it is done on pirate ships? We have to draw a line. You must be punished, not rewarded, or every rank on the ship is at risk."

Suzanne responded equably. "I have no idea about pirates or how your crew will react. But as for punishment, fine me. Fine me a month's wages or something. Reduced, of course, because I was not a crew member at the time."

"Oh, get out. Leave an old man to brood on the devils of mischance that have led him into your hands. Suzanne, you are Fourth Officer probationary, report to the First Mate for instruction. Tell him that I want the entire crew assembled on deck for me to address within half an hour. I need to finish this unsavoury business so we can clear the coast and out of reach of Spakka pirates."

Captain Larroche looked down on his crew. Every member arrayed on the deck in front of the poop, except for the helmsman and the First Mate. Brian was standing just to his rear. Suzanne was in the front row, now wearing the hat with insignia of rank.

"I am sure you are all aware of the events of this afternoon, but I shall repeat them for to ensure you know what happened.

"Fourth Officer Desmond Reilly, who was not due on watch till this evening, smuggled a lady on board ship and concealed her in his cabin. The lady was not aware that we were departing and on discovering the deception became very angry. Being a skilled close quarter fighter, she proceeded to strike Fourth Officer Reilly twice. The second strike broke his nose, and a piece of bone entered his brain and killed him."

He sighed, and looked at the crew who were watching him entranced, all eyes fixed on him.

"I have conducted an inquest and come to the following conclusions.

"Fourth Officer Desmond Reilly was guilty of kidnap for sexual purposes. This is a serious charge which carries a capital sentence in the courts."

There was a buzz through the crew at this, and he waited for it to die away.

"Further, this action by a member of the crew incriminated all aboard this ship, and as such would have merited beaching at the nearest port and forfeit of his shares in the cargo and profits."

The buzz grew louder and swearing could be picked out: reduced profits causing real anger.

"Suzanne Delarosa did kill Fourth Officer Reilly, and I am satisfied that it was not intentional. However, she has not shown contrition or remorse. Her actions are not mutiny because at the time of the event she was not a member of the crew.

"Before I pass final judgement on this, does any member of the crew wish to claim involvement or add evidence that I have not mentioned?"

Sara was surprised at this, and noticed Lieutenant Mactravis' eyes widen as well. Most commanders that she knew would not even have told their people what was behind a decision.

There was a moment's silence, and then Else stepped forward.

"Captain, I'm sorry to tell you but there was a lot of unease amongst the girls in the crew at the Fourth Officer's conduct before this incident." She was embarrassed and shy at talking in front of everybody, but determined to make her point. "I think, and I reckon I speak for all the girls, that his kidnapping of Suzanne was disgusting, and I thought it to be kidnapping from the start. He got what he deserved and all the girls will sleep more easily as a result."

There was a murmur of appreciation at this, many heads nodding. The Bosun pushed her way to the front, winked at the Captain and turned to Suzanne. "Three cheers for Suzanne! Bloody good job, girl! Come on lads and lasses, Hup, hup hurrah!"

All the girls in the crew joined in with a will, and most of the men, thought a few just looked puzzled. Suzanne looked a bit startled, and the Bosun went over to her, put her arm round her and looked up at the Captain. She nodded at him. Captain Larroche scowled at her and went on.

"Very well. I find Fourth Officer Reilly's death to be an accident, but with that judgement I also decree that his crime will not be posted to his memory on return to Rikklaw's Port. It is a matter for the ship and closed. The shares that he bought in the inventory revert to the ship."

This caused another cheer from the crew.

"These events leave us with two problems, we lack a Fourth Officer and we have a person on board who is not a member of the crew. Both the First Mate and the Bosun have tested Miss Delarosa, and we accept her as a Midshipman on the Queen Rose with the acting rank of Fourth Officer.

"Fourth Officer Delarosa has killed a member of this crew and I do not like her replacing the person she killed, even if it was an accident, as we are not a damn pirate ship!" He glared at the crew. Pat and other younger members shuffled their feet and hung their heads, even though they were not aware that this occurred.

"Oh, I dunno, Sir," said the Bosun cheerfully. "Helps keep the officers in line." A laugh ran round the old crew, who knew both the Captain and the Bosun and were treating the whole thing as excellent entertainment.

Captain Larroche ignored the interruption and carried on. "Fourth Officer Delarosa must be punished, and the punishment we have decided is a twenty five percent reduction in her share of the profits.

"Carry on!"

The crew burst into noise, all discussing the events at the same time, and Brian whispered into the Captain's ear.

"That went well sir. A few confused, most happy and none upset. The girls are particularly pleased."

"I hope so Brian. Not sure our soldiers, and I include Sara in that, are impressed."

"They're used to telling people what to do, not explaining it. I prefer our method. Better for people who have lots of skills, not just killing."

An hour later, the Captain and Brian were on the poop deck in discussion with the helmsman and Walters. The crew were scattered round the ship and Suzanne was no longer the topic of conversation, though most had managed to have a word and congratulate her on her appointment.

The farm boy, Sam, was encouraging the pigs to relax in the sun in which Mot ably assisted him, and he found himself treating her as a superior - the pigs trusted her a lot more than him. The chickens had not had the same instant trust, but were getting there. One had been bold enough to peck at her tail to suffer severe chastisement. This alarmed Meghan, Sam's assistant, who was not at all sure about a dog that seemed to know everything about animals and was clearly trying to instruct her. Sara and Pat were inspecting arrows and dividing them up, Pat cursing the fletcher and wishing he had been involved in the purchase.

A cry came from the masthead, "Ship on the larboard bow!"

Nils leapt into the rigging and went up so fast he seemed to levitate. Everyone stopped what they were doing and watched him reach the soldier, who was pointing. Nils looked for a moment, and then called down to the Captain.

"Spakka longship, about an hour off sir."

Brian moved to the poop rail, "Bosun, clear ship for action. Crew to stations. Topsailsmen aloft, get the topsail off her." With the topsail down, she would be harder for the longship to see, being lower in the water, and it might be possible for them to slip by unseen, while they could still see the longship from the masthead.

Pat and Sara jumped into the rigging while two soldiers took the bundles of good arrows to the poop and laid the arrows into racks, each rack lashed closed. They started testing the bows, and the rest of the soldiers joined them, four of which had crossbows. Sam let Mot get the pigs and chickens into their cages which he lashed down.

The helmsman put the ship over onto a new course well to the right of the longship. Within ten minutes, with the topsails lashed tight, the ship was driven by the main courses only, at a noticeable slacking of speed.

"Another longship to starboard, sir," came Nils' voice. "Same distance."

"Damn," breathed Brian. "Bastards have laid a net for us."

On the horizon, to the right of their course, a thin column of smoke rose into the air.

"Seen us," said the captain with finality. "Get the sails back up."

Brian rushed to shout the orders, while Perryn came up.

"Sir, I can do something about the fire. But I need fire myself."

The Captain looked at him for a moment. "Bosun! Get to the galley and bring us a small stove of lit charcoal. We have a Fire Mage aboard."

In moments, the Bosun was handing a small iron chest up the front ladder, and Perryn took it to a niche. He laid it down while the Bosun fanned it and stood by with extra charcoal. Carefully, he opened his own small chest and took out a lens, perhaps a handspan in diameter. Holding it above the charcoal, at a slight angle, directed towards the smoke on the horizon, he closed his eyes and started to intone quietly, almost under his breath.

One of the soldiers stepped forward, cranking back a large crossbow.

"Want me to fire a bolt down the line of force, Mage?"

Perryn's eyes opened; he looked at him blankly for a moment, then smiled.

"Yes! That would help, wouldn't it? How did you know that, soldier?"

"Worked with a Fire Mage before. Helped him focus the energy more quickly. You should be able to hit the fire with the bolt which will give them a bit of a surprise." He grinned happily.

"I'm sure I can. Give me a minute, and then fire when I drop my hand."

Perryn closed his eyes again, intoned a phrase, raised his hand then dropped it. The crossbow man released a bolt high in an arc towards the smoke. Perryn snapped a final word and the charcoal seemed to leap forward, through the lens and after the bolt.

They watched the horizon in silence for a moment, until the column of smoke seemed to shudder and puffed out at the base, then broke up and disappeared.

"Good lad," said the crossbow man, slapping Perryn on the back. "I reckon you hit that fire smack on and spread it all over the ship. Those rowers will be hopping in their chains."

"Well done Perryn," called the Captain, as he concentrated on getting speed to the ship.

"It never occurred to me to use a bolt before," said Perryn,. "Nobody ever mentioned it at the academy but it makes so much sense. You opened a perfect track for me to pour the energy down. It might have taken me half an hour to put it out otherwise."

The crossbow man grinned. "Not all magicians go to the Church. Some just don't like the Gods, and definitely not the priests. Then we have a fair few who prefer to be soldiers and we tend to think a bit more directly, if you get my drift."

"You have the touch yourself?" Perryn said, while Walters also looked surprised.

"Nah, but one of my mates did and I picked up a few bits. You gotta be careful that they don't have a Mage themselves - That's what happened to my mate, bolt came right back at him and skewered him."

Walters went white at this and retreated.

The crossbow man grinned some more. "You wanna check and see if they have any of that blasting powder?"

Perryn looked blank and Walters gasped. "That's a closely guarded secret. How do you know of it?"

"Ah, lots of people know about it. Anyway, if you scan that boat you should feel it, and you can blow it up. Why we ain't got none ourselves."

The two Mages stared at him in amazement. "I don't sense anything," said Perryn, not at all sure what he was looking for.

"Oh well, enough of that, can you overlook that longship? Useful to know what they are up to."

"Overlook?"

"Ah," said Walters, "we can use the lenses to see further but the longships are over the horizon and out of sight."

"You can create the lenses out of air, can't you?" asked the crossbow man.

"Yes," said Walters, "but we need an anchor and we use our hands for that."

"Use the cloud. That one looks thick enough. Do it big enough and we can all see what is happening."

"But, but, you use a lens to concentrate light, so you can see distance - the cloud"s in the wrong direction."

"Sir, I think I understand what he means," said Perryn. "If I put a shiny back on the lens, it would reflect as well as concentrate light."

"Yeah, that sounds like what our laddie used to do. He couldn't make a very big one though, but it helped."

"Let me have a go," said Perryn and started to concentrate on the cloud. A blurring appeared on the cloud, started to come together then collapsed. "I think I will need some practice - with the ship rolling I can't manage it."

"Not to worry, we'll find out soon enough."

The ship was scudding along at full tilt, with every bit of sail up and the Captain was examining the rake of the masts, calculating the forces. The longships had disappeared from view and he was worried.

Suzanne appeared. "Sir, permission to stand down the crew and get them fed. Any action will be an hour away at least, and I want them relaxed and rested before fighting."

He glanced at her. "Good thinking Fourth, but not sure food is a good idea. Ever seen an arrow in the stomach? Not good if there is food in it."

"That's why I want them fed now sir, so they have more energy and the food is past the first part of the gut."

"Very well. Warn the first watch they are on call."

Suzanne turned and called the Bosun over and the two went off. The crew started down the rigging and headed for the galley.

"Those two are as thick as thieves," murmured Brian. "Amazing how they get on. Have to say they have taken a firm hold on the crew in no time at all."

"I still worry she will be trouble, Brian."

"Don't think you have much to worry about, sir. Except for that damn longship. I want to know where it is and what it is up to. How many ships saw that signal?"

"They'll see us long before we see them, with this spread of sail. I think we will see him come at the port bow in about an hour. He'll have a hell of a pull to get there in time to hit us, though."

"They have speed on us, sir."

"Only for a short pull. This is a long chase."

Pat appeared with a tray of food for them, Walters and Perryn who were still on the poop. A soldier came behind him with food for his mates.

"Where's your damn dog, boy?" asked the Captain.

"With the Bosun, sir. They get on well, and she'll be sorting out boarders. Mot is good there, not much use to me. Mot'll take a couple down at least."

"With luck she won't have anything to do. Boarders will mean a hole in the side from the ram. You know what you have to do?"

"Yessir. Take out the helmsman about 100 paces away, so the longship swings. Take out the man beating the drum to keep time. But, sir, I would also like to give this arrow a go."

He proffered an arrow with a huge, heavy head, pointed and streamlined.

"I can hit a barrel with this at 200 paces; I reckon I can hit a longship at 300. Coming down from a good height, it should go straight through the hull around the rowers' feet, give them a scare if it doesn't hit one and kill him."

"Hummph. Yes, that could work. Try it out first."

"Also, sir, I think I can take out the helmsman at a lot more than 100 paces. Permission to try when I think I am in range?"

"As long as you take off a quarter of your range - you must make certain with your first shot or they will put up shields."

"Bodkin arrow, sir, will go through plate armour and most shields. I will make certain of a hit sir. I am taking off nearly half my range because of the roll of the ship, but it does help that the wind is with me. I'll need to be on the foredeck, sir."

"Why not the crow's nest on the foremast?"

"Pitches too much, sir. What I gain in range I lose in accuracy."

"Hummph. Fair enough, off with you now. Brian, who's in the nest?"

"Nils, sir. Best eyes on the ship, has seen longships before."

Spakka

The afternoon dragged on. The crew went about their business cheerfully, not thinking of an enemy - all they had seen was a smoke. The Captain fretted and marched about the deck impatiently, his forehead deeply creased. The day was crisp and clear, the sun warm on their backs and the breeze steady, the sea a rolling swell without a breaking wave. The dolphins played in the bow, every now and again setting off a delighted squeal when Mot went to talk to them.

The sun was still high when Pat came running back from the front, calling loudly, "To arms! To arms! Stand to! The enemy is upon us!"

As he came closer, he shouted up to the Captain as the crew boiled out onto the deck. "Sir! They have a deception spell. The longships are obscured. You can spot them by the seabirds following the ships, everything else is obscured. Get the priest on it. Nearest ship will be in my range in about ten minutes." He turned and ran back to the foredeck, while everyone turned to look for birds.

Sure enough, they could pick out no ships, but here and there were tiny flocks of birds, all either coming straight at the ship or on a converging course. Looking in front of them, the air was sort of squiggly, almost like a haze, very faint.

Perryn arrived on the poop, and started staring. 'His' crossbowman rapidly joined him. "A ship there, another there and a third there Mage," he said, pointing. "Can you trace the threads of power back to source?"

"What?" Perryn said, who did not have a clue what to do to break the spell.

"If you can follow the threads of the spells back to the Mage, you can direct my quarrel down it and give him a shock. Might even skewer him, but should blow out the illusion."

"Ah, yes, give me a moment." He concentrated on the nearest ship, and opened his mind to the spell, feeling it, absorbing it, knowing it. He saw with clarity how the spell was wrought, and saw the thread of power running back over the horizon, combining with other threads of power from the other longships.

"Yes! Give me a moment and I will be ready." The crossbow man started to wind up his crossbow.

On the foredeck, Pat put up his bow, pulled it back so his shoulders bulged, and casually released one of his heavy arrows, right down the wind. The crew watched as it sailed high up to catch the gusts, and travelled an impossibly long way to plunge into the closest mirage, a good three hundred paces away. As they watched, the mirage wavered, and cleared to reveal a longship, oars all over the place and men rushing around. The oars on one side caught in the water, and the longship swung broadside to them. A cheer came up from the crew.

"Well, I'd never of believed it," breathed Brian, while the Captain nodding in equal astonishment. "He must have startled them and smashed a board on the side. Put the fear of God into them."

"Now!" cried Perryn beside him, indicating a direction, and the crossbow man released a quarrel. "Damn, I missed it. I didn't pick up the quarrel. Can you send another?"

"Give me a minute," said the crossbow man, unperturbed, and already busily rewinding the heavy crossbow for the next shot. "Should be ready in a couple of minutes. Here, choose a quarrel from the bag and get to know it, drop it in the slot when you are ready. Better if I don't touch it."

Pat loosed another of his heavy arrows, with no result this time.

"Perryn reached over, selected a quarrel, noticing with pleased surprise that it had a flint tip not cold iron, closed his eyes and ran his fingers up and down the shaft, barely breathing. He wrapped his concentration around it, took his hands away and with his mind gently dropped it in the slot. The crossbow man raised the crossbow and released the quarrel without a word.

Perryn closed his eyes and used his inner sense to caress the quarrel and tweak it in the right direction. He felt it curve up and drop down on the thread of power, and slide down it away and over the horizon. He stood stock still, delicately balancing the quarrel and felt it increase speed and rush down. His eyes opened wide in shock, and he fell to his knees and vomited.

A murmur of surprise went up from all sides, as the illusion fell away and the longships were revealed, nine of them, all pulling for the Queen Rose, while Pat's victim was getting itself together and would be under way again soon. The crossbow man knelt beside Perryn, looking worried.

"You alright, lad?"

Perryn looked at him bleakly. "I was riding with the quarrel when it hit. I felt it go straight into an eye and a skull explode. Dear God, I just killed a man. I felt his death. It was horrible."

"Ah, lad, that's it, is it? Well you wouldn't be much of a man if you didn't feel like that on your first kill, and I am sorry I didn't warn you from riding the quarrel. Didn't really know, actually. Mage I worked with couldn't ride 'em. That's a good skill, lad. Now don't worry about killing the man, yeah, it ain't a good feeling, but you will get used to it. Just make sure you never lose the bad feeling 'cos ordinary men don't much like Mages who can kill easily. Just remember that killing that Mage gives us a better chance to win this battle. You can't fight an enemy you can't see. Bear up laddie."

He looked at the Captain, who raised an eye, and he nodded.

The Captain stepped forward. "Fine job, Perryn. Well done. You look exhausted and I am not surprised but we can take it from here. Get him to his master, soldier."

"Sir! Come on Perryn." The crossbow man helped him up and splashed some water from a bucket over his face, the remainder washing the vomit into the scuppers. He got Perryn"s arm over his shoulder and started him towards the wardroom. The door opened and Walters took over, releasing the crossbow man to go back to his duty.

Lieutenant Mactravis was standing beside the Captain, and nodded when he came back.

"Good work Little. Looks like you've earned yourself another promotion. Think you can last a bit longer this time before you make us bust you?"

Little grinned. "Hey, boss, this trip is looking to be fun. It's only when I get bored I make trouble. Have we got to stop all these little boats, or can we let a couple board so we can have some fun?"

Captain Larroche gasped and found himself speechless, but Mactravis answered. "We'll stop them without boarding today, thank you Little. Plenty of time for fun when you've taught some of the crew how to fight. Go and join your squad and tell Sgt Russell to look after the second longship."

"Sir!" Little turned and jumped down to the lower deck without bothering with the stairs.

Mactravis turned to the Captain and continued. "I think we can trust that cowboy to sort out the first longship, and I'll get another squad on the third. That should leave you to run on down the wind, Captain. How long before we will be out of reach of them?"

The Captain looked at him. "Not sure that any others are able to get in range, Mactravis. You think you can stop them from getting closer? The ballistas are not too accurate for hitting longships."

"Sure, Captain. Don't worry about it. I will go and make sure the second squad is ready." Lieutenant Mactravis did use the stairs.

Brian looked at the Captain. "Suddenly I am feeling a lot more secure, sir."

"Indeed, his confidence is infectious."

There was a peal of laughter from deck of the fo'c'sle, and they looked over to see Pat scowling at Linda and Terri who were laughing at him.

"Seems others are confident as well. Acting like it's a damn tea party for their entertainment."

"Don't they know anything about the Spakka?"

"Maybe the Spakka don't know anything about our military. Perhaps we should have had some soldiers aboard before - we might not have had that close a scrape off Sarl last year."

"That first longship is getting a bit close. When's Pat going to start?"

"I told him to take them at 100 paces - he said he would take them further out."

The Spakka longship was about two hundred paces out, and now the front of the longship was bristling with shields and bearded faces looking over them and shouting curses. The drums could be heard, echoing across the water. The voice of the master came faintly on the breeze, "Ram speed!" Clearly the command in their guttural speech, as the drums picked up the pace and the longship seemed to leap across the water straight at the bow of the Queen Rose.

Pat snapped something at the girls, picked up his bow, turned and fired off two arrows so quickly they were almost instantaneous. No height on these, they streaked across the gap, just over the heads of the bearded men, who ducked - far too late. The arrows disappeared into shields set up at the stern of the longship, passed straight through them as if they were not there. The drum cut off and a bald figure reared up, bare to the waist and with batons in each hand, an arrow through his chest. He fell backwards at the same time as the longship swung violently to the left, oars getting caught together and snapping with the impact. Screams came over the water and the slave oarsmen were standing up, many with bits of oar impaled in them. Overseers with whips came into view, but not whipping, more looking on with astonishment.

The Queen Rose rolled majestically on.

"Two arrows," breathed Brian. "That's all it took."

"Very special arrows. And a few years of training - plus inherent skill."

"How in hell did it have that effect so quickly?"

"I guess the oarsmen got confused without the drum, some stopped and some didn't, while the helmsman must have fallen on his rudder and pushed it hard over. Who would have thought it?"

They watched as the longship fell away behind them. It left five abreast thundering down on the Queen Rose. Pat pulled back his bow again, the arrow streaked across the water, through the barrier, and nothing happened. The second arrow also gave no response. The longships came on, water thrashing at their sides as the rowers strained at ramspeed.

Nils, up in the crow's nest, leaned out and peered at the longships, then simply dived into space. He twisted in the air, landed feet first in the foresail travelling at a terrific velocity. The sail changed the angle of descent, slowing him slightly. He turned and scrabbled at the sail edge, clutching at it to slow his descent. He grabbed the rope at the bottom of the sail and heard his shoulders pop as he tried to hold on, gripped onto a rope and tried to slide down it, squeezing hard to slow down.

Linda pushed Pat to one side, seeing this shadow above them, and both stood back in amazement as Nils smashed into the deck, blood splattering up from the impact. Nils groaned, tried to turn over and looked up at Pat.

"Pat!" he croaked, barely able to speak, "the steersmen are lying on the gunnel, to the starboard, holding the tiller with their feet!"

Pat whirled to look at the longships, and sent a bodkin arrow low and to the left. This time his reward was the sight of the steersman falling back into the sea. The longship came on. He was shocked, having expected more success. The longship was at ramspeed and the steersman was superfluous, Nils' sacrifice in vain.

On the main deck, Lieutenant Mactravis was lining us his men ready to take on the boarders, oblivious that they would be outnumbered about ten to one. The soldiers were looking eager, and preparing their feet on the deck. The Master Blacksmith, a dwarf, pushed out of the armoury and came up to him.

"Kaptin, I 'ave parasols for you," he grunted. He had metal shields over one arm, and poles on the other.

"Wonderful! Thanks. Russell! Distribute these! Parasols! Axe defence formation!"

Sergeant Russell came running up beaming, grabbed the shields and quickly gave them to the five largest men. He ran to the arms lockers and started pulling out long spears, which he gave to the others. The parasol holders fixed the shields on the metal poles and stood ready by the side of the ship. Each parasol was a small heavy metal shield, with a hand's breadth of soft wood above it. The metal poles screwed into the base so when an axe fell, the parasol caught it, trapped the blade and vibrated the wielder's arms. The harder he struck, the more it would hurt.

Five men stood behind them with long spears, ready to skewer the axe wielders, Strachan amongst them. Lieutenant Mactravis took the right side and worried about the left. Sara spotted this, and appeared on the left, smiling wolfishly at him.

"I've got this side, Lieutenant. I know what to do, fought with parasols against the Spakka before." He nodded at her and concentrated on the five longships

A loud twang echoed and thrummed from the bow as Else released her ballista. She had loaded it with a sheaf and it split perfectly a few yards from the first longship, sending over twenty long light spears in a shower along its length. The men in the longship seemed to explode, screams echoing, as the spears lanced through rowers and axemen alike. The drummer appeared from behind his shield, a spear through his body and he slumped over the side. Some of the spears had transfixed two or three men.

The longship stopped dead in the water, blood flowing away from it and turning the sea red with the sharks already appearing. The remaining four boats did not notice and kept coming.

The stern ballista fired, but its sheaf did not separate properly and the spears smashed into the second longship in a clump, killing a few axemen but not affecting the speed or direction. The Captain nodded at Brian. The sheaves were experimental, and the Captain was pleased with the result. The hours of practice paid off, despite the painful cost.

Captain Larroche had a hand on the wheel, with Taufik watching carefully while a huge brawny master's mate had the spokes in his paws. Brian watched the wind carefully, tracking its strength and direction through the movement of the sails. Captain Larroche measured the gap between the longships and the vulnerable side of the ship with his eyes. He had gone cold and focused, not allowing any feelings to surface, feeling his ship through his legs, moving gently with her motion.

"Now," he said, pulling down on the wheel a little. The master's mate immediately spun the wheel savagely, causing the ship to turn away from the longships and across the wind which caught the sails and high castles, pushing the ship hard over on its side so it leant over towards the longships. The crew on the deck were expecting the tilting deck, anchored, and ready, but the soldiers suffered, crashing into the side of the ship and Little would have fallen overboard if a brawny soldier, Husk, had not laid a huge hand on his upper arm.

The longships were moments away from impact as the big ship heeled over and turned away from them. Assuming it a manoeuvre to crush and swamp them, but mistimed and played too early, the galleys reacted gracefully like dancers, the drummers barking orders, the larboard oars digging into the choppy waves and spinning the longships to port.

It was too far for the outermost longship without its steersman, and the next longship fouled its oars as well, pushed it to one side and it slid past the Queen Rose to turn and beat back. The other three turned gracefully putting themselves broadside on to the ship. Accelerating, they slammed into the side of the great ship with a scream of breaking wood, despite losing full ramspeed. The great metal shod spikes pierced the side of the ship just under the waterline in a shower of water and splinters, impaling the great ship and attaching the longships firmly to the side. The Spakka, despite being braced for impact, were thrown forward and picked themselves up with a premature, deep guttural roar of victory.

The master's mate spun the wheel the other way and the ship swung back into the wind. The deck righted itself, as the Queen Rose majestically rolled upright, dragging the three longships up by their rams so the ram holes were above the waterline. The longships dangled at a steep angle from the side and the broken wood screeched at the strain put upon it. The Spakka, recovering from the impact and swarming to the bows, lost their footing and fell back as they found their decks slanted upwards and a steep and difficult angle to climb in order to board the carrack.

Howls rent the air as the axemen recovered, pushed to the front of the longships and swarmed up the side of the Queen Rose, throwing rope boarding ladders up from their prows. Sara watched expressionlessly as a huge Spakka warrior leaped up and used the deck railing as a springboard to soar high and smash his axe down at Little' head, where Husk deftly caught it with a parasol. The clang echoed with ear-splitting intensity, and the warrior cried out, seeming to vibrate in the air. Before he could land, Little lanced him in the belly and twitched him to one side as if he were spearing salmon at the rapids.

The soldiers were making short work of the axemen, but the pressure was building as more ladders were thrown against the side so more could come up at once. Sensing the pressure, Sara cried out.

"SING YOU BASTARDS! You're soldiers of the King, let them know who you are!" and she started to sing the battle song of the frontier, the House of the Rising Starr, with all the soldiers immediately crashing in, and singing as the wet work continued.

Behind the soldiers, the Bosun grinned demoniacally. She was gripping a long halberd, like an axe on a ten-foot pole, with a huge hook under the axe. Some of her mates stood beside her similarly equipped, while others held knives. Mot stood beside her, growling faintly, ruff erect and bristling.

Pat was still on the foredeck, methodically firing arrows into the axemen waiting to board, those not hidden by the side of the ship, and shouting for more arrows. He had loosed over a hundred and his fingers were bleeding. Terri climbed up the ladder with a sheaf in her arms.

Now a surge of axemen came up the side from the second longship, and the Bosun and her mates leaned forward. At first, it was the blade of the halberds, knocking warriors back down, but they pressed up the sides, eyes glaring, faces red and shouting hoarsely, lost in the battle rage. A hail of thrown axes pushed the sailors back, three falling, where they changed tactics and used the hooks to gaff a warrior as he reached the top, drag him wriggling over the side and back to the waiting knives. And Mot.

The soldiers could not cover the breadth of the boarding attacks, and Sara soon found herself in action, able to come from behind some rigging to stab the warriors as they attacked the parasols, firmly stopping them from coming round the side. She was seen from below, as a thrown axe cleared the rigging, just missing her ear and a warrior jumped up, grabbed the rail, pulled himself up and over in another prodigious feat of strength before she could react.

Landing lightly on his feet, he sent the axe whistling sideways toward her neck. Sara rolled beneath it, so close it took a few stray strands of hair, and sank her rapier into his exposed armpit while he changed the axe's direction. The blow petered out as the warrior slumped back, frothy blood pouring from his mouth. Sara pushed him off her blade with her foot, and turned to the next raider, oblivious of a shocked Dan who watched the man die and stood uncertainly with an axe. She was still singing with the men; her fighting style very different. She could not stand up to the axemen, as the soldiers did, and instead moved constantly, darting forward to stab between armour plates and immediately pulling back. She needed to, for somebody in the longship was looking out for her, as throwing axes fizzed through the air whenever she appeared.

On the poop deck, the Captain watched the battle unfold. Two of the longships were embedded below the main deck, while the third was under the poop deck where the side was too high to climb, and the axemen were trying to break through the side of the ship into the hold.

Captain Larroche nodded to Brian and pointed to this longship. Brian took a picked band to the aft mast where they used the spar as a crane and swung out a net of huge ballast stones, thoughtfully lashed to the mainmast in preparation for this event. As the net swung out, Brian made a chopping motion, a crewman pulled a rope, the net opened and the ballast stones rained down on the longship, smashing through its deck and hull. The longship shuddered, the stern falling back into the water as the ocean poured through the rents. It was caught strongly by the current rushing past the Queen Rose and the ram ripped out of the side, splinters and bits of board flying, and the longship was floundering in the wake, men scattered everywhere as she sank.

Brian roared an order to a boatswain's mate to take his sailors down and clear the hold of those Spakka who had made an entrance, if any.

Captain Larroche looked out for more longships, and realised that even with the two remaining embedded longships, the Queen Rose was now pulling away from the pirate fleet. He nodded again to Brian, who supervised ballast stones being swung out over the remaining longships. At the same time, he shouted down to the deck.

"Mactravis! Offer quarter!"

Mactravis did not hear, but Sara did and relayed the order. Mactravis leaned forward to shout down, and a thrown axe smashed into the top of his helmet, sending him flying backwards, stunned. The first stones swung over the longships, galvanising the longship slaves who jumped up from their oars, wailing and screaming. Those close enough to a Spakka grabbed him and hauled him down to their feet to be brained with manacles, and the drum master could be seen smashing at the nearest slaves with an axe, till an arrow from Pat knocked him overboard.

"Russell!" Sara shouted. "Lieutenant is down, you have command. Hold the line, defence only. Stop singing, men!" She moved to the side, staying behind the railing. She called out in harsh, accented but understandable Spakkan.

"Axemen! Bold Spakka warriors! It is done. Will you die or will you live?"

At first, there was no change, then the shouts died away, replaced by groans and cries of pain. Sara raised her head, wary of a thrown axe, and looked over, seeking an officer. The warriors were slumped, looking round, the axes lowering. The longship slaves were standing by their oars, looking at her while keeping apprehensive glances on the stones above.

"Do you have a noble left alive?" Sara called.

A figure in better armour rolled slightly, and a head lifted up, eyes staring with pain. He had clearly fallen back into the longship and been pulled back out of the way. He tried to lift himself up on an arm.

Grabbing a rope with her left hand, rapier ready in her right, Sara went over the railing and walked herself down the side into the longship, ignoring the warriors and picked her way through to the officer. On the poop, the Captain gripped the rail and cursed. The sailors all looked puzzled, only the soldiers understood.

Her point at his throat, she spoke. *"Noble sire, you have trained your warriors well. They have followed you to death and laughed. Will you have them sing your name in my feasting halls or will you take them with you?"*

"Your accent is terrible, girl, but you have honour," the Noble grunted. *"Your poxy blade already has my life."* She saw the blood seeping from his armpit, her favourite target, and the bloody bubbles on his lips from the lung strike. He lifted his voice, struggling with the effort. *"Warriors! You have a new leader who knows the code! Serve her well and with honour!"* He nodded to Sara, and said, *"I thank you for your honour. I regret I never met you on the frontier, blade to blade. Hurry now, before I shame myself."* He turned his head slightly and bent it, eyes misting in agony. Sara carefully placed the point just in front of his ear and leaned on the blade, sliding it into the brain and the Noble died without a sound.

She looked up at the warriors, *"You, you and you - go and free the slaves. Strip the longship of everything worthwhile and load it up to the ship. You will be given berths and instructed when on board."*

She strode to the gunwale and called to the other longship. *"Do you have a surviving Noble?"*

"No, mistress," came an instant response. *"We were sworn to the Noble Hilario whom you have honoured. We are yours."*

"You heard my orders. Free the slaves and take everything on the main ship. I want everything done within thirty minutes, then draw up in ranks on the main deck and introduce yourselves to me."

Sara hesitated a moment, wanting to sheath her blade before climbing back, but reluctant to sheath it without cleaning it. A Spakka warrior, really a boy, knelt at her feet, head bowed and hands up.

"I beg the honour of cleaning the blade, Mistress. It has done great service this day and is a Noble weapon even though so small." His voice was hushed and awed, breaking slightly and she saw his sparse beard, guessing he was even younger. She dropped it into his hands and swarmed up the rope back onto the ship.

Strachan was forming the soldiers up into a party to bring up the loot from the longship, while Little was tending to Mactavish. Russell was trying to get the Bosun to tell him if she wanted the wood from the longships, while she still expected an attack.

"Sara," cried an irritated Sergeant Russell, "go and have a word with the Captain, see if he wants to haul those longships on board or have us chop them away. Good job, by the way."

Sara smiled, threw him a snappy, regulation and totally unmercenary salute, and climbed up the ladder to the poop deck.

"Both longships and all survivors surrendered, sir," she snapped briskly, "the slaves are being released and the vessels stripped. Do you want the wood or indeed the entire longships pulled aboard? I gave instructions for the slaves and warriors to muster on the deck in half an hour so you can count them up and allocate them to quarters."

"Allocate them to quarters?" The Captain spluttered. "Damn it, I'll rescue the slaves, but we'll set adrift the survivors in one of the longships. I don't want the bloody things."

"Oh, I am so sorry sir," said Sara contritely, wondering how to get out of this. "I took their oath to stop them fighting. Spakka don't surrender, but they will change sides if their Noble gives them away. I got to him before he died, to stop us killing them all."

"Before he died?" Brian interjected. "You rammed your sword through his skull."

"Spakka honour, sir. It is their cult of a warrior. We learn all about it on the frontier."

"Funny how a mercenary would know that," said the Captain, suspiciously. "Such a young one, too. Never mind. So we have a bunch more crewmen. Brian, I want an injury and a damage report as fast as you can, and you and the Bosun can decide what to do with those damn longships. Sara, you took an oath from these warriors."

She nodded, smiling guardedly.

"So they are loyal to you. What about to me, and the ship?"

Sara opened her mouth to reply and stopped, mouth agape. Snapping it shut, she started. "I am so sorry, sir, I wasn't thinking. I assumed they would be taking oath to you and the ship, but I don't know. Honour is very important to them, but I don't know how it works when a subordinate takes them over on behalf of another officer. I'll ask Mactravis, he'll know."

"Do that," Captain Larroche dismissed her, and she went, chagrined. It was dawning on her she had not exactly been acting in character, but she was still high on adrenaline.

Lieutenant Mactravis had his armour off and was in the galley where Perryn treated his bruised skull, along with several other sailors with various gashes, bruises, broken bones and a highly embarrassed Pat who was trying to escape. Nils was unconscious on a pallet in the corner, Else tending him, with his shoulders wrapped in bandages. Two bodies lay wrapped in canvas on the floor, and one sailor lay unconscious with the stump of his arm raised in the air, smelling of the hot tar with which Walters sealed the raw wound

"What happened to you?" Sara asked Pat, where Terri and Rat had him cornered, waiting his turn.

"It's nothing," he mumbled, hanging his head and not looking at her, going bright red. Sara was immediately fascinated

"It's his fingers," said Terri, importantly.

"Silly bastard kept firing, ripped his skin off," said Rat, grinning.

"Often happens when you're out of practice," Pat mumbled, trying to leave. "I'll be fine."

"Archer!" snapped Lieutenant Mactravis from across the room in a very irritated tone. "You will wait and be examined by the priest. Is that clear?"

"Yessir," mumbled Pat, looking at his fingers.

"Look at me when I give you an order, boy!" Mactravis' tone had gone very cold. "A soldier's first job is to ensure he is ready to fight at peak condition. We might have another load of longships in half an hour, and you have a better chance of being ready with the priest."

Pat started and looked into Mactravis' level eyes. "Yes Sir. Sorry Sir." He made an attempt at a salute that made Sara bite her lip to keep herself from laughing. Mactravis returned to Perryn who was inspecting his eyes and Sara whispered in Pat's ear.

"He's treating you like one of his own men. Big compliment." She pinched his arm affectionately, not noticing Terri's glare, and went off to Mactravis.

"Sir, Captain's compliments, we need some information about the Spakka," she saluted, unconsciously giving a perfect Rangers salute.

"Well, tell him what you know, damn it," he answered with a growl, glaring at Perryn who was manipulating his skull. "That hurts, damn you!"

"Sorry," said Perryn, clearly not.

"I don't know, is the trouble, sir," Sara continued doggedly. "The warriors I picked up, do I just hand them over to the Captain? What do I tell them?"

Mactravis looked at her. "Well Miss Mercenary who just happens to speak Spakka, why don't you ask the Spakka?"

Sara flushed. "If you want, sir, but I thought you would know and it might be better to check with you first. I shall speak with them." She turned to go.

"Wait," he said, grabbing her arm, feeling the muscle. "What mercenary company were you with, that knows about parasols and can even form a decent wall? I've never seen a woman mercenary under thirty and you're, what? Seventeen?"

"Ah," said Sara, thinking furiously and cursing herself. "Well, I was with a few, since I was a kid. Mum was a merc, trained me up. Was with Constantine's last."

"No you weren't. I know Constantine's officers, you weren't one of them and he doesn't have any under 30."

"I wasn't an officer, sir."

"Then why were you giving commands to my men, and to me, damn it, and we obeyed you? How do you know the Battle Song? Why do you take an officer's position in a wall as if trained to it? Why do you speak Spakka and know more of their customs and rituals than I do?" Suspicion was glinting in his eyes, anger lurking behind it. "There's only been one girl on the frontier," he began and his eyes flared wide with shock and he fell silent, mouth still open.

The blood rushed to Sara's face and she pulled her arm free of his weakened grip. "I'll speak with the Spakka now, sir." She fled the room, hearing a sudden bark of laughter from the Lieutenant, conscious of all the eyes staring at her curiously.

Outside the longship, she pressed her shoulders to the door, hearing the questions flying at the Lieutenant and was relieved as he ignored them all. She felt hot tears behind her lids, and repeated her silent mantra from her childhood. "A Starr Princess does not cry!"

The emotion ebbed, she smiled grimly, took control of herself and went to look for the Spakka.

As she appeared on the main deck, the Spakka were bringing up the last of the spoils from the longships. The Bosun was assessing the ex-slaves, and she could see lots of tears. Presumably, many were Harrhein. The boy was looking round, holding her sword and he saw her first, striding over proudly, going down on one knee and proffering the sword.

She took it from him and inspected it minutely. As well as cleaning it, he had greased it and sharpened it, removing a tiny nick that had bothered her.

"I did not tell you to sharpen her."

The boy smacked down onto the floor, prostrate at her feet. He grabbed her left foot and lifted it up, putting it on his head. Not expecting this, she nearly fell over and just kept her balance.

"Mistress, yours is a sword of power, a famous weapon, such must always be tended. I feared you would kill me if I did not tend it correctly. Please, Mistress, may I know the name of your sword?"

"She is Lady Strike. Now, I need information. Can you give it to me or do I need to ask an older warrior?" She placed the rapier in the sheath on her belt and took her foot off his head.

"Mistress, I will answer if it is within my knowledge. I doubt the others will know more than I." He grabbed her foot and put it back on his head.

"Why not? You are but a youth?"

"I am Noble born, Mistress. Noble Hilario was my father."

Sara was shocked, and blinked several times, wondering what to say. She took her foot off. The youth replaced it hurriedly, hanging on more firmly now and spoke again.

"Mistress, as a dutiful son, I wish to express the thanks of my House for the honour you gave my father. It is rare for us to meet honour in battle and few of our people gain the honour of a true death as you gave my father. I will be your sword carrier for five years and a day, the full term, in gratitude, before returning to my house to sing your praises."

Sara was alarmed. *"Five years? Will all the men wish to serve the same term?"*

"No Mistress. Most will, but some have wives and children and will return to them after the first year."

"I am not Spakka, and I do not know your customs. I honour everyone where I can. You must help me to understand. Will you do that?"

"Yes Mistress."

""What is your name?"

"Janis, Mistress, Janis Cederroth."

"Well, Janis, I am a serving officer on this ship, the Queen Rose." She hoped the Captain would forgive her promotion. *"Does your honour go to me or my superiors?"*

"Superiors, Mistress?" In his surprise, Janis released her foot and she could stand properly. *"Are you not the Princess?"*

"What do you know of the Princess?"

"We were told you would be on the Great Ship, it was why we put such an effort into trying to capture it. A message was sent from our spies. Noble Hilario asked especially for the boarding honour as you honoured his friend on the frontier."

Sara sighed. Did everyone know who she was? *"Right, well tell your men that although I am the Princess, I am in disguise and serving on this ship. Nobody is to refer to me as Princess or Asmara. I am Sara, just Sara."*

Janis digested this for a moment. Sara noticed that most of the Spakka were listening in with great interest. *"We will call you Mistress, then,"* he said with great finality, and the listening Spakka all murmured in agreement. Sara ground her teeth.

"Very well. On the ship you will train with the Harrhein soldiers and report to their commander. The Captain of the ship is Larroche. You will obey him and his officers."

The Spakka murmured again, definitely not in agreement.

"No," said Janis, *"you have our honour. We obey you and only you."*

"I have other duties. I cannot nursemaid you all the time," she sneered in perfect Spakka style, as light dawned and she realised how to talk to them. *"You will train under Lieutenant Mactravis. I will check your training. I expect you to become proficient. You will also learn Harrhein language and customs. If required to sail the ship, you will do so and follow orders given by ships officers. When I decide to act as Princess, you will form part of my honour guard IF you measure up. Fail me and you will feed sharks."*

This was clearly correct as the entire contingent threw themselves to the floor and snaked over to her. The first reached her, grasped her foot and placed it on his head.

"I am Andreas Esbech. My honour is yours, Mistress, for the full five years." A huge bearded warrior, missing an eye in a long and livid scar. She nodded and the procession began, while crewmembers came out to watch. Sara noted that they were all saying five years, and it was not till they came to the last few, older men, that they started to say, apologetically, a single year. Sara was not quite sure what to do, and Janis whispered from behind her.

"They must see your blood. You must accept their honour."

Sara stood, legs apart, looking down on the still prostrate men, who were now looking up at her, though not meeting her eyes. She threw back her hair, or tried to, forgetting it was cut short, and ostentatiously unsheathed Lady Strike. The Spakka all breathed in deeply, and curved their necks, proffering their heads for her to take.

Lady Strike whirled high into the air, gleaming and catching the evening sun's rays, sending flashes and shadows round the silent deck. She whipped down fast, and there was a long streak of scarlet on Sara's left forearm.

"I accept your honour," she cried in a ringing voice, *"and bind you to me and to this ship, the Queen Rose, with blood, steel and wood."* She dripped blood onto the deck, and rubbed it in with her bare feet. She allowed the blood to drip down the blade, which she held to the wound, then strode amongst them, flicking blood over them. *"I bind thee to me; your honour is tied to my blood. I will protect you, I will honour you, I will kill you. You are mine, mine for the term, and will do as I command."* She repeated these words as she strode through them, flicking blood in their faces with Lady Strike.

The men were no longer looking at her. They were trembling, shaking when her blood touched them as if scalded, and quickly licking it from skin, cloth and deck. Janis was no longer behind her, but with the men. A loud groan built up from the men, coming to a crescendo and breaking into words.

"We are yours, Mistress. Command us! We are your children, our lives are yours to take."

"Enough!" She cried. *"There is work to do. Stand up. That man,"* she pointed to where he emerged from the infirmary to watch, *"is Lieutenant Mactravis. He will instruct you until I wish to see you again. He will see to your instruction in Harrheinian. Janis! Clean Lady Strike and bring her back to me, then report to the Lieutenant."* She turned and walked to the poop ladder, inwardly trembling in reaction, but feeling triumphant at the same time. As she walked, she looked at Mactravis who was smiling.

"They will take your orders now, Mactravis. They are expecting to be trained as elite Harrhein soldiers and taught our language."

"No problem, ah, Sara. I remember you now, from your mercenary stint on the frontier." His eyes twinkled with pleasure. Sara was not feeling guilty anymore. Instead, there was a huge rush of feeling, of pleasure and satisfaction. Adulation is so addictive.

Up on the poop deck, a number of people followed this ceremony. All the officers were watching, joined by the Bosun, Walters and Perryn. Walters was excited. "Oh, this is wonderful! Such a barbaric ceremony! Now, Perryn, make sure you sketch what is happening. I will pen a description to go with it. I don't think anyone has ever seen a Spakka allegiance ceremony before. Look at that monster of a man - Stiphleek he called himself - he's crying while he licks the blood off his arm. You can see how much it means to him." His voice was a whisper that did not carry far. Perryn was busy sketching.

Suzanne whispered in the Captain's ear, loud enough for those nearby to hear. "I think she may have earned a promotion, sir."

"I concur," said Brian. "I've never heard of a Spakka bothering to learn another language, even as a long term prisoner. Nobody else can talk to them."

"Yes," said the Captain, ruminatively. "I think we shall make her a Midshipman, rather than a Boatswain's Mate." He grinned evilly at Brian. "Then you can have the welcome task of teaching her navigation."

Pat came down from the galley, his fingers treated but he had refused a bandage. He made his way to the group of soldiers settling down to clean their kit. Most of them had been in the galley with him, the soldiers having a wound or three though none serious. Little was the exception, he was happily telling the others how slow and clumsy they were as he oiled his armour with the instinctive care of a veteran. He looked up at the boy approaching.

"Good shooting, laddie. You want to get some mail, though, as they are going to stick you soon, the way you stand out in the open. We've got spare. You stick with us, laddie, you're a soldier, not a sailor."

The tallest soldier stood up and stepped forwards, taking Pat's hand and looking at it. Pat tried to pull it back and started to flame up again, but relaxed at his silence. The soldier examined the wounds closely, sniffed at the treatment and frowned.

"What is it?"

Pat shrugged. "Some plant from the Port that I don't know."

"When you wash it off tomorrow, if it hasn't a good start to healing, bring to me. I have woundwort."

"Thanks," stammered Pat. "That's kind."

"May I see your arrows?" He took a shaft form Pat. "Elven," he said, and looked at the shaft, especially the seven full inches of hardened steel making up the bodkin tip. "How much carbon?"

"One and a half. Got to keep sulphur out."

"Sure." He smelt the wood.

Pat spoke in a strange, lilting language. "*You have a look and feel of the people. I cherish the chance to see you shoot.*"

The tall man looked at him solemnly and replied in the same language. "*My father. How do you speak the language of the North?*"

Pat grinned. "*Fighting and trading! One of my tutors was an elf, a farstrider.*"

"If you two bloody elves have quite finished," Sergeant Russell glared at them, "we only speak languages everyone can speak in this army!"

"Yeah" said Little, "but it's only Husky who can't speak Elvish and he's thick as pigshit."

"Enough," said the sergeant wearily before Husk could respond. "OK lads, so get the tension off the bows and oil them up. This salt air will kill them as quick as a wink. Inspection in half an hour."

There were the usual groans from the soldiers, but they set to straight away, taking great care of the weapons. Pat sat down beside the tall man and started cleaning his bow and putting the string away, while they murmured together in Elvish.

Lieutenant Mactravis climbed wearily up to the poop. He saluted the Captain who regarded him bleakly.

"Are you injured, Lieutenant?"

"Just a bang on the head, Sir. Helmet did its job."

"And your men?"

"Scratches, mostly, one broken bone, but all will heal. It's not an easy thing, climbing into a shield wall."

"Crazy," murmured Brian. "I can't understand the Spakka. They never had a chance."

"Oh, I'm not sure," said the Captain. "I think that was a well worked plan that had a very good chance. If they had caught us of guard, they would swarm over us and we'd have been disabled. They still had a chance till they found the shield wall, and if Pat and the ballista hadn't reduced the numbers, they could have come round the sides."

"Not sure what you did, sir," said Mactravis, "but I think that if the ship has slowed much after the impact, we would have had another load to contend with. That would have been warm work."

"Indeed, there are still a few longships astern of us looking for wreckage. Now, Lieutenant, tell us about these Spakka Sara has landed us with."

"I don't really know, sir. Spakka I have fought have always died, never surrendered. There are stories of how to get them to surrender, and Sara must know them." The Lieutenant eyed the Captain and Brian thoughtfully. "More than any mercenary would. She took command of my men without even thinking about it. Not many outsiders have heard us sing and fight."

"Yes," said the Captain slowly. "I wondered about that. She seems very young for a mercenary leader of such ability."

"Well, you'll need to promote her now, sir. All of a sudden your little topsails girl has thirty odd big hairy savages who will obey her and only her."

"Really?"

"You saw her welcome ceremony, sir. They put her feet on their heads. Drank her blood. But she has told them to do what I say, which apparently they have accepted for training purposes."

"Will they sail?"

""If she tells them to, I guess they will. They are all happily learning Harrhein this evening as she decreed it to be the most important thing. I never heard of a Spakka learning another language."

"Hmmmph. Well, I agree with you on the promotion anyway. She's now a Midshipman."

Sailing

With the Spakka galleys falling behind over the horizon, the Queen Rose maintained a steady south east course. She listed right over to one side as all the Bosun moved the ballast and cargo to starboard to keep the damaged side planks out of the water.

The carpenter managed a quick rough repair, stuffing the holes with canvas for the night, and the next day went over the side in a sling along with his assistants and experienced seamen. The Bosun oversaw from the deck, with the new recruits kept well away and out of mischief. Sara objected vociferously to her promotion but couldn't find a suitable argument. Once Brian pointed out that it was out of character for a mercenary to refuse more money, she submitted with bad grace, but insisted on remaining a topsailsman until the Spakka spoke enough Harrhein to incorporate them into the crew. She would need extra time as a Midshipman to learn her future duties.

While overseeing the repairs, the Bosun conducted interviews with the released slaves. There weren't many of them, for it seemed the Spakka preferred to row themselves for fitness. Slaves were not a permanent position - it was the bottom rung of society from which you could rise and become Spakka yourself. There were half a dozen Harrhein slaves, and she spoke to them first. They were a little reticent, one admitting to have been a slave for three years, the only one thankful for his release.

The Bosun came up to the poop to report to the Captain, with Taufik in tow. "Captain, I think we've picked up a right rum lot here," she reported without preamble. "I reckon most of them were pirates and wouldn't trust them an inch. Almost worth turning back to port to dump them."

Captain Larroche stroked his beard and prepared to speak when Taufik interrupted. "Captain, you must kill some of them."

Brian stopped his navigation lesson, he, Suzanne and Sara turning to listen with interest, as did Walters and Perryn, busy working on the report of the allegiance ceremony.

"Humph. I don't tend to execute many men, Master Taufik." Captain Larroche regarded him with a quizzical eye, hand still resting on his beard.

"Sir, they are Havant," said Taufik with the air of someone who has explained everything in full.

"Ah," said Captain Larroche, "I believe I have heard of Havant. Bishop, isn't it a country to the east of Spak?"

"Indeed, sir," replied Bishop Walters in his best tutor's voice. "It is supposed to be quite a large country and a veritable maritime power. They are always fighting with the Spakka, though, so we have little knowledge or trade with them. Most of our knowledge comes from Taufik here."

"So, Master Taufik, they are Havant and that is a reason to kill them? Why?"

"Sir, the Havant control all the Western trade with Hind. They are very jealous of it, and they are a very warlike people. We are expressly forbidden to trade to the West, and indeed it was only due to a storm we came this way. If the Havant find out we are trading in Hind, they will send warships to track us down and sink us."

"Do they have ships as big as this?" Captain Larroche asked, a shade contemptuously.

"Yes sir, many of them. This design is a carrack, and they also have caravels which they claim they invented. Caravels are smaller but faster. If they know about us, they will blockade the sea lanes. You must kill them. You cannot take the risk of them escaping. When we get to Hind, they will just steal a boat and slip ashore, then make their way home."

Silence spread across the poop deck. The sound of hammering rose from the side where the carpenter worked on the holes, and Little could be heard swearing in the distance. Hens cackled and a cockerel crowed

Captain Larroche looked at his officers, including Taylor, the third mate who materialised in time to hear. "Thoughts?"

Nobody said a word, though the Bosun began to look decidedly grim.

"Right, everyone," said the Captain, "imagine you are King of Havant and you are the sole trader established with all of Hind. Another country appears, one you don't trade with. Do you seek to encourage their trade, or repress it? If you repress it, how would you do so?"

Captain Larroche saw with interest the hard, determined expressions appearing first on the girls faces, as Sara and Suzanne came to the same decision as the Bosun. Bishop Walters joined them, while the other men still looked disturbed.

"Perhaps with some discussion and negotiation," began Brian and trailed off as he looked around and saw a lack of support.

"Who's going to kill them?" Taylor asked, a tough squat man. Married, and he saw no reason to put his wife in extra danger. "I can see the necessity, but I ain't doing it."

"And when?" The Bosun put in, her face troubled. "I don't want my crew upset by this. Needs to be done fast before they make friends. Not that they will. Take out the pirates too."

The silence deepened. Sara shook herself, and thought about responsibility. '*I'm growing up too fast,*' she thought miserably, '*this was supposed to be a fun trip. Go on girl, sort it out. They won't, and we must do this for the country. I must do it fast or they will find a reason not to do it.*' She stepped forward and cringed inside as she saw the faces brighten, a look of relief appearing fleetingly on the Captain's face.

"It's my fault they are here," she said clearly and confidently, no trace of her anguish. "I will sort it directly. Sir, you will explain why to the crew afterwards."

Captain Larroche nodded, "I can do that, but what will you do?"

"I will have the Spakka slaughter them. They will do what I say, and I will tell them it is a test. They must also slay any Spakka once of Havant." The iron grip she held on her emotions to stop the revulsion made her words come out hard and cold, which matched her face.

The Captain sighed. A way out, so tempting. Sternly he gripped the rail. "No. That is not the way. It would upset the crew who would never trust the Spakka. We need a trial before we hang them. I know, I know!" He put up his hand to stop Sara's angry protest. "This is a ship, not the army, we don't do decrees here. Every member of the crew is entitled to understand what is happening."

The Captain moved over to Sara, put his hand on her shoulder and murmured, "It is a good thought, but this is better for the ship." He stepped back and continued a little louder so others could hear. "If you could use your Spakka to arrest the slaves, we"ll try them straight away. I want them all held individually. You will do the translating at the trial."

The congregated crew grumbled and shuffled, not happy. Life as a galley slave amounted to the depths of hell, and they wanted to celebrate the rescue. Why put them on trial?

The first ex-slave brought forward came from Harrhein. Captain Larroche explained the tribunal consisted of an investigation to find out how he came to become a slave, and was rewarded with a long involved tale of a fishing boat being shipwrecked and his being rescued by Spakka who enslaved him. The crew listened appreciatively and hummed at his bravery. Sara translated his story to the Spakka, without him hearing.

The ex-slave finished his impressive tale and smiled at the crew. A large Spakka warrior grunted and muttered to Sara. "Captain, I have further evidence." The Captain nodded.

"This is Boersma. He remembers his capture." She indicated the warrior, who grinned theatrically at the crew through a large scar down his cheek, exposing several missing teeth. The crew frowned, not a popular witness. "He was a sailor on a pirate ship they caught. Along with four others over there. It was the Gull."

The crew gave a sharp intake of breath, the mood changing in an instant. The Gull had been a particularly bloody pirate ship. But Boersma wasn't finished.

"He says this one had no honour," Sara translated, stone faced. "He didn't fight to the death, begged for his life." Boersma took a step forward and spat in the direction of the ex-slave, who went white and sank to his knees. Other Spakka warriors pulled forward the other four men, and the five of them shrank before the glare of the crew.

Captain Larroche looked down on them. "Do any of you have

anything to say?" He waited, one sank to his knees and started to sob, the others just looked down. The Captain looked at his crew, to see if any of them wanted to speak, but mention of the Gull changed opinions. Even the recruits knew of her. "We will not have creatures like you in our crew. You will be hanged after the tribunal."

Sara spoke a few words in Spakka and the warriors laughed, dragging them off to the side.

Next up came a hulking young man with a flat face and black hair, who looked at them expressionlessly. A northerner who spoke only Spakka. His name was unpronounceable, and it wasn't clear whether he didn't understand the proceedings or didn't care. Seeing two others of similar ilk, the Captain called them in as well. The crew wanted blood now, and seeing foreign northerners in front of them were ready to see them hang as well. But the Spakka weren't helpful.

"Good fighters, hard workers. One day make Spakka. Have to knock them out to catch them." That was about the limit of their description. They shrugged when asked about their capture, and Janis said the Spakka were always fighting the northerners. Captain Larroche resorted to questioning them in Spakka through Sara.

"Will you work hard in the ship for us?"

"If you feed us." Sara tried not to smile as she translated.

"Will you run away?"

Shrugs. "Who knows? If the food better and the work not hard, we stay."

"Will you fight for the ship and the people in it?"

"Fighting fun. Give spear, we use."

The Captain looked at the Bosun, who shrugged. "Very well, they stay on probation. Who's next?"

A young boy with broad shoulders from rowing who claimed to be a fisherman. He said the Spakka had taken his ship and killed his father and uncle. He was from a fishing village on the east coast of Harrhein. A Spakka warrior confirmed his story, and added that he was a good boy who had stood over his father despite being small. The Captain passed him into the crew where one of the Bosun's mates took him under her wing.

A blonde giant came forth next, and a very similar one pushed out to join him. The second spoke up without being questioned, in broken Harrhein.

"We are Uightlanders! We on ship, raiding Spakka, Harrhein, anywhere we can. If not raiding, we trade. Sometimes we trade with Harrhein, sometimes we raid - depends on how good defences." He smiled. "Usually good, so trade! You take us, we part of crew, work, fight, trade. In maybe one year, maybe two, we ask for money and go home. We like to be on ship with women!" He grinned at the girls in the crew.

Captain Larroche spoke quietly to Brian. "They look likely lads. What do you think?"

"They'll be fine. Good lads, these Uightlanders, always an asset to the crew. Can start fights when they're drunk, but always in good spirits."

"OK Bosun, they're all yours." Captain Larroche called down to the deck. "Are the remaining ones all one nation, Midshipman Sara?"

Sara narrowed her eyes at the title, more so at a couple of titters from the crew. "Yes, Captain. All from Havant. They don't speak Harrhein."

"Very well. Find out if they have a spokesperson and what the Spakka have to say."

The Spakka herded them forward, a round dozen of them. Big men, with a browner skin than most Harrheinians, and prominent noses and black eyebrows. Sara spoke to them, one answered for the others. A Spakka intervened and the conversation went back and forth.

Sara turned, looked disdainfully at the Havants, and spoke. "All pirates, sir. Not very nice ones, either. Apparently they all liked to decorate themselves with human body parts when they went to attack another ship - hands, fingers, that sort of thing. This one," she pointed, "even wore a baby's head."

The crew growled, the mood turning black. The Havants looked worried, sensing something amiss and the spokesperson spoke urgently to Sara, who shrugged.

Captain Larroche felt something out of place. "All of them? From the one ship?

"Oh no, sir," said Sara with certainty. "Apparently there are lots of pirate ships in Havant, and these are from several ships. This one used fire arrows and looted the victim before it sank, leaving the victims behind, while these ones were slavers, raiding hamlets and fishing villages when the men folk were away, killing the old people and babies while taking the children and women."

The crew moved restively, an angry murmur coming from them. The Captain moved decisively.

"Very well. There is only one punishment for pirates. Hang them."

Some of the brawnier crew members pushed forward to help the Spakka, who seemed to guess their intentions and were not selfish. They and the Harrhein pirates were dragged over to the railings where Else and Pat had been busy putting nooses over the spars under the direction of Little, who had anticipated this with some relish. He grinned up at the Captain, seeing Brian reluctantly making his way down to the deck.

"Hey, Captain, you want us to get on with it or do you have a ceremony to go through?" Little shouted up, causing a number of crewmen to pause and look at the Captain for his reaction.

"Just get on with it," said the Captain with distaste. "But make sure it is quick, with a drop, not a slow death." He turned away, most of the officers going with him as the first screams rent the air, as the Havantines realised what was happening. Sara came up the ladder to join them and he eyed her, measuring her mood. He jerked his head. "My cabin. Now."

On the deck, Little took charge of the hanging detail and checked the knots for the nooses with Husk's assistance. "Got to be a big knot, Husky mate," he said, "so the head gets pushed over and the neck breaks."

Husk grunted. "Tell me something I don't know." He placed the noose around the neck of the first prisoner, one of the Harrhein pirates and grimaced in disgust. "Ah you bastard, you've shat yourself! Be a fucking man and die well." He pushed him over the side and watched the man fall, then his body twisted and he could hear the neck break as the weight hit the knot. When the body stopped jerking, Husk sliced through the rope just above the head, allowing it to drop into the sea and be washed away. Pat efficiently pulled the rope up to create a new knot.

The soldiers were brutally efficient in hanging the men, the

Spakka watching with great interest. Most of the crew gathered around watching, only a few mothers attempting to stop their children from seeing the show. Nobody spoke, content to watch. Hanging was a common enough event in Harrhein.

In his cabin, Captain Larroche helped himself to a drink of brandy, offering the bottle to Sara in silence, who accepted it. He knocked back a substantial slug and allowed the aroma to swirl up through his nose. Finally he looked up at her. She sipped her drink, ignoring him.

"You're a lying fucking bitch," he said. "Thank you."

Sara sighed. "It worked. But I can't let myself feel anything right now. How long does it last, this empty feeling?"

"A day or so. When it goes too quick, you know you're not human any more. That's when it's time to stop being a captain and take shore leave. I guess it's a good mark for a mercenary to judge themselves by as well."

"I've killed people, and it was hard the first time. But I've never ordered an execution before." She looked bleak. "Yes, I know, you did the actual ordering, but I set it up for you and I am responsible. It feels a damn sight worse than your first kill." She dropped her glass, her face broke and fat tears pushed their way out of her eyes. She cried in great, racking sobs and the Captain leaned forwards and enveloped her in his arms. His face sombre, he stroked her hair softly, as shudders ran through her. He let her cry herself out and felt her pull herself together, whereupon he released her and looked at her with a critical eye.

"Good girl. You'll be fine, but please don't get used to it. Here," he retrieved her glass and refilled it. "Take another dram and we'll get back on deck in a moment. Your Spakka will need instruction this afternoon. So, where did you learn to speak Spakka?"

"Uh, on the frontier," she said, confused.

"Sara, I am your Captain, you can tell me. I know you are not a mercenary. Who are you and why are you on my ship?"

She hardened and demonstrably pulled herself together. "Don't worry, sir, I am no threat to you - rather a help as I think I am showing. I can't tell you who I am, but I am here because I am running away, hiding."

"Very well," the Captain plainly wasn't satisfied, drumming his fingers on his desk. He looked hard at her, trying to place her. He remembered a fracas in Sarl, told to him by a fellow Captain over a flagon of wine. The feisty daughter of the Duke of Hardenwall had been married off to a known unpleasant rake, a Count of Sarl, rumoured to beat his women. The talk was that the Count had blackmailed the Duke. The daughter wasn't happy and stabbed him and ran away, only to be returned in sorrow by the Duke. The Captain put two and two together and made six. Poor lass, she looked far too young to be married to a swine like that. Frontier Hardenwall was a tough place, everyone could use a sword and fought the Spakka. Just the place where a girl might learn the language. "Off you go, sort out the Spakka. I don't care what happens in Sarl." He finished with a merry twinkle in his eye and a wink, to let her know he had worked it out.

Sara left, mystified. She had not heard the rumours from Sarl.

The Spakka did need instruction. Firstly they wanted Sara to explain why the Kingdom executed people by hanging them, rather than using an axe to cut their heads off. This would not only be efficient and use less resources, but help to train people in using an axe and allow the King to show off his skill. Was it because she was a girl she didn't like cutting heads off? Then they wanted an in-depth explanation of the techniques involved, whereupon Sara called over the fisher boy, Hal, and told him to take over teaching the Spakka Harrhein, and to translate for them in discussion with Little. Husk came over as well and she left them to it.

The ship settled down to routine. As Captain Larroche predicted, the winds stayed fair requiring little sailing work, though the new hands learnt to handle sails and all went through topsails lessons, including the soldiers, and the Spakka. The Uightlanders, northerners and the ex-fisherman melded in with the new recruits, and became part of the family, though the Spakka held themselves aloof. They spent a lot of time learning Harrhein with Hal, and didn't appreciate it.

The second day out, Captain Larroche called a meeting of all hands in front of the poop deck.

"Right, Ladies and Gentlemen, we have a lovely treat for you."

He grinned and the Bosun beside Pat groaned. "These lands we are going to have a mass of different countries, and just as many languages. There is no way anyone can learn them all, though Taufik seems to have done a fair job at it. However there is a trade language, Belada, which is spoken by traders and sailors throughout the countries. You will ALL need to learn it, and fortunately we have a teacher. Master Taufik speaks it fluently and will be conducting lessons. Everyone will take part - and here is a little incentive.

"Only fluent speakers will be permitted shore leave in the ports we sail to." He grinned and relinquished the rail to Taufik.

They all studied him, some for the first time. Unusual to their eyes, small, slender, though well made, with ink black short straight hair. Black eyes, and amazingly his skin was brown like leather, as if he was really well tanned.

Taufik smiled and spoke with his slight accent, rolling his r's. "The language is very simple - it needs to be as so many different people speak it. It has loan words from many languages and you will be pleased to know there are no irregular verbs or grammar to speak of. All you need is vocabulary, and the rest will come easily."

He started off with a few simple words, having the crew parrot the words back to him. This occupied the afternoon and all made progress to varying degrees. When the lesson finished, Pat grabbed Perryn and pulled him into the fo'c'sle. Interested, Sara followed, arriving in time to hear Pat.

"OK Perryn, have you got some dried sawblade root in your pack?"

"Yes I do, and that is a damn good idea."

"What are you two up to?" Sara interjected.

"Sawblade root is an aid to learning. We'll take some before the next lesson and one repetition will be enough. Can you take hypnosis?"

"Sure," said Pat, nodding.

Sara also nodded, and continued. "We don't need to wait till tomorrow. Let's take some and catch Taufik after supper and get him talking in Belada. Bet he will be happy to do it. By tomorrow we will be ahead of the rest and can get dispensation."

As they headed in a group up to the poop after supper, they passed Suzanne, who looked at them and stopped them.

"Going for extra lessons?" she smiled. "I'll join you. Give me some of the root."

"How did you know?" Perryn asked in accusation.

"Your eyes. Pupils are like pin pricks. I know all about the different drugs and what they are for. C'mon, give me some."

Perryn passed her a little dried root, she looked at it and snapped it in half, popped the half into her mouth and started chewing.

"I don't think that will be enough," Perryn started.

"It will be. I've used it a lot and know how much I need - I am very susceptible to it."

They found Taufik relaxing by the rail with a hot drink, and he was happy to talk to them in Belada. Far from being astonished at their speed, he grinned and speeded up, saying they had the same root in Hind.

Next day he dismissed them from the lesson.

Pat expected to lounge in the sun and talk to the dolphins, but Sara had other plans for him. Perryn managed to talk his way out of it, on the grounds he would never need the skill and should study his spellcraft, so Pat found himself gingerly holding a light sabre while Sara explained the skills to him.

"Oh, God! Careful with that pig-sticker, it's sharp."

"Of course it's sharp. Stop being a baby and concentrate or you'll get hurt. Now this is how you parry."

"Can't we practise with a stick or something?"

"No. The weight is wrong and you will get the wrong reflexes. Much better to practise with the real thing."

An hour later Pat dripped with sweat and blood, while Sara was cool and calm. They also had observers as school had ended, to Pat's intense embarrassment. The soldiers and the Spakka joined them. Little offering advice - he seemed to be the only soldier who talked much. Mactravis watched Sara with interest, as did the fascinated Spakka.

Finally, Pat muffed a parry and managed to knock Sara's blade the wrong way, receiving a nasty gash in his thigh.

"Enough," he panted, looking crestfallen at his leg, trying to squeeze the sides of the cut together. "I need to treat this, there is no mud to stop the bleeding."

"Ha! Piss on it lad, that's the best cure." said Little helpfully.

He took Pat off towards the heads on the leeward side of the ship. "You need to piss on it quickly to clean it. Piss is the best, as it stops infection. Yeah, that's the way. I know it stings, but you'll get used to it. You can't trust mud, could be all sorts of shit in it on a battlefield. It's alright in the middle of nowhere, but you're a soldier now, not a hunter."

Meanwhile, Mactravis replaced him as Sara's fencing partner and they went at it hard and fast. The other soldiers paired off and also started bladework, keeping an eye on the Spakka who hacked at each other with axes.

Sara disarmed Mactravis with a quick flourish then found she had to step smartly as he caught the blade in his other hand and continued as if nothing had happened.

She disengaged and stepped back. "Not seen that before."

"We're a little different on the battlefield to the salles. Sabres aren't much use, as some of the savages use huge heavy swords and are so strong they use them like sabres, with good skills. They snap sabres, you can't block them." He smiled at her. "You're no mercenary, ma'am."

"I am, though. Just haven't served on the northern frontier."

"Yes you have," Mactravis replied. "I was a cadet at High Peaks when you tried to lead a night patrol out. Thought the way Captain Parkes chewed you out was very stylish. He was horrified when he discovered who you were."

"Damn! Does everyone know who I am?"

"There's not a soldier in the army who doesn't love you and would recognise you, ma'am. I know Sergeant Russell as a corporal caught you trying to steal a sword from the armoury when you were eight. He was your Master-at-Arms, I recall, so he knows you. You've spent far too long around the army to find anyone who hasn't seen you. Your disguise is good, I only worked it out after the fight with the Spakka. I expect the boys worked it out right away, they usually do."

"Lieutenant, you know why I am here?"

"Not exactly, but I presume there was some sort of assassination attempt? Lord Rotherstone?"

"Yes, a good one. How did you spot it would be him straight away?"

"He's been trying to foment discontent in the army for years. Don't worry; we're with you to a man. I presume you selected us as your guard on this jaunt?"

"That's right."

"We are honoured ma'am. May I ask how long we can expect to be gone?"

"I don't know. I am planning to be gone about six months, but my spymaster will let me know when it is safe."

They talked quietly at the side of the ship, and she told him about the assassination attempt in detail. The soldiers continued to practice, making enough noise to keep the conversation private while ensuring they could hear themselves.

Sara came up on deck from the heads after the watch finished, and went looking for Pat. Awful sounds came from a cabin on the port side of the rear castle, which she thought was the smithy. It sounded like a fight was about to start, shouts and aggressive noises but the words were a nonsense.

Curious, she looked in the door and saw Pat shouting at the smith and his assistants. And one of them was shouting at Pat, waving a hammer at him. Pat stood there, glaring at him, then shouted back. Sara stared as she realised he was using the same language. *'Bloody cowboy, my eye,'* she thought. *'Speaking dwarvish, what next? I've never met anybody who could speak their language.'*

Brian pushed past her. "What the hell is going on here?" The Bosun was behind him, unobtrusively holding a marlin spike.

Pat and the smiths turned in surprise. "Nuthin'," grunted the smith. "We just talkin' about metal." The four of them stared at Brian for a moment; one of the smaller smiths barked something at Pat, who shouted back, picked up a poker and slammed it on the anvil. This got them all shouting at once, until Pat pulled out a bit of paper and a pencil and started drawing on it, using the anvil as a table. They all shut up and crowded around, looking at his drawing; they started arguing again.

Brian shook his head and departed, the Bosun following after giving Pat a hard look. Sara sat down and watched, hugely entertained.

The argument went on until finally the dwarves roared in agreement and pulled out some mugs, filling them from a barrel, a clearly illegal barrel hidden under some spare bits of metal. Sara was given one too, and as she sipped it, they all shouted a toast and drained theirs, promptly refilling them and starting work, pumping the bellows and staring critically at the flames, waiting for the right temperature.

Pat waved to them and left. Sara followed him and asked, "What was that all about?"

"Oh, I wanted them to make me some different arrow heads."

"What was the argument about?"

"Argument? What argument?"

"Well, you were shouting and threatening each other."

"No we weren't."

"Pat, explain please," she said patiently.

"Uh. That's the way you talk with dwarves."

"Really? I've never seen them act like that before."

"You seen them speak their own language?"

"No - and how come you speak it?"

"We went to one of their mines and borrowed some smiths a couple of years back. I hung around to see what they did and learnt the language. They always talk like that when discussing things."

Sara shook her head, thinking she had only seen about two dwarves in her life.

"Some cowboy you are. So what were you asking them? How to transmute gold from steel?"

Pat looked at her in incomprehension, deciding to answer the questions he could understand.

"I was asking them to make me some arrowheads of different designs. You can't transmute anything, but you can take it out of certain rock, if it is gold bearing ore."

Sara started to ask what ore was, then gave up. "Come on, let's make the sing-song. You learnt the songs yet?"

"Some of them," said Pat cautiously, worried she would drag him in for a duet. He hated being the centre of attention and Sara seemed to push him into it relentlessly. She put her arm through his and dragged him off to where the boatswain's mates were charging their fiddles.

Two days later Pat and Sara were relaxing on deck with hot tea made from a herb infusion popular in Praesidium. They were on watch, but nothing was required. The nightwatch was asleep, their watch was on call. A burly sailor came up to them. They knew him vaguely; he had joined a fortnight before them and considered himself above them. Pat didn't like him.

"Midshipman," he said. "I have a small problem with the cargo. Need your opinion."

Sara passed her drink to Pat and started after Kane as he turned and walked away.

Pat took the cups and started towards the galley. "I'll lend a hand as well."

"No need," said Kane over his shoulder, Pat shrugged and went to talk to the soldiers.

Sara followed Kane down a companionway into the bowels of the ship. He grabbed a lantern and opened a door that gave access to the main hold. Sara followed him in and looked around with interest. It was hard to see in the gloom, and the place smelt pleasantly of cotton and dyes. Kane worked his way along a gangway to the middle, where a narrow passage led deep into the cargo between bales.

He held the lantern high. "You're smaller than me, so go ahead. Go down here and take the first gap on the right. I'm worried about some of the bales in there."

Obediently, Sara set off and he followed behind with the lantern. She found the gap, turning sideways to squeeze through, finding a larger space behind it. Kane held the lantern behind him as he squeezed through and she couldn't work out the layout in front of her, so she paused.

Kane pushed through, brought the lantern behind him and hung it up on a peg. Sara stared in astonishment at where a small space existed on top of the bales, perhaps eight foot by six. It was a layer of bales with nothing on top of them, making a small cosy cabin in the middle of the hold. She was just about to comment when Kane pushed her hard and she landed face down on the bales which were soft and gave under her. Before she could react he was on top of her, his weight pinning her to the bales.

She tried to buck him off, but could get no purchase, nor could she shout with her mouth full of cotton. In outrage, she felt his hand curve round her buttocks, and heard his pleased chuckle. She tried to cry out in anger, and couldn't. His hand was working round under her now, feeling for the belt and fastenings of her trousers. Her legs thrashed ineffectually, and he used her movements to get his hand on the fastenings and undo the belt . He started working on the buttons.

Sara got an arm free from under herself and tried to hit him, but could not reach him on top of her. With a hard yank, he pulled her trousers down past her buttocks. She clamped her legs together but his hand was under her panties and pushing down into the crack of her buttocks. Sara squealed in outrage as one of his fingers pushed with brutal and painful force into her bottom, the nail rasping and tearing at her tender flesh. She clenched her buttocks together, relaxing her legs at the same time and in a trice he pushed her trousers down to her knees.

Kane moved higher on top of her, she tried to buck and he sat firmly on her back. He used his legs to pin her shoulders and leaned down and pulled her trousers off, taking the panties with them, despite her kicking. Sara began to panic and tried to scream again, struggling to breathe under his weight. Kane turned around, shuffled backwards, sitting on her buttocks. She reared up, pushing herself up with both arms. He grabbed her shirt at the collar and pulled it down and out, ripping open the top two buttons and trapping her arms to her side. Then he slipped off her and swung her onto her back, her arms pinioned to her sides, bare from the waist down. Before she could react he fell on her, pinning her down with his waist. One hand held the shirt and her arms, with the other he popped a straining button and revealed her breasts, grinning as he caressed her left breast and rolled the nipple with his thumb.

Sara stared at him in shock and astonishment - nothing in her life had prepared her for this, nor for the revulsion that welled up in her as her nipple hardened under the friction. Realising she was trapped, she started to shout for help, knowing Pat would hear. As her mouth opened, Kane was ready and he pushed some loose cotton into it. She choked and felt panic rising inside her, thrashing feebly. He saw the nipple firm up and grinned again, speaking for the first time as he rubbed the nipple further.

"Ha! Knew you would like it when we got down to it. You proud and hoity-toity girls always want it rough." He dropped his head to her breast and she felt hot damp warmth on her breast. She groaned, thinking how her nipples always reacted to temperature and friction and how annoyed it made her when boys thought they were responsible. Now this! His weight crushed the breath from her, and she felt a growing pressure in her groin where he pressed against her. His hand went down and she felt him fiddling with his own trousers that he pushed down and away and she felt something big, hard and hot against her thighs.

She sobbed in horror, and he laughed again, wiggling his legs. "Stop struggling, girl. Or should I say Princess." He grinned at her expression of shock, pushing the horror and outrage off her face.

He chuckled, looking down at her frozen form and squeezing her left breast painfully. "You heathen Starr bastards have lived off our backs long enough. Not even a proper Christian, are you, bitch?"

He bent to her breast again, biting and the pain lanced through her. She thrashed again, desperately trying to get her arms free and he used her movement to slip between her thighs, forcing them apart and wide. The hot thing was now pressed against her private parts, rubbing against her, causing more revulsion to erupt in her, combining with the pain from her breast. She smelt his rancid, unwashed body and felt a surge of bile rush up her throat, a shudder of horror and panic overwhelming her, her mind a screaming mass of panic.

Kane pulled back and looked down at her, grinding his groin onto hers and grinning. "The Count says goodbye, bitch." Without warning he smacked her hard around the head, and the flat taste of her own blood filled her mouth. "Yeah, I can smack you around too, Princess. Not used to that, hey? Well, here's a message from the Count. Before I kill you."

He thrust hard at her, grunting in pleasure as she felt the hard, hot bar rake across her skin, skidding upwards. "Your daddy won't be upset for too long, when you don't come home. 'Cos we're going to kill the bastard too, sweetheart." Another hard thrust, this time catching at her fold with a painful jerk before sliding upwards.

Something cold went through her at the mention of her father, and she was thinking rationally. *'Girl,'* she thought to herself, *'if you are going to get through this and sort this man, you're going to have to be an actress. Never mind your sweet virginity, worry about that later.'* Deliberately, she collected all her feelings of horror and revulsion, mentally put a big canvas sack over them and slowly lashed it down. She felt the horror recede as she lashed it tighter and started to think.

She let a little moan out, relaxed her legs and moved her hips against him in experimentation. He chuckled, relaxed his left hand and moved it up onto her right breast, holding it firmly. His hips moved and thrust at her again, the hard thing pushing up from her thighs right onto her stomach, catching on her sensitive parts again, and he growled in frustration.

She moaned in her throat and worked at the cotton, trying to get it out. Feeling the revulsion bulge up, she lashed it tighter, and blanked her mind, remembering listening into a lecture on how to survive torture. His chest was pushed into her face now, as he gathered himself. One hand went to her crutch, and her eyes widened in pain, shock and revulsion as the grubby fingers groped and parted her flesh. She groaned again and thought her head would burst as she struggled to blank it all out.

"In a minute, bitch, when I'm ready" he said in great satisfaction, misunderstanding the groan. "Well, well, well, little miss royalty really does like it rough."

He adjusted his hips, the thing went down and she felt it press against her, warm and now throbbing. His hand guided it into place and she could feel the heat against her as she tried to move her hips backwards. With an effort, she spat out the cotton just as he thrust, her eyes bulging as she felt the thing slither inside and push impossibly far into her, the friction tearing and hurting deep inside. His hands were still on her breasts, but his head was above her and her mouth was against his chest, and she moaned in agony, the pain igniting a white hot, calculating rage inside her.

"Ohhhh," she moaned, thrashing in virulent pain and he laughed again, still mistaking her noise but finally releasing her breast and bracing himself on his elbows, retracting and thrusting in again with studied deliberation.

"Ah," he said in deep satisfaction. "That feels good, doesn't it girly? Well, enjoy it while you can, because I'm gonna kill you after, Count's orders." He paused, watching her face to see how she took it while continuing to thrust into her. Seeing the disbelief, he continued. "I've set up a bale, see, right heavy one it is. When we've had our fun, I'll break your fucking neck." His words paused with each thrust. "Then you go under the bale, and I'll push it down. Thump on yer head." He grinned, with a particularly virulent thrust.

Sara steeled herself and concentrated on her immediate goal of gaining trust, ignoring her body rocking in a sea of pain. She raised her legs and locked them around him, moving her hips instinctively like a piston and speeding him up, ignoring the pain, blanking out feelings, intent with her purpose. She strained up towards him, raising her head.

"Oh, God, kiss me. Kiss me now," she cried, staring intently at his mouth.

Kane was pleased. He was loving this. This wasn't the first high born lady he had raped, but it was the youngest. Pity it would only be the once, so time to revel in it while it lasts. Awkwardly he ducked his head down to her mouth and she grabbed it with hers, sucking his tongue in past her teeth. With a feeling of intense satisfaction, she felt his tongue deep in her mouth, sucked in a lot of lower lip and crunched down hard, gratification flooding through her as she felt the hot blood spurt into her mouth. She bit harder and as he pulled his head back she went with him then yanked back with her head hard and fast, feeling the flesh tear. Blood flooded over her as Kane reared up and let out a garbled scream of pain and horror, his hands releasing her and coming up to his face. He slithered out of her, becoming limp. She spat out half his tongue and a lump of lip, finding her arms coming free as her jacket slipped away.

Sara's left fist came flying up from the bed and landed on the hand over the wound, smashing it into his revealed teeth, her strength finally released. As he went over on his side she slammed her knee into his groin and knocked him over the side of the bales into the crack between them. Getting ready to hit him again, she heard running feet, and grabbed her trousers, arching her back to get them on and give herself some semblance of modesty. She barely finished before Pat appeared, took one incredulous look at her still bared breasts and then the moaning Kane. He grabbed his feet and started dragging Kane back down the narrow way, while he thrashed feebly.

There were voices behind him which exclaimed as he pulled Kane out.

"What the hell happened to him? Look at the blood."

"He tried to rape Sara," said Pat grimly. He hauled Kane to his feet, turned him while twisting his arm behind him. Applying pressure, he started Kane towards the door. Seeing Katie, he snapped to her: "Go in and help her. Somebody get Suzanne. I'll sort this scum."

Word passed quickly, the nightwatch was up as he brought Kane to the deck. Suzanne passed him on the way, running down the companionway with barely a glance. The nightwatch stared as Kane came out, groaning, with his remaining lip flapping like a bird's wing, showing teeth that grinned white in the lamplight, rimmed with the black blood which still ran down his mouth, neck and chest in gouts. The stump of his tongue waggled visibly, still pulsing blood and he croaked when he tried to speak.

"Nils!" Pat shouted in an absolute fury. "Get a rope, tie it to the main spar and chuck me the end." He glared at the crew around him. "He tried to rape Sara."

"On it, Pat." Nils shinned up the mast in a moment and ran a rope from the spar so it would hang over the ocean. He threw the end to the waiting Pat, who started to fashion a noose, his movement precise and expert. Without a large knot.

Brian came up beside Pat and took his arm. "Wait, Pat. I understand how you feel, but on ship you cannot do this without the Captain making the decision." He looked at him. "Will you wait while I get the Captain?"

Pat looked at him, and Brian was inwardly taken aback. '*This is not a boy anymore,*' he thought to himself.

"I'll wait," said Pat flatly. He gave a twist to Kane's arm and threw him to the deck, kicking him as he landed. Brian turned to go for the Captain, wishing he had not heard the arm break, Kane's sobs in his ears, when Sergeant Russell arrived like an avenging fury.

"You fucking BASTARD," he cried, slamming a hardened fist into Kane's gut. "Where is she?" he screamed, as Brian wrapped his arms around Russell. "Where's my little girl?" Tears were pouring down his face as he tried to hit Kane again. Captain Mactravis arrived, to Brian's short lived relief.

"Is it true?" Mactravis asked, white faced and dagger in his hand. "Did this man rape Sara?"

"Never mind that," said Brian with some heat, "help me with your bloody soldier." Russell might be a small man compared to Husk, but he easily threw Brian around as he ignored the arms around him and continued to hit Kane.

"No," said Pat, watching Kane flinch to the punches and feeling the bone in the arm grate where he held it. "But he tried."

"You swine," said Mactravis at Kane, whose bloodshot eyes peered up at him in pain and terror. "Leave off, Sergeant, I want him still. Kane, I'm going to skin you alive." Mactravis' voice dropped to a hiss, and the dagger shot forward, slicing into the skin beside the eye and flensing it away back to the ear.

"Lieutenant Mactravis! Where is your discipline?" Brian shouted. "Get hold of yourself, man! BOSUN! Come and help restore order."

The Bosun arrived with her mates and eased the soldiers off Kane, although Pat refused to relinquish the arm. A flustered Brian went to find the Captain while Mactravis and Russell set off for the hold.

Sara sat on the bales with her arms crossed around her breasts, staring at the floor. Katie had her arm round her and was talking about her life back in Praesidium where she had worked as a serving girl in a tavern. Suzanne pushed in, having ordered all the men back.

"Katie, can you go and get a tea from the galley for her, please. I have asked the guys to keep a guard and not let anyone through. Thanks."

She watched her go, then turned to Sara, wrapping her in her arms.

"Oh, my darling. It's all right now, sweetheart, mama's here."

Sara broke, crying into Suzanne's neck.

She sobbed out her story, while Suzanne rocked her.

"All right, darling," said Suzanne, her thoughts racing as she rocked. "Did you tell Katie?"

"No"

"What did anyone see? What did Pat see?"

"I, I managed to get my trousers on before he got here. I don't think he saw anything, just my breasts and he's seen those when I am swimming."

"It's not the same, darling, but don't worry. OK, nobody knows it was anything but attempted. We'll keep it that way. It was an assassination attempt. They will buy that and they will understand you are shocked. Now, if you are up to it, I will take you to my cabin."

"But Suzanne, it was horrible. OK, I hid what I really felt and blanked it all out, but he took my virginity," she wailed. "I, I, I wanted the first time to be special!"

"No he didn't, sweetheart, you lose it when you make love for the first time. This was something else, an attack, an animal. That man has done this many times before. You would never have got away if you weren't so clever and brave and I am proud of you." She hugged her again and could feel the doubt. "Honestly, darling, you only saved yourself because you were so good at acting, and you did it the right way, blanking it all out. When you bit him you took a risk, a big risk. Rapists often break girls' jaws to stop the biting. And as he was going to kill you anyway, you are lucky he didn't."

Sara calmed, and Suzanne helped her up and along the gap just as Mactravis and Russell arrived. She looked at the guys, and spoke softly. "I'm taking her to my cabin. Swain, please check the area for evidence and bring it to the captain. Be careful. He said he had a bale ready to drop on her. It doesn't look like this is the first time he has used this place either, proper little trap he has in there."

The Boatswain's mate nodded and went down the gap, but Mactravis and Russell were riveted by Sara. Russell fell to his knees at her feet.

He started to speak, choking out his words, tears streaming down his cheeks while Suzanne's eyes narrowed and the sailors nearby looked on in astonishment

"I've failed you, ma'am. I wasn't there to protect you, Pr.."

"Sergeant Russell," broke in Suzanne, wise in the way of men's emotions. "If you can keep your apologies for an appropriate time, we shall be able to escort SARA to my cabin."

Russell started, jumped to his feet and swept her off her feet. "Of course, so sorry, I'll carry her."

Sara twisted in his arms, burying her face in his neck. "Not your fault, Andy, I was silly, let my guard down" she whispered, only audible to Mactravis and Suzanne, who raised an eyebrow.

Suzanne took them to her room, comforted her, left her with Katie and Russell while she went to the Captain's cabin, taking Mactravis with her. On the way, she spoke to the Bosun. Captain Larroche sat at his desk with Brian. She sat down at his nod.

"Captain, the man has a proper little bed laid out amongst the cargo. I expect you will find he stacked those bales himself - if he had an assistant, then we have another rapist." She nodded. "Yes, it was rape, very, very nearly, a much practised one too, although the primary attempt was assassination." She told them what had happened and how Sara had broken free, leaving out the penetration.

Captain Larroche looked puzzled. "What I don't understand," he said, "is why the Count is making such an effort when she clearly wants nothing to do with him. And how did he manage to get somebody on my ship?"

Brian started to shrug, until he noticed Suzanne and Mactravis looking at the Captain, puzzlement written on their faces.

"She's not the daughter of Duke Hardenwall, is she?" he asked, looking at their faces.

They both shook their heads.

Captain Larroche closed his eyes. "I'm not going to like this am I? All right, tell me, who is she?"

Mactravis and Suzanne looked at each other for a moment. He shrugged, while the Captain began to fume.

Forestalling his anger, Suzanne spoke. "She is Princess Asmara."

Brian sagged back in his chair, while the Captain looked stunned. There was silence for a moment; the Captain pulled himself together.

"Oh my," he said. He sighed. "Damn. We have to hang him, and fast." He glanced at Brian. "This is your fault, Brian, you selected the crew."

Brian gaped at him, nodding in slow agreement, guilt pushing him down in his chair.

There was a knock at the door. At the Captain's call it opened and the Bosun came in, with a small girl called Jane in tow.

"Thought you'd like to hear what Jane has to say," said the Bosun.

With some difficulty, in deep awe at talking to the Captain, Jane stuttered out her story. It seemed she had been subjected to Kane's attentions for the last week, after he inveigled her to his lair while still in port. She was in terror at having to tell it, as Kane had threatened her should she say a word. She kept saying she was only talking now because he had been caught, and please don't let him know she had talked. What would his punishment be? The poor girl was shaking.

The Captain sighed, grabbed his hat and headed for the door. "Come on, let's get this distasteful business over with." They followed him.

Pat still stood beside Kane, bristling with anger; the soldiers were up and surrounding the Bosun's mates holding him, Sergeant Russell also holding an arm. The Spakka were there, very unsure. Nobody had explained to them that Kane had tried to rape their mistress, but they sensed something seriously amiss and were questioning Hal, whose shrugs showed his own ignorance. Kane was looking even more worse for wear than before, the soldiers having exacted more retribution despite the 'swains protection. The entire crew was there, not a man looking friendly towards Kane.

The Captain strode to the rail and looked down on them in the darkness, faces looming out of the gloom below him. He could see the blood pooling around Kane's head. The man was barely conscious.

"I've looked into the matter, it is open and shut. Kane is another of those damn mercenary murderers. Not only did he try to kill Sara, but rape as well, and but for her quick thinking might have succeeded. Not only that, but it was a practised assault, not just aimed at Sara. For we have found another girl who has been subjected to his attentions and she has testified against him."

He looked around at the crew. Every face he could see hard and angry. His eyes dropped to Pat, who was standing scowling at the front, leaning forward listening.

"Hang him." The Captain nodded.

Pat yanked Kane up and Little dropped the noose over his head, a noose without a big knot, and Little took care to fit it snugly behind his head, not his ear. They bundled him to the side of the ship and pushed him over without ceremony. Kane swung down, one hand grabbing for the rope while the broken one dangled and his feet trailed in the sea, desperately walking on the water as he woke up.

Little grunted and spat dismissively. "Betcha 5 sovs he lasts less than 5 minutes," he said to Strachan casually.

"No bet," said Corporal Strachan. "The way the, uh, Sara bit him, he won't have the strength."

A wail went up from behind him. A young sailor knelt on the

deck crying and shouting incoherently. The Bosun walked up to him and grabbed him with satisfaction.

"Well, Hughie, thought it might be you. Another rapist here, Captain," she called over her shoulder with great satisfaction.

"No! No!" The kid cried out in terror, his trousers soaking wet. "I never! I didn't know what it was for. I thought it was just a den, like. I helped him make it and went there to sleep a few times, never took anyone there. I wouldn't hurt a girl. Please! Please believe me."

The Captain looked at him. "Bosun, chain him in the hold. We'll discuss him in the morning."

Howls of fury rent the air as the Spakka prised an explanation out of a shell shocked Hal.

Pat looked over the rail bleakly. Kane still twitched. One of the Spakka, Esbech, supported by his mates, hung down the side and carefully broke every bone he could reach with the back of his axe. Pat felt empty, no satisfaction in this death and he mourned for Sara, not sure what had happened and not knowing what to do. He wondered at his own feeling and started when somebody took his arm.

"Pat, she needs you now." It was Suzanne. "She's in my cabin. I won't use it tonight. You stay with her till morning. Don't talk a word about what happened. Just comfort her." She looked into his eyes as she walked him towards the companionway.

"Oh, damn, you're a bloody kid in some ways and a man in others. You don't have a clue what to do, do you?"

Pat looked at her.

"You go in there and put your arms around her and hold her. When she stops crying, take your clothes off and get into bed with her. Hold her gently, kiss her and do whatever she wants. Clear?"

For the first time Pat looked scared, really scared, his eyes wide, his anger gone as if never present. A little boy was looking back at Suzanne.

"Dammit, Pat, she needs you, a man, to give her love right now, she doesn't need another girl. She needs a man who cares for her to hold her and love her. You care for her don't you?

He nodded, mutely. They arrived at the door, she opened it and pushed him in with a smile, calling Katie out and sending her off.

Russell long gone to assist the hanging.

Pat stood flat footed inside the door, looking at Sara who sat up at the end of the bunk, her back against the wall. Her eyes were huge, luminous and uncertain.

"Is it over?"

He nodded, and shuffled over to the bunk. She started to shrink away from him and he looked stricken and went to his knees.

"Oh Sara! Are you OK? Sweetie, you look so..." he stopped, thinking on his feet, "so pretty. How do you feel?" Feeling he was doing something very wrong he leant forward and put his arms around her. Sara burst into tears and hugged him. As her tears subsided, he wondered at Suzanne's prescience, forgetting everything as she kissed him with fierce passion. Gently he took her clothes off while she removed his and he slid into the bed.

Sara felt his hands on her and shivered deliciously. She had been feeling defiled, dirty, and was terrified nobody would want her now. Her friend Pat wanted her and she felt her heart swell and almost burst with love for him. She took her tongue out of his mouth, pushed his head up and guided it down towards her left breast, needing to feel his lips taking away the earlier stain. She gasped as he went down and started to suck, contentment rushing through her as the feeling of his weight crushing her and the rising warmth of his manhood. She spread her thighs for him, feeling a rush of pleasure coming up into the very core of her being. She felt his head part her flesh, and a flashback overwhelmed her, the smell of Kane in her nose, and the tearing agony came searing back. She screamed and pushed Pat away; he floundered and fell off the bed while she curled into a ball and sobbed.

Pat didn't know anything about girls, but he knew how to handle a hurt wild animal. He slipped back into the bed and curled himself around her, holding her and making small soothing sounds.

Suzanne, outside the door, heard the soft sounds and smiled in total misunderstanding. Her Princess was fine and getting the best cure. Now she felt like some exercise herself. She recalled Lieutenant Mactravis had a cabin to himself, and swayed off, humming a happy tune.

Storms

Nils was a wonder in the yards. He took ten days to recover fully from the battle with the Spakka, having dislocated both his shoulders and broken his nose when he reached the deck. Then he began to show off his skills. He could run along the top of the spars, disdaining the cord below each one which most sailors used to walk along while holding the spar. Within days Pat was copying him, and of course the first thing he did was slip and fall. He landed on the mainsail, fortunately with a big belly, and slid down to the edge just above the deck. He turned as he slid, and caught the rope along the bottom, nearly jerking his arms from their sockets as he swung for a moment then dropped lightly to the deck. Moments later Nils landed beside him, having copied him and learnt from his previous experience.

"That was fun! Let's do it again."

That was the last time they used the rope ladder to come down, though Captain Larroche nearly had a heart attack when he saw them, and tried to ban it without success. It took them a while to work out how to use the technique in different winds so they were able to brake properly and not replicate Nils' crash into the deck.

The rest of the crew spent time in the rigging too. Changing sails was too big a job for four, it required a whole watch of twenty hands when the wind changed but it was still just the four of them who set the topsails, though the two blond Uightlanders were getting there. Most of the work was done by ropes and pulleys at which the Spakka excelled.

Pat was taking a section of four on a starboard yard, a good sixty feet above the sea, while Nils had the larboard. Linda was on the end, over confident in her abilities and determined to try spar walking. They were all leaning over the yard, standing on the cord beneath, pulling up the canvas, packing it down and tying it up with the cords that ran down the sails for that purpose. Linda over-reached for another length and her foot slipped off the cord as she pulled back. Her hands were trying to grab the canvas and they scrabbled desperately for a grip as she went backwards. One hand caught the foot cord as she fell. There was an agonising pain in her shoulder as it dislocated under her weight and slipped through her fingers. Her head bounced off a ratline and her body rotated as she fell down to land in the sea, flat on her back, about ten yards from the ship.

"Man over board!" Taufik shouted and Jim immediately hurled the safety barrel over the side towards her; it landed mere feet from her, its ropes trailing near her. She didn't move.

"Keep bloody working." Nils shouted. "We can't help her till the sails are furled."

The topsailsmen had all stopped and watched Linda fall; some like Pat had already started to react. Pat was up onto the yard about to jump, as was Sara.

"Pat! Sara! If you bloody jump I'll skin you alive. Get back to work, fast. It does more good to furl the bloody sails." Nils was really angry now, the first time they had seen it. Reluctantly, they went back to work, the sails furling faster than ever before. As they worked, they saw the little jolly boat being dropped astern, half a dozen sailors spilling into it, and rowing after her.

By the time they had all the topsails furled, the jolly boat was far behind. Taufik had swung the ship round and was painfully tacking back towards it. The crew could feel the different motion of the ship, and those that had just got used to the steady downwind motion found the different, choppier motion hard to bear.

By the time the topsailsmen could drop to the deck, the jolly boat was on its way back. They lined the rail and watched as the boat was hauled up. Dan's face was bleak as he stepped out of it, holding Linda's body in his arms. He wouldn't let anybody take it from him and the tears were streaming down his face.

The body was light because there wasn't much of it.

Pat felt Sara gripping his arm and heard sobs from amongst the crew.

The Bosun silently laid a length of canvas on the deck and gestured to Dan who gently laid the remains on it. Huge gashes were in the trunk of the body, only one arm and the stump of one leg were left. The Bosun rapidly wrapped it up and started to stitch the canvas into a closed tube. The dwarven blacksmith silently put a chunk of metal near where the feet should have been.

Captain Larroche held a funeral service immediately, and then Pat went off to talk to Bart the fisherman about sharks. After that Pat and Grey Fox, the half Elf, practiced archery at the back of the ship along with the crossbowmen.

They killed a lot of sharks.

Shark hunting caused them to develop a new fishing technique, with a cleverly barbed arrow, made by the smiths after long debate and copious draughts of dwarven ale. A length of fine chain attached to the head. They spent three days working out how to coil the chain so that the arrow was not deflected too much, and how to compensate for it. Bart was fascinated by this and created a teaser for them, a length of twine with a knot at the end to which he whipped several feathers from the chickens and some bits of silk and wire.

He would let this out some way behind the ship, until fish, usually tuna, started to strike at it. He would then retrieve it rapidly, with the fish chasing it, till it was in range and the archers would harvest the bounty. To attract sharks, they simply used one of the tuna.

Taufik was pleased with this addition to their diet, as he kept warning of a sickness that could afflict deep sea sailors, and insisted that everyone should drink his Yellow Remedy at least once a week. This was a disgusting mixture of citrus juices, grasses and herbs which he said was invented by a people far to the East. Apparently these people were the source of much of his sailing lore including the compass. He sniffed disdainfully at the Harrheinian compasses, bemoaning the loss of his own fine instrument.

All the officers were required to record the course and speed, thus calculating the distance travelled, at all times. Sara worked under Brian as well as being on the topsails watch. She tried to share what she learnt with Pat in the evening, but he wasn't much interested. Brought up in the wilds, he had an instinctive feeling of place that allowed him to navigate in his own way. Not that it was much use at sea. Walters would draw a chart based on the data, though Captain Larroche continued to keep his rutter, a sea diary that was a Captain's lifeline and enabled him to copy routes. Walters and Taufik would argue for hours as to exactly where they were, as Walters was worried about sea currents which would distort the dead reckoning they were using and Taufik was frankly disbelieving at the idea of a current in the middle of nowhere.

The Spakka learnt to speak Harrhein, some better than others, but remained stand-offish. They took part in sailing the ship, and were adept at anything they turned their hands to, but continued to prefer their axes to the Harhein variety of weapons. They revered Sara, and she would spend an hour a day with them talking in their own language and settling disputes. For some reason, they welcomed Little and Husk into their community, though this always seemed to spark some sort of argument. The ex-galley slaves also spent a lot of time with them, somewhat to the wonderment of the crew.

Perryn spent much time with Little and the soldiers, who were delighted to teach him the little they knew of battle magics, and his own skills grew rapidly as he experimented with the different techniques they told him about.

Other skills were learnt as well.

Captain Larroche was standing on the poop in the sunshine enjoying a morning brew when Brian came up to him.

"Going well Brian. Can't remember a voyage with such fine weather and such a constant wind."

"Indeed sir. Only problem is the new hands think they are real sailors."

"Ha! Indeed. They've settled in well. Don't know when the crew smiled so much."

"Yes, well you can thank Suzanne for that."

"WHAT! Don't tell me she is screwing them all? Surely the women would get upset."

Brian cursed himself under his breath. He had forgotten that the Captain was a bit touchy about sex.

"Ah, no sir. I am not aware of her having sex with anyone."

"Then what the devil do you mean?"

"Well sir, you are aware that the crew make relationships with each other? And that this usually causes lots of problems, arguments and resentment?"

"Of course. Reason that fool Black only has men in his crew. And makes half the profits we do."

"Well, it seems that she caught one couple arguing, the girl in tears and the boy shouting. She dragged them off to her cabin and discussed it with them, then, ah, had them make love to each other while she, ah, instructed them on it. It seems the instructions were quite detailed."

"Good God." The Captain was speechless.

"Word got around," Brian continued. "More couples went for lessons. Seems like everyone on the ship attended her class."

"Good God. What about the Bosun?"

"Ah, she was one of the first. She told me about it, sir."

"Good God." The Captain stared unseeing into the horizon. He jerked as a thought struck home. "Brian! You have had a lesson too?"

"Oh no, sir. Regretfully I don't have a partner. Wouldn't do for the First Mate to be thought of as having a favourite."

"Partner? What do you mean?"

"Oh, she doesn't actually do anything herself, sir, she insists everyone brings a partner and she teaches them together."

"So you and I the only ones not to ..."

"I believe so, sir. Apparently it saved a couple of marriages amongst the older hands. Suzanne is one of the most popular officers I've sailed with."

"Next thing the ship will be full of squalling brats. It's all your fault, Brian. I never wanted women on board."

Brian ignored this. "Actually, sir, I think you will find we will have less than ever before."

"Eh?"

"It seems that the actual making love is just one of her talents. She is also accomplished at the consequences."

"Do you mean to say she is carrying out abortions on board? Put a stop to it at once. She will kill those poor girls."

"No sir. She has a store of herbs, well, actually she found them in the galley stores and took some from the magicians. She makes teas for the girls which stop them becoming pregnant. She also apparently can cure that Spakka disease some men get from whores."

This was too much for the Captain, who changed the subject

but it was noticeable he started treating his Fourth Mate with more respect.

Nineteen days out from port, the wind failed.

It was hot and sweaty without it, and tempers grew short. Walters was constantly testing the air and looking worried. The sails flapped loosely to the odd gust. The Bosun had the crew cleaning and repairing and kept watching the horizon. Pat asked Else why, and she told him shortly that a flat calm was often followed by a storm. But nobody knew what it would be like out here in the middle of nowhere.

Sure enough, Walters came running to the Captain who started barking orders, and Pat and Sara found themselves working hard in the heat, releasing the spars from the masts which were lowered to the deck with their sails tied round them and stored away. After four hours of brutal work, the masts were bare poles with most of the rigging removed, just the essential ropes that kept the fixed masts in place.

The pigs and chickens complained at being locked away, while Sam and Meghan checked each fastening. Dan and Billy got into a fight which Little dealt with quickly and efficiently by the simple method of knocking them both out. The Bosun threw a pail of water over them and told them to get back to work.

The sea started to rise, waves getting bigger by the hour, and they watched apprehensively a rough patch of sea getting closer as fast as an eagle in full stoop. It hit in a similar manner, with a rush, the masts bent and moaned, singing a strange song over the rush of wind. The crew were huddled in the fo'c'sle, some sitting but Pat and Sara had copied the experienced seamen and were in their hammocks. Only experienced seamen were on watch and above deck. Both Captain Larroche and Brian were on the poop deck, with Taufik himself at the wheel, two brawny boatswain's mates to help him.

The Queen Rose seemed to buck beneath them and the hammocks swayed, while those not in them were thrown across the cabin. Nobody laughed as they climbed into their hammocks.

"What will we do?" Pat asked to the room in general.

Bart answered from the far end. "Run before it lad. All we can do. You don't fight the sea, you live with it."

"Get some sleep if you can," added Jim. "This could last a few days, and you'll take your turn on watch and helping the officers."

"Watch? What can you see in that?"

"Rocks, lad. Listen for 'em, you can hear them roaring far away, then we need to get ready as the ship will go down if we strike them. We pray that the Captain knows what he is doing."

The room fell into silence. Pat noticed Sara looking at him, and she pushed down one side of her hammock and opened her arms in invitation. After a moment's hesitation, he got out of his hammock with difficulty, and made his way to hers by clinging to the ropes as the ships swayed. He slipped in with her and she grunted as he kneed her thigh, but they managed to twist around till they were comfortable. Pat noticed most of the other hammocks were either empty or double as others followed their example.

The lights dimmed, and Pat jumped as he felt Sara's hand slide down his trousers.

"I'm not sleepy," she whispered in his ear. "This could be fun!" It had taken a couple of weeks, but Sara had recovered from her experience. She had not yet allowed Pat to make love to her, but she enjoyed experimenting and playing with his body. She was beginning to allow his ministrations in return, but still clammed up on occasion.

They weren't the only ones to seek such recreation, and shortly shouts of complaints came from the singles at the noise the various couples were making, but this stopped when Gerry leant out his hammock and was copiously sick.

The older hands were furious with him, and had no patience, driving him up to the deck to get a bucket of water and forcing him to clean up. They made damn sure that all the others knew where to go to vomit in future. The room stank, and Pat was pleased when Suzanne stuck her head in and called to Pat and Sara.

"I've got the watch - you two are in it. On deck, come to the poop in five." She grinned at the sight of them in one hammock.

Getting up on deck was a challenge, but one they relished. Neither were bothered by the motion, though several of the new crew were being sick in the scuppers while a boatswain ensured each had a rope tied round them in case they were swept over the side. Some of the waves into which the ship plunged came up and into the scuppers, over the moaning bodies wishing they were dead.

For a moment Pat thought the door had been locked, till he realised it was the pressure of the wind. Coming outside was a shock, as the wind whipped the ship along and the rain was horizontal, smacking into unprotected flesh with a painful, smarting blow. Waves were huge, and despite her size the Queen Rose was wallowing, with an uncomfortable corkscrew motion. After the heat that had been building day after day, it was wonderful to feel so cool again, though it was still not cold.

Pat and Sara dragged themselves to the poop deck using ropes to cling on and haul themselves against the wind. They were soaked to the skin by the time they climbed up, both grinning from ear to ear. Suzanne was standing in the lee of the Captain's quarters looking smart in a great coat with her hair wrapped up and down her back, inside the coat. She shouted at them over the wind.

"Nils has the fore watch. Pat, you are to join him and learn from him." Pat nodded, grinned and turned. As he started to make his way down, there was a loud crash from above and the central topmast snapped off, swinging down in a tangle of rigging and started banging against the main mast. The ship leaned hard over and groaned as the wind caught the obstacle and pushed.

Captain Larroche was out of his cabin in a trice, and called to Pat.

"Get Nils and tell him to cut that away."

Pat jumped to the deck, the wind catching him and blowing him so he landed several feet further along than he expected. Travelling to the bow was hard, having to time his movements with the pitching of the ship and after one close shave when he nearly went overboard, he learnt to pick his next handhold and let the roll of the ship and the wind take him to where he could grasp it with a death hold.

Just past the main mast he met Nils coming back. Nils turned his ear to hear the shouted instructions.

A determined, grim expression spread across Nils' face. "Stay down here Pat, I'll sort it."

"You can't do it on your own. I'm with you."

Nils grinned at him. "On your own head then. Grab an axe and tie it to your belt. You'll need both hands and the axe is vital. Keep three points of purchase always. Stay away from me so I don't knock you off if I fall."

The two of them started up the mast. Pat couldn't believe the force of the wind. He tried to keep it on his back so the rain didn't blast his face. Without looking up or down, he concentrated on each step, planning where he was going to put his hand or foot next. As he climbed he grinned, remembering times in the past scaling trees and cliffs, then thought that crossing the desert had been more similar in terms of sheer endurance. His arms straining from the constant pulling of the wind, he glanced down and was surprised how little distance they had travelled.

Putting it out of his mind, he concentrated on a foot at a time. Reach up with a hand and grasp the rope. Take a firm hold, look down and watch the foot rise up to the next step. Wiggle the foot and slot the rope between the toes and grip. Move the next hand up. Straighten the leg and watch the second foot come up into place. Repeat. Over and over while the wind buffeted him, his clothing rubbing against him and weighing him down as it more than doubled in weight from the rain.

Almost in trance he moved up steadily, and then banged his head. Looking up, he found it was Nils' foot. They were at the first spar location.

Nils shouted something down that he couldn't hear, and pulled himself up. Coming up carefully, Pat saw that the mast was greasy. One of the protective beads had split and gone, spreading slippery grease over the mast and ropes in the process. He checked, there was no way around, he had to go through it. Nils inched past, and he could see his foot slip on the grease. Pat was thankful for his bare feet and stretched his toes getting ready. His first step landed on a greasy rope and he slipped. Buffeted by the wind, he couldn't see and pain seared through his fingers as they caught a grip. Digging his nails into the unforgiving wood, he tried taking tiny steps and inched his way up.

Past the spot he went faster, and felt the mast ringing with every gust. He held on more tightly, seeing Nils was going slowly. While he watched Nils, he saw the top mast crash back just above his head and Nils stiffened, then grabbed the rope with rigid arms. Pat watched the topmast swing out again and saw broken rope slashing after it. Nils didn't move. He was in a dangerous place and now was inching back down. Pat looked at the other side of the mast. The rigging remained in place, but it was a stretch to reach. He swayed in the wind, then timed a gust and swung with it, risking a hand and foot across the gap. The gust pushed at his back and gasping he grabbed the far rope, pulling himself across, breathing rapidly. Pulling himself level with Nils, he sensed something wrong.

He reached out with one hand as he came level and grabbed Nils' arm. Nils turned his face towards him and Pat gasped. Nils' left eye was gone, just a gaping hole with blood trickling out of it.

"Rope end" screamed Nils, "slashed me across the face. Can't see properly."

"Your eye!"

"Is it bad? Hurts like the devil and I can't see a thing. Give me a moment and I'll go up and free it. Got to get past this bit where it slams into the mast. This is where we earn our pay, lad!"

"Nils, you're not going to be able to do it. Your eye is bad. Go down a bit out of range and leave it to me."

"Thanks Pat, but it's my job. You're back up. Aaah! Damn, it hurts! Salt in a cut by the eye!"

"Nils! It's bad! Get down and leave it to me! You won't be able to see well enough to do it, no chance!"

Pat pushed past and watched the topmast. It would be held out at right angles from the mast for a while, then when the gust passed it would slam back into the main mast. That was the killing moment, when bits of rope whistled around. It came down again and Pat buried his face in his arms, eyes closed. A line of fire erupted across his back but he held still. He felt the wind pick up, looked up and saw the mast going out straight.

Disdaining care, he raced up the mast, the wind picking at him with insistent fingers, levering at his hands constantly. He came to the part where the topmast was attached and it was a mess. The careful lashings, lovingly put on and expertly tightened, were splayed apart and the butt of the topmast waved free, bits of broken lashing hanging about.

The wind died, and the mast fell again. Pat clung on tightly, out of the danger area now, and watched how the mast was connected. He picked out the ropes still attached to it, which would cause more problems if the mast was freed first. Locking his legs around a rope and the mast, thin here, he took a turn of rope round his left arm and released the axe with the other. Not the moment to drop it. He swung at a tight cable, caught it perfectly and nearly went flying as the mast side of the rope sprang back, whipping past his head and grazing his skull.

'Close,' he thought, feeling blood dribbling down his skull.

The next one he swung at, he ducked his head at the last moment and protected it in his tethering arm. Looking up after a moment, he saw he had missed. Judging the moment again, he swung again and parted it. One more to go, but it was out of reach to one side. He could only get to it when the wind gusted strongly and he needed a good 30 seconds to get to it, cut it and get back. The gusts usually lasted up to five minutes, never less than a minute, so as soon as the next one started he pushed up, leaned out and cut the rope. It slammed back into his ribs and he groaned, but didn't release his grip.

Getting back, he took a breather and glanced at the topmast. The lashings were looser, a few swings and it should be free.

He swung, the sharp axe sliced through three ropes of lashing and the rest unfurled and fizzled away after the topmast which shot away on the wind. He felt the ship spring back up to the vertical, seemingly lighter without the burden of the broken mast. Gasping, he rested a moment then inched his way down to Nils.

"It's done, Nils."

"Took you long enough. Pat, I still can't see. Am I blind, Pat? Have I lost my eyes?"

"No mate," lied Pat, sensing Nils would let go and be blown away if he thought he was blind, remembering how he loved to stand high and watch the sea birds and the dolphins. "But it's bad, could be awhile till you can see. I've seen a few of those injuries where a rope smacks somebody across the eyes. Can take a week before you can see again." He had to shout across the wind and hoped Nils could hear. "Come on, I'll help you down."

The trip down took forever. While the mast did not sway so much with the topmast gone, Nils couldn't see where to hold or step and Pat had to place his feet. If Nils hadn't been so good, they would never have made it. His shoulders were a raging sea of pain by the time they reached the mainsail spar socket of the mast, and

Else and Sara were there to help. Pat turned and shouted at them,

"Nils can't see! Took a rope end across the face! Help him down and get him to the galley." With his free hand he pointed to his eye and shook his head, then put his finger on his lips. The girls looked at him strangely until Nils tilted his head down on hearing Else call to him.

The gaping socket leered horribly out of his skull, washed clean and staunched by the rain, but still with the thread from the eye ball hanging part way out, looking like the tail of a worm burrowing into his skull.

Else went visibly white, even in the night storm. She was up alongside Nils, going round to the opposite side of the net where the wind could pull harder at her.

"Step with me, darling," she said quietly and started to move his hands. Sara took his feet, moving them one at a time. Nils moved slowly as the wind and blood loss started to take effect. Pat, himself exhausted, lowered himself to the deck, braced himself against the wind and reached up to help Nils the last few feet to the deck where he collapsed.

A pair of huge arms swept him up and he felt himself being carried; looking off to the side he could see two men had Nils. It was the Bosun that had him, and she tenderly laid him on the galley table, with Sara beside her, squeaking over his hands.

Wearily he picked them up and examined them, eyes widening as he saw that he had lost four nails, three from his left hand. Sara was peering at his head now, while the Bosun peeled off his shirt and was looking at his back.

"Ach, laddie, you're a one, you are. Grand job you did there. Your back looks like you've shipped on a pirate and they've given you the lash!"

Nils was brought in and sat beside Pat, Suzanne coming in behind him already arguing with Walters, while Perryn pushed in behind them.

Somebody pushed a hot mug into Pat's less ruined hand and he took a gulp. Feeling strength returning, he listened to the medics squabble.

"No I will not let you put hot pitch in the socket," said Suzanne forcibly.

"We have to stop infection," cried Walters.

"I think hot pitch would make it worse," said Perryn worriedly.

"Shuttup," Pat cut across them. "Have any of you ever operated on an eye before? Successfully?" He glared at Walters who had started to answer. "Well I have, maybe ten or twelve. There's a fly that gets into the eyes of horses and cattle, if they are scratched by a branch, lays its eggs and buggers off. Next thing you know the eye is a ruin, full of maggots. We have to cut out the remains."

He pushed himself off the table and went over to Nils, turning his head so the lantern light fell on the socket.

"You said my eyes were alright," whispered Nils accusingly.

"You would have jumped if I told you anything else," said Pat tiredly. "Anyway, it's only one that's gone, I can fix the other. You'll be running along spars in a day wearing a patch."

Pat put his hand towards the eye and saw it shake.

"You can't do anything now, you're done in." Suzanne forcibly took charge. "Else, wash it out gently with a tea of euphrasia, eyebright flowers. Steep about four flowers in boiling water for 5 minutes; let it cool to blood temperature so it doesn't hurt him. Oh, put some of those orange flowers in too, the ones for cuts, some sinjunswort and a monkshood flower. He can sip it while it cools. I'll sort him in the morning."

Perryn and Pat were nodding at this, while Walters looked worried.

"When you clear the eye on the cattle, what do you do?" Suzanne asked, peering into Nils' eye.

"Sockets clean from the rain, but you have to get out any bits that may be in there, and tie off that string so it doesn't bleed. You can snip it off above where you tie it. If there are some bits of the eye ball left, stuck to the sides, they need to be cleaned out. Cheer up, Nils," he slapped Nils weakly on the shoulder, "Else will stop Steve from pissing in it! He reckons that's much better than Elven remedies!"

He sagged slowly forward and braced himself on the table. Sara gently supported him. "We need to sort out your injuries too. What does he need, Suzanne?"

"Some tea with monkshood, and put some wolfsbane in it. Bathe the cuts with sinjunswort and marigold tea." She replied briskly,

Perryn nodding enthusiastically while a glum expression spread across Walters' face.

Pat slumped forward on his face. "No fucking hot pitch." He said and passed out.

Morning dawned bright and clear, the storm having blown itself out in the night. Sara and Else were right up the top in the rigging, checking for damage while others replaced the main spars.

Captain Larroche looked bleakly off to the north, brooding on the two seasick sailors who had been lost. Washed from the scuppers, one had broken his safety rope and gone, while the other when dragged aboard had drowned. That had been Hughie, and he wasn't sure the lad had been tied up correctly. He should have been more forthright in clearing him of the rape accusations. He worried about Nils, who had been with him for seven years and had taken to topsail work in the new ship as one born to it.

In the sick bay, Pat groaned and opened his eyes, to see Nils looking at him with one bright eye. They stared at each other for a moment, then Nils said, "Thanks Pat. I would've jumped. I'll not forget this."

Pat went red and blustered. "God, I'm starving, isn't there any breakfast for sick lads? Have you scoffed the lot, Mr Greedy?" Nils hardly ate anything.

The door banged open and the Bosun came in bearing a wide tray which steamed.

"Hah, you lucky laddies, see who's your nurse today! Your pretty birds are up in the rigging looking for damage so I thought I would come and play with their toys! Who needs a bed bath then? If you need a piss, I've got a bottle and I'll even hold your willy for you, there's an offer you don't get every day!"

She laughed happily and leaned over and kissed Pat as she put the tray down.

"I suppose I will have to feed you, the way your little bird wrapped your hands up last night, you wont be able to get at the food."

Pat pulled his hands from under the covers, and found them like huge mittens with bandages all over the place.

"Oh, god, Bosun, this is no good. The wounds need to breathe! Can you take the bandages off please?"

"Really? Breathe? Well, I don't know..."

Impatiently, Pat attacked the bandages with his teeth and the Bosun leant forward muttering, pulling out a huge knife from her boot and slicing off the knots. Pat inspected his ruined nails critically, then went over to Nils and removed the bandage that was over his eye.

"Borrow you knife, Bosun?" he asked holding out his hand. She placed it there, and he went over to a lantern that was still burning. He opened the window and stuck the knife in the flame for a moment.

"Why do you put it in the flame?" The Bosun asked.

"My Elven healer made me do it. Don't know why." Going back to Nils, he said, "Hold still, mate."

With his right hand he held the knife half way along the blade, and resting his hand on Nils' cheek, he used his fingers to delicately lift up the cord that dangled uselessly in the socket. He grasped it firmly with his left hand, and saw that one of the girls had tied it off low down with a thread. Very gently he sliced it off just above the thread. Nils didn't move. He peered into the socket, then moved Nils to the window where he could see better.

"There's still a bit of the eye in there, Nils, need to get it out."

Pat slowly inserted the tip of the knife under a shred of eye, lifting it slowly away from the side of the socket. An absorbed Bosun was watching over his shoulder.

"There," he said, "that's fine mate. Will heal up in no time. Leave it open to the air till it is healed up, then you can put a patch over it or chuck a false eye in."

Unconcerned, Nils simply said, "Can I have my breakfast now? I thought you were hungry. By the way, did I understand you right? You've never done that to a man before? Just on a cow?"

An hour later, Captain Larroche dropped in to see how they were doing and to compliment them on their work. Pat was embarrassed, and Nils brushed it aside with his own question.

"Did you select a new topmast yet, Captain? Will it need a lot of work?"

"We pulled up several spare spars, and Else picked one. The shipwright and his mate are working on it now. Should be ready this afternoon."

"Right sir. We'll be rested enough by then and we'll get it up."

"You stay here. Else can set the ropes and we'll pull it up from down on deck."

"I know sir, but she hasn't the strength to set it on the block. You can't do that from below, it will sway around. Let her do that and she'll lose a finger or two."

"Can't any other of the topsailsmen help her?"

"Only one I would trust is Pat," said Nils with finality. "They are fine down on the main spars, but up on top of the world, no chance. Got to be me, with Pat helping. Else can set the ropes and do all the preliminary work."

"Are you up to it?"

"I reckon."

Pat just nodded, the idea of not doing work because of a little injury like missing fingernails and eyes hadn't occurred to him.

Predictably, the girls kicked up a fuss. Else backed down when Nils smiled at her from his ravaged face and said, "Else, it has to be. You know that. There is no one else."

Else tightened her lips and said nothing more. Not so Sara. She glared at Pat.

"What are you thinking of?! There is no way you can climb the rigging with your hands like that!"

"Nils needs me." Pat was puzzled and didn't understand the fuss. Sara stamped her foot.

"You stupid little idiot! What sort of good would you be in your condition? Your hands won't work properly! You are not going up, do you hear me? And that's final! I forbid it!"

"You forbid it! Who do you think you are? You are not my boss." Without waiting for an answer Pat turned and opened the infirmary door, fuming with anger.

Sara glared, and her eyes narrowed. "Who am I? I'll tell you who I am, I'm your fucking Princess, that's who I am!" She bit her tongue, even more angry that she had said that.

"Only at night!" Pat threw back over his shoulder and went out.

"Pat!" Sara called out urgently, and when he stopped and turned back, she went to him. "Please, darling, I don't want you getting hurt again, I couldn't bear it, and I love you." She whispered this to him.

His eyes softened and he reached out and touched her face. "It'll be all right. This is nothing - Mikkel rode three days with a broken leg once. I've had much worse injuries and carried on working. I have to do this."

"Pat, on Fearaigh you know what you are doing. This is different, it's a ship, and you are right up in the sky where you need your hands working properly to hang on, let alone work. Don't go." She stroked the back of his hand.

"Honey, I can't let Nils go alone and there is nobody else who can do this."

Sara frowned. She wasn't used to being baulked, and her patience snapped. She slapped him, not hard but enough to rock his head. "I said you were not to go. I am concerned about your safety. If you go off and work now, that's it, over between us! Understand?"

Pat's eyes filled with anger. His mouth worked a couple of times, as he started to speak, "Fine." He turned and stalked off, bristling with fury.

Sara's eyes blazed then filled with tears. "He doesn't understand," she whispered.

Else put her arms round her. "It's OK, honey, he'll be fine. We can't stop them when they want to be stupid." She wiped Sara's eyes and motioned Nils to leave with her head. He left hurriedly.

Nils called from the top of the mast. "Easy now! Bring her up!" Pat was just below him, Sara and Else off to the side. Pat hadn't said a word to Sara since the argument, and was ignoring her. He still seethed inside at her words, not having been spoken to like that for years. He kept replaying her words and worked up his anger more and more. Recalling how she called him a stupid little idiot again and again, getting angrier every time. Deliberately, he put it out of his mind to concentrate on the work in hand, not wanting to slip now and prove her right.

The Bosun had a team pulling on a rope, which went up the mast from the new topmast, attached to the thin end of the mast and through a large ring near the top of the main mast, from there to a pulley, then back down to the deck where it went through a block and tackle, an arrangement of pulleys that increased the strength of the pull while increasing the distance the rope had to be pulled.

The team hauled the rope back six feet and the mast went up

a foot. This continued till the new topmast reached the top of the mast, where Nils and Pat manoeuvred it to rest on the topgallant spar, the penultimate one. Here they removed the rope from the top of the mast and attached at the bottom, while attaching four other ropes to the top of the mast, which also went up through the metal ring, one going back to the top of the mizzen mast, one to the top of the fore mast and the other two went sideways to the ends of the royal spar. These kept the topmast straight, and all went down to the deck where four teams kept them taut, overseen by boatswain's mates.

Nils waved, and the teams took up the strain again, slowly raising the topmast up the last short length of mast. As it came up through the ring, it became a tight fit and Nils and Pat were carefully easing it through, attending to the rope. Nils was sharp with Pat, careful he didn't lose a finger as the ship rolled and the foremast pinched the side of the ring. The wind was steady and applied more and more pressure on the topmast as it rose, requiring a careful balancing act of tension on the top four ropes, which Else co-ordinated down to the Bosun in a phenomenal exhibition of skill. As it came higher, the stub end inched past its support block and Nils pushed it into place, waved, the main rope relaxed and the topmast sank onto the block. Pat started lashing it in place while Nils tightened the ring. For two feet the rope was lashed around both masts in coils that butted up to each other.

Pat held off while Nils went over it checking, then he waved to the deck. The main rope was untied and drawn back to the deck while the four support ropes were tied off. Nils and Pat went wearily down the rigging while Else and Sara did the finishing touches of waxing the lashings and getting the topsail up and set.

When Sara came down, she found Pat asleep in his hammock, which he had moved to a spare spot some way down the fo'c'sle.

The next day he ignored her, and Sara seethed inwardly. She saw him take a mug to the starboard rail, lean on it and look out to sea while Mot leaned against his legs. She went to the rail a few yards away, knowing he would sense her, and waited. She glanced at him a few times, and finally caught his eye. She smiled tentatively. He stared at her levelly and her smile petered out. Sighing, he moved closer.

"Sara. Are you going to strike me again?"

She dimpled. "I'll try not to. Pat, I'm sorry." She frowned. "But you took a fearful risk. I was so scared for you, every time you grabbed a rope I thought you'd fall."

Pat shrugged. "You don't need nails to hold a rope. I thought we were finished."

Sara moved closer. "I was angry, darling. I didn't want you hurt. Forgive me? Please?"

"Well," Pat hesitated, unsure what to say. Sara leaned over and kissed him.

Lovers

On the thirty third day of the cruise, Pat jumped up from where he was brushing Mot and scurried up the mast to the crow's nest. He came down after a few minutes, fast down the sails, and settled back down again, winking at Grey Fox.

"Needed some exercise!"

Shortly afterwards, a cry came from the masthead.

"Smoke, fine on the starboard bow! Smoke!"

The Captain rushed to the poop deck, bringing his telescope with him. The officers joined him, Grey Fox, Little and Pat taking up their archer stations surreptitiously, Perryn close by.

"What do you think, sir?" Brian asked. "Pirate action? Burning a merchantman?"

"If so, it's the biggest bloody merchantman I've ever seen. Would dwarf the Queen Rose."

Taufik spoke as he scanned the horizon. "It is a Fire Mountain, sir. They make the islands."

"You recognise it?

"Oh, no sir, there are many of them. They make a long chain along here. The eastern men, they say it is a window on the jail of a dragon, captured by the gods. It melts the rock trying to escape. "

"Hummph" the Captain noticed Walters nodding thoughtfully and wondered a priest would believe in dragons.

"These islands, Sir, they are made of molten rock that has cooled and become hard."

Walters nodded, "Lava islands. There are a few in the north, Captain, it is a known phenomenon."

Taufik spoke again. "There will be coral reefs, sir, spiky rocks in the shallow water. They can kill a ship, and sometimes they are near the surface with nothing around to indicate them. Only the water colour."

"You are the Sailing Master. Take us to this island."

The island was huge, with the smoking volcano at the south westerly end, and a couple of dead ones making up a range of hills stretching away to the north east. Taufik did not know the island, and had not heard of it, but he said there were many in the chain.

As they came around a rocky promontory, there was a gust of wind from onshore, and it brought with it new and different smell. It was damp, rotting, briny. Strange trees covered the beach, right out into the sea. They weren't tall and had a multitude of trunks, most thin but the odd one towered higher with a thick trunk. Multi-coloured birds, squawking raucously, wheeled over the sea and the forest. One huge bird, with a deeply forked tail and a scarlet throat, soared around the masts crying excitedly. A river slowly flowed out from the middle of the forest, bits of grass and branches floating in it. The trees moved out into another promontory and ended in what appeared to be a number of small, thin stumps. Taufik called them mangroves and they seemed to be full of life. As the tide went out, thin roots appeared, arcing out from the trunk and into mud which seemed to be moving. Little fish skipping, according to Taufik, and loads of crabs. At one point the mud emitted a constant flashing of orangey white light. Taufik said it was crabs waving their claws and wasn't much interested, but Pat and Perryn borrowed the telescope and spent an hour watching them, discussing what the crabs were doing. Rounding the forest at last, the trees gave way to a blinding white beach that curved into a natural harbour with a river running out over the sand, crystal clear water with coloured rocks visible on the bottom. And a large village of huts made apparently of grass at its edge.

The water was flat and calm. But several hundred yards out from the beach the waves broke on rocks.

"Coral reef," said Taufik. "Protects the village and the harbour, but kills any ship blown onto it. The gap near the swamp is because the mud from the other river kills the coral."

"Kills it? How can you kill rock?" asked Walters.

"I do not know," he replied, "but the rock grows and is coloured.

When it dies, it turns white. Always it is getting bigger, never is it the same. It is alive, this rock."

The harbour was full of canoes, mainly small ones with a single outrigger, no sails. There appeared to be traffic with another village further up the bay, and fishing canoes as well. As the ship came into view and sailed slowly and majestically into the harbour, all the canoes turned and started to race towards her, with more people rushing down to the sea from the huts. More canoes were launched, but some people just started swimming.

"Taufik! Are we being attacked?"

"I don't know sir, some of these villagers are cannibals."

"They are not carrying any weapons beyond the odd fish spear, sir," said Pat.

"Confirmed," said Grey Fox, "and most of them seem to be laughing." To the half-Elf this seemed an extraordinary observation.

"Anchor her well out to sea, Taufik, in a good 6 fathoms. About 500 paces from the beach. Bed seems to be sand so use a hook. Lieutenant Mactravis, prepare to repel boarders. Brian, reef the sails."

The first canoes were getting closer and they could make out the nearest native. A girl with white flowers in her long black hair. She had dark brown skin, which caused a murmur to go round the crew, and was completely naked. She was also beautiful.

She paddled her canoe with sure, powerful strokes, straight at the ship which was still going at a good clip. She waved happily at the ship, a laughing smile on her face, grabbed a basket and leapt with sure agility from her canoe to grasp one of the trailing ropes that came down the side of the ship. Quick as a squirrel she was up and over the side, chattering away constantly in her own language. She pulled a strange fruit out of her basket and which she thrust into the hands of the sailor, Dan, moving to stop her, smiled at him and jiggled her breasts with studied deliberation.

Dan stared at her and clutched the fruit, his mouth falling open. As soon as his eyes dropped to her jiggling little breasts, she squealed with pleasure, leant forward and started to kiss him. Dan knew his orders, not to let them on board, but couldn't hurt a girl. He wondered at the strange brown skin, marvelled at her nakedness.

Her lips against his burnt like fire and he was conscious of her breasts pressing hard against his chest.

Desire raged through him, and an erection blossomed under his trousers, hard and excited further by the constriction of his clothes. The girl felt it, and ground her hips into him, giggling with pleasure. She ran her hands under his shirt, pulling at the unfamiliar garment. Unthinking, Dan helped her, baring his hairy chest which distracted her. She started cooing and stroking the hair. Dan's mind seemed to explode; one hand clasped the girl firmly towards him, the other ripping at his trousers till they fell to the deck. The girl laughed, rubbed herself against his nakedness and fell back to the deck, spreading her legs and smiling. Dan plunged into her, his mind afire and with no thought but the girl and the sensation of her body against his.

On the poop, Captain Larroche stared in astonishment as a swarm of brown people poured onto his ship and immediately started kissing his crew. Unsure what to do, he turned to a hand pulling at his sleeve and found himself falling into a pair of beautiful brown eyes.

Pat didn't understand what was happening. He was kissing a girl, urgently, and felt himself getting hard as her hands fumbled with his clothes. He was vaguely aware of Suzanne swearing.

Suzanne was thoroughly alarmed. All over the ship, beautiful brown girls were climbing aboard, uncaring of their canoes, grabbing the nearest sailor and the sailor would grab back, all discipline forgotten. They would fall to the deck and start to make love. She could sense, feel, the magics crackling in the air. She felt herself getting aroused, and when an arm came around her to cradle her breast, she relaxed back into a strong body, her buttocks detecting his readiness, which caused her lower belly to tighten and a liquid rush started deep inside as her thoughts fled under the pressure of erotic emotions escalating to lust. Turning in the strong arms, she found it was Mactravis and she responded to his urgent kisses.

Mot left the Bosun, who had grabbed one of the male sailors, and came leaping up the vertical stair to the poop deck. Distracted, Suzanne saw her rush over to where Pat was thrashing away under a girl, growl and dive forward, biting into the girl's wrist. The girl screamed, looking at Mot in terror. Pat didn't notice. A knife spilt away from the girl's hand but nothing registered as Mactravis chose that moment to thrust deeply into her as she stood against the cabin wall, legs apart and uniform skirt up. She moaned and pushed back strongly, meeting his frantic movement and matching his rhythm.

Sara was curled up by the helm, arms hugging herself as she fought to control the pounding of her blood. Mot's bark reached her and she focused on the dog barking at Pat who was fucking somebody else! Incensed, she made her way over, grabbed the girl by the hair and pulled, not noticing the knife in the hand that Mot was holding and shaking. The girl dropped the knife, leaving Pat as she came to her feet and Mot released her. Her eyes filled with tears as she cradled her arm, turned and ran to the side where she dived into the sea. Sara ignored her and fell on top of Pat, pushing down her breeches and hopping out of them. He did not seem aware of the change in mount.

Dan wasn't thinking, he was blindly thrusting away, as fast as he could, urged on by the girl's cries of delight while her movement was taking him beyond the limits of his imagination. As he climaxed, he shuddered dramatically as a brief, blinding pain erupted in his head. The girl rolled him over gently, expelling him as he went. She slid the obsidian knife out from behind and under his ear where it pierced his brain, and absently wiped the blood away on what was left of his shirt, while she surveyed the scene.

Everywhere people were having sex, though she frowned as she realised many of the crew were with each other - she thought it strange there were women in the crew and then stared. To her astonishment some of the men were taking each other! She shook her head in amazement; the ways of the Gods proving strange and impossible to understand, as always. She checked her friend Monata, unsurprised to see her carried away, forgetting her duty. Lying back with a brawny sailor plunging between her legs, her eyes turned up into her head showing the whites and she grasped the man's shoulders to her as she moved easily with the sailor's rhythm. Clucking with annoyance, Hinatea moved over to help, carefully cutting the sailors throat, timing it with his lunges. The obsidian knife was cruelly sharp, cunningly flaked from the mother stone, with a long fine blade, the handle wrought from carved wood bound with greased thread. He didn't seem to notice; neither did Monata, as he bled to death while still moving, the blood pouring down over

Monata's face forcing her to open her mouth wider to breathe.

Hinatea grunted with contentment, looking around for another victim and moved cautiously towards a ship's couple, two sailors, male and female. She paused her approach, as the sight of them inflamed her. She scanned for another man, but seeing none returned her attention to the couple, her breathing starting to race as she felt herself tense inside and she knew she needed the man inside her as the magic started to take possession of her again.

The couple pounded away as she came alongside, the girl underneath, but when she grabbed a leg and pulled it up, she found it easy to roll them over without interrupting. Once the girl was on top, it was a simple matter to cut her throat, pull her off and replace her. As she matched thrusts with the sailor, she carefully slipped her knife back into its sheath hidden in her hair, resolving to thrash the magic out of her system before culling him.

Suzanne clasped Mactravis' head to her shoulder, both legs off the ground and wrapped around his thighs, her eyes rolled back with the intensity of a prolonged orgasm, when she became conscious of pain lancing through her thigh. Her eyes swam back into focus and the aftermath glow receded as the pain came into the present, forcing her attention to it. Looking down Mactravis' back she saw Mot, front legs resting on her right thigh where it wrapped around Mactravis, looking straight back at her. Mot barked.

Suzanne jerked repeatedly as Mactravis kept going and a thought swam into her head through the clouds of eroticism. *'Mot bit me! Why?'*

Mot growled loudly and bent towards her thigh again. "No," she cried to the dog, which looked at her and wagged her tail slightly. Suzanne shuddered as the pleasure mounted, and started to close her eyes, then opened them wide in fear the dog would bite again. As she did so, an errant thought drifted across her brain. *'Why am I fucking? I am on duty.'*

"Oh Gods," she cried out loud. "Magic! Why?" She looked down the poop deck past Mactravis' shoulder to where the second mate was enthusiastically coupling with a girl. As she looked, she saw the girl's hand stab down at his back, and blood fountain out. It didn't seem to disturb the second mate, who kept going and

Suzanne tried to make sense of what she was seeing as Mactravis kept thrusting into her and she tried to postpone her own orgasm. She saw the second mate start to slow down, and then Mactravis was spurting into her, tipping her over into her own pleasure.

She felt Mactravis' legs go, and quickly got her own down, as he fell to his knees, managing to keep herself somewhat aloft on shaky legs. Holding his head tightly to her stomach, she stared in horror at the second mate, blood pooling from his back, while the girl underneath him was still moving and stretching herself languorously.

"Oh God," she moaned, "we're being attacked." Her head was still fuzzy, and she fought the desire to turn Mactravis on his back and get him going again. Instead she dropped him, and reached for Mot. Grabbing the dog by the scruff of the neck she dropped to her knees and stared into the dog's eyes, trying to ground herself. Mot stared back, and licked her with enthusiasm.

Mustering a huge effort of will, she dragged herself to her feet and staggered to the railing. Wherever she looked, the crew were having sex. There seemed to be blood everywhere and several corpses, all crew, with gaping scarlet gashes across their throats, immobile on the deck. The murderous island women seemed to be deeply involved in fucking and she couldn't see anyone being killed.

The magic pulled at her, and she turned, ready to go back to Mactravis, her loins aching with need. However in the brief moments she left him alone, one of the island girls had revived him and was astride. Suzanne felt anger and jealousy course through her, then determination filled her and she made her way unsteadily to her cabin, fortunately close by. A quick rummage in her bags and she pulled out a pendant, which protected against magic. She draped the thong around her neck to cut herself off from the magic. Immediately, the pressure eased and she could think.

She took a moment to arrange her thoughts, with Mot watching her with expectant eyes from the door. She pulled out her quarterstaff, turned and went back to the poop deck, looking for Perryn.

He was with a small, delicate girl, who was clutching him tightly with both hands, both her eyes closed as they moved slowly together.

Suzanne tapped the girl carefully on the head with her staff. She kicked Perryn firmly in the rear, knocking him off the unconscious girl, and was assisted by Mot who rushed to help and bit Perryn on the left buttock, hard.

Perryn moaned and looked up. Suzanne grabbed his ear firmly, and pressed her thumbnail into his earlobe.

"Perryn, come back! It's a magic attack! Sort it out! Get your defences up! Oh, hell," and she intoned a short phrase in a crackly language while leaning forward so her pendant touched his forehead. Perryn, shuddered, his eyes rolled back in his head, then rolled forward and snapped into position as he was cut off from the magic.

"Wha, what did you do? What's happening?"

"Magic attack, from the island. It's made everyone desperate for sex, and the islanders have come aboard and started screwing the crew. Just like you were doing."

Perryn, frowned, his head hurting, and looked to the girl sprawled unconscious by his side. He blushed at the sight of her exposure, and it deepened as he recalled what they had been doing. His first time, and he hadn't even known anything about it.

"Perryn, it's worse." Suzanne felt tears start from her eyes. "They have knives, hidden I don't know where, and they are stabbing the men as they fuck them!"

Perryn looked at her wide-eyed, and watched as she leant over and searched the girl. This was easy - she was naked. In moments Suzanne found the knife, tied into the hair. She pulled it out, long, wickedly sharp, and black. It looked evil.

"You saved my life," whispered Perryn.

"Never mind that, what's happening? What sort of magic is this? I've never seen anything like it!" There was a note of panic in Suzanne's voice and she was close to tears.

"How the fuck should I know?" Perryn was scared.

"You're a magician, damn it. Find it, stop it!" Suzanne was on the edge of hysteria.

Perryn peered up at the sky, frowned and tracked something through the air.

"It's from back of the village. Suzanne, it is strong. I can't send something down it to the summoner, I would need an arrow, but maybe I can block it, I think. Give me your hand; I need your strength as well." His fright fell away as he concentrated, and Suzanne felt better, using him to ground herself.

He grasped her hand, closed his eyes and frowned. Nothing

happened. Perryn's brow furrowed and she felt something drag at her, flinched as it poured down her arm into Perryn.

Suzanne felt the magical aura fluctuate around the ship. Even the pigs were fucking.

"They're still at it, Perryn." Suzanne had reclaimed her arm, and was rubbing her shoulder where there was a residue of pain. She felt weak and tired, though that was nothing to the wreck Perryn had become.

"Umm, it's too strong for me. I can't undo it or block it over the whole ship." He looked regretfully at his earlier paramour while rubbing his head. "That hurt! Uh, is that blood?" He was staring at the second mate.

"Yes, damn it!" Suzanne cried, finding her confidence and needing action. "They are killing us while fucking us. Come on, we need to get the island girls unconscious and to snap anyone we can out of the magic. I'll work on the first; you get cracking on the others. Uh, hang on, I think I may be able to get Mactravis back and he can work on his soldiers. They should have magical protection. Is there anyone else who has any protection against magic apart from us?"

"Umm, I'm not sure. Not thought about it. Why do you have protection?"

"Don't be silly. How many times do you think somebody has tried to use magic to seduce me? Of course I have to have protection. Sara! She will have some."

"Sara? A mercenary? Why?"

"She isn't a damn mercenary, that's why. Now get on with trying to break the spell on people, use some herbs or something."

Suzanne strode over to Mactravis who was enthusiastically showing his soldierly endurance. She tapped the girl accurately on the head, who slumped away, then leant down and viciously dragged him off by a mixture of hair and ear, feeling him squirm and wince with a considerable degree of relish.

"What..." he looked round angrily, bracing himself on his arms.

"Get up Mactravis and do your duty! The ship has no defence, we're being attacked and none of your men are fighting! Stand To, Mactravis!"

This last, with its inherent call to immediate danger that was drummed into his blood from years of military service, provided the desired effect and he staggered up, looking questioningly at Suzanne, the light of his eyes still obscured but a semblance of intelligence in the depths. She lifted up her pendant and touched it to his forehead.

"Mactravis, it's a magic attack. It's making everyone want to have sex; they send girls aboard with knives in their hair and they kill the men while fucking them."

Mactravis' eyes widened, and he looked down the poop deck, seeing the second mate in a pool of blood.

"Get a grip, Mactravis, and get your soldiers sorted. I need some defence on this ship. And put your trousers on." She kicked him vengefully in the thigh, his instinctive movement protecting her real target confirming he was almost back to normal.

She turned and stalked over to the Captain, keeping an eye on Mactravis as she did so. Mactravis, looking totally shocked, moved towards his men as he fastened his trousers. Little was lying on a girl and he kicked him viciously in the side. Little grunted and pushed himself upwards from the girl, revealing he was holding her hands down while he was inside her. Mactravis saw the knife in her right hand. Clearly Little was not unused to having his paramours stab him.

Mactravis kicked Little again. "Stand to, damn you! Get off that woman and get your section in order. Find me Sergeant Russell and have him report."

Little raised himself up slowly, looking down at the girl who watched him through half closed eyes. "Bloody hell," he murmured, his hand going into a pocket and pulling out a charm. He brushed it against his lips, then his forehead. His eyes cleared and hardened. "You go help with the officers, sir; I'll sort out the men. This ain't officer work. We've all got charms against this sort of magic, just didn't expect it here, I reckon. Gotten soft."

Mactravis went over to Suzanne. She had knocked out the girl with the captain, and the one with Brian, and was carefully easing a knife out of Brian's shoulder. She looked up at Mactravis.

"Nasty looking thing," she gave him the blade. "What is it?"

"Lava glass," he answered. "Sharpest knife you can get, but brittle. Make sure it doesn't snap off inside when you pull one out."

"It didn't. Here, bind this up will you, I need to get Sara back."

She left him and went over to where Pat was enthusiastically ploughing into Sara, and leaned over and touched her pendant to Sara's head. Sara's eyes flew wide and she looked up.

"What the hell," she cried. "What's going on?"

"Magic attack. Have you got a defensive charm?"

"Yes. In my bags." Her answer was a little cut off as she had to speak in time with Pat. Sara started to colour up as she realised what was happening to her and she was having sex out in the open where everyone could see.

"You need to get them and you can help me."

"Sure. What about Pat? Don't hurt him," she cried as Suzanne tapped him on the back of the head with her staff.

"Not a chance," she said. "He'll wake in an hour with a slight headache but hes fine."

"What's happening?" Sara asked as she adjusted her clothing and fondled his cheek gently.

Suzanne sighed and repeated her explanation, looking carefully at Sara, pleased at the speed she came back to reality.

Sara stood up and turned away, looking over the side as she did so. "Oh no," she cried. "The ship is still moving. We'll run aground."

"Shit." Suzanne shouted. "Mactravis! Get some men organised and get the anchor down!" She looked up at the rigging. The sails were reefed, so it would be a question of getting an anchor down. At that moment there was a creak and a groan, the whole ship seemed to shudder and she came to a slow stop, canting over at a slight angle, run aground. "Never mind, Mactravis. Let me know when your men are ready, we need to incapacitate all the islanders."

"Sure Suzanne," he responded, looking down to the main deck, his eyes narrowing as he counted out his soldiers. Corporal Strachan was covered in blood. "Strachan!" he shouted. "If that's your blood, you'll lose a stripe! Report!"

Strachan's voice came up from the deck, strained and a little shocked. "Not mine, sir. All Royal Pathfinders accounted for, uninjured and ready for duty, sir!"

"I want every islander on board incapacitated and tied up. Knock them out first if they are still fucking. Then start to revive the crew."

"Sir, we'll have the girls sorted in a couple of minutes. With regard to the crew, how?"

Mactravis hesitated. When officers didn't know what to do, sergeants and corporals usually did. They weren't supposed to need instruction. "Get up here and we'll take advice from the experts. And find me Sergeant Russell!"

"He's not responding, I'm afraid," said Perryn, relaxing back from Walters, who was clasping an unconscious girl with a beatific smile. "I'm not sure how much help he would be, to be honest. He really doesn't do any religious work, let alone magic. He is very much just a scholar."

"All right," said Suzanne in frustration. "Here is Sara back, and Mactravis."

Mactravis came up to her, then turned and watched Sergeant Russell and Corporal Strachan come up the ladder and join them. He turned to her. "Can you give us some instructions to revive the crew, Suzanne?"

She stared at him blankly for a minute. "No," she sighed. "Perryn, Sara, any ideas?"

The two looked at each other. Sara shrugged. "How long will your pendant work, Suzanne?" Perryn asked. "Could we use it to clear people's minds?"

"Frankly, I've no idea. So far, I've only tried it on people who already have some training in magical protection and their own charms." She looked over the five of them. "Is it just us six and the other Pathfinders who are able to work and fight?

"Yes, Suzanne." Mactravis looked at her steadily. "The Captain is not capable at present and for how long I don't know. Until he does, you are the ranking officer, ma'am."

She stared at him for a moment. "Fine. Report please."

"Russell?" Mactravis said.

"Sir. We have fifty eight island girls unconscious and tied up on the main deck. There are twenty three confirmed dead crew, mostly male with two girls, and another thirty with some sort of injury, six of which are terminal. That's not including those here on the poop. We have not been all over the ship, there may be others."

Suzanne stared at him, speechless.

"Don't take it so hard, Captain," said Mactravis. "If it wasn't for you, we would all be dead."

"It was the dog," whispered Suzanne. "She woke me." They all looked at Mot, who was lying beside Pat's unconscious form. Her tail thumped the deck. "And the Bosun? Is she alive?"

"Yes sir. She's still fucking, sir."

Suzanne looked over the rail, and realised what members of the crew she could see were all copulating. "Twenty three dead already. In moments. I can't believe it. That's nearly a quarter of the crew." She shook herself. "Perryn, the spell seems to be gone. Did you do that?"

"Err, no Captain, but I agree, it seems to have cut off. I expect it is very difficult to cast and the mage won't be able to keep it up for a long time."

"The crew are still going and I can feel the pressure in my mind, still."

"It seems to engrave itself in the mind, creating a sort of loop that keeps on even when the original spell is no longer active. It's an interesting spell, almost with a life of its own that feeds on the people who it hits. Gosh! I've never imagined anything like this. It's a whole new application." Perryn started to get enthusiastic.

"Yes, yes, Perryn, but how do we break it?"

"I have no idea," Perryn began, when a scuffling alerted them. They looked over to see the girl who had been with Perryn sitting up, rubbing her head. She looked over at the six of them, saw Perryn and smiled. She got up casually and walked over, linked her arm in Perryn's and smiled shyly at the others.

They looked back at her in some amazement. "Do you speak Belada?" Suzanne asked in that language. The girl looked back blankly.

"She doesn't appear to be under the spell anymore," observed Sara. "Maybe knocking them out has reset the spell."

"Not entirely," observed Mactravis as the girl gripped Perryn's hand.

"Strachan," said Suzanne crisply, "make sure all the girls up here are secured. We just knocked them out."

"Ma'am!" Strachan saluted as he proceeded to carry out the order.

"Perryn," continued Suzanne, "You're research. Find out how to revive people. Make sure there is a protective spell over us to ensure it cannot happen again." Perryn nodded, muttering slightly under his breath.

"Sara, you're promoted to mate. Check out the situation with the ship. Get the anchors out behind us and attached to the capstan. I want us pulled off at the highest tide and anchored out in deeper water. Plan it out, work out how many men you need. And check on the Spakka. I presume it affected them as well but I haven't seen any."

"Captain!" Sara nodded crisply.

Sergeant Russell came to attention. They all looked at him, and he spoke, looking at the sky. "Captain, the spell badly affected the Spakka. Their buddy system had something to do with it. Perhaps half the dead are Spakka." There was something about his report which made them think he was holding something back, but after a moment's pause he closed him mouth in a tight line.

"Thank you Sergeant. Mactravis, no prizes for guessing your duty. Defence! I don't want anyone within two hundred paces of the ship. Grey Fox is to be on permanent guard with his bow. He can sleep when there is somebody watching nearby who can wake him in need. Now we need intelligence. As the women wake up, see if any speak Belada. Then we can question them and find out what is going on. Anyone you can spare to help Perryn? I was thinking Little might be useful." Perryn looked back and nodded.

"No problem," responded Mactravis. "Shall I also get those of the crew who are unconscious put in their cabins or hammocks, and prepare the dead for burial?"

"Yes, do it. Oh my, what about the dwarves? Have you checked on them?"

Mactravis answered carefully. "I have not. I have served with dwarves a few times and know them quite well. They are unusually resistant to magic attacks, but if they got the urge we will find out if any of those on board are female because the others will be fighting. But judging from the lack of noise from the forge, they are all dead drunk. That is a frequent reaction to crisis of this sort."

Strachan came back. "All secured, ma'am. You may want to look at the woman who was with the Captain. She is older than the others and she looks to be stirring."

"Good. Carry on, people. Mactravis, after you have detailed orders for your men, join me. Oh, and reviving ship's officers is a priority."

Suzanne went to where the Captain lay and looked at the girl who had been with him. She was indeed older than the others, perhaps thirty though it was hard to tell with these different people. She gestured to the Captain and Strachan and a soldier picked him up and took him to his cabin. She concentrated on the woman.

Really, she could be a Harrheinian, if it were not for her skin, she thought. Her features are regular, no difference, It's just the skin colour and they all have black hair. No blondes, redheads or even brown. Her thoughts went on as she dropped to a squat beside the woman, looking at her body now. Thin, but not unfit. No boobs to speak about, and none of them do really. No fat showing. Strong, though, the muscles are lean and long.

The woman's eyes fluttered, and focused on Suzanne. They went wide in surprise and fear. She tried to make a gesture with her hand and realised she was bound. She started to babble in her language.

"Do you speak Belada?" Suzanne asked, beginning to wonder if the hours spent learning had been worthwhile.

"A ship with women on board?" The woman replied in Belada.

"Why not?" Suzanne snapped, "Is this how you always welcome traders?"

The woman blinked. "Trader? What is trader?"

Suzanne was taken aback. "Um, we discuss the value of goods we have, and exchange them. That is why we have a big ship, to carry cargo to swap with you. Our cargo is from far away and valuable to you, yours is very valuable to us when we get home."

"You no take?" The woman was calming down with this prosaic talk.

"No. Not good. We come every year, exchange goods; you make better goods for us, grow and become richer."

The woman looked at her. "People not goods," she snapped with heat.

"We do not trade in people. You see any on this ship?"

The woman sat up and shook herself, seeming to take stock and examined Suzanne. "I Rereau. I junior priestess of the Pahipi. I sorry we welcome you this way. We think you Umayyads."

"What is an Uma-yat?"

"They come in ships, not so big as yours. One sail, they come, take our boys and girls, kill others, steal our food."

"How often do they come?"

"Not often. I think long way. Maybe once, two times in 5 years. Very bad when come. We not fighting people. We girls make this plan. It works on them. Two ships at bottom of sea here." She looked around at the ship and smiled tentatively. "Magic very strong. How you escape?"

Suzanne did not smile back. "Twenty three of my sailors are dead and another six will be soon. What sort of a welcome is that?"

Rereau blinked. "I sorry."

"Sorry? That does not help my dead men. And what will the survivors think? Their friends killed while they were beside them, fucking, sometimes fucking their friend's wife! I watched that man die," she pointed at the second mate. "He was my friend."

Rereau looked calmly at her. "I six years old when I see my mother raped till dead by foreigners like you, while my father watch with arms and legs chopped off, bleeding to death. My village burn down, and only twenty escape. You foreigners come and destroy us, every year, and now you upset we fight back? This is last island, nowhere else for us to run."

Suzanne blinked and settled back on her haunches. The woman pressed her attack. "How we know you any different? You come in big ship, we think you take our young people as slaves. And now what you do? You catch us, tie us, now go ashore kill old people? Steal food? Burn houses? Chop up children? Well, you can. We women have failed in saving our people, and you have killed all men."

Suzanne stood up and turned away, she hadn't thought anything beyond getting the ship in order. The woman's words echoed in her head and she called Mactravis and Sara over to her, Sara coming up from the bows where she had been diving into the sea to inspect the damage.

Mactravis spoke first. "We've cleaned up the dead; they're being sewn into cloth for burial. Wounded are in the galley, ready for you to have a look at them. Perryn and Little are working on ships officers, not much luck. I can lead the Pathfinders on a reprisal raid when you are ready, Captain."

Suzanne looked hard at him, but didn't respond immediately.

She needed to think first, so she nodded at Sara.

"Doesn't seem to be any damage, no split planks, but the bows are wedged pretty deep into sand. I've no idea how much effort it will take to get them out. But we can run out anchors behind the ship and try and pull her off at high tide, which I think should be in about four hours. I will need all the soldiers to turn the capstan, if the crew haven't recovered. Can we do that before any reprisals? We don't want to risk losing any men."

Mactravis snorted at this. "We won't lose any men. These people are not physically strong and they have no iron - their weapons are stone."

"It's priorities as well," answered Sara, "we need to have flexibility as we don't know what is ashore. There may be thousands of villagers waiting for us and we haven't seen any men yet, they may be twice the size."

"Oh, I know, you're right, but it is frustrating. We just want some afters."

"I think you will find the sailors do, too, and it may well be the best remedy for them, to take out their anger and frustration."

"Enough," cracked Suzanne. "I am not at all sure we should attack them."

"Pardon, ma'am, but we must." Mactravis looked oddly at her. "Otherwise they will think we are weak and always attack us. You would put us in grave danger if you don't. We need to show them the rewards for attacking our people - ten deaths for every one of ours at least."

"Ten's not enough," snapped Sara, going red in memory of what had happened. "It should be at least...." Her voice trailed away seeing Suzanne's troubled face.

"We have walked into an ambush laid for other people. Somebody called Umayyads. These islanders are a remnant of what they were. The men have been killed off, and the girls are the fighters. They fled down the islands, trying to get away from slavers." She told them what she had learnt, troubled.

"Slavers," said Sara flatly. "I hate slavers. We caught a slaver when I was on the frontier. It was horrible."

"No men?" Mactravis asked, troubled. "You sure? Damn, it wouldn't feel right slaughtering women and kids. But they must be punished. What are you going to do, Captain."

"I don't bloody know," she snapped. "I'm a whore pretending to be a fucking officer. I'm not a captain, you be bloody captain and decide!"

"Me? I'm a soldier, I don't know a thing about ships. Besides, dealing with this sort of thing is outside my training. It's not in the manual." He spoke defensively, and two pairs of eyes slid over to Sara.

"Don't look at me! I'm just a topsailsman."

"You are the Crown Princess of the Realm," stated Mactravis flatly. "You are trained to take these decisions. You have a better idea of what to do than we do. Give me a battle and I will win it for you, but this!"

"Oh, damn you!" Sara's eyes moistened. "Give me some time." She turned and went over to where Pat lay, and sat down on the other side of Mot, leaning down and cuddling him while she thought. After a while she looked up to see the older island woman watching her curiously from a few feet away.

"How many people in the village, and on the island?" Sara asked tonelessly in Belada.

Rereau hesitated, but she had a fair idea of what had happened from the body language. One thing she understood was young princesses, and it was clear the others had asked this girl for a decision. "There five villages on island, this biggest and maybe three hundred people. No men. Plenty young boys and some old men."

"How far have you come, running from the slavers?"

"All my life we run. Three islands. Five years ago we here, and we make plan to kill Umayyad. Twice they come, each time we kill all. My grandmother, she tell stories of time before Umayyad, of brave sailors who travelled far in their canoes."

"You fight for your people. Are you the leader?"

"No. Grandmother is leader. I princess, leader one day."

"I am also a princess of my country, and one day I will lead it. It is one month by this ship over there." She pointed to the North West and Rereau's eyes widened. "Takes longer going back, we have to find the way." Sara sighed and looked at Rereau. "My people want to fight you, because you attacked us. They want blood to pay for blood. But you are nothing. We cannot fight women and children. If I go home and say you attacked us and we helped you, my people will be angry. So instead we will take you over. You will become part of my country and accept me as your ruler. I will send you strong men to marry your women and make babies. We will build homes and farms. And when the Umayyads come we will destroy them.

"I will go back to my people and say we have a new land, part of us, that we had to fight for it and some of our people gave their lives to win it. They will cheer and honour them, and we will call streets and buildings after them."

Sara looked at Rereau who was following her words intently. "You understand me? You accept?"

Rereau nodded slowly. "I understand you meaning. Not all words. It not my place to accept. Grandmother must say. But I think good. Strong men like him?" She pointed at Pat.

Sara smiled for the first time. "Yes, there are lots of lovely men like this one in our lands, who will be happy to come here."

Rereau thrust her arms forward. "You untie me?"

Sara looked at her steadily. "Will you do us harm?"

"No. I help you." Rereau returned her gaze unflinching.

"And the others?" Sara gestured to the lower deck and the other girls on the poop.

Rereau hesitated. She nodded at the ones close by. "These good. Down there is Hinatea." She shrugged. "I cannot say for her. Maybe. I must talk with her first. Angry girl."

Sara leaned forward, looked at the knots and simply drew her knife and slashed through the rope, sawing at it while Rereau held her hands steady. Then she helped her to her feet. Rereau was a good hand shorter than Sara, and they stood looking at each other. Rereau put her arms around her and hugged her, whispering in her ear as she did so. "I put my people in your hand. Take care of us. Please, always we scared the Umayyad come again."

Sara felt wetness on her cheek and hugged hard back, feeling deep racking sobs come through the woman. In a moment she was crying too, the pain of a people being destroyed reaching deep into her soul.

After a moment, they braced themselves and stepped back,

smiling at each other.

"Explain to your girls here, I will talk to my people, then they will release these girls. You must all stay up here, though, until we revive our crew, and get them over the effects of your magic."

"Yes. I help make better. They need sex. Gets rid of magic. That and exercise." Rereau went to her girls and Sara went over to Suzanne and Mactravis who were watching her uncertainly. "Call all the men over. I will talk to everyone at once. Anyone who is conscious and capable, have them come to the bottom of the poop stairs."

Mactravis nodded and called instructions down to Russell who was on the lower deck. Suzanne squeezed Sara's hand in support and went into the cabinway to recover Perryn and Little who were in the Captain's cabin.

As they assembled, Sara untied her hair from the ponytail in which it hung down her back. Not as long as it used to be, it was beginning to show its true glorious colour, gleaming red at the roots and in places where the dye wore away

She shook it out into a mane, and stood tall and proud at the head of the stairs. The soldiers were all standing up and looking at her, plus some of the crew on wobbly legs. Most lay around, still copulating.

"I speak to you now, not as your shipmate, Midshipman and Topsailsman Sara, but as your Crown Princess, Asmara, Lady of High Reaches. I have been in disguise, but this current crisis requires my presence." She paused and smiled down at them. The soldiers were grinning widely, only Perryn was looking shocked. A few of the crew looked up from their exercise and seemed to pay attention.

"I congratulate you. You have survived a battle, a strange but noble battle with a desperate enemy who fought with the bravery and trickery of those with their last hope in the balance. It will be known to history as the Battle of the Pahipi, the name of this isle, and it is the most important battle fought in the last four hundred years of our history. Not since King Bernard Starr accepted the sword and axe of Trehaun, and welcomed into the Kingdom Fearaigh, has Harrhein enlarged her borders as we have done today. Thanks to your skills and courage, your names will go down in history." She could see the soldiers grinning, perhaps with some bemusement, but nevertheless thrilled.

"For these girls were the last army of this island. Their defeat here on the ship leaves them with nothing. Their princess has ceded the island to us, and we are the conquerors. The entire island belongs to us, and we will bring colonists from Harrhein to farm and develop it." Now the soldiers looked uncertain.

"As is customary, every person on the ship will receive a parcel of land, which you may own or sell as you so wish." That brought a cheer and restored the mood.

"Now we have won the war, we need to win the peace. And that will be more difficult. You need to understand some things. These girls are a remnant of a once powerful people who lived to the north. They were defeated in battle by a people known as Umayyads, who are slavers." She hissed the word at them and they responded with growls. "These slavers are particularly cruel, raping and torturing those they don't want as slaves, killing even the little children, burning the villages. The men of these women died to a man, to enable them to escape with the children and the elderly. They sailed as far away as they could to escape the Umayyads, and developed this effective technique to protect themselves. To date, every slaver ship that arrived here suffered the crew slain to the last man." She paused, and they looked at her, entranced.

"It took Harrheinians to survive! It took Harrheinians to win!" Her tone changed now, her voice ringing with passion, stirring up the soldiers who started to bounce on their feet, itching to cheer. "And now Harrheinians will show how magnanimous we are, for we will assist our erstwhile foe, our brave enemy, who have become our friends and countrymen. Are you with me? Will you help these poor orphan people to recover their spirit and lives?"

"Yes!" They roared, "We're with you Princess!" And to her surprise, many of the crew were shouting too, and Suzanne, who had been equally in the Princess' thrall, realised her speech and words had cut through the magic in them. It was the passion in her words, she guessed, thinking ruefully that she knew what made royalty.

The crew were not instantly cured. The Princess' words were so full of passion they ignited in the crew, who listened happily, gone along with the words, cheered the princess and now returned to the important business of more sex.

Princess Asmara smiled, and looked down at the soldiers. "Princess Rereau will speak with her ladies, after which you may untie them. They will help to dispel the magic still afflicting people. Please ensure none are untied until she indicates they are ready, as we don't want them continuing the fight." She turned to Rereau and switched to Belada. "Please speak to your ladies below. Can we release these ones?" She indicated the girls up top.

Rereau nodded. "I go."

She went to the stairs, while Mactravis moved through the six girls on the poop deck, cutting their bonds.

Suzanne turned to Sara. "Well done, Princess. Happy with that, and you did brilliantly. Now, where are the Spakka. You didn't report earlier."

Sara's face took on a strange look. "They are, well, recovering. I hadn't realised, but it seems Spakka like each other." Suzanne looked puzzled. "Their warrior creed, they buddy up and do everything with their buddy." Suzanne's eyes widened as comprehension dawned.

"You mean...."

"Yes, with each other. Something the island girls didn't like. A good dozen of the dead are Spakka. I doubt they understood my speech, and they are still away with the fairies, well under the magic spell."

Hinatea surfaced slowly through throbbing pain, taking a moment to place herself. She was on the ship, three kills only to her credit. Uggh! The deck was hard, and cold. She tried to move her hands and froze as she realised they were tied. She took a quick mental note of her state. Her head hurt, she was lying down with her wrists tied, but not her feet. She was on her back. Clearly she had been hit and tied up. Damn. She was a slave! Not for long, she vowed to herself, and opened her eyes a crack. She could hear somebody speaking in a stupid language that sounded like somebody gargling. It was a girl. Men were listening to her, and she opened her eyes fully as she realised nobody paid her any attention.

She tested her bonds. Tight. Would take her time to work them loose. She checked for the magic. Quiescent. There was no impossible urge to fuck anything that moved. Good, keep it down.

She wouldn't be able to escape if it woke in her again. Around her, all her comrades. All unconscious, no, Rerata was showing signs of waking. Stupid girl, making a noise and attracting attention. One of the men leant over and checked her bonds.

Surreptitiously, she swung her hair and felt from the weight her knife was still there. Good. She strained her arms, and felt the rope give slightly. She wriggled her wrists, feeling the rope move a little, and felt something touch her neck. Taking a chance, as the girl stopped and the men made a noise, she turned and looked behind her. Silmatea was looking at her. Good girl, no noise. Hinatea hunched her body and proffered her wrists to Silmatea, feeling her grip and worry them with her teeth.

Through her lashes she saw the girl stop talking, Rereau come down the stairs and walk over to where they lay.

She spoke, asking who was not awake. Reluctantly, Hinatea opened her eyes and nodded at her. All the girls were awake. Hinatea was pleased and proud so many had pretended unconsciousness. She listened to Rereau's words and didn't know what to think. Anger chased frustration around and around. She snapped, and spoke words in anger to the priestess, instantly regretting them.

"So, at your word we lay with these strange, unknown men and killed them, and you were wrong? They are not enemies? The gods were wrong? The gods have been wrong for many seasons! And now these people will kill us for killing their people without reason."

Rereau looked at her sadly. "Yes, Hinatea, best of our warriors, I was wrong. I was wrong to think these people were Umayyads; that only Umayyads would come here. The gods were wrong to not tell me they were coming. Maybe we have not followed their wishes correctly, and they have forsaken us. These people have different gods, maybe stronger gods, and maybe our gods are frightened of their gods. I don't know. I do know that they are strong, much stronger than us and much stronger than the Umayyads, and they will protect us."

"So now you give us to slavery of these pasty, uncooked people instead of to the filth, the defilers? That is our punishment for killing them? We, who killed the Umayyad and now these people, are to be punished by going tied into slavery? And you? Will you escape and we are your price?"

Rereau sighed, knowing that Hinatea was the one she must convince and the others would follow her lead. But she had never managed to relate to Hinatea, who seemed to be more a man than a woman and gloried in the hunt and the kill.

"Hinatea, they will not enslave us. They hate slavers, and they will hunt the Umayyads down for themselves, not for us. They are angry at us for killing them. But the leader accepts it was a mistake, an honest mistake. As reparation, they are taking over us, our people and our land. We are becoming part of them. But they offer us something we had not dreamed could happen. Husbands! They will bring us men, Hinatea, strong men to father strong babies, who will live on this island. They are going to bring new things to us and protect us."

Hinatea subsided, knowing she had lost. Indeed, she too thrilled at the word 'husband', and sensed all the other girls straining to look at the men of the crew. The girls had grown up knowing little of men, sharing the scant few left on the islands, and the thought of one for yourself, alone... She questioned herself. Lost? She had lost nothing. Instead it was Rereau who had lost, Rereau's gods was false. She, Hinatea, had just stopped following her.

"Hinatea!" Rereau called urgently. "Will you stop killing these people?"

Hinatea rolled onto her back and sat up; lithely rose to her feet, holding out her bound wrists to the white man standing beside Rereau, while at the same time pushing herself forward in a blatantly sexual way.

"Why would I kill them, False Priestess? They have penises, and that we lack. Tell him to release me and I will take him to paradise."

"Hinatea! Do not play with words with me! Take your oath in the face of the Gods that you will not kill these men!"

Hinatea looked at Rereau, her face blank. "I will not kill them. I will learn their ways and grow strong in their society. I will find their heroes and I will fuck them. The best of them I will let him give me babies. This I give you my word on my honour, but on your weak and faithless gods, I will not speak."

Rereau inhaled in anger, and a deep sigh went up from the girls. For a moment Rereau was tempted to withhold release.

Sara watched Rereau talking to the girls, and felt for her through the altercation with the tall, pretty girl, for whom she developed an instant dislike. She watched the power play, and saw Rereau lose all the girls, then to her amazement Rereau told Strachan to untie the girls. She left them and climbed heavily back up to the poop deck.

"That didn't seem to go well?"

"Oh, is fine for you. But they unhappy with gods. Say your gods are stronger."

"Ah." Wisely, Sara said nothing to this, just embraced Rereau who sobbed briefly on her shoulder, then pulled herself together.

"In truth, is long ago that our gods deserted us. But I still love them. Is that wrong?"

"Not at all. And I promise you, I will build you a temple to honour your gods, and you will remain their priestess. And your children can follow you."

Rereau's eyes filled with tears, but before she could speak there was a ruckus from the cabins, and Captain Larroche appeared on deck, looking extremely worse for wear. He looked around wildly, and his glance fell on Rereau and he rushed over.

"There you are! Are you alright? I awoke and you were gone! Come, my love, come to my cabin." He spoke in Harrheinian, grabbed her hand and started to pull her towards the cabin.

Rereau didn't need to speak Harrhein to understand his intention, and allowed herself to be pulled along, raising an eyebrow to Sara as she went. "The magic still in me, I feel it. Must get rid. Is all right."

Sara felt an answering tingle in her groin and looked over at Pat, who was still unconscious. She clamped down hard on herself and thrust her hand into a pocket to hold her charm.

Strachan was having a hard time releasing the girls. They all clustered close around him, the tall one's hip jostled him with every movement and every time he leaned forward to cut rope, she leaned with him to help hold the hands which caused her bare breasts to run along the back of his wrist. He could barely walk for the swelling, the magic drumming in his blood, the sweat beading on his brow and he kept plunging his hand into his pocket to grasp his charm. Finally he dragged it out and held it between his teeth, which helped, though he nearly cut one poor girl's hand off when Hinatea's erect nipple flicked his elbow and she managed to catch his eyes with hers.

Lieutenant Mactravis came to his rescue by calling him to the poop deck, and he left the girls to release the last of their friends despite being almost overcome by a cunning, hidden farewell squeeze from Hinatea which made it difficult to mount the stairs.

Hinatea watched him go with a smile, having enjoyed the game. It had brought the magic back with a vengeance though, and she blinked slowly at the warm pleasurable feeling coursing through her veins.

"What do we do now, Hinatea?" Monata asked.

"I know what I want to do," she smiled, "and I am sure you all want the same. But best we make friends first. They will be upset with us as they recover. What did they do with the wounded?"

"Through that door there," pointed one of the girls.

"Well, let's go and make them better. Maybe some are well enough to make us better."

As they headed off towards the galley, Hinatea saw Pat in the corner of the poop deck, and peeled off, telling the others to keep going. She grabbed a rope and swung up, climbing quickly over the rail and dropping beside Pat.

Gently she rolled him onto his back and his eyes fluttered. As his face appeared, something strange raced through her, an emotion causing her breath to become short and her heart to beat fast. Perplexed, one hand stroked his brow as he looked up at her, and with the other she checked for injury, when she felt something coming at her and whirled around, ready to take the figure lunging at her. It braked to a stop at her readiness, and she saw it was the girl who had been speaking, with the funny hair, normal at the end but red at the base. The one Rereau said was a princess. She was angry and shouted at her.

Hinatea moved protectively between the girl and Pat and the girl's eyes narrowed.

"Get away from him!" she grated in Belada, which Hinatea understood slightly.

"Is all right, I help him. He hurt." She jumped slightly, because Pat was recovering and watching the scene with interest, and chose this moment to run a weak hand up her thigh.

Sara moved up beside Pat and tried to push Hinatea away. "I can look after him perfectly well, thank you." She glared.

"He has magic in him," she explained throatily as it rose heavily in her. "You busy, I look after. He need lots of sex to get rid of it."

"NO," flashed a furious Sara. She truly did not like this girl. She pulled out her charm and pushed it down onto Pat's head. Pat was beginning to look at Hinatea's nakedness with far too much interest.

"Suzanne!" Sara called up her heavy artillery. "Can I borrow your pendant please? Pat is waking up."

Hinatea stared at Sara, and sank down beside Pat, who put his arm around her.

Suzanne came up and took in the scene instantly, pulled out her pendant and reached over Sara's shoulder to place it on Pat's forehead. Pat's eyes cleared and he looked around in some wonder, went bright red and hastily removed his arm from Hinatea.

Hinatea shrugged and smiled. She leaned forward and quickly kissed him, vaulted over the rail and dropped to the lower deck, heading over to the galley where the other girls had gone. In something of a daze, she wondered what she felt. Suzanne watched her go, and called down to Grey Fox.

"Fox! Can you go to the galley please and make sure the injured are safe." He nodded and followed her.

Pat was scarlet with embarrassment, hunched over as he stood, trying to conceal his erection. Sara was helping him up and he was flinching away from her, to her distress.

"Steady on, love," she said. "It's been a magical attack on us, which caused everyone to have sex with anybody near them. The islanders used it to kill us, they have knives in their hair. They have killed twenty three of us, with more injured. It's over now," she continued hastily at his expression, "but it's been tough."

"But, but, that girl, she was an islander..."

"Yes, it is over now. We have won and we are taking charge of the island. Now they are on our side."

"Who died?"

"I don't know, not yet. But we can go to the carpenter's workshop and see. They are laid out there."

"They died in the fighting?"

"It wasn't proper fighting. It was an accident, they mistook us for slavers. It happens, Pat, and you must get used to it. They are on our side now, and helping us get over the magic."

"Magic? Get over it?"

"Yes, it's a compulsion to have sex. Still affecting many people. You will see they are still having sex."

"Who is dead?" He pushed her away, staggering slightly. "The ship feels funny, wants happened?"

"We've run aground. Waiting for high tide to float her off. Come on, let's get to the carpenters shop."

One of the first people they saw was Dan, and Pat flinched, holding his friend's cold hand for a moment. He peered closely at the wound in his head, nodding to himself at the precision of the cut and taking small comfort in the knowledge it was quick and painless.

Others drifted in slowly, as some of the crew were getting over the spell, and went round the bodies. As they were leaving, the Bosun came in, looking drawn and tired, supported by Jim. She gave Sara a hard look, but said nothing.

"Bosun. Glad you are back with us and safe," said Sara. "Are you up to duty?"

"I'll manage," she said shortly.

"We need to get the ship off the sandbank. High tide in an hour, Suzanne has taken charge as the ranking officer and told me to sort it out, but I think it would be better if you did."

"Thought I saw you take over?"

"Only for a little bit, to handle negotiations. But Suzanne has promoted me to Lieutenant, acting mate while she is acting Captain. There wasn't much choice..."

"Very well, I'll sort it. Sir. I don't like your decision, Sir. These are my friends and charges lying here dead. Sir."

Sara bristled at the insolent, truculent tone, and iced up. "That's because you are not aware of all the information, Boatswain. For your information, I don't like it either, but it is the correct decision. We sprang a trap laid for slavers, and if we do anything to these innocent people, we are as bad as the slavers. It is the slavers that killed our friends, it is the slavers I hate, and it is the slavers I blame for our friends lying cold and dead. So keep your hatred and need for revenge, Boatswain, keep it cold and merciless, bottled up in your thoughts. Feed it, keep it strong, keep it ready. Keep your cutlass sharp and a marlinspike to hand. For we will meet the Umayyad slavers soon, I am sure, and when we do, then bring it out. Bring it out with dripping blade and ice-cold fury, and I shall be alongside you as we slaughter them. But do not take it out on an easy target. We must help these islanders, not hurt them. They are part of our country now, our people, equally wronged and hurt by the slavers."

"Yes, ma'am!" the Bosun said, her demeanour changed and eyes level. The others in the room were also nodding, pleased to have a target. Sara swung out of the door, pleased with herself and how naturally command came. She caught Pat's face as she did so. It was stricken.

"Your decision? Your orders? Why?" Pat's whisper was low, fast and urgent.

They were outside on deck, nobody nearby. Sara turned to him with a sad smile. "I'm sorry I didn't tell you before, Pat, but I couldn't. I am Princess Asmara Starr. I had to flee an assassin and shipped as an ordinary sailor to keep safe." She smiled fondly at him. "But don't worry, you can keep calling me Sara, love. I like it when you do." She leant forward and kissed him again, then frowned at the lack of reaction.

"What's the matter?"

"It was you," he whispered, "you who decided not to punish the killers of Dan and the others."

"It is the correct decision. Do you need me to explain it to you?"

Pat stood tall and looked straight ahead. "Of course not, ma'am. Whatever you say. If I may be excused, I must prepare the jolly boat to take the anchor out."

"Damn it, Pat, don't give me that. Come on, I need you, I need you here beside me." She slipped up beside him and whispered in his ear. "The magic is still in us, the charms just hide it. We need to work it out. We can borrow Suzanne's room later."

Pat kept looking straight ahead, an obstinate expression across his face. Sara lost her temper, slapped him hard across the face and stormed off to the poop deck.

Suzanne was listening to Grey Fox's report. It seemed the girls were indeed looking after the injured, doing a good job of treating the wounds too, and keeping their minds off the pain by fucking the hell out of those that could. All in all, Suzanne decided, this was a good thing, and was glad the Captain wasn't there to hear about it.

She saw Sara's face as she approached, and guessed the cause. She decided not to give her time to brood.

"Starr!" She called out smartly; secretly pleased at the way Sara jumped hearing her surname. "Tide is reaching a high, get than anchor out and ready men on the capstans."

"Aye, aye Captain," replied Sara quickly. "The Bosun is somewhat recovered, enough to take charge of the operation on the deck. I shall instruct her from here."

"Very well. Carry on."

In moments the jolly boat was heading out, and the Bosun was detailing crew onto the aft capstan, thanking the Captain's foresight and insistence of having a capstan at each end of the ship. The noise brought some of the island girls out of the galley, and they all tried to help. The Bosun wasn't at all sure, but she had difficulty in rousing enough crew to man the capstan, so didn't object when Hinatea copied the first three sailors, grabbed a short spar and shoved it in the hole and stood possessively beside it. Several other girls did the same, all chattering with excitement.

Despite herself and her misgivings, the Bosun found she was smiling at the girls, and was silently astonished at herself. Word of what the girls had actually done, especially in wiping out two slaver ships, had passed round the boat, and she shook her head at their bravery. They seemed so young and innocent. Well, she thought ruefully, it is better to die by the hand of brave warriors than by slaver scum. She said a little prayer for her departed shipmates, and started shouting at their replacements in Belada, at which she was about as proficient as many of the Pahippian girls.

This caused shrieks of laughter. The Bosun cut it off as Sara called down to her the anchor was being dropped and she passed the hawser round the capstan twice before feeding it down to two sailors in the hold.

"Alright you horrible animals," she shouted in Belada, getting even her crew laughing, "take the strain and let's pull the rope in."

The capstan turned easily as they took in the slack and the girls chattered and laughed. The hawser tightened and it became hard work, the capstan finally tightening and not budging no matter how they pushed. The girls were all silent now and sweating as they pushed. All seamen, they could understand exactly what the Bosun was trying to do.

The jolly boat returned, and its crew jumped up and joined them on the spars, Pat finding the girl next to him was Hinatea who smiled broadly and winked at him. He grinned back briefly and threw himself into the spar. The capstan creaked, the hawser became as solid as an iron bar, water spurting from it as the threads tightened, causing little rainbows along its length. The Bosun watched it critically, fearing it might break.

"Right, avast there. We'll try putting in a tackle."

The capstan was slowly released, and the hawser was passed through a series of pulleys, which increased the power of the pull. This took a good fifteen minutes to organise, and the sailors working the capstan rested, easing their muscles. The island girls jumped on them, checking their muscles and massaging them.

"Must keep warm," Hinatea scolded a bemused Pat as she tested his shoulder muscles with approval, and kneaded away enthusiastically. He had another girl on the other shoulder, as did the other crewmen. He saw Billy begin to get aroused again and felt the magic straining inside him. His trousers swelled and instantly Hinatea smacked him firmly on the side of the head.

"No," she said, "bad. Not now. Fix canoe first, then fuck. Lots of fucking, very good for you." She smiled happily, and all the girls took up the mantra to Pat's intense embarrassment. Billy's too, as he also got a smack. The Bosun laughed.

She sorted the tackle and chased them back on the spars. The capstan creaked as they started it turning, moving smoothly round as they took up the slack, then braced themselves as the hawser tightened. This time more pressure was placed on the anchor, with its huge flukes buried deep in the sand, and the ship groaned and shuddered.

"Good lads," cried the Bosun, "keep it going now. Backs into it."

The men on their spars had turned, the spar across their shoulders and were low down to the deck, walking backwards, putting the strength of their legs into it. Hinatea copied them, shortly followed by the other girls, though Rerata was unceremoniously dragged out by the Bosun when she tried to get over Billy and push. Her indignant squeals caused everyone to laugh, and the Bosun noticed they used the laugh to give an extra push each time.

Slowly the ship eased backwards, faster as they came free and she floated away. The Bosun kept them going till they were over deeper water, dropped another hook and tightened the hawser till the ship was firm and going nowhere.

Rob, a big burly Bosun's mate, was sent off to check the hull for damage. He stripped naked in the bows before diving over, to the delight of the island girls who flocked forward to help him. Pat found himself alone at last. Husk, easily the biggest of the soldiers, sidled up to him.

"Listen sonny, and listen well. Upset our Princess and you won't be a pretty boy much longer. Understand?"

Pat gaped at him. "Not really. I'm not upsetting her. I'm being respectful and doing what she says."

Abruptly, Husk's fist flew forward, totally unexpected, from a few inches away, leaving Pat with no chance to evade as it cannoned into his face, knocking him to the deck. Pain slammed through his head and his vision blurred.

Husk's huge hand reached down and lifted Pat effortlessly up. "I saw her slap you. You don't upset her. Understand?"

"For fucks sake, leave me alone! I'm a royalist too. But I'm not royalty, or a fucking courtier. She should be with an officer, or a duke, not a bloody commoner like me. It's like she just wants to have me do whatever she wants."

Husk's other hand slammed into his stomach and Pat bent over and retched. It was like being kicked by a horse. As the gasping stopped, Husk lifted him up to look into his face. "So do whatever she wants. Understand?"

"Bastard," gasped Pat, "goat fucker!" He twisted in Husk's hand, brought up both feet and lashed out, catching Husk in the stomach and face. Husk didn't flinch, but released his shoulder and caught a foot as he fell. He bounced Pat twice on his head, then abruptly dropped him and left. As Pat groggily tried to get up, the Bosun came round the side of the cabins to check the anchor cables. She stopped short at the sight of Pat and came over, looking at him critically.

"No secrets on a ship, Pat. I've a damn good idea what's just happened and why. Can't tell you what to do, but make sure you don't disrupt my ship."

"Why is it my fault, Bosun? I only just found out she is the Princess. So if I do something to upset her, she slaps me and the bloody soldiers beat the shit out of me? She's always getting upset with me. I'm just a pet to her." He looked at the deck mournfully and kicked it.

"What do you think I am, a bloody priest? It just is your fault, because she's the princess and you're not. Live with it. Either you're her pet or the soldiers will beat shit out of you. Your choice laddie." With these happy words she left him and he wandered morosely down to put out the washing raft and clean his face.

On the poop deck Suzanne was feeling tired. She had the ship working again and slowly the crew were coming together, but they were lethargic and prone to staring into space, the soldiers as well. She and Sara had an unpleasant scene when they retrieved Rereau from the Captain's cabin, causing the Captain to weep uncontrollably. Hinatea was despatched to retrieve a canoe and take Rereau ashore. She was delighted to do this as it was Mactravis who asked her, but she delegated the paddling duty to another girl.

Suzanne decided she would try and get some sleep, and give Sara the watch. She was in the process of handing over when they heard Hinatea squawk in outrage from the lower deck, and looking down they saw she had caught Pat trying to go into the fo'c'sle, and had gripped him by the ears while she tried to study his face. Pat was trying to break her grip and cover his face at the same time. Hinatea was shouting at him in her own language, and appeared to be cursing him. Now she shouted at one of her other girls without releasing his ears. The other girl shot off and came back shortly with the remains of one of the fruits the girls had brought on board earlier.

While Hinatea held a struggling Pat's face, the other girl rubbed the skin of the fruit into his eye.

Suzanne and Sara looked at each other, and with mutual purpose headed down the stairs. As they got closer, they saw others coming to see what was going on and Pat was scarlet with embarrassment, still struggling to escape.

"What is going on?" Suzanne asked in Belada.

Hinatea looked up. "We fix eye. Hurting."

Now they could see Pat's eye, black and swollen. Sara took a sharp intake of breath, and Suzanne asked, "How did that happen?"

"Slipped," Pat muttered, whereupon Hinatea smacked him on the head.

"Not true. Fat man hit him. Trieste see him do it."

"Pat! Have you been fighting? With the ship in this condition? What about?" Sara was infuriated, not sure whether to be angrier with Pat for fighting or for letting Hinatea treat him, when she wanted to bathe his eye herself.

"Please," begged a mortified Pat, "just let me go to bed and sleep it off. Alone." He glared at a persistent Hinatea, remembering to use Belada.

Sara started to speak, but Suzanne cut her off. "Of course you can Pat. Off you go. Hinatea, leave him alone. Come, Sara." She turned, her hand gripping Sara's elbow tightly. Pat escaped into the fo'c'sle. She could feel Sara fuming in her grip, but said nothing till they were back on the poop and no chance of being overheard.

"You realise why Pat is injured?"

"NO! Why did you not let me go with him?"

"Because he needs to be alone to sort out his thoughts. Who do you think the fat man was, and why do you think he hit him?"

"I don't care. I am worried about Pat."

"The fat man will be one of the soldiers. There are a couple who fit the description, though it is muscle not fat. Those soldiers are loyal to you to the death. Did you do anything to Pat earlier?"

"Well, yes, I slapped him when he was being an idiot."

"I guess one of the soldiers saw you."

"You're kidding." Sara looked stricken as she made the connection. "Surely nobody would do something like that. What do they think I am? Do they think I would want somebody who was forced to be with me?"

"Men do strange things. They are the most illogical of creatures and can be relied upon to do something ridiculous at every opportunity. It's a typical male reaction."

"Oh God. What can I do?"

"Be happy. Don't brood. Make sure nobody can think you are upset by his actions. I know it is difficult, sweetling, but it's part of being a woman. Now, I want to hold a council of war. Round up any officers who are capable, including the Bosun."

Sara and the Bosun were there, with Perryn and Lieutenant Mactravis. Captain Larroche and Brian were unable to make it. Taufik was there but not much use. The Second Mate was dead and the Third in bed with his wife.

"Right, first things first," opened Suzanne. "We need to get the crew back into shape. Perryn, what's wrong with them."

"In essence, they have had their libido overwhelmed and brought up to a peak. All they can think about is sex. It's particularly hard on the Captain, because it is not a subject that has been important to him, and the same for Brian. Bishop Walters is also in deep shock because he always thought he was celibate."

"Celibate? What the fuck does that mean?" The Bosun asked.

"Ah," stammered Perryn nervously and uneasily.

"He never had sex," stated Suzanne calmly. "Carry on Perryn."

"There's a major difference between men and women. Men are just interested in sex, and the spell keeps them going far longer than normal, and able to come back for more again and again. For the women, it cements the bonds if they are already there."

"What are you talking about?" The Bosun asked suspiciously.

"Um, the married women and those in a relationship are much more in love than previously."

"Are you telling me I'm in love with Jim because I let him shag me? Fat bloody chance."

"No, no, there has to have been feelings already."

"But Maisie was with Bill instead of her hubby."

"And who is she with now?" The Bosun subsided. "I do think that the older you are, the harder it is to recover. Umm, I want to talk with the priestess who cast the spell to find out more about it, I've never heard of anything like this. Exercise seems to help, though and the younger are definitely less affected."

"Well, that's a start. Mactravis, your department. Starting tomorrow, I want all the crew on an exercise regime."

He nodded. "What about the women? Not sure they need it."

"Use any you need to help, I'll use the rest to run the ship. Sara, you've laid the basics out for them, you carry on the negotiations with the islanders. You are released from other duties."

Sara nodded, thinking.

"Bosun, I want the crew checked and re-organise the watches. How are the craftsmen getting on?"

"Dwarves, no problem, the masters are pretty much recovered, as they are younger than the captain and they all have their wives along. We got them off girls and onto their wives." She grinned. "Nancy hasn't had such a good seeing to in years. Now they've screwed it out of their systems, they are getting back to themselves, but I think some exercise will be good for them!"

"Right, well get them sorted and I want reports on each of their departments, and staffing levels. Sara, how are the Spakka doing?"

"It's hard to tell. They have withdrawn into themselves, spending all their time in their wardroom. They seem to be able to work, not well, but they can do it. They are clearly under a lot of shock at having something like this overcome their discipline. You know they were screwing each other? Their blasted honour doesn't cover this."

"Well, make sure they join Mactravis' exercise regime. She looked round at them. "One last thing. Perryn, I want Taufik and Walters working on a chart soon. Anything else?"

"We need to survey the land," said Sara. "I want to know what is available here, whether there is any metals."

"Do we have anyone who can?"

"I don't know."

The Bosun heaved herself to her feet. "I'll go and ask the dwarf." She went down the ladder and was back shortly.

"Well, that was simple. He just said 'Pat.' He could do that instead of exercise, take Grey Fox with him."

Suzanne spoke low to the Bosun. "Bosun, get somebody up to clear Lieutenant Stevens old cabin. We'll give it to the Princess now she is an officer. And get her kit up from the fo'c'sle. I don't want her to go down there to get it herself."

"Good idea, Cap'n. Will sort it out. You got the watch, Sara? Your cabin will be ready tomorrow. Want me to take the dogwatch Cap'n?"

"It's alright, Bos'n, I'll take it."

"Beggin' yer pardon, ma'am, but you shouldn't. Officers stand watch, Captain doesn't. He turns up when he feels like it and keeps us on our toes. You leave it with me, ma'am, and I'll set up a roster with the Princess, Lieutenant Mactravis, Master Taufik and myself. We'll teach that bloody soldier how to sail, sure we will." The Bosun smiled widely and slipped away before Suzanne could come up with an objection.

"I'd feel a damn sight more like the Captain if I had his cabin! Now, I will make off to my little cubby hole and get some much needed sleep. You take care, Asmara." With a squeeze of her arm, Suzanne left her there and went to her room.

It was dreadfully hot and stuffy in there, she opened the tiny window to get some breeze and stripped off her clothes, reviewing the day's events. She felt quite pleased with herself at the way she had managed, especially at getting the Princess in control, ruling, where she should be. She had a pail of water in the cabin, and now she washed, dipping a cloth into it and rubbing it over her body, getting rid of the sweat. It felt glorious and cool. She took a while longer than usual enjoying the simple pleasure.

She was aware of the magic in her blood, and it thrummed as she washed herself, particularly when the cloth went between her legs. But she stamped down on it firmly, stroking her amulet where it stuck out of her shirt. Must get some exercise tomorrow. Wouldn't do for the captain to do anything naughty with the crew, would it? She felt quite pleased with herself - all this way and she'd only been to bed with one man, Mactravis, and that just twice. She laughed quietly to herself, thinking she was acting like a nun.

Her hair was a mess, but she untied it and a quick brush through had it crackling and shiny, though it was very hot in her little cabin. She climbed onto her cot, pushed her hair up and away from her body and face and pulled a sheet over her nakedness. She took off the amulet and put it on her shirt nearby, letting the magic strum through and relax her as she prepared to drift off to sleep, still feeling very pleased with herself.

Just as she began to drift off, something aroused her. A gentle tap on the door. Irritated, she dragged herself out of bed, clasped the sheet to her breast and went to the door.

"Who is it?"

"Pat."

"What the hell do you want, Pat? I am trying to sleep."

"I'm sorry, Suzanne, I'm having trouble with the magic, and wondered if I could borrow the amulet. I don't really want to ask the soldiers."

She sighed and opened the door. A woebegone Pat was standing there in his shorts, looking utterly delicious. She started slightly and slapped the thought down. "Come in, I'll get it for you," she said without thinking and turned to get it from by the bed.

Pat felt like he had been hit by both Husk's fists at once. He staggered into the room. Suzanne had opened the door half asleep, her hair up in a magnificent mane behind her and trailing down to her shoulders, her big blue eyes wide and sleepy as they blinked innocently at him. Clutching just a sheet to herself, exposing disquieting bits of flesh, her breasts pushing out past her hand and one side exposed. He'd always thought she was taller than he was, but now he realised she barely came up to his eyes.

Now she turned away from him, forgetting she was naked and he was treated to the sight of her bottom swaying in mesmeric fashion as she went over to the bed, bending over exposing a tuft of hair, which caused his knees to tremble.

She came back, one hand clasping the sheet to her chin, and one hand wasn't nearly enough, the other holding up her shirt. "It's in here somewhere," she said, waving it vaguely.

The door closed behind Pat as she waved the shirt at him. He reached for it, not looking at it with the distraction she was giving him, biting his lip to try and keep control. Suzanne let go of the shirt, Pat missed it and it dropped. Suzanne grabbed for it with both hands, missed and the sheet fell away. She stooped and picked up the shirt, forgetting about the sheet, and her breasts swung forward, swelling magnificently in Pat's entranced eyes.

Suzanne picked up the shirt and proffered it to Pat again, smiling triumphantly at this little accomplishment, and admiring Pat's bare chest. To her astonishment, Pat knocked the shirt and the amulet from her hand, sending it skidding across the floor. She looked at him, wide-eyed. Pat took a step forward and she felt her nipples touch his chest. Something ignited inside her, and she lifted up her mouth to him as he crushed her to his chest, and pushed her back on the bed urgently, desperately seeking for him with her hips. Scrabbling with her hands to drag down his shorts. Sighing with pleasure as he sank into her and the magic took her, raising her up to a constant rush of sensation.

A couple of hours later, she awoke, Pat underneath and still inside her. She smiled, and worked her internal muscles, feeling him become rigid again. Gently she leaned forward and woke him, watching his eyes as he looked up and found his world bounded by her face, circled by her hair and breasts, resting on his chest. Delighted by his reaction, she resolved to somehow acquire this spell; it put such strength into men it would make her very, very wealthy on return to Harrhein.

Sitting up, she put her hands behind her head, brushing out her hair, knowing full well the effect it would have on Pat, and smiled as she rode his immediate frantic lunges. Rolling her hips with the motion, she cast her thoughts outside, oh, yes she was the Captain and would need to go on deck soon to make sure all was well. No hurry, the Captain could go when she wanted. She thought she would see how many times the magic could raise him before burn out, biting her lip with anticipation, then having to reach down and arrest his progress as she felt him tense. Didn't want him going too early. Now who had the watch, ah, yes, Sara, that was fine, she was capable...

Sara! Oh no, this was Pat under her! In her confusion, she lost control and Pat pulled her down, kissing along her jaw and stroking her back. He started to whisper in her ears, telling her his feelings and how she looked and felt. The magic thrummed hard and she forgot all about Sara for a few hours.

She next awoke to find a smiling Pat kissing her gently. He was dressed, and whispered in her ear. "My watch will be called soon. I must go. Thank you. Till tonight." He kissed her again, gently with closed mouth, and slipped out the door. Suzanne smiled with pleasure, her heart swelled with love and she slowly writhed in the bed, savouring the smell of him. Damn, that had been good. Now, how to explain to Sara? She felt guilty for a moment, but then thought she hadn't chased him, Pat had come to her, Pat had chosen her. Damn, if it hadn't been for the magic, it would never have happened, but now it had, well, she might as well enjoy herself.

Honeymoon

S uzanne came up to the poop deck after dawn, and found Sara sitting on the deck talking with Rereau and an old woman, who she introduced as Rereau's grandmother, Poema.

"How are the negotiations going?"

"We're just about there. They need to send for the principals of the other villages, but it won't be a problem."

"Good. I need to check on the injured and see if Perryn got anywhere." She left them and went to the galley. One of the injured had died, but the others were stable. Suzanne was actually quite impressed with the way the island girls were nursing them. She was concerned to realise none of the injured had recovered from the magic.

The ship was quiet, she prowled around finding most of the crew either asleep or having sex, usually with another crew member but also with the island girls. The same went for the soldiers, and she left Mactravis alone after finding a girl in his bed. She gave the Spakka a wide berth as well. Pat, she noted, was eating, ready to go watch. She smiled at him, which he returned. As she turned back, she saw Sara had noticed and was giving her an odd look.

The bell rang for the watch change and Suzanne went up to the poop to see the Bosun take over from Sara. The island women had gone. Sara said Rereau was with the Captain and Poema back to the village.

"Did Perryn speak with her?"

"Not exactly, she can't speak the complicated Belada needed to explain. It wasn't much use; they don't know how to get rid of it. It does pass, and exercise and sex helps. That's only with young people; older people like Rereau have it a bit harder. We're seriously worried about the Captain and Walters."

"Bosun, please inform Mactravis I want a word with him. He is to start the exercise program for the entire crew this morning. I want everyone on parade immediately after breakfast. Including the Captain, Walters and the cook. Walking wounded can join us, leave the galley doors open so the others can hear. I'll be back to speak to Mactravis in five minutes."

She strode off, ignoring Sara who started after her and set off on another circuit of the deck. She could just hear the conversation behind her.

"She's acting a bit strange, Bosun? I wanted to talk with her."

"Leave her alone, Princess. She's finding it tough as Captain. She don't have your training but she's got good instincts. She's worried about everyone, and discovering more things to worry about all the time. Besides, she needs to get rid of the magic, and as Captain she can't go round screwing the crew. Mactravis is what she needs, and he's got an island slut in with him. I'll have a word with him when he comes on deck, selfish bastard."

Suzanne paused round the corner of the cabin, where she could hear more, out of sight.

"Whatcha gonna do about the magic, Princess? You need to get young Pat into bed, and he's on watch now. Don't keep slapping him, neither"

"What do you mean?" asked Sara sharply. "He was being obtuse and horrible."

"You can't tell strong young men what to do all the time, Princess. If they're no good, they'll stay and take it. If they are any good, they'll piss off. You've got to be careful, too, because some of the little bastards will try and thump you when they can't take it anymore." There was a noise Suzanne interpreted as Sara spluttering and stamping her foot. The Bosun continued.

"You need to lead them, get them to do things by letting them think it is their own idea. Always pretend to be thicker than them. Let them think they're boss till you've got them tied up and ship shape." The Bosun gave a chuckle that was quite evil.

Even early in the morning it was already hot. The crew lined up raggedly on deck, waiting while the last of the men who thought themselves too important to join were dragged protesting from their cabins, Captain Larroche the last. The Spakka formed up to one side in a sullen group, with Sara in front of them where she could ensure they understood. Suzanne spoke to them from the poop deck.

"The magical attack has affected you all badly. We don't know exactly how it was done or what it means to you. Perryn is talking with the priestesses to try and find a solution."

There was a commotion as Walters tried to get back to his cabin on the grounds he should help Perryn. The Bosun grabbed him firmly. "He's not in your fucking cabin, Bishop, and you're not getting off to go shagging." Walters was shocked, never having been spoken to in this fashion. He subsided and hid himself amongst the rest of the men.

Suzanne tried not to laugh and carried on. "We have found exercise helpful, so you are all detached from duty and put under command of Lieutenant Mactravis who will be putting you all through a fitness schedule." She moved backwards, allowing Mactravis to take over. He leered down at them.

"Right my lads, you're going to enjoy this!" A groan went up from the company. Some of them had been soldiers, and all knew enough about soldiering to know when an officer said that it was going to hurt.

"Now, we can't do any exercise properly on board ship, so we all need to be on the beach."

The crew looked at the shore, sand glistening as the wavelets ran up it, a good 300 paces away. Some looked hopefully at the boats, all lashed down securely. Captain Larroche made an ineffectual gesture.

"And you can't do any exercise in your normal clothes, so strip. I don't care if you're naked or have shorts. Get a move on, you have one minute, then off you go to the beach."

Pat was first into the water, quickly followed by the Pahippian girls who weren't going to miss out on something as exciting as swimming, though they didn't have a clue what was happening. The rest of the crew quickly followed, most stark naked, a few with shorts on. The older men were slower, and a few had to be thrown in. Brian squealed about his injury as the Bosun stripped him naked and threw him in. Rereau tried to protect the Captain, but Suzanne and Sara stripped him and pushed him over.

Pat was already on the beach by the time the last of them were in the water, surrounded by girls all trying to feel his muscles and chattering at the same time. They spoke little Belada, so it was tricky for him to fend them off, particularly when one took an interest in his member. So he set off to run, knowing this was the next step. He headed off down the beach, and as others came ashore, they saw him and followed.

Mactravis was in the jolly boat, keeping an eye on the Captain who was floundering, even with Rereau swimming beside him. Corporal Strachan nudged him. "Trouble," he said, pointing to the beach.

It took a moment for the sight to sink in, and then Mactravis cursed. "Pat will run them into the ground. We need to head them off. Sergeant Russell!" He shouted to the other boat. "Send Grey Fox to bring them back, then get them organised into squads according to who comes ashore, ten to a squad, one soldier with a squad, get them running. See how far they can manage, turn back when they start to flag. I'll look after the officers."

Russell called out orders, Grey Fox dived off the ship and swam to shore, several other soldiers doing the same. Grey Fox swam to the beach and sprinted fast after the runners, sending them back as he overtook them. Some of them collapsed on the sand in relief.

On the ship, Suzanne found she and Sara were the only ones left, apart from the dwarves and the wounded in their hammocks, with a couple still in the galley. The female crew were ashore, supposedly in support of their men but really not trusting them with the island girls.

"Don't you want to exercise, Sara?"

Sara frowned. Suzanne didn't seem to be quite the same, a little more stand-offish. "I'm fine for now, Captain. A bit tired after my watch, not slept much. Once I get Pat into bed, I'll be alright!" She grinned happily at the thought.

Suzanne frowned. "Well, that will be some time. You might as well take some exercise."

Sara turned to her. "What about you? Aren't you going to exercise?" Her eyes narrowed slightly, she wasn't quite sure why she was uncomfortable, but Suzanne felt strange.

"Oh, I don't need it. Didn't affect me so badly."

"Yes it did. I saw Mactravis with you."

Suzanne flushed. "That was before I got my amulet."

"It's not that strong, no more than mine is, against this spell." She looked closely at Suzanne. "You had a man in your cabin last night didn't you?" Sara started to smile, but it wiped off her face as an awful thought struck her.

"Well," said Suzanne, desperately, "I might have done. So what?"

"You smiled at Pat this morning. I saw you." Sara's tone was accusatory, harsh.

"I often smile at Pat. So what?"

"Not like that. You had him in your room last night didn't you? You lured my boyfriend into your room." Sara was staring at Suzanne, her voice beginning to rise. Suzanne flushed, then struck back angrily.

"I didn't lure him in. He knocked on my bloody door when I was falling asleep. He wanted to borrow my amulet, so he said, but when he opened the door he changed his mind. The magic took us both. We couldn't help it."

"You bitch!" Sara flared. "I can't believe you. I thought you were my friend. You know how I feel about him, I've talked about him, asked you if I should have his babies! And you, you slept with him!"

"It was the magic, alright! It wouldn't have happened otherwise. But it did and it was great, and we both enjoyed it. And we'll do it again tonight!" Suzanne glared at Sara, both girls getting more and more worked up.

"Aaaaaaagh! You fucking bitch! Whore!" and Sara flew at Suzanne, both hands slapping at her, grabbing for her hair. Suzanne retaliated, a short, sharp punch laying Sara back on the floor. Sara looked up at Suzanne, her eyes narrowed and she pulled Lady Strike from her scabbard with an ominous hiss.

On the beach the oblivious object of the fight cut a distant figure now, still gamely pursued by three of the girls, the others having turned to other sailors. Billy floundered along the soft sand when

Grey Fox went past.

"Stop running, form up into squads and wait for a soldier to take you running," he called as he went past.

"Fuck that," said Billy and fell to the sand. He looked back and saw Rat, Pete and a couple of others under a palm tree a couple of hundred yards behind him. He grunted and went back to them.

"What the fuck is going on?"

Rat grinned. "Pat's being pestered by those girls and took off, they followed him and everyone followed them. We were supposed to wait on the beach."

"Ah, shit, why can't he take them into the bushes and shag 'em."

"Hah! He's probably too knackered. I ..." Rat's voice trailed off. The others looked at him. "Hey! I'm not thinking about sex. Perryn was right. Exercise worked."

The others looked at each other, wonderingly.

"Great," said Billy. "We're cured, we don't need to fuck about running in this heat. Come on, let's go back and help out or we'll be rounded up for more exercise."

The Spakka, all together, watched from nearby shade and followed them sweating profusely and pulling at their clothing. Rat wondered if they would finally relinquish their sheepskin.

In the jolly boat, Corporal Strachan grabbed Lieutenant Mactravis' arm. "Sir, there's something strange happening on the ship."

Mactravis looked up from the floundering Captain, and heard the unmistakeable thunk of a weapon striking wood. "Oh hell. Are the island girls attacking again? Husk, take us back to the ship. The Captain will be all right."

The Captain swam badly, but Rereau was with him. The jolly boat turned and quickly went back to the ship, where Mactravis gripped the rope ladder and started up, with Little right behind him. He reached the railing, looked over the top and stopped dead. Little pushed up beside him and looked onto the deck.

"Cor!" He said with feeling.

On seeing Lady Strike appear, Suzanne picked up her quarterstaff from where it rested against the ship's wheel. She bounced lightly on her toes, gripping the staff nearer to one end with it pointed towards

Sara. She was an expert with the weapon, and was totally confident in her ability to beat a swordsman. She feinted at Sara's face and quickly reversed the staff to take out her knee, but Sara was easily equal, leaping backwards and coming in with a fast lunge at her hands. Suzanne blocked it and found herself breathlessly blocking a series of slashing attacks with Sara's foot stamping relentlessly as she forced Suzanne backwards.

Sara switched from lunges at Suzanne's body to slashing at her hands, and Suzanne retaliated by trying to catch the blade sunk into the wood and trap it. Both girls pulled back, breathing deeply and oblivious to the rapt audience building up. Suzanne smiled, she felt she had the measure of Sara now, and she would put the damn girl in her place. Punching the Captain indeed! Drawing a blade on her! It was not to be tolerated. She began to consider how she would punish her, and which bones to break now. She switched her grip on the staff, holding it equally between both hands, and advanced on Sara with rapid blows from alternating ends of the staff, aimed at head, hands, leg, body, neck; none too powerful, but fast, oh so fast, a swordsman couldn't live with it. The arm, she decided with satisfaction, the left arm.

Sara retreated slowly, watching Suzanne's eyes. She wasn't so much learning her style as her rhythm. She noted the stronger right hand, and casually deflected the odd blow with Lady Strike, but mainly she used her feet to avoid them. Her anger had congealed into white hot fury that misted in front of her brain. She wasn't thinking of anything but the need to spit Suzanne's lying, deceitful body on Lady Strike, to wash the deck with her blood. Suzanne's eyes tensed ever so slightly, Sara swayed out of line and lunged, her tip gently disappearing into Suzanne's left forearm. Blood spurted out and Suzanne screamed in shock and pain, almost dropping her staff at the unexpected shock. She had never been touched before. She pulled back instantly, preventing damage to the arm, but it hurt, although it still worked.

Sara coiled up like a spring, put her foot against the rail and pushed herself forward, dropping at the last moment to slide underneath the defensive block on her back, flat against the deck, then jerking upright to stab at the exposed midriff.

Suzanne threw herself sideways, no attempt to block or strike, but rolling away from the attack while squalling with pain and fear. She thumped into the fo'c's'le wall, and turned to face Sara running at her with a face like death incarnate. With nowhere to go, she lashed out with the staff at full extension, caught Sara's upper arm more by luck than judgement and turned the killing strike that stabbed into the wooden wall right beside her body. Suzanne was still squalling in terror and tried to get away as Sara wrestled to pull Lady Strike from the wall. As the sabre came free, a marlin spike whirled into the back of her head and she slumped to the floor. Suzanne, still sobbing in fear, tried to pull herself upright and finish her off, but the marlin spike came back and thumped into her midriff. She subsided beside Sara, and a wary Bosun came up to them, leant down and grabbed each of them by the hair, kicking their weapons away. She shook them, till Sara's eyes opened and she had both girls looking at her.

"You stupid fucking bitches," she hissed. "You sorry excuses for officers. This is my fucking ship and I won't have you fucking tarts destroying it. Get a grip of yourselves! We've been attacked by natives and you two think you can fight each other? Over some worthless boy?" And she smacked their heads together, hard.

She glared at Sara. "You think you're a fucking princess? Then fucking act like one! Sort out this bloody mess. You're the one who told me not to kill those girls. Now prove you're right. Sort it out."

"She attacked me!" Suzanne gasped in outrage. "I'm the Captain. That's mutiny, lock her up Bosun."

"Captain? The Captain doesn't go round shagging the crew. You wanna be Captain, well fucking act like it! Now both of you will forget this, go to your rooms and sort yourselves out. Understand?" She shook them and banged their heads together again. "Understand?"

"Yes Bosun," whispered Sara, her voice dead and her face white.

Suzanne couldn't speak, just nodded, and the Bosun dropped them. They crawled off to their rooms while the Bosun rounded on the spectators, fortunately few of them.

"If you breathe a fuckin' word of this, so help me I'll skin you alive. It never fuckin' happened, alright?"

They nodded, mute.

Suzanne stepped ashore from the jolly boat, wearing extremely short shorts and barefoot, the sea going up past her knees. Her arm was sore, but the wound wasn't deep and would heal. She walked over to Lieutenant Mactravis, enjoying the feel of the sand under her feet, but conscious of the heat. Inside she was still fuming over the row with Sara, but the makeup was doing its job and her face was a mask. She looked sensational and she knew it. One look would be enough and Pat would be trapped, she thought to herself with satisfaction.

"How's it going, Lieutenant?"

"Pretty good, Suzanne. All the young guys are fixed. The Captain now hates me more than he wants Rereau so we are making progress."

"You're holding something back."

He twitched uncomfortably. "I'm sorry, I made a misjudgement."

Suzanne arched an eyebrow.

"I should have had somebody ready on the beach. Would have done for soldiers, thought these guys wouldn't be so fit."

He waited for a response, but Suzanne gave him no encouragement, just looked at him levelly.

"Ah, we've lost Pat."

"What do you mean, lost? Is he dead?" A hint of emotion crept into Suzanne's voice and she looked at the village, wondering if Sara had run off with him.

"Oh, no, well, at least we don't think so. He took off down the beach, running, and hasn't come back. He set off without being told."

"Alone? Unarmed?"

"I'll say he was unarmed. He's stark bollock naked. I don't know if he's alone."

"What do you mean, Lieutenant?" Suzanne was getting angry now, dragging the facts out slowly.

"At the last sighting, he was still being pursued by three of the girls."

Suzanne closed her eyes for a moment. At least he wasn't with Sara. "Well, of all the crew, I expect Pat is the most likely to survive alone on this island. Where's Mot?"

"Pigging herself in the village. Some of the girls took her off and they've been feeding her some sort of boiled root which she loves. They've washed her and are busy braiding her hair."

"Well, if she isn't worried, neither am I. If Pat isn't back later, Mot will track him down. How many men are back to active?"

"All the young ones, most of the middle aged."

"How long to get the Captain back?"

Mactravis sighed. "To be honest, Suzanne, there is no real change in either him, Walters or even Brian. You're stuck with the job for the foreseeable future."

Suzanne walked up the path to the village, considering her feelings. Mixed, she decided. On the one hand, it was fun being the Captain, in charge of all! And she was damn good at it, she told herself smugly. Maybe not so hot on navigation, but we're in port now. But, oh, God, some of the decisions! And then the fight with Sara, who was being quite out of order. She really needs to get used to it and accept the situation.

She saw Sara sitting in the shade of a frangipani tree in front of a house, its strange blunt branches, long glossy leaves and copious flowers casting a dappled shadow. Unlike Suzanne, she had scorned make up and her face was clear, unmarked by the earlier emotion, with her hair tied back. Like Suzanne, her face was a mask. Poema sat opposite her, carefully dissecting one of the many fruits from the island. This one was massive, with orange flesh and lots of black seeds in the hollow centre.

"Hello darling," she said icily to Sara in Harrhein, "how are you getting on?" She switched to Belada and addressed Poema, "Greetings High Priestess. I trust the day sees you in health and happiness."

Sara nodded expressionlessly, imaging a scene back at court where she had regained Divine Right and Suzanne was being impaled on a jagged, splintered stake, right through her offending organ, while Poema beamed, oblivious, and offered her some fruit. "Please, try this papaya. It has a bland flavour, but it is cooling in the high heat of the day."

"Thank you, just what I need. Where is Perryn? I thought he was working with you?"

"Ah, he is a clever one, that boy. He is so talented, I cannot follow him. He wants to understand our magic, but it is a gift of the Gods, given to only a few."

She paused, and Suzanne smiled. Silence worked on women just as well as men. So did her charm.

"I sent him off with Moea. She has a talent that complements his and I hope she can show him what we do, for I cannot. I hope when he understands, he will be able to cure your people, and our girls. They suffer as well."

Suzanne looked at her levelly. "And how are they studying?"

"I think you have guessed. It helps them to get their minds together if their bodies are also together. Power comes from the Goddess and she gives it to us when we are together as a man and a woman. It is the most basic way to worship."

"You realise Perryn follows a different religion?"

Poema smiled. "The Goddess does not care."

Suzanne changed tack. "Are they making any progress?"

"I think so. They are sweet together. Maybe the Goddess will call him and he will stay with us. In time, all things come."

"The Pahippians do not measure time as we do, Suzanne." Sara's voice was emotionless, flat, and Poema gave her a startled glance. "They do not understand why we should be in a hurry. The island gives them all they need with little effort, which is why they spend so much time being happy. It is a good life, here. Probably helps there are no men."

Poema smiled, Suzanne said nothing. Sara sighed and carried on. "Which is what causes me a problem. There is nothing here to trade. If we want anything, we would have to bring in workers. And I bet the Pahippians would turn them from being workers in no time at all."

"Oh, I think I can think of something." Suzanne smiled. "Import a few of these girls to Praesidium and I would see my business in a sorry state in no time. Oh, I don't mean myself, but I own a couple of elite houses and another in Riklaws Port."

"I'm sure at least a hundred of your regulars would stay loyal," said Sara sweetly, to which Suzanne bridled.

"Don't worry about me, dear. I've always specialised in a few, rich, aristocratic, even royal friends. But I don't mean to take the girls from the island. Bring the customers here!"

"But it's such a long way, I don't think you would get many coming."

"Sure, it is now. But before long, I expect they will do it in less than a month each way. It would become a special tour for the rich playboys, a trip round Pahipi and Hind, with a month sampling the girls and boys here. They would pay, and pay enough to make it worthwhile. Don't worry, darling, I'll set it up. I bet you I can make more than you need." She smiled brilliantly and tucked into her papaya, content she had reminded Sara of her expertise, replaced quantity with quality, reminded Sara of her relationship with her father, not told her Pat was missing and especially that Pat wasn't with her.

Sara didn't react, but replayed the impaling sequence more slowly, noisily and graphically.

Anticipating the cool of the evening, a big bonfire was built in the middle of the village. Several of the sailors were dragooned into helping. Little felt a sharp crack on his behind, and turned to find a large Pahippian woman brandishing a stick at him, telling him off loudly and pointing to the woods. She jabbed Husk as well, and the two of them went off to get more firewood, Little muttering she wasn't just big enough, but also acted like Husk's mother.

Suzanne turned to Sara. "Looks like the rest of the Pahippians are getting used to us now." The girls had declared an unspoken truce, both relieved the other was not with Pat.

"I think so. Haven't seen any men yet, and there don't seem to be many old people."

"Have you noticed how new the village is?" Lieutenant Mactravis came over and overheard them speak. "These people have not been here long. I have been talking to old Manuarii, he led them here five years ago. Their whole history is one of flight. These are survivors, gentle people."

"Did you learn much about the other islands?"

"Not really. They are very scared of the next island in the chain, but it is a long way away. They came round the south of it and sailed a long time to get here. Most of the old people died on the trip. There aren't many men, either. Perhaps three."

"Where did they come from?"

"A chain of islands to the north, but these Umayyad people preyed on them, nearly devastated the entire race. Lost their history and most of their men. They were fleeing from them, these are all that made it."

"What did you find out about the Umayyads?"

"Not a lot, really. They have ships, much smaller than ours, with a single sail. Lots of men on them, come ashore, burn the villages, kill the old people, the sick and the young, then take the rest off in chains."

"Slavers," spat Sara, "I hate slavers. Probably in league with the Spakka."

"I expect so. We will have to be careful as we go to the north."

"We'll need Pat. Any sign of him?" It was the first time she had mentioned him and she spoke carefully.

"No. I told Strachan to get Mot and track him down. Shall we see how they are getting on?"

They walked over to a hut on the edge of the village that was basking in the late sunshine. A hugely bloated Mot was lying on her back while several soldiers stood around her. Grey Fox looked up.

"She is not interested in Pat's clothing."

Corporal Strachan was looking worried. "These damn islanders have filled her up with this poi muck. She won't move."

"Poi?"

"It's a root they boil. It's their main food, what they grow in the fields. Damn dog loves it. First time we need her and she's pigged herself."

Mot looked at Sara, thumped her tail and wriggled slightly to make it easier for Sara to scratch her stomach.

"How can she eat so much? Look at the size of her stomach!"

"She looks like she should have given birth a month ago. Oh! She's moving! Maybe she finally registered Pat's clothes!"

"Nah," said Strachan with fine scorn. "It's that bloody girl with more poi for her." Indeed, they saw a girl returning with another banana leaf full of what looked like porridge, most indignant at being chased away from the god dog.

"What is the matter, Suzanne?" Poema asked, coming up to a concerned huddle of officers.

"One of our men is missing. We are discussing organising a search party to look for him."

"The one who ran down the beach? Oh, do not worry, Hinatea went after him with her girls. They are wild, those ones. They like to go all over the island. They know how to live in the wilds, how to make a shelter for the night. They will come back when they are ready. There are some beautiful spots on our island, and I expect she is showing them to him."

"Hurr, hurr," said Little from beside the bonfire, "I reckon she's showing him a pretty valley all right!" There were several other laughs from the soldiers.

"Couple o' hills, to see the view, like." "I reckon she took 'im caving." "Or round the back."

Sara flushed with a mixture of anger and embarrassment. Damn, she thought, as if Suzanne isn't bad enough He'd better not have touched those damn girls, especially not Hinatea! Surely the spell will have kept him for me? It makes people fall in love. She saw Suzanne looking gravely at her and turned away, hiding the tear in her eye, for the first time appreciating the magic had tied Suzanne to Pat as well.

"Well, if you are sure," said Suzanne, ignoring the soldiers, "we won't go looking. Do you think he will come back in the morning?"

Poema shrugged. It clearly wasn't important. "Unless they want to climb the mountain and talk to the Gods, they will probably come back tomorrow."

"Talk to the Gods?" Perryn interjected, getting up from where he sat by the fire and coming over. "How do they do that?"

"The Gods live in the mountain. You can see the smoke from their fires. We climb the mountain to hear their voices and find out their wishes."

"Could I do that?" Asked Perryn eagerly.

"Ask Moea. She is young enough to go. I only go on special occasions, and I am not due to speak to the Gods till the rains come."

"How do you speak to the Gods?"

"We go to the mouth of the mountain, and we cast presents into the fire. Then we sing and meditate. If the Gods wish to talk to us, they speak into our minds. We don't talk to them, they know what we are doing and what we want."

"What sort of presents?" Perryn asked with deep suspicion, dark thoughts of human sacrifice filling his mind.

"Fruit and food, and of course sex. Every time we make love it is a present to the Gods."

Suzanne and Sara spent the night on the ship, as did most of the girls in the crew, who made certain their boyfriends were with them. The unattached men slept ashore, except for the Spakka who weren't happy ashore. They were still deeply suspicious of the island girls whom they banned from their wardroom. Sara didn't trust them to not take their axes to the Pahippians, but she worried about them, they were introspective and even Janis was short with her when she tried to spend time with them. Even Willem Stiphleek, their noisy tone-deaf bard, was silent, no painful tunes emanating from the cabin.

After breakfast the girls took the jolly boat and went ashore, coming up to where the men were relaxing beside a fire, being given breakfast by the locals. Lieutenant Mactravis stood, unusually dishevelled and slightly embarrassed.

"Morning, ma'am," he said to them both. "Trust you slept well and all is shipshape aboard."

"Did you get any sleep?" Suzanne asked with a twisted smile. It had not been an easy night for her or for Sara with the magic still coursing through their veins. He went red, but was saved from answering by a chorus of shouts from the men, who were standing up and waving. Looking in the same direction, they saw Pat coming up the path from the fields.

He was wearing a grass skirt and looking acutely embarrassed. Behind him, three girls were walking, clearly in considerable discomfort. Legs apart, one leaning on another, expressions going from satisfaction to wincing. The men's shouts died away, and they could hear Pat trying to tell the girls to stop it. They kept coming, and now everyone could hear them moaning with pain as they limped along.

"Bloody hell, Pat," said Little, "did you do that to them? All of them?"

"No! Of course not! Well, yes, but I haven't hurt them, they are just fooling," he replied.

Hinatea looked at the men, her eyes wide, and indicated Pat with her hand. "Verra strong! No stop! All night!" Her broken Belada was sufficiently understandable.

Pat cursed. The men stared at the girls, who staggered on into the village. Hinatea had what appeared to be copious amounts of dried blood over her thighs. In fact she had been dribbling fruit juice over them shortly beforehand without Pat noticing. The girls went into one of the huts, from which the distinct sound of giggling came over the hum of insects and birds, the only sounds in the village.

"Oh dear God, what have they done to you?" Pat cried into the silence, not looking at Sara or Suzanne.

A bloated caricature was advancing on him slowly, her tail wagging uncertainly, the flowers woven into it waving in the wind. Mot's entire body was covered in flowers, all woven into her hair. She could barely move, her stomach was so distended. Pat fell to his knees beside her and she collapsed happily to the ground.

Sara's cheeks were flaming as the men all gathered around him and started asking questions she didn't want to hear, let alone the answers. Pat was gruffly answering, mainly in the negative, and getting quite upset. Serve him right, she thought furiously. Beside her she could feel Suzanne equally angry, but didn't dare look at her.

"Well Pat, when you have quite recovered," Suzanne's icy tone cut through the voices, "we have a task for you and Grey Fox."

Pat looked up guiltily, panicking at the severe angry expressions.

"We need to survey the island for metals. The dwarves say you know what to look for."

He nodded eagerly. "No problem. I will go as it gets cooler this evening, it's very hot in the middle of the day. I have seen quite a bit of the island, will take me a few days."

The soldiers were milling around, clearly itching to continue the questions, while both Suzanne and Sara groped for some reason to take Pat off alone to talk.

Hinatea came running from her hut, followed by her troupe which had expanded to a good dozen girls. She was clutching something in her hand, and as she came closer, Pat could see it was some sawblade root. Everyone fell silent as she took his hand affectionately and spoke in her broken Belada.

"Words, learn?" She looked at him expectantly, her girls around her, all traces of injury gone, all with their eyes like pinpricks, a clear sign the drug was working.

"Belada?" Pat asked, unable to resist a plea for help.

"No. You words." Pat looked puzzled.

"She wants to learn Harrhein," explained Mactravis, oblivious of the feelings of his superior officers and greatly enjoying the drama. "I think it is probably a good idea. Poema says she can come with us, along with a few of the other girls, to replace the missing crew. Some of them haven't recovered from the spell and apparently these ones are too wild to stay on the island. I can believe that!"

Suzanne desperately searched for something to say and found nothing. Sara beside her had gone wooden, and when she reached tentatively for her hand, she grasped it instantly and squeezed, both girls feeling better for the contact, joining forces against the common enemy. Sara wondered if she could ban Hinatea from coming with them. Suzanne was determined not to let her on board. Suzanne pulled gently and both girls walked away, down the path towards the bathing pool in the stream, unused at this time of day. They didn't speak until they reached the pool, standing in the deep shade of a fig tree.

"All men are bastards," said Suzanne bitterly, and both girls were crying, holding each other.

A few days later, Suzanne was conducting her daily report session under the shade of the palm trees, when Pat and Grey Fox came up the beach with Hinatea and Silmatea. Mot followed them, back to her usual shape. They came up to the group, and joined it, the others moving slightly to let them in. Suzanne felt her breath catch at the sight of him while Sara went still.

Pat nodded to them, apparently oblivious of any feelings, Hinatea holding his hand in a way he had never permitted Sara. "We've been right over the island, no metals of any sort. Quite certain of it. Lots of the sand called yellow flowers, though, up on the craters. Whole pool of smelly water you can't drink."

"Is it any use?" Suzanne looked at Sara, who shrugged, her face unreadable.

"You can use it a few ways," said Pat. "It helps things to grow, if you use a little of it, and for some illnesses. And you can use it to start fires easily."

Perryn nodded at this. "Walters will be interested. We don't use it much in Harrhein, but it certainly has some usage."

"How is it sold and how is it packed?"

"Well, it's quite expensive. I'm not sure how much, there isn't a lot available. I have only seen it in small quantities."

"If we took a few barrels back, would they sell?"

"Oh yes. I wouldn't take too many though; there is no market for lots of it. Check with the dwarves, they may want some."

"Good thinking. Pat, do that later. Perryn, carry on." Both girls ignored Pat pointedly though he didn't notice.

"Sure. I think we can sail when you are ready. The Captain will slowly improve over the next few weeks, as will Brian and Walters. Everyone else is about recovered. The spell was concentrated on the poop deck, which is why it has a deeper effect on the men there, especially the three older ones. I have learnt a lot about it and the religion here. The Gods do talk to them, they have spoken to me." He looked troubled and infinitely sad. "My own God has never done that."

"Really? What did they say?"

"They told me to go away. They said Moea was not to go with me, but she would have my child. They wanted my magic, but said in me it was tainted by my own God. They said their magic was not for the people of Harrhein, but they were not against us, they approve of us." He looked at Sara. "They like you, and they thank you. They are gentle Gods and they say this is their last refuge. They are under attack from other gods, especially those of the Umayyads and those of Hind. They ask for protection from other gods, including ours." He looked down at his feet.

Sara was sitting next to him and touched his arm. "It's all right Perryn, I understand. I will do as they ask."

There was silence around the group, broken by Lieutenant Mactravis, who let out a long sigh.

"Not sure what I think about gods who talk to you. At least as soldiers we don't have to worry about that, usually. I hope to the nine pits of hell Little doesn't upset them."

Hinatea answered him, surprising everyone with her Harrhein. "The Gods like him. They understand him, and how he thinks. They have asked the girls who are staying to have children by him and the others like him. They want his soldier blood to protect the island." She looked around the group, smiling quietly. "All the girls who stay are already pregnant. The Gods say we need the men, and the new blood."

Suzanne took a breath angrily. "The girls who stay? And how many are coming with us? And why do you think you will come?"

"The Gods have told us we can go. You will need us, and some of your men will not be happy to leave us behind. We are not pregnant."

Lieutenant Mactravis cleared his throat. "I am afraid this true. If some of the girls do not come, some of the men will not leave. They will take to the hills."

Before Suzanne could reply, Perryn spoke. "Some of the men need to stay. They won't be able to leave."

"Well, it's not too bad. We need to leave some men here, some soldiers and some sailors, to build an outpost. So let's consider who stays and we'll take the girls to replace them." Lieutenant Mactravis spoke as if it were already decided, but before Suzanne or Sara could think of a suitable reason to object, the Bosun spoke up. "Better to leave the third mate, Taylor, and his wife. They're not right for working, and they've taken to island life. Also gets you promotion to second, Suzanne. Got maybe a dozen others who can stay."

"Walters should and wants to stay, but I am not sure he should," contributed Perryn contradicting himself.

"Indeed," agreed Suzanne, giving in to the inevitable, "Brian and the Captain ought to stay, but we shall take them and see if they recover on the journey. It's all the older people. We'll leave the non-essentials."

"I am not happy about leaving any soldiers," said Mactravis. "I doubt any of them actually want to stay, and they could be a bad influence. Bloody Little, I caught him, ah, having sex with a girl in the middle of a crowd of people! They were all watching and telling him what to do!"

Hinatea looked at him in puzzlement. "Why is wrong? We often do, is nice to get compliments from others, and it helps people to learn. If we learn more, we get more pleasure."

Suzanne looked at her incredulously. "You often do it? Really? In the open?"

"Oh yes. I think I understand from talking to Pat you have

competitions in Harrhein? Archery? Running? Riding on animals? Kicking a ball? We do too. Sometimes it is fishing, but usually it is sex. We all know who the best are, they are popular. I am one of the best!" She answered smugly. "Very popular!" Both Pat and Grey Fox looked embarrassed, the first time any of them had seen an expression on Grey Fox's face.

Sergeant Russell broke in suspiciously. "How can you have competitions when you have no men?" Clearly he was worried about hordes of men coming out of hiding.

"It is difficult," replied Hinatea seriously. "We share the seven men on the island, they move around the villages, plus we use the old men and soon the first boys will be old enough. But also we go with two girls. That is fun!" She smiled brilliantly and looked around, projecting an invitation at Sara, who looked shocked. Hinatea's smile grew wider and wicked. "I have special stick I carved. You want to see?"

"No!" Suzanne said, trying to take back control despite the thought of Grey Fox taking part in these competitions. She really didn't want Sara to work out what the stick would be. "Bosun, make a list for me of those who want to stay. We'll aim to sail in two days. Pat, speak to the dwarves and work out how many barrels of yellow flowers to take with us. It's a powder, right?"

"Powder and crystals. The crystals are more expensive. I will pack the crystals in the powder so we have both."

Later, Suzanne took a walk by herself in the heat of the day down to the bathing pool. She needed to be alone with her thoughts. She sat on the bank, her feet trailing in the water, idly kicking at the little fish that came to nibble, and allowed her desolation to flow out. The sight of Pat brought a huge up-welling feeling of love for him but it felt odd. Letting it flow over her, she felt it was tainted, adulterated by the magic, and she felt used, for it felt like the love she had experienced as a young girl, before life took the complicated turns which left her in a brothel. She realised it wasn't Pat with whom she was angry, or even Hinatea and the Pahippians, but simply with the way the magic had not only taken away her control, but tried to impose feelings on her. She sighed, thinking she needed to have this conversation with Sara and wondered if she would be allowed.

A fish nibbled her toes, tickling, and she giggled slightly, welcoming the interruption to her thoughts. She felt a presence and jumped to her feet, to find Pat watching her from a few yards away.

"Damn it Pat, don't do that! Creeping up like that. What do you want anyway?" She asked crossly, clamping down on her heart which raced at the sight of him.

Pat hung his head and looked at his feet. "Don't know," he mumbled. Pat was in considerable turmoil himself. His had sorted out his feelings for Sara, which had fizzled out in the revelations after the attack, but the sight of Suzanne had wakened others. While he didn't love Suzanne, the night with her had been sensual and physically rewarding and he wanted a repeat, but had no idea how to say it. The running and the Pahippian girls had worn the magic out of his system and he was becoming very fond of Hinatea, a rewarding partner on many different levels. Hinatea and her friends were off to talk with their families and friends, exchanging stories and catching up, so he had responded to the emotional turmoil he felt at the sight of Suzanne by slipping away and following her. Now he took a step towards her.

"Stop!" Suzanne cried, alarmed at how closer proximity made her feel. "Pat, you've made your choice, now go to your girls and leave me alone. I am trying to plan."

Pat had learnt a surprising amount about the magic from talking with the girls, and now hatched his cunning plan with immense subtlety. "I was worried about you, Suzanne, and how the magic was affecting you. You haven't had much opportunity to exercise, it must still be coursing in you, and so I thought I would help you get rid of it." He smiled hopefully at her, pleased with how delicately he had spoken.

Suzanne's eyes narrowed. "You filthy little boy," she hissed. "You didn't come here to make me feel better; you just wanted to rattle me. Well think again, farm boy! You will never, ever, touch me again. In fact, I'll make sure you don't touch anyone!" With that she started to spin towards him.

Pat fled, the memory of her kick to Fourth Lieutenant Reilly running through his brain, and felt the waft of air as she missed him, barely. Suzanne watched him leave, fuming. As her anger dropped she realised it had blown away the last of the magic within her and her mood turned. She laughed, thinking Pat was just like every other seventeen year old boy who had discovered sex.

In the evening Suzanne discussed trade with Poema, while Sara listening in without much interest. It was difficult, as the main traders were the Captain and Brian, laid up by the magic, but the girls understood the importance. The only valuable trade products seemed to be copra, pearls, and trepang. Sara couldn't understand why Suzanne was so happy and cheerful. She had even winked at her.

Trade talk did cause the Captain to perk up a little and come and listen, but although he saw the value in pearls, none of them knew what copra and trepang were. No, Rereau and Poema didn't know what they were used for, but they planned to trade them to the next island along, one day.

Taufik was consulted, and they discovered copra was a large dried nut, the source of oil that was a basic commodity in Hind, while trepang was sold to countries to the East, who valued it highly and was worth its weight in gold. It turned out to be a huge sea slug, about a foot long before being dried, that looked totally revolting, both before and after being dried. Suzanne couldn't help laughing at the sight of one and had to hold one, while Sara was shocked at both her behaviour and the indecorum. She didn't find what the slug looked like remotely funny.

The Pahippians wanted many of the Harrhein trade goods, but did not have much of anything with which to trade. They weren't prepared to put in the hard hours gathering either. Life was easy on the island and it was more fun to party than work. Nevertheless, they had a small store of copra and trepang, and more of pearls which they used for decoration. They were happy to give this to the Queen Rose in exchange for knives and mirrors. Eventually Sara cut through the problem by stating Harrhein would rent land and employ local workers in return for their goods.

Surfing

The following morning Captain Suzanne Delarosa convened her meeting on the poop deck rather than ashore. Present were her officers, Lieutenants Mactravis and Starr, the Bosun, Sailing Master Taufik and Priest Perryn. Taufik gave them hope for the recovery of Captain Larroche, for he was much improved over the last two days.

"Thank you for attending Gentlemen and Ladies," started Suzanne. "I called the meeting here rather than ashore because I want to remind you and all the crew that we are a crew and will be sailing shortly." She looked around at them, and they nodded.

"Now there are two major problems I foresee, and I want you to contribute any others you are aware about. First is the state of the Captain, the Mate and the Bishop. It is my opinion, given Master Taufik's strong recovery, we should ignore their requests to stay and take them with us, by force if necessary. I intend to enter the command in the log, but first I wish to give each of you the opportunity to lodge any opinions or objections to be entered in the log." She looked around enquiringly, but met with looks of approval and nods.

"You log it, Cap'n," said the Bosun. "We're with you. I've sailed with Wilbur for more than ten years and it's what he really wants, whatever he may say when that skinny brown tart looks at him." The others looked a little startled to discover the Captain's first name, but nodded their agreement.

"Very well. It is so noted." Suzanne wrote in the log while the others admired her penmanship.

"The next problem is more interesting. So we sail on." She looked at them with level eyes. "How? I have been a ship's officer for barely a month. I can run a watch, and follow orders, but I do not have the slightest idea how to plan a route or judge the wind. I don't know where to go next." The lieutenants and Perryn looked blank but the Bosun chuckled.

"Don't worry about the sailing. It's me and Taufik does that anyway, whatever you bloody officers think. As for the route, dig out the Captains rutter and see what it says."

Perryn leaned forward. "I can get out Bishop Walters' maps, and perhaps Taufik can explain?" He looked at Taufik who nodded, so Perryn slipped off to collect the maps.

"Captain, don't worry about the sailing," the Bosun went on. "I know you and the Lieutenants don't know a blamed thing, but me and Taufik can set the course alright. You just decide when to go and where to go. You're doing a right fine job if you ask me so keep it up." The others murmured agreement.

"Captain," began Sara, "it seems to me we need to proceed along the chain of islands, checking each one out to ensure there are no dangerous surprises for following trade ships. We need safe ports like Pahipi all along the chain." Sara and Suzanne had conspired overnight, during which Suzanne told her about Pat at the pool. Sara cried, threw a tantrum and slapped Suzanne, then burst into tears while the girls hugged each other. Suzanne told her how the anger wiped out the last of the magic, but Sara confessed she still had some in her, in a small voice, though the slap helped. They hugged again, exchanged apologies and were almost back to their old selves, though Sara vowed to herself never to trust Suzanne with a boyfriend again.

Suzanne nodded. "Yes, that makes sense. What else is in the bigger picture? I am thinking of us as a trade ship, but you have other ideas?"

"Oh yes," Sara nodded . "Of course we need to find trade opportunities, but politically it is difficult at home. There are lots of dissidents at the moment, and this damn parliament is causing problems for the Crown. They are trying to restrict the Crown's ability to tax, which means our income which means our power. This trip could be really important for us. If we can set up trade routes, with established partners, they could cause money to flow to the Crown and we won't need to worry about the machinations of parliament. It's just some of the barons and traders trying to take power."

"If you say so," said Suzanne doubtfully, as she had friends in Parliament. She traded on both sides. "But I do understand about the trade routes. The whole country will benefit from those, as well as the Crown."

"Sure will," said the Bosun. "We're the first, but the ship yards are keen for us to succeed as they want to make more carracks like this. You know the carpenter's mate is the son of my cousin, who owns the yard that built the Queen Rose? If we start building loads of these ships, it will make lots of people rich."

"The Crown will need to build warships to patrol the trade routes," mused Mactravis, alternative career paths opening up in his mind.

Perryn came back with the maps and also with Captain Larroche's rutter. This was an astonishing book, full of not just beautifully drawn maps, but very specific descriptions of winds, currents and weather, with specifics on sail setting, stars and directions. It ended at Pahipi.

Looking down at the rutter, her fingers tracing one of the maps, Suzanne spoke. "Can we sail tomorrow, Bosun?"

"Three days, please Captain. I want to change all the water casks, and the cook will want to take on as much dried fish as he can. I suppose we'll need some of those bloody poi roots if we're taking some girls. I need three days to finish the re-provisioning, wood and other stores. Sara, can you work out how to pay for the provisions?"

"No problem, Bosun. That helps me, we need to buy cargo from them."

In fact it took another week before the Queen Rose sailed, leaving behind the Third Mate, Taylor, and nine crew with orders to build a Harrhein embassy and trading post. The oldest of the crew, hardest hit by the spell, they were taking the longest to recover. Sara charged them to protect Pahipi from intruders, using the threat of Harrhein retribution. They were married couples, ones the girls hadn't subjected to temptation, plus a couple of gentler souls.

Suzanne, on advice from the Bosun, promoted several people. One of Taufik's assistants, Stevens, she promoted to fourth mate, while Pat found himself a Bosun's Mate in charge of the second watch, under Lt Mactravis, with additional responsibility for the ship's archers. She hoped the Captain would ratify them when he recovered. He had agreed perfunctorily, but she doubted he would remember. Captain Larroche's recovery moved at a snail's pace, and he threw a tantrum when he discovered Rereau was not coming with them. She took him into the hills for a night, and afterwards he agreed to sail. This was better than Walters, who was older and making up for a lifetime of abstinence. He needed to be carried bodily aboard by the soldiers.

Sixteen of the girls sailed with them, all excellent sailors, possessing greater sailing lore than most of the crew. They were agile and loved working in the rigging, all competing with Pat and Nils in the upper yards. Crew morale went up, as the girls were making up for a lifetime with few men, and would spend their time off watch debating the merits of each one while deciding which one to settle down with. The idea of having a man for your very own, without having to share, was exciting, not something they had imagined they could ever have. They were determined not to make a mistake in the selection, which meant intensive research. Nor did they possess the Harrhein attitudes to sex, being very open about it and indeed happy to make love in front of each other. At first horrified, the Harrheinian girls deemed the debate a good idea and joined in the discussions with enthusiasm. The men found it intensely embarrassing. Pat's explorations were curtailed, as Hinatea didn't allow him to join in the free for all; he was hers. At least she wasn't sleeping around.

Suzanne's fears eased as they sailed from Pahipi without any problems. She stood on the poop deck, with a critical eye on the sails. Taufik tried to explain what she should be looking for, while Captain Larroche stood beside her moping and on occasion interjecting unhelpfully.

"You check the sail to see if wind changes. If sail starts to flap, it means...."

"Luffing," said Captain Larroche gloomily. "Called luffing."

"Yes," said Taufik, after a pause to see if the Captain wanted to explain more. "If it luffs, you are steering too close to the wind and are losing speed. See: watch the sails as I turn into the wind slowly. There! See it? Usually in these waters the wind is very steady, but around islands it can be different. But also I will use it to slow the ship, or to go into harbour."

"How do you tell how much sail to use?"

"Always we are careful not to use too much. If too much, the ship she can blow over. Very bad. We look to see how the sail shapes and we feel the stays, the ropes. Most important, listen to the song they play."

"Song?"

"Yes. The noise of the wind blowing through them. If too high, we have trouble and we must ease them. In strong winds, better to have lots of small sails than one big sail. More ropes, but more control. Never use too strong ropes. Better they break than the mast."

"Tack," said Captain Larroche. "Can't tack."

"No," agreed Taufik, "this ship is very good running before the wind but the high castles mean we get pushed sideways faster than we go forward when we tack. We can do a close reach, but very slow. When the wind hits the sails at an angle, it is funnelled backwards which makes the ship go forward."

Suzanne's eyes glazed over as Taufik continued with enthusiasm.

Sara spent quite a lot of time with the Spakka, becoming friendly with Janis. She found it helped her emotions heal, as she still felt awful at the sight of Hinatea and Pat. Janis explained to her why the magic had backfired with them, once he recovered and felt comfortable enough.

"In Spakka we marry for life. Our parents decide, when we are small. We marry when we are twelve, the ceremony that makes us a man. But we cannot live together or be alone together until after our first battle."

"What happens to the girls when their man is killed?" Sara pounced on the flaw instantly.

"If they have no children, they take a new husband, or become second wife of successful warrior. If they have children, they run the farm. All farm work is run by the women." Doggedly, Janis came back to the point. "Spakka is run by women. Men are for fighting. We guard the border, we guard traders and we harvest."

"Harvest?" Asked Sara suspiciously.

"Like when you won our honour. We tried to harvest this ship, and you harvested us. We know our women wait for us. They do not come with us and trust us on our travels. Our honour demands we respect that trust."

"What about..." Sara groped for a word, realised she didn't know it in Spakka and switched to Harrhein. "Love?"

"I hear the word," agreed Janis in Harrhein, "and I don't understand it. The Harrhein girls use it for sex, but the men don't. It seems to be something that hurts a lot."

"It can hurt," agreed Sara, "but it can also be wonderful. It is the feeling between a man and his wife. We wait for that feeling before we decide to marry."

"How strange! You must wait a long time, as often I hear the feeling does not come for many years, and grows out of mutual respect."

"No, it can happen instantly. Sometimes as soon as you meet somebody."

"Ah! I hear your men talk of that. It is not honourable. It does not last. We know and ignore it. It only takes discipline. We see it causes problems for you." He said this with undisguised contempt and radiated superiority. "It is no wonder honour is so rare amongst you."

Sara's annoyance levels peaked, but she didn't show it. "So this discipline kept you from the island women. But you still reacted to the magic."

"Yes," he replied equably without the embarrassment she expected. "You understand we partner with a friend early, and that man is our shield? We do everything together and know each other, our moods, our strengths, our weaknesses. As we learn discipline, we help each other. In the early days, we exercise in the hills. At night it is cold, if we do not come together for warmth, we die. The body reacts." He shrugged. "It is not with a woman so there is no loss of honour."

They sailed north east through a chain of atolls and small islands, arid and dry. An outlying village of the Pahippians perched at the end of one with water. The girls there received them with fascination - no ship had come from the main island first in living memory. They barely qualified as a village, being at most three huts. Suzanne couldn't see the point of the village, but Hinatea explained it harvested the best of the oyster beds and also gave them early warning of Ummayads. There was indeed a good view of the ocean, and a myriad of little atolls into which the canoes could escape.

They left the last of the atolls behind and sailed out of sight of land for a week, before sighting a substantial island. This was not a volcano, or at least not a live one. The Pahippians concern mounted; Hinatea remembered sneaking past as a child, her mother wary of disturbing the inhabitants.

On the second day of circling the island, they came upon a small village, with a larger one further up the beach, again on a river. The river flowed wide, slow and brown, full of silt carried down from the hills. The larger village sat upstream of the mouth. Again, the beach was fringed with the feather trees they now knew to be coconut palms producing copra.

This time the canoes and fishermen fled for the shore and disappeared.

Suzanne called a council of war on the poop deck, with the Queen Rose anchored in the mouth of the river.

"We need a landing party. Mactravis, take however many men you need and make contact."

"What a wonderful idea," said Sara. "The natives will see us land a boat full of heavily armed soldiers and come rushing out to kiss them. Come on, Suzanne, you know the Ummayads raided Pahipi, you can bet they raid here as well. The way the natives fled indicates they will expect an attack."

Nettled, Suzanne shifted uncomfortably, reflecting it would be better to make Sara Captain. "So what do you suggest?"

"It needs a woman leading the party, so we don't look dangerous or threatening. I'll go down with some of the Pahipi girls and half a dozen soldiers."

"We not go," interjected Hinatea with some force. "Bad island, bad men, bad god."

This set Sara back on her heels, but before she could question her Mactravis broke in.

"I agree with your thoughts, your Highness, however I strongly oppose you going ashore. You are the Crown Princess of the Realm and no way should you go into a situation like this where we know nothing of the terrain or the intentions of the locals. Yes, you have been in serious situations in the past, but each time you knew all about the enemy and their intentions. Here you do not even know if they are enemies, let alone how they will react."

"Well," replied Sara, ready to battle for this adventure, "I don't see there is an alternative. It is not possible to send Captain Larroche or Brian and who else would have the experience?"

"Send the Bosun; that would frighten the fuck out of them!"

"Corporal Little, I do not recall you being invited to attend this meeting?"

"Thought you might need a soldier's view, Sir!"

"Yes, yes, that is quite enough," said Suzanne, intervening at the sight of the Bosun swelling up. "Bosun, kindly keep your hands off Little till after this meeting." She drummed her fingers on the chart table for a moment. "Perhaps Pat might do? He is experienced in meeting other peoples - do you know anyone else who can speak Dwarf and Elf? A young boy would be equally un-threatening."

"He may be experienced in talking with them, but not in opening negotiations. We would be at a disadvantage for sure. We need some experience here, which is why it must be me. There is no alternative." Sara's certainty convinced the Bosun and Taufik, while Mactravis' expression showed did not agree and Suzanne's own brow creased with annoyance.

"If it is experience required, you don't have any in meeting new people." Suzanne spoke with finality ignoring the rising heat in Sara's cheeks. "You are well trained, I admit, but not with experience. I, on the other hand, possess plenty, as I am sure you will agree men are a different species, never mind race. I'm not really the Captain anyway, you can manage without me."

"Fine," said Mactravis quickly, before a furious Sara could speak. "I'll come with you with the soldiers and we'll take Pat and his dog, they'll be useful. I want Rat too, the boy is good at sneaking and I want another scout. No Spakka, though, they frighten the life out of everyone."

Sara settled back on her heels, her thoughts flying. She realised she needed to think politically, rather than with her heart, if she wanted to win arguments. She knew she had lost this one.

"Very well. I don't agree, but I shall abide by the decision. I will prepare a force of Spakka and Pahipi girls ready to land at a moment's notice to support you."

Suzanne nodded. "Good. It is agreed."

The pinnace, the largest of the ship's boats, went up the river and tied up to a well-constructed jetty made from bamboo, a new wood to the Harrheinians. Mactravis sent out scouts - Pat and Mot to the right, Grey Fox and Rat to the left. The rest of the party came out in arrowhead formation, Mactravis and Suzanne in the centre, leaving Sergeant Russell and Garson guarding the pinnace.

Mot checked a clump of bushes a hundred metres to the right and went in, Pat on her heels. Grey Fox went into a small stand of trees a similar distance to the left and faded from sight, Rat went up a tree and disappeared.

The point man, Graves, walked forward, eyes scanning, Corporal Strachan behind him and the arrowhead moved up the path to the village. Every now and then a brief movement on either flank showed the path of the scouts.

The village consisted of wooden huts made from bamboo on stilts made from coconut trunks. It was empty, without a sound bar a few chickens scratching in the dust. Beneath one hut an animal stared at them malevolently, hauled itself to its trotters and waddled into the woods. Suzanne stared in astonishment. Hugely fat, black and with a great sag in its spine as if broken, it looked decidedly pregnant, but enormous testicles proclaimed otherwise. Peculiar looking beast, whose familiarity nagged at her till she realised with a start it was a pig. There were bushes outside the huts, some fruit trees with curious looking red bell shaped fruits, and the flamboyant red flowers the Pahippians called hibiscus.

The village was clean, and the odd bush with spidery green-yellow flowers lent a sweet scent to the air.

There were no people.

The arrowhead reached the gate of the village and stopped. Pat appeared from the right and shook his head. "In the huts," he hissed, turned and slipped back into the bushes. No sign of Mot.

Suzanne spoke to Mactravis, who set the men down in all round defence with no weapons showing, signalled Pat first, then Grey Fox and gave the patrolling command.

They waited.

Suzanne laid out gifts in the street in front of the gate. She stood and turned carefully around in a circle, her skimpy outfit proclaiming she was not armed.

They waited.

Pat slipped wide through the bushes to the edge of the village, where the fields grew strange vegetables. He crouched low under a shrub and studied the countryside. A distant movement caught his attention and he saw three heads in the long grass on a hilltop about three hundred metres away. They were watching the centre of the village.

Moving through the bushes he came upon a trail leading up the hill and could see the signs of passage in the dust. Bare feet, lots of them, no animals. Looking across the trail, he saw a bush tremble, but Mot showed no concern, so he showed himself and indicated the hill. Grey Fox appeared and nodded, then used Elven sign language to tell him to report while he watched the hill.

He circled the village and slipped up to Mactravis and Suzanne, who jumped as he appeared. "Tracks leaving the village. Looks like all the women and children have gone into hiding. I think the men are still here, in the huts, in ambush."

Mactravis nodded and spoke. "Get Grey Fox back, tell him to take the left, you cover from the right. Close by, not far, and we'll have a section with each of you for support if you're rushed." He nodded at Corporal Strachan who issued quiet commands.

A noise came from the village. It was like a deep, long sigh, very quiet, but seemed to cause silence as it passed. Pat noticed the chickens all disappear and nocked an arrow.

The sigh came again. As it reached the end, it rose in volume to a crescendo, whereupon men leapt from the huts, landing on the ground and giving a loud grunt at the same time. This caused a huge wave of sound which rolled down the village and over the soldiers, who turned not a hair. Suzanne was shocked, and felt fear rise up in her, but took a strong hold of herself at the actions of the soldiers. She took especial heart from Little, who always broke the emotions when they threatened to affect people.

"Cor, that's not bad, is it Corp? Should tell 'em to fart when they land, that would improve it!"

"Fart? They'll fuckin' shit themselves when we get hold of 'em!" Husk didn't speak much and Suzanne saw him smiling for the first time she could remember and realised with shock all the soldiers were keyed up and grinning. Her resolve hardened; it was up to her to stop a fight breaking out, as all these bloody men wanted to fight. It gave her new strength and she concentrated on the approaching men.

They were huge, all well over 6 feet, broad shouldered and with a shock of frizzy hair sticking out from their heads a good two feet more, making them look even larger. They were black, rather than brown, with fine features and grinning faces. Each clutched an odd stick, though a couple brandished spears. She looked for a moment at the bent sticks in puzzlement.

Mactravis saw her glance. "War clubs, ma'am. Might look like nothing, but they will be effective. They'll use them like pick axes, no back lift, shatters the skull. Not to worry, we know how to handle them. Ready to form a shield wall, men."

The black men stopped. All crouched, ready to attack, all still with enormous grins and flashing teeth. With annoyance, Suzanne realised they were also relishing the idea of a fight. She could feel the rush of pleasurable excitement coming off both sets of soldiers and wondered with part of her mind. The rest concentrated on frustrating them.

The native men sighed again, louder, and at the crescendo all stamped hard. At the same time a huge man leapt from the main hut, bouncing on his feet, the impact throwing up dust and adding to the noise.

He was very dark, with his hair tightly curled and sticking up like a bush all round his head, feathers tied into it. Streaks of grey shot through his hair but he strode forward proudly with menace in his stride. Pat stared. The brown Pahippians seemed strange enough, but he had never seen anyone so dark.

The man was huge, taller than anyone he had ever seen and with a big frame. He stalked up the path, carrying a massive jabbing spear. Muscles bulged under his skin, with blue marks whorled on his face - Pat guessed they were tattoos, never having seen anything like them. He walked straight up the centre of the village to the gate, ignoring the Harrheinians, till he stopped in front of the gifts. He looked at these, raised his head and gazed at the landing party, leaning on his spear.

Suzanne strode forward and a look of surprise went over his face.

"Greetings, Great Chief." She spoke in Belada. "We are from a land far across the sea, over a month we travelled to get here. We are traders and would seek permission to trade with your people. If it is successful for both our peoples, we will come again each year. Please accept these gifts as a token of our esteem for you."

He stared at her for a moment, and spoke to Mactravis in accented Belada. "Do you not speak the trade language that you let a woman speak for you? I will take her as a gift."

Mactravis grinned without humour. "You will find it difficult. This woman is our leader, and capable of beating any two of us. We are warriors of renown, and appreciate battle skills wherever they are found. She speaks for us."

"A woman is your best fighter?" He laughed, exposing strong white teeth in his handsome face and turned his spear around so the blade stuck in the ground. He looked at Suzanne with interest, measuring her and grinning.

"So, woman people, what do you seek in trade? Flowers?" He roared with laughter at his own joke. His men started forward to come up level with him, unhurried.

Mot streaked across the clearing and came to a halt beside Suzanne, turning and facing the chief, her tongue lolling out. As one, all the soldiers brought their weapons to the ready.

The chief stepped back, frowning.

Suzanne looked at the chief. She realised Pat had sent Mot as a message, and she had missed something all the men recognised. The spear turning blade down was a signal to his men, ready to fight. Because she was a woman. Damn. "Your men are ready to fight. My men are asking for my permission to kill them. How many would you like me to kill?"

He laughed. "Women who kill? My warriors will play with your women men, while you, you I will show you what a real man is!" But he looked a bit uncomfortable as he looked at Mot, who bristled, growled and showed her teeth.

Mactravis spoke, enunciating each word. "Form a shield wall on Strachan. Scouts, fall back behind the shield wall. Ma'am, step back into the shield wall, we'll swallow you." The men flowed like a well-oiled machine, heavy shields coming together with a ripple to form the wall behind her.

Suzanne hesitated, convinced she could stop the fight. Out of the corner of her eye, she could see Pat, arrow nocked, running from the bushes towards the men behind her, Grey Fox and Rat coming from the other side. Mot whirled away and returned to Pat. She stepped towards the Chief, looking deep into his eyes. "Great Chief, why fight? What is the need? You have great warriors, we have great warriors. We fight, they die. Instead let us talk. We can trade and nobody dies."

The Chief threw back his head and laughed, deep and ringing with genuine humour. His eyes sparkled as he answered. "How can we trade when we know not each other's strength, Ghost Woman? Why is your skin pale, Witch Woman? Are you sick? Do you bleed power from your people to make them sick and pink? And your hair, like dead grass, falling down. If you are so strong, why does it not stick out? Ha! I think you have no power, your men no strength!"

His leg shot out and knocked Suzanne's legs sideways, and he caught her as she fell, realising bitterly she had come too close. Lifting her high, the Chief stepped backwards as his men came forward at speed, stepping uncaring on the gifts laid out prettily in front of the gate.

They came in a mad rush, each striving to reach and brain the white intruders before their friends, and crashed into the shields. The biggest soldiers wielded the shields, like Husk, who grunted and leaned their shoulders into the shield backs, while smaller soldiers slipped spears through strategic gaps into naked bodies on the other side. Husk cursed Little, whose left hand held a smaller shield over his head which rang as a war club thumped down on it.

The two lines strained against each other, while Pat and Grey Fox shot the few warriors coming round the sides. Pat tried to see Suzanne, but could see nothing behind the press of warriors trying to push over the shields. The closing of the shields under pressure snapped the few spears thrust through, and it degenerated into a shoving match, with the soldiers retreating inch by inch and the smaller soldiers helping to brace the wall, leaving Mactravis and Pat to pick off active attacks round the side, Grey Fox having added his strength to the wall. This took less than thirty seconds.

The Chief had not gone far. He twisted Suzanne down and ripped off her skimpy top, admiring her breasts and grinning as he moved his thigh to block her driven knee. "Ha! Little one, you are fiery! I will enjoy you and maybe I will keep you a little while!"

Suzanne twisted in his hands and tried for leverage, but could do nothing as he kept her in the air and laughed at her struggles. He only needed one hand, and with the other started to caress her. She slumped, and the Chief clucked in annoyance at her cutting his game short by fainting. He turned her upside down for a close inspection, holding her legs, and lifted his eyes to check on his men's progress overwhelming the women soldiers. He frowned to see the stalemate developing and the bodies of more warriors than expected on the ground, a couple staring at small sticks projecting from their bodies.

He sucked in air to bellow instructions, when there came an excruciating pain from his groin and the bellow came out as an agonised scream as he fell to the ground, dropping Suzanne, who had come to life and grasped his testicles in both hands, grinding them together. She slid out from under him as he fell, and with a clever shuffling of her hands kept his testicles under control as she swung around onto his back, yanking them up so the skin stretched into the crevice of his buttocks, the strands of his grass skirt splayed on either side. He shouted in pain again.

The shout reverberated down the beach, frightening some wading birds into the air, and it froze the fighting; the warriors backed off and looked at the scene behind them.

A furious, red-faced and bare-breasted Suzanne glared at them, one dainty foot planted on the Chief's buttock, both hands grasping the royal testicles.

A couple of warriors started to their Chief's rescue, war clubs raised.

"STOP" shouted Suzanne in Belada. "Any further and I will rip them off! You will be ruled by a man defeated by a woman, a ball-less man! Will you do that to your chief? Stay where you are and he keeps his balls!"

The warriors hesitated. Not a situation they were expecting. The

Chief broke the momentary silence by laughing.

He shouted something in his own language and the warriors started to laugh as well. They grinned at the soldiers and went to look at their injured men, ignoring the battle in which they had moments earlier been involved.

The soldiers relaxed, settling down their shields and rubbing their bruises. Little, at a quiet word from Mactravis, pulled out two men from the front line, one of whom unconscious and the other with a damaged and broken shoulder.

The Chief switched to Belada and spoke to Suzanne. "You are cunning and clever! Now I know your strength, so we can talk."

"Talk!" Suzanne glared, her earlier pacifism replaced by a lust for vengeance. "You wanted to rape me and felt my body! Why should we talk?" She tweaked his testicles, hard. He grunted.

"Why you come here? What you want?"

"We came to trade, as friends, but you met us with war, rape and violence. We came in peace and you met us with anger." Suzanne was becoming more and more worked up, as they gathered an interested group of spectators, both warriors and soldiers. One of the warriors, a young man, tall and spectacularly muscled, leant forward holding out a cloth.

"Please, Great Mother, accept this cloth to cover yourself. My father is sorry for exposing you."

"Yes, yes," said the Chief. "I apologise for the manner of testing you, it was unseemly. It has allowed you to demonstrate your great strength and power. It was your hair, falling not standing, that misled me. Come, we drink kava and I will call my women to tend you and make your hair stand strong!"

"Come on Captain, let him up," Mactravis joined the circle and grinning at her. "We need to tend the wounded when you stop playing."

Suzanne glared at him, released the Chief with a final savage twist, accepted the cloth from the strapping young warrior with a glare that made him hurriedly avert his eyes from her chest, and stood up, wrapping it around her breasts. The warriors gave a deep sigh of regret, in which the soldiers joined to Suzanne's annoyance.

"I've sent the pinnace back to get Perryn and Sara. The wounded need treating and we'll teach these people how to clean arrow and sword wounds."

Suzanne looked down the path and saw Pat and Little with a crowd of natives around a warrior with an arrow through his leg. She could hear Pat trying to explain a bodkin arrowhead, without barbs, designed to go through armour, so could be pushed through without damaging the muscle. Little was making them piss on the arrow shaft before pulling it through, to cleanse the wound. Suzanne scratched her head in puzzlement, unable to comprehend how the two sets of fighters could become friendly so quickly.

The Chief rose up gingerly, checking on the damage to his essentials. His son assisted, clucking in sympathy and trying not to laugh. He didn't disguise this well enough, receiving a powerful clout round the ear. The Chief adjusted his grass skirt, gathered his dignity and turned to Suzanne.

"I am Ratu Ilikimi Nailatikau, the Great Ratu of the Vitu Levu, the strongest and most feared warrior in the kingdom. We are the great warrior people of Vitua, the kai Viti, feared throughout the islands, all come to us in fear to offer tribute."

Suzanne took a moment to restore some equilibrium to her emotions before responding to this formality.

"I am Lieutenant Suzanne Delarosa of the great ship Queen Rose out of Rikklaw's Port in Harrhein. We are the great warrior people of the Northern Ocean, so great we treat all people as friends for they fear to fight us."

The Chief chuckled at this, turned and shouted with awesome force, "Kava!" The one word echoing down the valley. He sent a volley of commands at the watching men. They swung forward and formed a half circle behind him, all grinning, white teeth flashing in their handsome faces, as happy at this new command as to fight. The injured men were brought up and sat at the ends of the half circle, while Suzanne tried to work out the lack of corpses. Surely it had been a lethal engagement? She noted Pat's arrows all pierced muscle, none in dangerous areas.

The soldiers gathered behind her in a similar formation and she realised that in some manner she couldn't understand, these two different little armies had measured each other, respected each other and amazingly liked each other. She saw Husk rub a massive swelling on his head and grin at one monstrous warrior, who laughed, waved and indicated a deep stab wound in his thigh.

She still hungered for revenge, so forced the desire down in the face of this incomprehensible camaraderie. She concentrated on the scene unfolding in front of her.

Some girls, again huge, also with tightly curled black hair rising out in a bush, came running down from the hill behind the village. They were dressed in a brief loincloth and necklaces of shell and teeth bouncing on their breasts as they ran. They went up the steps into the Ratu's house, and the first came out holding two stools. She stopped in front of the Ratu, knelt, held one of the stools above her head after placing the other on the ground and looked at him.

He nodded to the sand in front and she swept the stool from her head in a graceful arc that ended where he indicated. He nodded again at Suzanne, the girl's eyes widened but she retrieved the second stool, went behind the Ratu to come round to Suzanne's right, where she knelt, placed the stool on her head, bowed to Suzanne and swung the stool round in the beautiful ritual.

The Ratu sat, and nodded at Suzanne who seated herself on the stool. He barked an order and several men came forward and sat in a semi-circle, cross-legged on the sand.

Suzanne called out, "Mactravis, select half a dozen men to join us, you to my right, copy them."

The Ratu nodded in approval and grinned, showing his teeth. He smiled at a young girl who knelt before him with a pack of large, thick leaves and a quantity of fleshy roots.

"My daughter. Virgin still, very clean. Good girl." He grinned.

Mystified, Suzanne nodded and watched the girl accept some water from another girl, rinse her mouth out noisily but somehow daintily at the same time, and spat it to the sand behind the circle. Another girl placed a large, reddish-brown, shallow bowl, with a dozen tapering legs, in the sand between the Ratu and Suzanne. A greyish-white coating inside gleamed like a rain-filled cloud at sunset.

The girl proceeded to bite off a chunk of root and chew it, then spat it onto a leaf, a very liquid and copious squirt. Another girl gathered this with care not to spill any, and poured it into the bowl, where the third girl picked up a whisk of fibrous wood and started to stir it as the second added a little water. They repeated the process and the bowl began to fill up with a dirty, greyish liquid.

Mactravis leant forward and whispered, "Have fun!"

Suzanne replied without moving her lips. "You're going to be drinking it too!"

The third girl removed the whisk, passed it over her shoulder and to be collected by a fourth girl who flicked it in a ceremonial manner, bits of root going flying, and passed the whisk back again.

The Ratu stood and started to speak in his own language, to his people, his voice loud and sonorous. He translated to Belada.

"We welcome you to our land of plenty, this very island Vitu Levu given to his people by Kalou-Vu. You demonstrated you are mighty warriors and we give you our respect. By this ceremony we are pleased to welcome you and get to know you. If it is the pleasure of Kalou-Vu, we shall talk trade later."

The stirrer stopped sat back and nodded to the Ratu, whereupon his daughter stopped chewing. The Ratu looked up, grinned again, and said, "I must act as Orator as well as Ratu as only I know your name! You must help me by doing the same for the rest of your people and I will do it for mine!"

Suzanne nodded.

"When you are introduced, you must clap with your hands like this." He cupped his hands and clapped once, with an echoing sound. "Then you say 'Bula,' loudly. Then drink, all, quick. Then you clap three times and say 'Mat-hey!' Understand?"

She nodded again.

"Lieutenant Suzanne Delarosa, Great Witch Woman, Leader of Men, Mighty Warrior, Great Trickster, Possessor of Succulent Breasts and Eyes from the Sky, welcome to the land of Kalou-Vu."

A warrior stepped forward, and taking a polished half shell of coconut, swept up some of the dirty grey water. With a courtly bow, he offered it to Suzanne with a sweeping right to left gesture.

Suzanne blinked, clapped once with some hesitation, then again fearing it hadn't been loud enough, shouted "Bula," accepted it, and drained the draught in one. She handed back the shell, clapped three times and shouted "Mat Hay!" The locals all grinned, slapped their thighs and "hau, hau" echoed from their lips.

"No," said the Ratu, laughing . "Very good but you clap twice before saying bula. You must do it again."

Suzanne glared at him but accepted the shell again, grimacing at the taste. This time she made certain she followed the instructions with precision. She got to her feet, smiling although she found the liquid flat, insipid and bitter. "Thank you, Ratu Ilikimi Nailatikau, the Great Ratu of the Island Vitu Levu, the Strongest and Most Feared Warrior in the Kingdom, Violator of Women, Possessor of the Mighty Penis that creates Beauteous Daughters.." She got no further as the locals all roared with laughter and the warrior re-filled the shell and gave it to the Ratu with a much less precise gesture as he tried to suppress his laughter.

The Ratu was delighted.

He proceeded to introduce his councillors and three of his sons, alternating with Suzanne introducing her own subordinates. Each drained a cup of kava after being introduced. Only Mactravis got it right first time, while Little needed four goes which Suzanne suspected and Mactravis knew to be deliberate.

After the kava ceremony the Ratu assured her anyone greeted with such a ceremony benefited from safe conduct throughout his kingdom until a formal declaration of war. Instructing Pat to come with her as escort, which ensured Mot accompanied them, she accepted the Ratu's invitation to tour the village.

First though, the Ratu wanted to meet Mot, never having seen a dog before, though he realised her potential for war. Suzanne realised this was no ignorant savage, but a very intelligent and capable leader of men.

Then he wanted to see Pat's bow, and was delighted when Pat knocked a coconut out of a tree some 100 paces away. The arrow skewered the nut dead centre and caused an excited murmur and some undignified shoving amongst the men who all wanted to see the bow. The Ratu managed to pull it to full draw and release an arrow when he tried, to Pat's astonishment . This earned Pat the respect of the Ratu who slapped him on the shoulder and pronounced to his warriors he was a very strong man.

Several warriors with arrow wounds came over to be inspected by the Ratu, who gave Pat a measured look at the realisation Pat's arrows had removed four warriors from the fight.

Before the tour could start, a commotion from the beach claimed their attention as Perryn arrived with his medical chest. He was not alone, Sara waded ashore with an escort of Spakka and Pahippians, Hinatea's girls, all equipped with long spears resplendent in their new metal heads. Lady Strike shone naked in Sara's hand, a grim and determined Hinatea beside her. Suzanne smiled to see the two girls in harmony for the first time.

The Ratu was delighted to see more female warriors and rushed down to the beach with Suzanne to welcome them, loving the way the spears were levelled at him. He marvelled at the metal spear points and promptly cut his finger on Hinatea's blade as he checked the edge, chortling with delight as he sucked his finger, moving on to examine the axes of the Spakka. Esbech eyed him with distrust, not used to a man larger than himself, very reluctantly relinquishing his axe, then dodging as the Ratu swung it dangerously, just missing him.

Mactravis arrived behind Suzanne, and Sara asked for his report, a succinct summary. The Ratu watched with interest, returning the axe to Esbech and beckoning to Suzanne. Suzanne sighed, and explained to him some of the complexities of their line of command. The Ratu grasped the main thrust with impressive speed.

"So, she will negotiate for trade? Good! I will get my counsellors to talk to her. Come, we will look at my village." He grasped her arm and steered her away. "She looks very angry and not much fun," he whispered as they moved off and Suzanne bit her tongue to stop the laughter, her earlier lust for revenge fading to nothing. He shouted at a nearby warrior who rushed off to collect counsellors.

Sara had brought Taufik with her and found herself seated with him in front of a line of village dignitaries, while Hinatea's girls stood guard. Mactravis collected the Spakka and established a mixed watch of soldiers and axemen by the wounded, allowing the remainder to fraternise. The Ratu displayed no interest in the negotiations, trusting his councillors. Suzanne was much more interesting, and she found herself answering a stream of questions, impressed with the speed he acquired knowledge and the questions he asked. She delighted in the little children arrayed for her inspection, who dragged her away to see them hurl themselves off the cliff into the swimming hole.

The Ratu came to rescue her, and brought her to a range of fruits and vegetables laid out for lunch. The Ratu sat on the largest stool, pulling one a little closer on his right. He indicated to Suzanne to sit there, while placing Sara on his left, when she arrived. The dignitaries he chased off with a staccato sentence, taking Taufik with them. Hinatea he sat opposite, though she refused to relinquish her spear, sticking it in the ground beside her and ensuring a couple of her girls stood behind her. She continued to watch the Ratu with mistrustful eyes. He allowed Mactravis, Little and Pat to make up the numbers at each side. They did not sit at a table, but around large banana leaves on which the food waited. The Ratu pointed at what he wanted and a girl immediately passed it to him or the guest he indicated.

'Hinatea,' began the Ratu, "you island girl, yes? Where you from?"

Hinatea considered her response, before giving a guarded answer. "Pahipi. Long way."

"Why you travel with these people?"

"Do deal with Princess." She indicated Sara and the Ratu's eyes sharpened. "She protect Pahipi, Pahipi now part of her country. She give us husbands, we fight for her now." Hinatea indicated Pat as she said this and Sara ground her teeth.

"Protect? Who from? Why not ask the Great Ratu? I give husband too!" He smiled as he said this, eyeing Hinatea with close attention.

Hinatea wore a simple shift, instead of her usual nakedness, and sat straight and proud, ignoring his gaze. "She not like Ummayads, stop them coming. With her, one girl, one husband. You have six wives."

"Ummayads," spat the Ratu, "not come here. I kill. Seven wives. What do you mean, part of her country?"

"Hinatea not speak Belada good. Ask her," she pointed at Sara with her chin.

Suzanne started to answer and received a hefty prod in her thigh from the Ratu's finger, silencing her. The Ratu stared at Sara. "Tell me of your country. Who are you to reach across the sea and take these girls?"

"We are Harrhein," Sara answered, her head high. "Over the years we fought with our neighbours. With two, different people, we reached agreement and leave each other's countries alone. The young men fight when they wish, but the countries do not." The Ratu grunted in approval.

"Two other countries we fought with and they became part of us, now we are one. Suzanne is from one country, Pat from another. Now they are part of us and only think of themselves as Harrheinian." Suzanne wasn't sure of that, she felt the cultured part of her hailed from Galicia, but stayed silent as the Ratu's hand closed on her thigh, preventing interruption.

Sara indicated the Spakka by looking at them. "Those warriors are from a neighbour with whom we fight, always at war. They do not wish peace, and live by a strict code of honour. These ones I took in war and now I am their leader, their Ratu."

The Ratu stopped her with a hand and called to the nearest Spakka, Esbech, who stared blankly at him. The Ratu gestured and Esbech lumbered forward, accepting the proffered bread fruit with dark suspicion.

"This one says she beat you in battle and is now your leader. How did this happen?"

Esbech blinked at him while he bit into the breadfruit and grimaced in distaste. He was slowly learning Harrhein, but was damned if he was going to speak this bloody language.

"He does not speak Belada, and his Harrhein is not very good," said Suzanne. "I can translate his Harrhein for you, but you are better getting Sara to translate his Spakka. She speaks his language."

The Ratu watched Sara speak in Spakka, Esbech's brief reply which Sara translated to him, repeating the story Esbech recounted. The Spakka warriors were not literate, and consequently were skilled story tellers. Esbech told the story, and the other Spakka warriors came up alongside, now and then interjecting a correction. Esbech's hands moved with his words, his axe grasped by the hilt and swung at remembered Harrheinians. The Ratu watched in rapt fascination, as indeed did the Harrheinians, hearing the story from the other point of view.

"We had the ship, but they did not know it," translated Sara. "We were ready, about to unleash the rage, the valour, and overwhelm them."

"What is the rage?" asked the Ratu, and Esbech hesitated, seeing all the questioning looks. He looked at his comrades, who appeared troubled but Stiphleek the Bard nodded to him.

"When the God takes us," explained Esbech. "We drink the fiery Milk of Fryssa, the God takes us and nothing can stop us."

"It is a fury they experience," Sara clarified. "Once in this state you must kill them to stop them, or take off a leg."

"What is this milk?"

"Fryssa is the War Goddess," cut in Stiphleek, casting his eyes down with her name. "I am her acolyte and I make the milk from grain. Fryssa blesses me and the Milk comes alive to allow the God into us."

Silence greeted this revelation, Corporal Little's eyes lit up and he slipped off his stool to join Stiphleek. Esbech ploughed on with his story.

"The fury took Havic first, he leapt up too early, struck the shields and died. Erin followed him and a few others who could not restrain themselves. Then the singing started. We heard the Princess, for whom we had come. Thorvald leapt to see if he could see her and we all saw her kill him. Thorvald was the Noble Hilario's shield bearer, and the Noble saw his death and went too early, before the rage could take us. The Princess struck him back into the dragon ship, pierced through the lungs and we were dying as we rushed too few at a time. We faced our death when the Princess called to us, fearless as she came alone aboard the dragon ship. We stayed our axes. She blessed the Noble Hilario and gave us honour."

Esbech fell silent and would speak no more, ignoring the Ratu's questions and turning away, followed by the rest of the Spakka. The Ratu's voice rose, demanding to know what he meant by blessed.

"She ran her sword through his shitty head," said Corporal Little, grinning as he stole a mango and followed after Stiphleek. There were no swear words in Belada, so Little created his own.

"She gave the Noble an honourable death," interjected Suzanne, with a glare at Little. "As is their custom, a great honour to receive from the enemy."

The Ratu turned to Sara, still and lost in her memory.

"So, Princess, you fight wars." Sara inclined her head.

"In wars you need warriors. Always you want more." She nodded again.

"You give me axes, I give you warriors. Best warriors in all the world." He pointed at Mactravis with a bit of breadfruit. "This man train them. I come too. We conquer everywhere." He beamed enthusiastically and patted her knee. "You not need to put sword through my head."

In the afternoon, Captain Larroche, Master Taufik and Mage Walters came over to continue the negotiations, as Sara was no longer allowed to take part. Instead the Ratu took both girls off to discuss various plans, with an arm around each of them.

Sara packed off Pat with a couple of local guides and Grey Fox to locate ore bodies, while Hinatea took some of her girls and spears to protect them.

They inspected the wounded, and the Ratu watched in fascination as Perryn set the broken shoulder. He loved Little's insistence on pissing on fresh wounds and thought this likely to be highly effective against the malignant spirits that brought infection. On the grounds royal urine would be the most effective, he insisted on producing an impressive member and giving extra irrigation to his own wounded warriors, who meekly submitted. Suzanne was darkly suspicious as to the real reason behind this, though she did admit to herself she was impressed.

They settled down in the shade of coconut trees, each with a fresh young coconut to drink from, Suzanne tucked up close to the Ratu with Sara and Mactravis opposite, discussing warfare. This fascinated the Ratu, who required minute detail of previous campaigns, descriptions of the enemy tactics and weapons with the action portrayed in the sand.

In the mid-afternoon, the Ratu declared there would be a feast the following night, apologising the lack of time to arrange it that night because the pigs took all day to cook. Suzanne asked what the ship could contribute, which meant a boat had to be sent for the cook and some bottles for the Ratu to sample.

A variety of women came over and the Ratu gave them instructions. The ship's cook arrived, and began a long discussion with the women, with the assistance of the Ratu's translation as the women did not speak Belada. At the same time, Sara offered him various bottles to sample. Brandy was interesting - the first mouthful sprayed everywhere amid a fit of coughing. Sara was concerned, but

Suzanne simply poured him another glass and waited. The Ratu recovered and reached for the glass, which Suzanne hung onto, and only permitted him a sip. She told him it needed to be sipped and the aroma inhaled. She demonstrated and the Ratu was hooked, requiring a glass to accompany him for the rest of the day. He loved the glasses and Sara earned a lengthy hug by presenting him with a crystal balloon brandy snifter together with a bottle.

Tomorrow's feast having been organised, the Ratu felt peckish and insisted the girls joined him for supper.

Sitting at the back of the jolly boat while six sailors rowed them, the last, back to the ship, Sara said to Suzanne, "Oh, I thought we would never escape. Why, oh why did you give him so much brandy? He was so drunk, he passed out."

"Next lesson in handling men, love," replied Suzanne, sounding tired. "When drinking, first they are happy, then they think they are funny when they aren't, then randy, then they get aggressive, then sad, then they go to sleep. It is best to leave when they are funny, or you are in trouble. Otherwise, you need to get them pissed and passed out fast, or they'll fight over you or worse. The brandy made it easy; they don't know how to handle it."

"Dirty old goat kept feeling my bottom," complained Sara, "after you got him drunk."

"You should be so lucky," answered Suzanne. "My right tit feels like it's gone through a mangle. I wonder if he's bruised it." And she proceeded to take it out and examine it in the moonlight.

"Suzanne," cried a scandalised Sara. "What are you doing? In front of everybody? Put it away!"

"Huh?" Suzanne said vaguely, looking at the crew and seeing four men goggling at her and two girls looking annoyed and upset. She realised two of the men were the girls' partners. "Oh, sorry, was worried he'd bruised it." She gestured towards it, and slipped it back inside her dress.

"Are you drunk?" Sara asked, curious. "This isn't like you."

"No, not at all," frowned Suzanne. "I was careful not to drink much brandy. Drank quite a bit of that bloody kava muck though."

They came to the ship, tied up and climbed aboard. A frightful noise came from a group of soldiers on the far side. The girls went over to find out what was happening, and found Little vomiting and retching over the side.

"What's wrong with him?" Suzanne asked, pushing through the soldiers and inspecting Little with a critical eye. "Is he drunk?"

"Nah," said Husk with a grin. "He reckoned kava was alcohol. He drank a couple o' gallons of it and still isn't pissed. Tryin' to get rid of it now." He cuffed Little round the head and spoke to him. "Hey mate, if it's slowing down, shove yer finger up yer arse then dahn yer throat, that'll fix it. Get rid of that girl spit, that's the way."

"Ah fuck off Husky," gasped Little, "it's even worse coming up than going down. Feel better though."

Husk looked up at Suzanne and started to speak, saw Sara behind her and coloured. He stood straighter and stammered, "Sorry ma'am, didn't see you there."

"No harm done, Husk. Carry on." Sara answered with a smile and turned away. She started to head off to her cabin when she heard Suzanne, who had lost interest in Little, marching towards the fo'c'sle rather than the poop, muttering to herself, something about Pat. She followed her and was surprised to see her stop by a stored jolly boat, rap on it and pull back the canvas cover.

"Pat," she ordered, "come out, I need you tonight." She stopped dead, and moved back as a spear slipped out of the jolly boat and pointed at her.

"Pat is off duty," hissed Hinatea viciously, causing Suzanne to back up further. "He's exhausted from looking for rocks all day while you drink kava." She spat this last without emerging from the boat.

Sara grabbed her arm and pulled a spluttering Suzanne away. "She can't talk to me that way! I'm the bloody captain!"

"You're not acting like one! That was disgraceful behaviour and she was well within her rights." Sara did wonder how Suzanne knew where they would be, impressed at the clever little love nest put together out of sight. Her heart ached, but she was over Pat, she told herself. She saw Suzanne to her room, and, after a moment's thought, called on Janis to set a guard on the door with instructions to keep the Captain in her room till the morning. As an afterthought, she told him to use Boersma who certainly wouldn't be tempted by Suzanne. Thinking about it, she deduced the magic was making a comeback in Suzanne, maybe caused by the Ratu's close attention.

Sara was on watch with the sun well up when Suzanne appeared on the poop deck. She looked at the captain curiously. She knew Boersma had repelled a couple of attempts to leave during the night and was more than a little grumpy at the indignities Suzanne had tried to perform on him. "How are you feeling today? You were a bit worse for wear last night, as if the magic had come back."

"Well, I feel fine this morning," said Suzanne with a frown. "But I wasn't myself last night. Thank you for looking after me." She smiled and Sara sighed her relief at getting a sensible Suzanne back.

"Have you eaten, Captain? Shall I call the officers for a meeting?"

"Yes please. Give me five minutes to get a hot tea."

It took a bit longer, as they needed to involve Captain Larroche and Brian as much as possible, and it took longer to roust them out. After running through the daily duties, the Bosun went to get Pat for his report. He came up the ladder with Hinatea in tow. Sara felt a little worried and wondered if Suzanne remembered her performance the night before. Clearly she did, for she coloured.

"Hinatea, I am sorry for last night. I wasn't myself." She prepared to go on, but Hinatea's ferocious expression changed into sunny happiness.

"It's fine. I understand. You must be careful with these men. Bad men, eat people, much fighting. No drink kava with them." She shook her head and folded her legs underneath her as she took her place next to Pat. The dwarf master appeared and sat beside Pat.

"What did you find, Pat?"

"Oh, there's plenty of different ores on the island," he answered and proceeded to lay out samples on a cloth in front of him. Rocks of various different colours and shapes which the dwarf bent and inspected minutely, grunting as he did so. Sara couldn't tell if the grunts were words.

"Look like rocks to me," said Suzanne distastefully. "How do you know they are ores?"

"Bit of colour, but the weight is the main thing. I don't know if they are any good, the master will know."

The dwarf discarded a couple but retained four samples. "This one very good," he banged one in front of Pat. "You remember where you found it? Was there lots, easy to get?"

"Yup. It's a big slab sticking out of the ground. Just need to break bits off."

"We'll test it, see what it's like. Any clay?"

Pat proffered more samples.

The dwarf was less impressed with these. "Are these the best you could find? Well, I expect I can make do. I will need lots of people to work with me."

"If you can make axes out of these rocks, the Ratu will provide as many as you want," said Sara.

"Axes, no problem. Fine work, good swords, maybe more difficult. Don't know yet. I'll go get ready." He scrambled to his feet and slid down the ladder, rather than stretch for the steps.

Captain Larroche stirred and everyone looked at him, Suzanne and Sara with their pulses racing at this sign of life. "What have they got to trade?"

Sara slipped into role. "Copra, sir. I think it is a different, ah, type to that from Pahipi. I wouldn't say quality, but perhaps the curing process is different. There is plenty of land here, and the locals are good farmers, but I don't recognise most of the crops. Not sure what could be transported home. Perhaps dried fish?" She shook her head doubtfully. "Of course there is trepang."

"They make oil from copra. Make the oil and put it in barrels. Take that instead." The captain sat back.

"It's difficult." Taufik said mournfully. "I know they press it and heat it, that's all. Easy to make a mistake. Copra is easier. You have to watch for mould or it can all end up rotten and worthless. Otherwise copra is easy to transport and sell. Not a lot of money, but some. Better to learn how to make the oil in Hind and to take the copra to Harrhein to make the oil there. Oil doesn't travel well."

"Would you and Brian like to take a watch, perhaps together?" Suzanne asked hopefully.

"Yes," said the Captain slowly, with an enquiring glance at Brian who nodded. "I think that would be a good idea. Must get back into the swing of it."

"Sara, ship's business is taken care of. Do you want to discuss anything with regard to trade?" Suzanne looked at her.

"A few things. It seems to me these people don't understand

money, and will exchange service for service, or barter goods." Sara looked at Hinatea, who nodded at her. "I have some ideas as to what we should offer them, and I want your thoughts, please." She looked at them. "I am not talking about goods for barter, but more serious trade. The Ratu will offer me warriors, and wants me to train them. He wants axemen and shields." She looked round the meeting, to see interested faces, with Mactravis nodding but Hinatea looking alarmed. "There is metal on this island, so we can teach them metal work, which we will need if we are going to arm them. There are many different trees, and I think the carpenter can teach them something about building larger ships. I am sure there are many other ways we can improve their lives."

"Don't be too sure it would be an improvement," murmured Suzanne. "Remember how Pahipi didn't want most of what we can offer."

"Hinatea, you look worried," said Sara with a nod to Suzanne. "What is the matter?"

"You must be careful with these people. Very fierce. Just because he laugh and hold your bum doesn't mean he is safe. You give him axe, and ship, he go straight to Pahipi and kill my people, rape the girls."

Mactravis nodded. "It's a good point. You can't just give him weapons; he could turn them on us, kill us all and steal the Queen Rose. You'll need hostages or something to emphasize it isn't worth his while to break faith."

"Faith?" Walters said, breaking out of a reverie. "I shall convert them all, bring them safely to God, then they will become a host, the Glorious Army of the Lord, bringing His light to the world." He lapsed back into silence and contemplated his feet.

The Bosun, uncaring of politeness, groaned loudly. "No sign of the Bishop recovering then. Why did he have to get bloody religion all of a sudden? Want me to confine him to ship while we're in port?"

"No, leave him. He's not doing any harm," said Suzanne, "but keep an eye on him. Hello, what's this?" She looked down to the main deck where a young Kai Viti climbed aboard. "Sara, it's the Ratu's son. Maciu, isn't it?"

Maciu spoke to Little, who pointed up at the poop and Maciu

climbed up, delighted with the ladder. He smiled at Sara as he went up to Suzanne, ducked his head and knelt in front of where she sat, cross legged on the deck.

"Lady," he spoke in Belada, "the Great Ratu asks for your help. Demons entered his head in the night and struggle to get out. He shouts in pain and his belly is sour. He asks for more brandy to quieten the demons."

Suzanne's mouth quirked, but she managed to maintain a straight face. "I am desolate to hear the Great Ratu suffers so. I fear the brandy would feed the demons. I suggest he drinks lots of water, which will help to wash them out of his head. It would be unwise to drink more brandy before the demons depart. Please tell him I shall come to see him as soon as I can."

"As you say, Lady." Maciu bowed and turned to Sara. "Lady Sara, the Ratu's advisors are ready to talk with you when you are ready, and asked me to offer you passage in my boat to the shore." His eyes twinkled at her.

Sara smiled. "Thank you. That would be pleasing." She turned to the company and switched back to Harrhein. "I will keep in mind your thoughts, especially yours, Hinatea. If nobody has any further suggestions, it's back to the salt mines for me." She looked around, nodded to everyone and got up to follow Maciu, hearing Hinatea whisper to Pat, "Salt mine? What is salt mine?"

Sara sat in the canoe for the first time, and discovered just how narrow they were. She climbed in gingerly, accepting Maciu's hand and was surprised at the depth, though barely a hands breadth showed on either side of her slim hips. There was a yoke at each end, going out to port to connect to a long log, parallel to the canoe. Maciu called the log an outrigger which kept the canoe stable. Four paddlers knelt in the canoe, with barely enough room in the small vessel, and Sara thrilled at how fast they moved it, giving shrill cries of excitement as they paddled. She admired the muscles playing in front of her and thought them all superb physical specimens. She looked at the water flying from the wavelets in the bow, flying fish erupting from it, and spray streaming off the paddles onto the paddlers when a question occurred to her.

"What happens to your hair when you go swimming?" She turned awkwardly to look at Maciu.

"It falls down and straightens!" he laughed. "You like to go swimming? Later after you talk come and see waves, I show you paipo, how we ride them fast like the boat goes now, without paddling."

"Sure," she said. "That sounds like fun." It did too, and Sara liked the idea of taking a break from responsibility. She also liked the way Maciu looked at her.

Suzanne found the Ratu recovering from his hangover and being berated by a huge woman. He left his house with alacrity and announced he would show her the sights. Yes, the water helped but not as much as the sight of her, he assured her gallantly. Today he played the part of a perfect gentleman, paying her compliments, making her laugh and explaining how the island functioned. Even when they walked round the swimming hole with its beautiful waterfall, he didn't suggest they swim.

They joined the negotiators for lunch where the Kai Viti advisors brought the Ratu up to date and Sara did the same to Suzanne. The Ratu attempted to cut through the negotiations by extolling the savagery of his warriors. Captain Larroche, Brian and Walters looked alarmed.

Sara smiled and changed the subject. "I think we are finished for the day, Great Ratu. After lunch Maciu is taking me to see paipo."

"Paipo," roared the Ratu. "Yes, I am superb at paipo and will show you as well. Suzanne, this afternoon we go swimming in the sea on the south beach."

"Really," said Suzanne. "I will be happy to watch, but perhaps I shall sit out the swimming."

"You should just watch as well, father," said Maciu with a grin. "You are too old and fat now and will sink through the waves."

Before the Ratu could respond, a calm voice punctured his anger.

"Paipo? If your waves are good enough, I will show you alaia." Hinatea walked up to the lunch table and selected a piece of breadfruit, Pat, Grey Fox and the other explorers behind her.

"A woman?" Maciu hissed . "Impossible."

"We have no men on Pahipi, so we girls do the rituals. I am alaia." Hinatea answered and sliced a mango expertly, offering a piece to Pat.

"You are the warrior leader of Pahipi, the War Ratu," mused the Ratu, his play anger gone and betraying his ready grasp of unmentioned politics. "I wish to see your alaia."

A holiday must have been proclaimed, for the entire village and most of the crew trooped down to the south beach, a walk of a good half an hour. A long beach revealed itself through the ever present coconut palms, white sand sparkling in the sunlight, breathtakingly beautiful. Standing under the palm trees, Suzanne and Sara stared at the ocean. Huge combers rolled in, breaking a good five hundred paces out and rolling majestically to shore, smashing down into the sand with a roar.

"They swim in that?" Suzanne whispered in horror, while Sara looked at the death maelstrom with her mouth open.

"How high are those things," whispered Sara, "they must be twice the height of a man."

"A tall man. Oh, what are they up to now?"

The Ratu rummaged in a ragged hut, a roof without walls, and pulled out a monstrous board, three times as long as he was tall.

Hinatea ran a hand along it. "Olo," she breathed. "I never ride one. You can ride it?"

"I fall off," laughed the Ratu. "Better on the paipo. Easier when you land. We hear about alaia, but we never see anyone who can do it. If you are truly a wave rider, I will give to you."

Hinatea smiled and went to Maciu who offered her the choice of a smaller board the same size as her, or one twice her size. Hinatea inspected them and selected a board a little longer than her height. Maciu raised his eyebrows at her twice. She smiled, slipped off her brief tunic and started smearing coconut oil over her body. Maciu did the same. Pat came forward and helped her, smearing the oil over her back. The Ratu grinned at this and offered a pot of oil towards Suzanne who turned away, as did Sara, and they went down towards the beach.

"Careful, darling, it might be nice the way he looks at you, but don't lead Maciu on. He won't stop if you do."

"Ohh, I'm not sure I would want him to, he makes me tremble inside. But you are a one to talk, the way you lead the Ratu on."

"Lead him on? I'm desperately trying to slow him down!"

The girls giggled as they watched the first kai Viti rushing into the sea, carrying boards half their height. They carried them towards the smaller waves; wading out till the wave came, then dived into the wall of water, pushing the board in first and following.

The girls watched them climb on the boards and, lying along them, paddle out to sea. As the waves came in, they would turn and paddle with the wave, riding up high and either slipping back or catching it. They rode the wave, lying flat on the board, and being smashed flat on the beach. The girls watched in astonishment.

"Huh! They are not very good." Silmatea appeared beside them. "This old style paipo. For men. They see who is tougher, who can stand and walk away from the highest wave. It hurts." It looked as if it did. While they watched, one young boy twisted as the wave came down, and stayed flat on the beach. His friends pulled him up and he cradled his arm, whether broken or bruised they couldn't tell.

"Hinatea is an artist in the new style. She will dance on the waves. These savages are in for a shock when they see true beauty." Silmatea emanated her contempt for the kai Viti.

"Can you dance on the waves, Silmatea? Why aren't you taking a board?"

"Later we all will. But first we enjoy watching Hinatea. See, she goes now. She will not take the little boys waves, but go further out. The boy should be careful; he will not have ridden such a big wave as she will choose. Come, let us go down the beach to those rocks. They will make a good seat and she will come in there."

The other Pahippian girls were arriving at the rocks, bringing the crew with them, so they went to join them.

Maciu and Hinatea went into the water, followed by the Ratu, still arguing good-naturedly with Maciu. They came to the first wave and Hinatea went through it like a seal, bobbing up on the far side of the wave, lying on her little board, while the kai Viti chased after their bigger boards. With sure strokes, she paddled hard out to sea, rising gracefully up and over the non-breaking waves.

"See there," Silmatea explained. "The sea goes back out there and it makes the waves smaller. It is easier to go out to sea, it carries them. She will ride it to where they start to break and will come round outside them. The men will turn off earlier or they will have trouble. Ah, see? The Ratu is clever; he is stopping there where he has the best view. He will sit on his board and watch."

Maciu doggedly followed Hinatea, but most of the other surfers were now sitting on their boards, watching. Hinatea turned and moved parallel to the beach, only occasionally visible over the waves. Behind her something humped in the water like a leviathan rising, a seventh-seventh wave, a man killer. Foam flashed beside her board, and keen eyed Pat called out, "She isn't paddling, she's doing big arm strokes! Going really fast!"

Pat stopped talking, Grey Fox grunted with surprise, the others could see her change shape. "She's standing on the board," breathed Pat. "Oh, I've got to try this!"

"Me too!" Sara said, while Suzanne was not alone in thinking 'No fucking way!'

"It takes time to learn," said Silmatea, "but if there is another beach with different, smaller waves we can teach you."

All the kai Viti along the beach stood and watched Hinatea, for unlike the boys and men earlier, she wasn't going straight into the beach. Instead she slid sideways along the wave, travelling much faster than the others and creating a wake behind her. Now riding high, now swooping down at speed, once speeding to the top of the wave and almost flipping up in the air as she turned and came down again.

"No tricks, darling," whispered Silmatea. "Come in now, come in slowly and beautifully." Sara looked at her, wondering if she even realised she spoke in Harrhein.

Hinatea seemed to hear her, for she moved to the crest of the wave and struck a dramatic pose on her board, a dark shape silhouetted against the bright sky, arms held wide. The beach held its breath, this was the highest wave, surely the impact would kill her, yet she had taken her board higher up the wave. The board tilted up, she floated over the top of the wave and down the back of it as the front crashed hard into the beach with a roar, then she slid up the beach in the foam as the wave disintegrated, stepping off the board daintily in the shallow water as it came to a halt. She pirouetted in the sand then picked up her board, going over to kiss Pat. She accepted an opened coconut from Trieste and smiled at everyone looking at her.

"Good wave." She drank.

There was a thump as Maciu landed flat on the beach, coming

down hard off a smaller wave. He got up, shook himself, picked up his board and walked over to Hinatea who was sitting down now. He looked at her steadily, raised his eyebrows and sat down beside her. She passed him the coconut.

"I think it is sign of respect, the eyebrows." Silmatea whispered, continuing her self-imposed cultural interpreter position. "They do things differently from us."

A monstrous walrus erupted out of the next wave, scattering water everywhere and the Ratu appeared, disdaining to thump down onto the beach. He also sat down beside Hinatea and accepted a coconut from Trieste. The silence dragged on while kai Viti gathered from up and down the beach, nobody speaking.

The Ratu stood and looked at his people. He spoke to them in Vituan, sonorously rolling out the words. Half way through he extended an arm to Hinatea. She stood and smiled at the audience, who cheered. He switched to Belada.

"Hinatea of Pahipi, we acknowledge you as alaia. We believed our skill surpassed all others, that alaia rode the board to the beach as we do. Now we know a hard truth. But we are kai Viti! We love skill and ability. We grant you the title of Queen of the Southern Ocean and the name Biau Lala, Wave Dancer. We grant you freedom to live here in Vitua, the Land Beloved of the Gods for we proclaim you an honorary kai Viti." He leaned down and gave her a formal hug, which she returned in similar style, both oblivious of their nakedness.

"Tomorrow, Biau Lala, you will teach me alaia."

"With pleasure, Great Ratu. Perhaps we start at a different beach?"

They returned to the village, everyone talking and Hinatea the centre of attention, where the cooks rushed off to bury the lolo, the feast. All the food was wrapped up in leaves and placed on a bed of coals from a fire that had been burning all day at the bottom of a pit. They covered the food parcels up with a few feet of earth and left, to the deep fascination of the ship's cook and his helpers. A cheerful young warrior was assigned to translate. He found it hysterical to be interpreting about cooking, as his command of Belada tended to be more martial, but with the aid of gestures and showing items, they established communication and the day saw the ship's cooks gain a fair command of Vituan culinary terms. The Harrheinians knew most of the food from Pahipi, including a stunning dish of tuna cooked in coconut milk by leaving it in the full glare of the sun.

Most of the ship's company attended the party, Pat volunteering for guard duty as he wanted to keep Mot away from drunken kai Viti. He commanded a skeleton guard crew of Spakka who viewed the kai Viti even more suspiciously than the Pahippians. One exception was Stiphleek, who was not going to miss festivity and had recently formed a fast friendship with Corporal Little, a friendship which revolved around a mutual admiration for alcohol.

Villagers lit fires in a circle around the centre of the village and everyone sat inside the ring of fires. Many of the villagers acted as waiters, while the ship's cook collared half the crew to do the same in doling out beer and brandy from the ships stores. Kai Viti and Harrheinians got on tremendously well; recognising many similarities and all around the fires could be seen people exchanging close examinations of each other's skins. The kai Viti had never seen white people before.

The Ratu leaned from his seat to Suzanne, sitting in the place of honour to his right. "Is this the normal dress for you Women People?" he asked, indicating over to the side, where she saw Terri and Katie sitting with some young kai Viti boys, both naked to the waist. Sighing, Suzanne went over to them.

"I thought you would like to know nice kai Viti girls cover their breasts with necklaces of shells." She said this in Belada and glared at the young kai Viti who fell about with laughter, before placing necklaces over the girls' heads, who were scarlet with embarrassment.

Smiling girls served copious amounts of kava, while two brawny young kai Viti went to the centre for a wrestling bout, with lots of shouted encouragement. On the finish, Husk and the carpenter's assistant jumped up and conducted a boxing bout, to the huge delight of the kai Viti. The Ratu had to be shown how to box and make a fist, after which he laid one of his guards unconscious to great applause. Wisely, he retired as a few impromptu bouts started between kai Viti and Harrheinians. A couple of crewmen managed to win wrestling contests and a couple of kai Viti won boxing matches to general satisfaction all round. The kai Viti chefs, all women, drove the wrestlers and boxers from the middle with sticks, showing no respect for age or nationality, and started to serve the food on banana leaves.

The Ratu was distressed at how little Suzanne ate and kept trying to force delicacies upon her. She matched him cup for cup with the kava, though, beginning to get a taste for it.

The meal came to an end with fruits, and Captain Larroche rose to his feet to make his apologies and retire to the ship, when the kai Viti went quiet. Sharpening her attention, Suzanne noted the thinned ranks of kai Viti, and some careful, considered examinations of the shadows from Mactravis, Russell and Strachan. The Ratu looked outside the fires with obvious anticipation and the warriors marched in, each bearing a thick length of bamboo of different lengths. Lining up in front of the Ratu, they began to slam the bamboo onto the ground in turns, causing them to resonate with the force of the blow. Each different length of bamboo made a different sound, so the team acted as a band, creating a haunting music. Strong voices opened up and the Harrheinians found themselves silenced by the magic of the moment, strong, beautiful voices backed up by the unusual melodic beating of the bamboo, while sparks floated up from the fires to the clear sky adorned with the brilliant diamonds of the southern stars, framed by the fronds of the coconut palms.

The kai Viti sang for an hour, after which Captain Larroche declared himself exhausted and needing to return to the ship. Suzanne stood as well to the Ratu's obvious horror and dismay. He exclaimed the dancing would start in a moment, at which she smiled, and agreed to stay a little longer.

Sara came and took the Captain's place as the circle adjusted, those remaining coming to the Ratu's side. Accompanied by the haunting singing, kai Viti girls danced dressed in skirts consisting of a belt of twine suspending long strips of coconut palm leaves. Lots of strips, very narrow, coming down to below the knee, but the dancing revealed the legs. A lot. The girls also wore the shell necklaces. The dances were slow, rhythmic and beautiful, and Suzanne and Sara were entranced. Perryn remained, as did most of the young members of the crew, all riveted by this dancing so unlike anything they had ever imagined.

After the first few dances, the Pahippian girls joined in, wearing borrowed skirts and with different moves. They made a stunning contrast, with their long, straight, black hair, lighter skin and smaller frames. This inspired the Ratu to genius, and he challenged Suzanne to join in, offering her a beautiful grass skirt, cunningly woven and dyed. High and happy on the euphoria kava inspires, Suzanne leapt at the opportunity. She went with Sara and the Ratu's daughters to change in his hut. They brushed out her hair into a mane, rubbed in a wax made of pig fat and clay and brought it to a wild array similar to the way the kai Viti hair stood out. They twisted her hair into ropes to make them stand, over a foot long with the ends waving so it looked as if a forest of palm trees grew from her head. They rubbed her torso with oil so it gleamed, placed a carved shell necklace round her neck and topped it with a wreath made from scented flowers.

She entered the circle to a hushed awe, broken by a great "Hau! Hau!" of appreciation from the Ratu echoed by every man there, including the sailors. Her hair was stunning, making her look huge, while her natural grace and swaying movement entranced the men.

Suzanne gestured to the band, and improvised a sensual and seductive dance to the thumping of the music. The shell necklaces, pretty effective at concealing the kai Viti women's breasts, lost the contest with her impressive array and the frequent exposure made her even more enticing. On her conclusion, the crowd leapt to their feet cheering, the Ratu embraced her and offered her a celebratory draught of kava which she drained dramatically in the fire light, standing proud and oblivious of the fact her breasts conquered the shells and squeezed them into the valley. Euphoric with the attention and the kava, she pulled up the girls from the crew and shoved them off to the kai Viti girls to be dressed up.

Suzanne sat down with the Ratu, smiling happily and accepted more kava. She felt euphoric and couldn't remember being so happy. She became aware of the disarray on her front and ineffectually tried to correct it as the girls returned along with the giggling kai Viti girls who started to teach them the steps to one of their dances.

As the fires died down, the kai Viti pulled all the girls into a line and they started a slow and sensual dance in front of the men. Suzanne found herself in front of the Ratu, whose eyes were riveted on her breasts. The girls kicked high, leant right forward and swayed. Now everyone was showing off, not just Suzanne. The Ratu's eyes glazed. He leapt up with a shout and started to whirl in front of Suzanne, followed a moment later by the rest of the kai Viti men, the crew joining in behind them.

Sara found Maciu in front of her, startlingly handsome in his finery, who mirrored her movements and she responded to greater heights of agility, as did the other girls. Which inspired the men to greater heights. Suzanne changed the dance from athleticism to eroticism, as the euphoria washed over her, the steps becoming slower, the body swaying more, and all the other girls followed suit. The men followed the lead.

She didn't notice Hinatea break away and drag a protesting Sara out of the dance, nor the other Pahippian girls pulling out the rest of crew members. The Pahippians hustled them back to the ship.

"Wait," cried Sara, still smiling and not wanting to go, especially with the way Maciu looked at her. "Don't forget Suzanne."

"Fuck her," said Hinatea, displaying a disgraceful fluency in Harrheinian. "She drink too much kava. Her own fault."

"What do you mean?" Sara asked climbing into a boat as Hinatea pushed it off.

"Too much kava makes you want to fuck," said Hinatea succinctly. "Why Ratu give her so much. He happy tonight, tomorrow you get good trade terms. But if you fuck Maciu then he get good trade. See, Hinatea save you trade treaty tonight." Hinatea started rowing self-importantly while Sara tried to process this information, wondering if she should insist on going back to rescue Suzanne.

Suzanne groaned, without opening her eyes and tried to remember. Her head pounded and ached, something heavy lay on her side and breasts while she felt sore all over. Her eyes shot open as she recognised the heaviness as an arm with a huge hand enclosing her left breast. She recognised the ache in her breasts and throbbing in her groin and groaned again as bits of memory returned.

She blinked her eyes as the headache told her she how little sleep she had managed, and rubbed her breasts, feeling the tenderness. Sitting up, she looked around and saw the Ratu lying beside her, his member still impressive in the slack, and she rubbed her belly ruefully, becoming conscious of a very full bladder.

She started to get up and the Ratu awakened, eyes lighting up and grabbing her leg. She smiled at him and indicated her bladder, asking where she could pass water in Belada. He jumped to his feet, fast and agile for such a big man, leading her to the back of the hut. She stopped and went to grab the grass skirt, the only item of clothing she could see, but when she picked it up she realised it was torn to pieces, and she also saw bits of her beautiful shell necklace on the floor. Suzanne scratched her head, wondering how she managed to get herself into this predicament, while the Ratu's attentiveness showed his impatience to get her back into the hut.

A Tender Embrace

P at stretched his long limbs in the sun and tried to look at Silmatea's breasts without Hinatea noticing. He and Rat were out with the girls in a dugout canoe with a bamboo outrigger, taking the luxury of a day off work to go fishing, after three exhausting days looking for ore and clay deposits over the island.

Hinatea, dazzlingly beautiful with a large red flower behind her ear, expertly paddled the canoe along the inside of the reef. Standing in the prow of the canoe was somebody who refused to be left behind. Mot loved fishing, barking at the flying fish and searching the horizon for her friends the dolphins.

The boys wore their rough canvas trousers, cut off into shorts with ragged edges, bare feet and torso; their skin tanned to a dark mahogany brown by the tropical sun. The girls were nude. They disliked wearing clothes, not seeing the point of them and actually getting ill when their clothes got wet. They had submitted with bad grace to wearing clothes on the ship, but now with a day off they were revelling in their normal freedom.

Pat idly watched a big scarlet-throated frigate bird flying low, its deeply forked tail almost touching the water. As he observed its flight, his head turned towards Silmatea and Hinatea cracked him hard on the side of the head with her paddle.

"No look at Silmatea's tits," she said severely. Hinatea was hardly jealous of Silmatea, and it would not have bothered her for a moment if Pat were to make love to Silmatea. However, the Pahippian girls had discovered that Harrheinians didn't think that way, and the boys would submit meekly to chastisement for any transgressions involving other girls. So actually, she was just enjoying herself. Hinatea and her friends had taken a few days to realise that they could actually have one boy to their very own, and didn't have to share. Once this realisation dawned, the free for all the male crew had enjoyed, which also infuriated the female crew members, ended abruptly as the girls selected their men. Hinatea had toyed with the idea of having several, but decided it was too much hassle and, besides, she had noticed the Harrheinian girls only had one each. She was trying very hard to be a Harrheinian, even if they were very stupid about so many things.

Pat rubbed his head, checking for blood. "I wasn't looking," he growled, inspecting his fingers. "That bloody hurt, and it wasn't necessary."

"You bad boy," said Hinatea contentedly. "If not this time, then other time I don't notice." She kept paddling while Silmatea smirked in the front. The girls turned the canoe through a gap in the reef and into the open sea. Immediately, Mot started to bark excitedly, paws up on the prow. Flying fish were gliding away from the front of the canoe, and it was Mot's life's ambition to catch one of the glistening toys. Silmatea kept an eye on her, for she would jump in after one if they weren't careful.

The canoe slowed, going parallel with the reef, and the girls were peering down into the water. Pat and Rat unpacked the fishing lines and prepared them. Hinatea called out urgently and the two girls spoke rapidly to each other in Pahippian. Silmatea stood up, a stick in one hand and a net in the other, and dived neatly over the side, with hardly a splash.

Leaving their lines, Pat and Rat leaned over the side to watch her. The reef was like a bulging cliff and Silmatea was swimming alongside the drop off about fifteen feet down. She went past several holes, looked into each briefly, then selected one into which she inserted her stick. They could just see her jiggling it in the clear water, then she was pulling it out and *something* was attached to it. She stuffed it in the net, quickly as lots of quite large fish came charging towards her and seemed to attack the net. Silmatea pushed hard for the surface, still pursued by the fish, and threw the net into the boat, where it landed on Rat. It exuded a long arm covered in discs which *attached* themselves to Rat, who screamed and ineffectually tried to scrape it off.

Fascinated, Pat leaned forward, grabbed the tip of the arm,

carefully pulled it free and inspected it. The animal seemed to be all arms and it came out of the net, gripping his arm with several of its arms, which undulated. The discs proved to be suckers which were able to grip his flesh, while the arms all came from the base of a bag with two big eyes in the middle. It was changing colours rapidly, going from white to dark to brown to white again.

"Careful it does not bite you," said Hinatea, leaning forward, pushing an interested Mot out of the way and grabbing the body of the creature, restricting its arms. She pulled it back and away from Pat's arm, exposing the two big, soulful looking eyes. Bending over she seemed to kiss it between the eyes, it shuddered and went limp.

Seeing Pat's perplexed look, she showed him a bump between the eyes. "You bite this, he dead. Very good to eat. Here, try." She tore off an arm, bit a chunk off and offered it to Pat. He copied her and had to admit it was very tasty, chewy and delicious. Hinatea turned it over and showed how the arms all came from around the mouth, where there was a hard, sharp beak like the parrots Pat had seen on Vitua.

"We call eight legs, also best bait. See, when Silmatea catch all fish come to try and eat. So put bit on hook and you catch."

Silmatea surfaced with another octopus, from which Rat cringed away. Mot stuck her nose into it and yelped as the octopus attached itself to her muzzle, desperately shaking her head and trying to scrape it off. Hinatea came to her rescue, killing it swiftly.

Pat watched Silmatea underwater again, as Hinatea controlled the canoe and Rat dropped a line down, the crude hook baited with a chunk of octopus. He caught a fair sized fish instantly and was hampered in bringing it into the canoe by Mot who considered it her job to actually catch the fish, clearly hoping it might be one of her nemesis, the flying fish.

"Silmatea look for holes in rock," Hinatea explained. "If hole has stones in front of it, then eight leg inside. He put stones in front of hole, make pretty for his house. When he go out, he push stones to one side and go other way. But you never find him on reef, because he too clever at hiding. Change colour and look like rock. Have to find in hole."

"How do you get him out?" asked Pat, watching as Silmatea probed at a new hole. She was able to stay under water for a long time, and Pat wondered how long he would be able to manage.

"You put stick in hole, he grab stick. You turn stick and he hold, grab with more legs. When more legs on stick than holding him in hole, you can pull out slowly and he don't let go. If he big, kill straight away. If small bring to canoe. Must go quick as fish try to steal."

"How big do these things get?" Pat asked, looking at the beak again.

"These not big," said Hinatea, holding her hands a fair distance apart.

"That's bloody enormous," said Pat, looking at the octopus and again at the distance between her hands.

"I rest now," announced Silmatea as she climbed aboard. Hinatea took her stick and net and dived overboard, while Silmatea gave Rat a quick kiss, then pushed past Pat to the stern of the boat, ensuring he was able to have a good, close look at her breasts on the way. There she took up the paddle and held the canoe roughly on station.

Hinatea surfaced with a huge shell in her net, a snail the size of a person's head with a shell that coiled out to a long point. She shouted something to Silmatea, swapped nets and was gone again.

"She has found some clams," explained Silmatea. "Good eating."

Pat liked clams, but was unprepared for the enormous thing that Hinatea brought up next, the size of two hands side by side. Very different from the little ones in the sand at home.

"They good to eat when small like this," said Silmatea grinning.

"They get bigger?" Pat asked in astonishment.

"Oh yes." Silmatea's Harrheinian was a bit better than Hinatea's. "This one is a baby. They get this big." She held her hands as wide apart as they could go, pushing her breasts up as she did so.

"You're kidding," said Rat, as he hauled up another fish.

"No, honestly, they get that big. Not good to eat, very tough, and you must be careful. They shut quickly when you come near, and if you get your hand or foot inside you cannot get out and drown."

"Everything is bloody huge around here," muttered Pat.

"Except tits!" Rat said with a straight face and tried to dodge the water Silmatea splashed at him with her paddle.

Hinatea swapped places with Silmatea and it was Pat's turn to be kissed. The girls were very demonstrative, always touching and stroking, which was something the boys were finding difficult. The thought of a girl behaving like that had been the stuff of fantasy growing up, but the reality was disconcerting in the extreme.

Pat was distracted from his fishing, but tore his lips away as his hand was smashed down to the gunwale of the canoe and the line pulled through his fingers so fast they tore and bled. He jammed his foot on the line, gripped it with both hands and it promptly broke. Looking over the side they could see a large, humped fish angrily racing around the canoe, snapping at other fish and trying to work the hook out of its mouth on the coral.

"Eeee!" Hinatea said, looking at it. "A trevally - they very fierce, too big to catch on line. Break it every time. Don't fish while he here. You no catch anything, he take bait and break line every time."

Rat hurriedly pulled his line in, and indeed the trevally raced after it, snatching the bit of octopus tentacle off without hooking itself. They watched the trevally in silence as it circled about underneath them, all its fins raised and clearly highly annoyed.

Silmatea surfaced, some distance away, shouting shrilly in Pahippian. Hinatea shouted back and started the canoe racing towards her. Silmatea climbed aboard in great excitement, stammering out her story and shaking as she did so. The two girls conducted a long conversation in Pahippian, big smiles on their faces and the level of excitement going higher and higher. All the time Hinatea paddled slowly, keeping the canoe over the same area.

Pat and Rat wondered what was going on and eventually managed to get the girls to speak Harrhein.

"Is a grandfather!" Silmatea squeaked in excitement. "The biggest ever!"

"You help us catch him," stated Hinatea, looking down into the water. "We cannot catch normal way."

"We will be so proud," said Silmatea. "Not many people ever see a grandfather this big, and very rare to catch one."

"Remember one at Hula'ao," said Hinatea. "It kill and eat girl who try catch it."

"Oh, yes, that was Moana. I liked her. She was very silly to try and catch one on her own."

Pat and Rat were feeling slightly alarmed. "What is a grandfather?" Pat asked.

248

"Like the little ones, but bigger," Hinatea waved at the octopus vaguely.

"Bigger? You said they only got this size," accused Pat, worried and holding his hands apart. "How much bigger?"

"Is not eight leg. Is grandfather. Is different. Look, there is one of his legs." She pointed through the waves.

Pat looked, but all he could see was a large moray eel, actually a huge eel nearly twice as long as he was. In fact he couldn't see its head and with a sinking feeling he realised that it was an octopus tentacle.

"Dear God," Rat said quietly, while Mot, who was also looking over the side, barked and licked his face enthusiastically. "The fucking thing is enormous. Wait, if that is one of its legs, how big is the bloody beak?"

"Oh, probably about like your hands together," said Silmatea matter of factly, adroitly manoeuvring the canoe to get a better look at the hole the monster lived in.

"How are you going to catch it?" Rat asked. "I don't think your sticks are big enough."

"No, you right," said Hinatea. "We need him out of hole. So we use bait. He come out, start to hold bait, Silmatea and I swim down and catch him."

"What do you mean, 'catch him'?" asked Pat. "You won't fit him into a little net."

"We pull head back and bite between eyes, like with eight legs. Must bite hard, but he die, easy."

Pat and Rat digested this slowly, as the enormous tentacle slowly retracted into the cave. Another one came out and moved a rock around in the entrance. This tentacle looked different.

"That his catching hand," said Hinatea. "See, is flat at end? Also has claw to help hold."

"Charming," said Rat in a shocked tone. "Are we safe in the canoe? Can it reach up and grab us?"

The girls looked at each other and shrugged.

"Probably," said Silmatea. "I think I hear of it happening many years ago."

"Fuck this," said Rat, who was as brave as anyone, but courage tended to evaporate in the eggshell of a canoe. "Let's get out of here before it notices us."

"No," said Hinatea firmly. "We must catch it. Very good eating, and stop it catching people fishing and the Gods will be pleased. They hate the grandfathers."

"What are you going to use as bait?" Pat asked, picking through the fish they had caught and pulling up the largest, inspecting it critically. It was a red snapper and he thought it would be suitable.

"You," said Hinatea, looking at him with her eyes twinkling.

"What?" Pat said, startled, while Rat's mouth dropped open.

"You swim down, hold onto that rock there. He reach out and taste you with arm. He try pull you into hole. You hold rock tight. Then he come out to you, and hug you. Me and Silmatea swim down and kill him. Easy."

Pat stared at her in shocked silence for a good minute before he spoke.

"ARE YOU FUCKING CRAZY? NO WAY!" he shouted. Pat hardly ever swore.

"What mean crazy?" Hinatea asked with interest. "New way of fucking?"

Pat didn't reply, his mouth was working with nothing coming out. Rat was staring over the side at the monstrous tentacle, his face white. Mot thought it was all wonderful and barked excitedly, wagging her tail.

Hinatea turned to Silmatea, and spoke in Pahippian. *"Which one do you think we should use?"*

Silmatea eyed the two boys, both now looking over the side of the canoe. *"Yours, I think. He is bigger. The grandfather might not come for mine, too skinny."* They were both careful not to use the boys names. *"How are you going to make him go down? He is very scared."*

"Yes, I agree." Hinatea reached to pinch Pat's flesh and check how much fat there was, and restrained herself just in time.

"Will you threaten not to have sex?"

"No, he won't respond to a threat. I will make him want to do it. Watch me."

"I hope you know what you are doing. Will you tell him you have never done this before?"

"Ha! Of course not. But I hope the old stories are right!"

"It didn't work for Moana."

"She tried to do it on her own, without a person as bait. We will do it properly. This is very exciting! I have never seen one before!"

Hinatea leant forward and placed her first barb. "You Harrheinians never see animal like this?"

"No," agreed Pat suspiciously, while Rat nodded carefully.

"Aiee, the Captain will be happy when you bring him back. They not believe it if not see it." She watched carefully to see the effect of her words, looking for those tiny clues which girls see so effortlessly and of which boys are completely unaware. She saw his breathing speed up ever so slightly, and his lips part slightly. But pride would only go a little way with this one.

"They very dangerous for fishermen. I wonder how many he eat." She waited, till she saw his eyes widen slightly. "Poor kai Viti, I bet he catch and eat lots of them. Is why lots of fish here. They cannot fish here." Pat shifted uncomfortably.

"Fuck 'em," said Rat succinctly. "If they want to fish here, they can be bait. Let's go back and tell them."

"Kai Viti very backward," said Hinatea disdainfully, with the casual racism of one people for their near neighbours. "They not know how to kill, is why still here. We must help. Is Duty." Hinatea didn't quite understand what duty meant, but she knew it was a very powerful word that the Harrheinians reacted to strongly. "Poor little children, grandfathers like to eat very much." This was especially cunning, as she knew the boys liked the small children and had endless patience with them.

Rat moved uncomfortably, while Pat went very still. Hinatea knew she was winning and it was time to play the trump card of curiosity. She knew Pat's buttons and how to press them.

"Grandfather very clever. He make hole nice to live. Arrange rock way he like. Even he plant soft things outside." She waved her hands, desperately trying to find the Harrhein words. The boys looked at her blankly. Silmatea scratched her head, not knowing the word either. "You know, much colour, like plant but alive. Has lots of arms and stings little fishes."

"Ah," said Pat with realisation. "You mean anemones. We only have small ones in Harrhein."

"He like. He plant big ones by door and feeds them."

"Feeds them? Really? How?" Pat allowed his interest to show and peered over the side of the canoe.

"Look, you can see big an'money there?" She pointed over the side with her paddle.

"Yes. Wow, it's huge!" Pat was impressed.

"When he catch fish, he drop bits in it." Hinatea thought for a while, and then her innate honesty led to an addition, as she had made up the story on seeing the anemone. "I think is so, I not watch much."

Pat peered into the water, hoping to see the giant octopus feeding its anemone.

"Look at big rocks. He put them outside, make pretty. Inside much nicer. Outside for hiding, inside for pretty. He choose pretty rock." This was pure fabrication, but she knew that Pat would now want to see inside the cave. "How long can you stop breathing?"

"Uhh, not as long as you," Pat replied without thinking, caught off guard, and cursed the admission that he could hold his breath.

"You must make boom-boom slow," she said, patting his chest over his heart. "And you breathe deep before dive. Like this." And she proceeded to hyperventilate, a process which caused her small breasts to rub up and down his arm, a further distraction.

"Why do I go to that rock?" Pat asked nervously, and Hinatea knew she had won.

"He have long arm. He reach out and pull you into hole. If you by rock, you hold rock and he cannot pull you. Arm strong, but not enough."

Pat grunted unhappily. He looked at the rock, and had to admit that it was pretty big and solid, but there were some solid projections he could hold, maybe even get his feet the other side of it.

"What about that big beak? Won't he bite me badly? If it's as big as you say, he could do some damage."

"He not have time," said Hinatea, hoping it was true and not thinking about Moana's body, the bits they had recovered, with horrendous gashes where the octopus had bitten her. "Anyway beak not strong, maybe not go through skin."

Silmatea tensed at this calumny, and Pat noticed. "I don't want to do it," he said grumpily, but without much certainty. Hinatea started to massage his shoulders and Pat knew he was volunteered. Even

Rat had worked this out and had released his death's hold on the seat in the canoe.

"Practice stop breathe," instructed Hinatea and he half-heartedly started to hyperventilate. "Properly," she tapped him gently on the side of the head. Now was not the time for the usual clout. "Now stop breathe." Pat did so, and she was quite pleased with the result. "Is good. Long enough. Rest now, eat, drink. We go in a bit."

Hinatea told Pat to get ready and he started to hyperventilate. He cleared his mind and suppressed his excitement. A natural hunter, he was now enthused about the project and the challenge of pitting himself against a monster in an alien environment. Legends of the great heroes from the past, fighting all sorts of monsters, were flitting through his brain and he was seeing himself up there with the stories. These thoughts all had to go, he knew how dangerous they were. As an expert hunter with a knack of understanding animals, he didn't for a moment believe Hinatea. He evaluated the octopus, understanding the brain was the weak link and that all those tentacles would be dragging him towards the beak. He carefully looked over the small octopus, examining the brain and the eyes, and was confident the plan would work.

He dove over the side, straight down to the rock, finding his vision a little blurry under water despite the clarity. He quickly reached the rock and tested the handholds, discarding the first as too rough but getting a good grip on the second, when something tapped him on the shoulder. Twisting, he saw that it was a long tentacle already checking him out. He looked at it with interest and didn't resist as it wrapped itself gently around his right upper arm. He felt the suckers get a grip, then there was a sharp pain as the claws around the suckers sank into his flesh. Pat was expecting this, and just grimaced, inured to such slight injuries.

Another tentacle shot out, wafted through the blood released and retracted abruptly. Pat grinned, reckoning correctly that he was being tasted. He couldn't see anything in the hole, which was a lot smaller than he had expected. The tentacle around his arm tightened, pulling him towards the hole, and he resisted, thinking that he must taste good. No problem, and he waited for the octopus to come out.

Two big tentacles came towards him and he looked past them

where there was a gleam in the shadow, and he thought he could see the eyes looking at him malevolently. He shuddered slightly, not used to being prey, and braced himself as the two tentacles wrapped firmly around his left leg and his torso. These didn't hurt at all, and he realised they didn't have the claws. They contracted slightly, pulling him gently but firmly towards the hole and he resisted, not budging. Quickly, they contracted firmly, effortlessly pulling him from the rock, ripping his hands in the process and whipping him swiftly across the ten feet to the hole.

"Fuck," said Hinatea from above. She preferred Harrhinian for swearing and was becoming quite adept. As one, she and Silmatea dived down, not hearing Rat calling out.

Seeing the girls go, Rat panicked slightly, leaning over and watching them go down. He saw them drift away, then realised that it was he who was drifting. He went to the back, picked up the paddle and tried to copy the effortless way in which the girls manoeuvred the canoe. He promptly spun in a circle. He lost his bearings, and it was only because Mot barked and pointed in the right direction that he managed to get the canoe heading back, following the dog's directions.

Hinatea went down to the cave quickly and found Pat was jammed against the entrance. She leant down and took his left arm, while Silmatea came down and grabbed his right.

Pat had not lost his nerve. He was in a higher plane of thought, watching what was happening in an almost out of body situation, with time slowed down and creeping by. He felt the impact as he crashed into the rough coral, and felt his flesh tear as the octopus tried to pull him through the hole. His body strained, but was never going to fit as the octopus rapidly realised. Instead it came forward, and he saw the huge eyes, each bigger than his fist, coming closer and looking straight into his face from inches away. His imagination lent meaning, telling him that the octopus was salivating at the prospect of eating him. His breath was tight in his chest, but he still had awareness as he felt an exploratory tentacle run over his face, probing his ears and nose. He tried to bite it but it whipped away.

His legs were free now as the monster changed its grip, no longer pulling, just holding. Pat inched his legs up his front, tilting his body slightly so he could get his feet between himself and the octopus. Its inspection finished, he saw the front tentacles spread apart and the eyes tilted backwards as a monstrous beak appeared from underneath. It was huge, easily capable of engulfing his whole head and it looked hard and razor sharp. As it reached with its beak to disembowel him, he felt the girls grip his arms and at the same time he placed his legs on either side of the hole and pushed back sharply, with the girls pulling.

This unexpected push caught the octopus off-guard, and he came flying away from the hole as the suckers lost their grip. The octopus came boiling out in pursuit, unwilling to give up such a tasty morsel. Two long arms stretched after Pat, while other arms moved along the ground, pulling the body after them, leaving two anchored to the hole.

Pat kicked frantically for the surface, beginning to ache with the need for air, while Silmatea supported him, Hinatea letting go. The octopus grabbed his left foot and stopped him in mid water. He was desperately trying to kick it off and feeling the talons sinking into his calf, blood blossoming through the water. He could feel Silmatea pulling him and saw Hinatea arrow through the water, now behind the octopus.

More tentacles gripped his leg, moving higher up his body. They tensed and suddenly the octopus, horrifically, shot through the water and attached itself to his stomach. He looked into its eyes, right in front of his face, hearing Silmatea at his shoulder scream under water as she kicked at it, and the great beak was straining at his stomach. He could feel it rubbing against him as it snapped, not quite at the right angle yet. He put his hands either side of the beak, careful not to get one actually inside it, and tried to push it away, but was unable to get effective leverage. It flexed backwards and time slowed as he felt the point of the huge beak slide into his flesh. The agony was intense, and he strained desperately not to wriggle and lunge which would slice his flesh against the cruel beak.

Through mists of pain, he saw hands come down over the monster's eyes, huge in front of his face, and haul them backwards. Hinatea's head came between him and the eyes, her long hair swirling around him like a death shroud, caressing his cheek in the tide.

The pain was too much, his chest bursting with the need to

breathe, and he felt himself going, breathing out the air and water trying to flood into his lungs. Then he was free of the octopus and Silmatea was pulling him to the surface while he thrashed weakly.

Rat was desperately fighting the canoe, already exhausted from going round in circles and convinced Mot would bite him if he messed up again, as the dog was going mental around the canoe. He was finally getting to grips with it by paddling on alternate sides, when Mot barked like crazy and jumped over the side, swimming strongly towards a mass of bubbles roiling to the surface. Silmatea burst out of the bubbles and pulled Pat's head up. It lolled weakly to the side and Mot was beside them, trying to grab his shoulder and lift him up in the water, unsuccessfully. Rat aimed the canoe awkwardly in their direction, while Silmatea left Pat with Mot, took a couple of quick strokes and eeled into the canoe, relieving Rat of the paddle and telling him to pull Pat aboard.

Quickly she manoeuvred the boat alongside Pat, and Rat pulled him aboard as the blood sluiced out of him. Mot barked wetly through a wave as he forgot her, so he had to pull her in as well. As soon as Pat was aboard, Silmatea stopped paddling, rushed forward and pushed on Pat's chest, causing him to vomit water. She turned him on his side and he coughed weakly, while she worked his chest till he was breathing to her satisfaction. Through this he continued to bleed.

This took moments, and as soon as she was satisfied she simply leapt over the side with a rope in one hand. Rat hesitated, not sure whether to take the paddle or help Pat. Mot was beside Pat, licking his wound, so he went to get the paddle, but had no idea where to go.

"RAT! Throw me spear, quick!" It was Hinatea, her head just out of the water not far away. He saw her fish spear and threw it to her, cursing as he saw it was going to hit her, but she ducked under water. He wasn't sure if he hit her, and then blood welled up on the surface, followed by thrashing in the water that moved away from the canoe. A fin appeared in the thrashing, and he wondered what was going on.

An arm came over the edge of the canoe and Silmatea was aboard, the rope between her teeth. She started hauling and shouted at him to help. It was heavy, and he strained, nearly dropping the rope as he saw the octopus was attached to it. Silmatea cursed him, leaned over the side and with difficulty hauled it up into the canoe, with Rat's fairly ineffectual help. It flopped into the bottom. Rat could see that a couple of tentacles were missing, and he wondered if they were old wounds.

Silmatea was back at the side, banging on the side of the canoe, splashing the water loudly, then Hinatea was sliding into the canoe, blood dripping down the side of her leg where a large patch was rubbed raw. She was panting for breath. She lay gasping in the bottom, while Silmatea checked her leg and quickly looked for other injuries.

Hinatea hauled herself upright, grabbed a paddle and staggered to the front, while Silmatea went to the rear and slowly the girls paddled the canoe back though the gap in the reef into the lagoon. Rat stepped gingerly over the octopus, using the sides of the canoe and went to Pat, helping him to sit up. Mot stopped licking him and growled at the dead octopus.

"Give him coconut water," Hinatea said over her shoulder, her voice hoarse and strained.

Rat wasn't adept at opening a coconut, but managed to slash the top open with an old short sword carried for the purpose. He held it to Pat's lips, who swallowed greedily. Rat looked Pat over. He had really been in the wars. Both hands were ripped to shreds by the coral, the feet not much better. There were round marks all over his body where the suckers had gripped him, some of them surrounded with deep slash wounds where the claws had bitten deep. And there was a deep gash in his groin, where the beak had gone in, still seeping blood, but despite the flapping skin, superficial.

The canoe rode a small wave back into the limpid calm waters of the lagoon and the girls rested, Hinatea turning and taking the coconut from Pat.

He fixed her with a look. "Have you actually hunted those things before?"

She squirmed and shrugged. "Not that big."

"How big?"

Hinatea looked down, then at the horizon, hoping for a quick squall to come in to change the subject.

"I bet you've never even seen one before, never mind caught

one," said Pat tiredly.

"We have old stories," said Hinatea in a small voice. "Our men used to catch them this way."

"I think they were smaller," said Silmatea in an apologetic voice. "Our people always used to kill them before they got big, as they were too dangerous when they got big."

"How big is it? All I could see was its bloody eyes, glaring at me as it started to eat me."

Hinatea pulled out the longest tentacle, one of the feelers with the pad at the end. It slurped out from under the body sac, the noise making Mot and Rat retreat, both clearly worried it was still alive.

"You sure it's dead?" Rat asked nervously.

Hinatea ignored him. She was looking in astonishment at the length, more than two tall people, almost three.

"Not even the hero Tafa'i took a grandfather so big," she whispered. "I never think I see one this big."

Silmatea came forward, stepping over Rat and Mot along the gunwale of the canoe and squatted there looking down at it. Then she prodded Hinatea's leg, just missing the wound.

"Mao?" She asked. "How many?"

"I think three sharks," said Hinatea. "Two get tentacles, I get one."

"One come very close," said Silmatea, inspecting the leg. "From head or tail?"

"What does she mean?" Rat asked, looking more closely at Hinatea's leg. It looked as if something had shaved the skin off a large patch.

"Shark come close," Hinatea said dismissively. "Their skin very rough. This from head, hit leg." She prodded Pat's side, finding a patch without a wound. "Hey, hero, fun, hey? Tomorrow we catch another?"

Pat grinned at her. "Sure. If we can find this baby's daddy!" They laughed together and Rat shook his head.

"How did you kill the thing? Last thing I saw was you being pulled into a hole!"

"I didn't fit," said Pat. "While it was trying to get at me through the hole, it half let go and I kicked off the rock just as the girls got to me and pulled. It followed us out of the hole and grabbed me, started to eat me." He indicated his groin. "Hin came up behind it, pulled its head back and bit it."

Hinatea smacked him half-heartedly. "My name is Hinatea, not Hin. Very rude Patraigh."

"Sorry," said Pat automatically. "So what happened next?"

"He tough," said Hinatea absently, rubbing her arm where they now saw some bruising and gashes on her back. "Hard, very hard to bite his brain. He spin when I do it. Hit me against rock. Then he dead. Shark come to eat him, have to chase off. Cannot come up or lose grandfather to shark, but no air. Silmatea bring me rope. Kiss me to give air. I stay down while you pull up grandfather, keep shark off."

The boys looked at her, letting this stark account sink in. Pat, who had been feeling very brave and heroic, suddenly felt a lot less so. Silmatea smiled and went back to the stern, where she started to paddle them back to the village.

"What do you mean, kissed you?" Rat asked.

"Bad boy," said Hinatea tiredly, without looking at him. "Not sex. She blow air into me so I don't need go up."

"Wow," said Rat. "I would never have thought of that."

"When we go into the village, Patraigh must go first with Hinatea, Rat and I follow with grandfather," said Silmatea. "Important we look good. Very special to take a big grandfather. They make a big feast in our honour tonight." She rubbed her hands together gleefully.

"How are we going to carry it?" Rat asked in alarm. "I'm not letting that thing touch me!"

"Is not thing," said Hinatea indignantly. "Is grandfather, show respect like to Captain."

"I still don't want to touch it," muttered Rat with a worried look.

"Don't worry about it," said Silmatea. "We will carry it on our fish spears. We put them across our shoulders, and Hinatea will arrange grandfather over them so they can see how big he is."

The canoe grounded gently into the white sand, with Mot leaping for the beach and barking at the children who came running and screaming to welcome them, all shouting out asking what they had caught. Pat eased over the side and limped ashore, causing the children to redouble their questions, all shouting at once. In Vituan so he couldn't understand a word.

They fell silent all at once.

Hinatea had proudly lifted the grandfather up so they could see it.

None of the children said a word as Hinatea arranged the grandfather artistically on the spears, being careful to ensure it didn't touch Rat. Silmatea carried more of their catch in her net, while Rat had the fish in Hinatea's net. Mot took up her accustomed station in the lead, tail held proudly high as if she alone were responsible for the catch. As they started forward, the kids silently split apart and followed. A couple of fishermen mending nets at the edge of the town stood up, looking at them.

Pat was in a lot of pain, especially from the bite in his groin, but the wounds in his feet from kicking the coral were very bad on the walk. Hinatea helped a little, but she was also hampered by her thigh which she was careful to keep on the other side of Pat. It was very slow progress. They could see the Great Ratu sitting under the palm trees by the council rock, one arm around Suzanne and talking earnestly to Sara. Captain Larroche had seen them, for he stood up.

Pat looked back at the octopus, seeing the two staggering under the awkward weight. He could feel the quiet falling around the village, and people were appearing from everywhere to watch silently as they made their grand entrance. He tried to stand straighter. It wasn't every day you limped into town a hero, having battled a monster from legend.

They staggered proudly up towards the Great Ratu, and Hinatea mentally rehearsed what she would say. She held herself higher, reminding herself not to disparage the kai Viti for not slaying this monster, but to be gentle and kind. After being named Biau Lala, Wave Dancer, she wondered how she would be honoured for her bravery and skill in despatching the monster of the reef.

Pat limped along bravely, trying to forget the pain, half smiling and finding himself looking forward to telling the tale. It wasn't every day you were bait for a monster! As they drew closer, he could see the officers' eyes drawn to his amazing wounds, the suction marks of the octopus now looking like cicatrices all over his body.

The Great Ratu's mouth was open as he looked down on the procession, not looking at Pat or Hinatea, but fixed on the octopus.

As they neared, he suddenly let out a bellow like the bull whale that had followed the Queen Rose for a week. He jumped forward, amazingly light and agile on his feet for such a big man, shouting hoarsely in Vituan. All the kai Viti villagers started howling. As he came up to them, he started ripping at his jewellery, sending shells flying everywhere, still bellowing.

Pat, Hinatea, Rat and Silmatea stopped, confused.

The Ratu kept bellowing, and to their horror they saw tears pouring down his face. For a moment, Pat wondered if they were for him and his injuries, but the Ratu pushed past him. Rat and Silmatea eased their burden down and the Ratu knelt beside it, wailing loudly. All the other kai Viti were joining in with the weeping and wailing. The fishing team stood about, wondering if they should say something and not knowing what to do.

The Captain came storming over, his face a thundercloud, with Sara beside him and Suzanne just behind.

"What the hell have you done now, Connorson?" The Captain snarled.

"We, uh, were fishing, sir, and we caught this monster. They prey on fishermen and children. We have saved lives," said Pat, trying to be defiant, all his pride eking out into the ground.

"It is a god," said Suzanne with a stony face. She was rapidly learning Vituan. She was listening to the Ratu as he wailed out his torment, holding one of the dead tentacles, tears streaming down his face. He banged his forehead into the dead octopus. "It guards them from the wrath of the sea. The Ratu calls him his brother. They mourn his death, no, his murder. They fear for the future with the Guardian gone."

"Oh no," said Pat, closing his eyes, whilst Rat looked around wildly for somewhere to run. The Ratu started to thrash on the ground and all the kai Viti did the same.

"Is grandfather," said Hinatea obstinately, leaning on her fish spear. "Eat people, very dangerous. This one very big, catch, eat people."

"It's *tabu* to kill them," said Suzanne, using a strange word that Pat didn't understand but Hinatea and Silmatea clearly did, all the bravado going out of them in a rush.

"We are not on Pahipi now, Hinatea," said Sara. "The kai Viti obviously have a different relationship with the fish. Damage limitation in order, Captain, we must ensure this desecration does not reflect badly on us and affect the new relationship we have created," she continued crisply. "Place them under arrest and have them taken back to the ship. You will need these two in the sickbay, I think. Suzanne, up to you to find out what we need to do. I would prefer not to have to execute them, but we will if we have to." She ended grimly, not looking at the boys.

Captain Larroche issued a quick few orders and the fishing team were marched off to the ship under close arrest, heads hanging, thoroughly chastened and all dreams of glory vanished. Hinatea was still muttering in Pahippian.

"Now, Captain," continued Sara in full Princess mode, eyeing the kai Viti carefully. "I think we might remove ourselves from danger. We don't know how they are going to react to one of their gods being slaughtered by us. Suzanne, sorry but you will have to stay. I can leave you a small guard."

"Don't worry about me, I'll be fine." Suzanne was confident of her safety with the Ratu. "He's watching us, you know. Seeing how you react."

Indeed he was, and as the fishing team went into the boat to take them back to the Queen Rose he let out another loud bellow then stood up and came back to the Princess and her negotiating team. He gestured to his people to continue the lamentations and spoke to them in the trade language rather than Vituan.

"What do you do with them?" He asked Sara directly, with no honorific and no expression on his face.

"They are under arrest and will be placed in a secure area on the ship while we decide what to do with them. They will first be placed in the galley for their injuries to be treated." Sara responded directly and honestly.

The Great Ratu looked at her briefly then looked at the horizon. "We will discuss what to do tonight. Please return to your ship, all of you, and return here in the morning to hear our thoughts. It will be the decision of the *Bete*." He turned and went back to his people.

Suzanne bent her head to Sara and spoke in a low tone, loud enough for the Captain to hear as well. "The *Bete* is the priest, who talks to the Gods. *Tabu* means forbidden by the gods. Lots of things are *tabu* and they kill anyone who does anything *tabu*."

Sara closed her eyes for a moment in pain, and Suzanne went after the Ratu.

It was nine o'clock by the hour glass as the ship's boats slid up the sandy beach, sailors leaping out to run them further up from the tide. Sara jumped lithely ashore and walked up to a welcoming party of Suzanne, Maciu and a young Kai Viti, Maru, another of the Ratu's son and Pat's friend from his explorations. Both looked fairly grim.

"Have you brought them with you?" Suzanne asked.

"Yes, I got your message. In chains, as you suggested."

"We must bring them to the Bure Kalou." Suzanne looked at the Princess' youthful face. "You know this is a test, don't you?"

"Oh yes. On a great many levels, as well. Does he care at all about that damn fish?"

"I don't think so. He's over the moon at the opportunity to test you, and to test you on all the levels." Suzanne continued to look at her Princess, unsure as to how many of the levels she was aware.

"I thought as much. Is he equally aware that this is a great opportunity to test him on a number of levels?"

Suzanne looked startled. "Uh, no, I don't think so. Do you want me to let him know, ever so gently?"

"I don't think that will be necessary. I am sure I can do it perfectly well myself, thank you," said Sara sweetly. "What is the Bure Kalou?"

"It's the odd building, the tall one on the rocks. That is, well, not a church exactly, but where the priest, the Bete, lives and worships. I don't quite understand it all."

They turned and watched the Bosun bringing the prisoners up the beach. She was gentle with them, being fond of Pat and she genuinely liked Hinatea and Silmatea. They clanked as they walked, eyes downcast, the gashes all over Pat red and angry with inflammation. Without speaking, Sara led them to the Bure Kalou where the Great Ratu sat waiting, the entire population of not just the town but the neighbouring villages sat around in a semi-circle, watching the proceedings.

The Great Ratu was in his finery, grass skirt, shell necklace interposed with the mummified fingers of enemies killed personally in battle and his hair done up into a magnificent frizz, with flowers interlaced through the strands. He watched expressionlessly as the prisoners were marched up and displayed in front of him.

On either side of him stood two enormous warriors, naked torsos gleaming in the sun where they were freshly oiled, massive muscles coiled under the skin and holding the wicked Vituan war clubs, dainty sticks with a crook in them, and a raised ridge at the end for smashing open skulls. These were the Ratu's guards and his executioners.

The Princess watched the Bosun array the prisoners, then turned to the Great Ratu and spoke loudly in the trade language for all to hear.

"Great Ratu of Vitua, we bring before you the prisoners. We accept our responsibility not just for the prisoners, but for their actions, as we have brought them to your lands." The Ratu's eyes flashed at her with interest, and she continued. "While I regret the misunderstanding that has caused the death of your Guardian, I am delighted to have this opportunity to see and learn the justice and wisdom of Ratu Ilikimi Nailatikau, the Great Ratu of Vitu Levu, who is famed far and wide for his fairness and good governance."

The Ratu grunted at that, he liked to think he was famous for being a vicious fighter who massacred his enemies. He waved his hand, and asked for the prisoners to be unchained. He looked at them closely, grunting in disapproval of the rough canvas clothes they were wearing. Rat did not meet his eye, looking down at his scuffling feet, while Pat's eyes rested on the horizon and he didn't seem to be present, his mind ranging elsewhere. Hinatea and Silmatea looked him straight in the eye, standing tall, proud and not particularly repentant.

The Ratu spoke first in Vituan, for the majority of his audience, then repeated himself in the trade language. He recounted what everybody knew, how the four had come ashore with the Reef Guardian making no attempt to hide their actions. He asked the prisoners to tell what they had done, and Hinatea stepped forward and recounted the fishing trip, in simple, stark terms that were the more dramatic for their brevity. Pat looked up briefly when she admitted they had not taken a grandfather before, but had the stories of their forefathers. Under questioning from the Ratu, she revealed the sad tale of Moana's end which made Pat blink.

Sara didn't think the questioning very thorough, but on the other hand it wasn't as if the facts were in dispute. She wondered if it would be possible to save Pat, appreciating that the prisoners were clearly reconciled to receiving a death penalty, each handling the thought in their own way, Rat very badly.

There was a slight commotion in the crowd, as a tall youth stood up, immediately followed by another from a different location. The Ratu frowned at them, but they picked their way through the seated watchers and stood beside Pat. The first was Maru, and he looked at the Ratu and spoke in Vituan. The Ratu looked pained briefly, but nodded.

"Maru and Wiwik just claimed responsibility for Pat and the others breaking *tabu*," Suzanne whispered to Sara. "Say they will share their punishment, they should have been with them. Makes it hard for the Ratu."

"Brave boys," whispered back Sara, her eyes full of unshed tears.

The Ratu closed the questioning abruptly and stood. He turned to the crowd and spoke at length in Vituan. They all nodded their heads and made gestures of approval. From the corner of her eye, Sara noted Suzanne trying not to smile and wondered. The Ratu switched to the trade language, looking Sara straight in the eye.

"I blame myself for this incident," he surprisingly announced. "It is a misunderstanding caused by being different peoples. It often happens, and I should have foreseen it. Our peoples are too alike, we think the same way and get on together so well that we forget how different you are.

"In future, all visitors to our island who leave the town must have a kai Viti accompanying them, to ensure they understand the correct customs. This will ensure no repetition of this affair nor the breaking of tabu.

"Now we must hear the words of the *Bete* who will decide the *soro*, what must be done to placate the gods." The Great Ratu sat down heavily, his guards remained standing on either side.

For a moment there was silence. A lone, quavering voice split it, an old man at the back raising his voice in song. One by one, others joined in, till most were singing, but not the Ratu nor his guards. Tears were rolling down Suzanne's face, though she didn't bother to translate, and Sara could see many tear-bedewed cheeks amongst the kai Viti women. As the song went on, the Ratu slumped slightly where he was sitting, and with his frame diminishing, Sara's hopes followed. Desperately, she searched for a way to save the fishermen.

The Bure Kalou was a peculiar building, built on a bed of rocks themselves higher than a man. A ladder led up to the entrance, simply a woven bamboo screen in the front wall. The building on the rocks was a simple narrow box with a roof like a tall, thin pyramid, not much smaller at the top than the bottom and about twice as high as it was across. The screen moved slightly and a head stuck out from behind it. The figure came out from the room, turned and came backwards down the ladder to the ground. The Princess looked at the Bete with interest.

He was a mature man, but slightly younger than the Ratu, she guessed. Unlike the Ratu, he was thin, and his hair was quite short. He wore an elaborate grass skirt, and his chest was painted with an intricate red and white design. A long snake of woven leaves was around his neck and trailing down on either side of his chest.

He ignored the foreigners and made his way to stand in front of the Ratu.

"The Guardian of the Reef is an Elder God, a Kalou Vu. An insult to him is an insult to all Gods," the Bete said abruptly in Vituan. "I shall tell his story." A sigh went up from the audience. Suzanne translated his words for Sara and the Captain, and she noted that Maru was doing the same for the fishermen.

"Kaduvu looked down on the kai Viti and he was pleased. He enjoyed the daughters of the kai Viti and fathered the line of the Great Ratu. He knew that the shark god, Dakuwaqa, was hunting for victims and determined to protect his people. He entered the body of a Giant Octopus, and waited by the entrance to the reef. Dakuwaqa came to the reef, swimming swiftly to come in and go up the river to eat the kai Viti. Kaduvu grabbed him with four tentacles as he went past, using the other four tentacles to hang onto the rocks of the reef. Dakuwaqa was a proud god! He was strong, he was big, he was fierce; he beat every god he faced. But he could not beat Kaduvu.

"Kaduvu squeezed him till the great god yelled, and cried for mercy. Kaduvu kept squeezing, until Dakuwaqa cried that if Kaduvu released him, he would never eat the kai Viti again. Kaduvu thought about that, and decided it was good. He released Dakuwaqa who swam away immediately.

"Since that day, no kai Viti has been eaten by a shark and we can swim where we like in these islands, safe from sharks."

The Bete seemed to have grown while telling his tale, and was striding around the sand in front of the rapt villagers. He was working himself into a rage, and pointed dramatically at the fishermen.

"Desecrators!" he shouted. "Murderers! Our Guardian has gone and we are not safe to fish and swim in the sea!" A murmur went through the crowd, and Hinatea's eyes flashed angrily as Maru translated. She took a step forward, Silmatea a step behind her. She reached up, put a hand in the collar of her rough shirt, and yanked, ripping it off and leaving her naked. Silmatea did the same. Standing tall and proud in her national costume, Hinatea spoke to the amazed and horrified Bete in the trade language, which he did not understand.

"I swim where I want and I am safe from shark because I good swimmer and shark killer. Grandfather is not god. Is food and dangerous fish. Stupid tabu. I think you wrong, stupid man, not speak to gods."

The Bete didn't understand but was inflating rapidly and turning purple at the flagrant disrespect and heresy of this awful girl standing naked in the sight of the gods. An assistant whispered a translation to him, and he understood why the Ratu was trying to hide a smile.

The Bete snatched up a war club from a nearby warrior and stalked towards Hinatea, his mouth working uncontrollably. Hinatea watched him come, a slight smile on her face and turned slightly so she was side on, ready. Pat and Silmatea moved up slightly on either side of her, Maru and Wiwik just behind them. The two kai Viti blanching in terror at how the gods would respond, but staying with their friends.

The Bete suddenly whirled in a circle, the war club went flying into the crowd where it was caught by a warrior, and he collapsed on the ground, his body humping and shuffling while he frothed at the mouth and screamed inarticulately.

The crowd gave a great shout, and Maru whispered to Hinatea, "The god takes him."

The Bete twisted horribly on the ground, then pulled himself to his feet, and looked at Hinatea. His eyes were turned in on themselves so only the white showed, and despite herself, Hinatea took a step backwards.

The Bete spoke. In the trade language.

"You are right, brave girl from faraway. He does not speak to me. But I can use his body to speak, which is why he is a Bete." The voice of the god was rough and dark, but it had depth, substance and rolled around the village and the beach. Many in the crowd threw themselves face down. The god had not spoken like this for a few years. Usually he took the Bete is a far less dramatic fashion, and spoke very respectfully of the Bete.

"I did beat Dakuwaqa and my people are free of sharks as a result. But I do not live in the octopus, the Grandfather as you name it like my cousin does. If I did you would not have killed him. But his death called me and here I am. That is the true purpose of the Guardian of the Reef, which the Bete must remember in future." He turned from the fishermen and spoke to the crowd and to the Ratu. "Hear me, Ratu, Great Grandson. Killing the Guardian is not tabu. You must do it every five years, and replace him with a young one. I will enjoy the contest. It must be done as the girl did it, with no weapon. And afterwards the victors must walk the stones in my honour. As these ones will. Their kai Viti friends will walk with them to show the way. They will walk tonight, and then I shall know the girl."

There was a stunned silence, before Hinatea stepped forward. "Oh Great Kadavu, I am honoured that you select me. Please know that I am under a geas from my own Gods, to travel the world and protect another, important to our Gods. While the geas is upon me, I cannot bear a child."

The God laughed. "Wise as well as beautiful. Very well, Ratu, you will send your youngest wife to accompany this girl and she will bear the next Ratu so I strengthen the line." He looked down at the Bete's emaciated chest. "I shall choose another vicar tonight, maybe even you, Ratu." And the Bete slumped to the ground like a rag doll.

The silence stretched. It was broken by Pat, who spoke low to Maru but loud enough for all to hear.

"What did he mean by walking the stones, Maru?"

"The blessed of the Gods walk over fire as a ritual," answered

Maru, still staring at the Bete. "We cannot eat coconut today, really we should fast till after the ceremony. It is not usual to do it so quickly. But we trust in the Great God Kadavu."

Sara and Suzanne stood together looking at the fire with some incredulity. Young men were pulling it away with green sticks and vines, chanting "O-vulo-vulo" as they did so. As they cleared away the burning logs, they revealed a bed of large stones, the heat shimmering off them as they glowed dully in the huge pit.

A long tree fern branch was laid on the stones, pointing at the Bete who was overseeing the process, looking rather worse for wear. He shouted angrily at two men who were pulling a vine across the stones, easing them into place. Seemingly in a fit of bad temper, he proceeded to jump onto some of the stones. Suzanne gripped Sara's wrist without realising it, but he just jumped out of the incandescent heat with no ill effects.

The people were arriving now, standing around the fire place in a big circle. The Great Ratu arrived to stand with the girls. A gap had been left at one side and the Bete went there now, adjusting the branch to his satisfaction. The young men were now placing bundles of grass around the fire pit. The Bete checked them, and shouted suddenly and loudly, "Vuto-O!" Suzanne jumped.

Maru appeared from the bushes, followed in single file by Hinatea, Pat, Silmatea, Rat and Wiwik. The Bete pulled the branch from the fire, smoking badly, and laid it to one side. Maru did not stop but walked straight into the fire pit, walking over the stones in a circle, followed by the others. Hinatea and Silmatea were of course naked, each with a serene smile on their faces, while the others wore grass skirts. Each looked confidently forward and strode over the hot stones without looking down. Pat and Rat followed their girls, looking straight at the back of their heads. As Maru completed a circuit, he moved into the middle of the fire while, at a shout from the Bete, the young men threw the bundles of grass onto the outer stones, where they smouldered. Maru and Wiwik started a chant in Vituan, while Hinatea and Silmatea sang their own song in Pahippian, and the Princess could make out that Pat and Rat were chanting, 'cool, deep sea' over and over again as they marched in the middle of the fire, and then Maru was leading them out.

Later, at the feast, Pat found himself seated between Hinatea and Sara, opposite Suzanne and the Ratu. Hinatea and the Ratu were discussing the differences between their fire walking, while Pat was finding it very difficult to explain to the girls and the Captain exactly what he had done and why it hadn't hurt.

"I thought they weren't really hot, at first," he said, "because we had these little amulets of dry grass tied to our ankles and they didn't burn, but then they threw the grass on the stones and they did burn! Weird! Hinatea got me into the same state of being that I go into when I shoot arrows, which is a sort of higher plane, and then she said the God looked after me. I don't know. I just felt really strong and powerful. And look! All the inflammation from my cuts has gone, nearly healed too."

Battle

The next few mornings were busy, though they devoted the afternoons to surfing. Prospectors went out with burly warriors and came back with not just iron ore, but gold and copper too. The Dwarven smiths built a furnace and started instructing volunteers, one of whom, Waru, promptly burnt off all his impressive mass of hair. Rather than take this as a mark of disgrace, as customary, he roared this was his badge of acceptance by the fire god. All the other apprentice smiths burnt off their hair.

Captain Larroche and Taufik spent hours going over charts with the local fishermen and war leaders, some of whom travelled great distances, and helped create accurate charts. Once they understood charts, they pinpointed shoals, unfriendly tribes, currents and irregular winds.

Sara tested the military prowess of the kai Viti, and started training them in modern tactics, bringing in the soldiers and the Spakka to assist. It proved easier to teach them axecraft, not dissimilar to their warclubs, and the Spakka excelled with the weapon. The kai Viti fought individually, as did the Spakka, so Mactravis taught them to use a shield and form a shield wall. This took a long time, but the warriors soon appreciated her expertise and picked up on the respect with which the soldiers treated her. They called her the Little Queen, decided she needed a personal guard of picked warriors and set up a competition to choose them. This caused a squabble with the Spakka, forcing Sara to intercede. Both the title and the guard, led by the Ratu's son, Maciu, irritated her beyond words.

Maciu attended her at every opportunity, arriving aboard ship early to take her away on his canoe along with the guard. Sara found herself not just anticipating his arrival, but taking care with her appearance, noticing his reaction to different outfits and ways of brushing her hair. She took care not to ask Suzanne for advice, on the few occasions they spoke each day. Hinatea decided to protect her from Vituan treachery and two girls accompanied her everywhere, their presence developing into further irritation. She mused to herself, *'More security attends me in friendly Vitua than ever back in Praesidium where Count Rotherstone hunts me. And I thought I would get some extra freedom on this trip.'*

Pat tried to teach the kai Viti archery, with singularly unsuccessful results. No suitable wood grew on the island. Bamboo could make a bow, when split, but not a powerful war bow and so the kai Viti disdained it. While they could send an arrow with great force, none of them possessed a knack for aiming. It didn't help that they would all close their eyes as they fired and shout loudly to frighten the spirit of the arrow into going faster.

They concluded his skill was supernatural, so there was no point in trying to copy him.

Instead he delighted in their field craft and he and the Pahippian warrior girls joined the hunters on long treks where they exchanged tracking skills and scaled the cliffs for the prized eggs of the big booby birds. These mobbed them as they robbed the nests, inflating their scarlet neck pouches and screaming in their ears.

Suzanne moved into the Ratu's hut, joining his seven wives who welcomed her with pleasure and spent time teaching her the language, customs and bedroom specialities, none of which last were new to her. They welcomed her reciprocal lessons and the Ratu began to look tired.

The Ratu had an official hairdresser. This was his only job, as the Ratu's hair was sacred and hands which touched it could do no other work. The hairdresser even needed to be hand fed by his wife. The Ratu appointed him as Suzanne's hairdresser as well, and she enjoyed a very soothing morning ritual, watched by many of the village, as he set about repairing the damage to his handiwork inflicted by the Ratu during the night. The Ratu felt it important that her hair stood high and proud to show her strength and magic, so no other poor male would fall into the mistake of attacking her.

Various members of the crew went out with the locals on different tasks. Sam found the pigs fascinating and the kai Viti were equally fascinated by his. The whole village came to enjoy the spectacle as his boar impregnated their sows, to great cheers. Not so many came to watch the cockerel treading the local hens, and Sam found himself hard pressed to stop the locals using his cockerel in a cock fight with horrifically sharp bamboo blades strapped to the legs.

Bart and several of his friends went out with the fishermen and spent long hours arguing about different netting and line techniques. The kai Viti used the same coral fish traps as the Pahippians, which harvested fish with every tide. The fishing boats were dugout canoes, with an outrigger and a triangular sail. The sailors spent some time working on improvements and showing the fishermen how to build jolly boats.

The smiths created an axe first, to the huge excitement of the kai Viti. Their weapons were spears and clubs, the spears either fire-hardened or flint headed. One blow with the new steel axe went straight through a banana tree so immediately needed to be tested on a real wood tree. The ringing sound of the blade on a kapok tree brought people running including the Ratu. He appropriated the axe after watching the smith for a few minutes, and with a couple of lusty blows went straight through the trunk to massive applause and delight from the crowd.

Sara asked the smiths and their apprentices to concentrate on making shields and war axes, along with spear heads and found her guard would do exactly as she said, showing incredible discipline under as difficult conditions as she could create. After a trial judged by the Ratu in which her six guards withstood and 'killed' an attack by a dozen warriors using the traditional tactics, all the warriors volunteered for the new training and the soldiers became busy. Sara's guards became section leaders and started training their own sections. Finally Sara lost her personal guard.

The Spakka needed training as well. Their tactics differed from Harrhein tactics, much more individual and down to feats of skill. Janis spent hours with Mactravis, working out suitable tactics to incorporate into their training. Esbech and Stiphleek found themselves section leaders, a promotion that occasioned considerable suspicion.

Sara strode into the village one morning looking radiant, beaming smiles around, closely attended by Maciu and two Pahippian girls. Maciu's eyes seemed to fixate on the Princess.

Suzanne's eyes narrowed. She invited Sara off for a chat, waving the guards away, and made them both some tea. Sara grinned, looking forward to sharing her news. She accepted the steaming tea and sipped, spluttering at the bitterness before looking with accusing eyes at Suzanne.

"This is the tea for stopping babies! How did you know? I wanted to surprise you."

"Your face rather gives you away, darling, while Maciu has that particularly silly look of the man helplessly in love."

"Does he really?" Sara craned her neck to inspect him.

"It was yesterday, wasn't it? When you went off surfing. How did you manage to get off alone?"

"It was a mistake, actually. I didn't intend anything." Sara bubbled out the story, delighted to confide in Suzanne, but determined to avoid the graphic details Suzanne included in her descriptions of the Ratu's performance.

"Hinatea went fishing, all the girls wanted to go as well, so I sent them off. The men carried the food and Maciu and I decided to take the cliff climb to a new beach. The men took the main path with their burdens which is much further. I told them not to worry. The cliff path went by the cutest little cove; Maciu said the deep water was warm and great for swimming. He dared me to jump in from on top of the cliff. It was quite high."

Sara smiled as she relived the moment.

"You dived, didn't you? Little show-off!"

"Oh yes. He has never seen a dive, never mind from so high and was so impressed. He jumped after me, swam up to me and started to go on about how great I was. So I kissed him." Sara blushed. "I'm not sure why, but I felt so good and pleased with myself. The water was deep and we sank down quite a way before I needed to come up for air. I was worried we were too deep but he pulled me up and while I was gasping for breath he pulled me towards the shore. As soon as his feet touched the sand he started to kiss me again, and, well, he didn't stop."

"What, he did you in the water? Naughty boy!" Suzanne arched her eyebrows, smiling. She loved this and readied to press for all the gory details.

"Well, on the edge. He started in the water and we finished on the sand. Suzanne, I smuggled him into my room last night. He swam ashore before dawn. We were very quiet. "

"Were you indeed? No doubt the entire ship heard you screaming and the Captain will tell you off at some point."

"You think so? So there is no point in hiding? Can I just move him into my room?"

"Well," said Suzanne, "I am not sure about that. We don't have anyone who is totally conservative now the Captain has had his epiphany and nobody knows what Walters will do. Probably try to marry the two of you."

"I was thinking. He is a prince, you know."

"It's more than a little early to think long term, darling, and won't your father want a little more political match for you? Besides, he won't inherit the Vituan throne."

"I will never marry officially," said Sara, surprising Suzanne. "My father and I discuss the politics all the time. Far better to promise always and never carry through, which lets us keep so many different factions trading off each other. None of them are powerful enough individually to make marriage worth our while. If I can turn up with an army of a thousand kai Viti in return for marrying this Prince, that makes the contract worthwhile.."

"The church will never accept him. They set their hearts on you marrying a true believer like Raphael." Suzanne knew how far advanced the plans were, but refrained from mentioning this inflammatory news.

"That asshole! As if I would let him touch me. A thousand kai Viti axemen with their discipline will shut them up. Thank you for the tea, Suzanne, time to chat with the Ratu, I think. I will move Maciu in later, thanks for the advice."

Suzanne felt a little nettled, the conversation not following quite her intended path, and she found herself left unsure. Sara would change from little girl to sophisticated courtier in the blink of an eye, so unsettling.

Sara installed Maciu brazenly and openly. She did this so casually that nobody turned a hair, not even Captain Larroche. Suzanne watched without comment, her help unnecessary. She reflected that Sara made a pretty good ruler all ready, persuading people to follow her desires without thought.

On the ninth day, the Ratu discussed tactics with Sara, Mactravis and most of his senior warriors, while nearby Suzanne and Captain Larroche compared Harrhein pottery with the style the local women called Lapita.

A warrior came running up the path, dropped in front of the Ratu and started reporting with his face in the sand. The Ratu stood, fury contorting his features, kicking the warrior's head.

"What is the matter, Ratu?" Sara asked.

"The filth from the outer islands attack us. They take two fishing canoes, also the fishermen, including two of your men."

"Where is their village ? Will they take the captives there and what will they do with them?"

"They will take them to their village and they will eat them." said the Ratu, with a final furious kick and the poor bearer of bad news.

"How big is the village and how many warriors?"

"Maybe two hundred warriors. Same size as this one. The island is three days away by canoe."

"Let me take a hundred of your warriors and we will flatten the village and take our people back."

"A hundred? Not enough! We do not have the power to take their village. We need three or four hundred, they are behind a wall. They fear us."

"A hundred will do the trick. We have big catapults on the ship to bombard them, and with the new tactics we will take them. Besides, our warriors have other talents you have not yet seen."

"Ilikimi, if you tell Sara the situation at the village, she can plan what she needs to rescue our people and take revenge," said Suzanne, unerringly getting him on board with the use of the word revenge.

"Do you have anyone who has been there to build a model?" Sara asked.

"What is a model?"

After an explanation, they sent for Walters along with his charts and Captain Larroche came to join them. Both were pretty much recovered now, Captain Larroche having reclaimed the captaincy on board, while leaving the girls in charge of negotiations. Walters' lapses into religion became less frequent, particularly as he had persuaded an older crew girl to move into his cabin. He proceeded to build a scale model of the enemy village from his charts and details filled in by the kai Viti who knew it - not many, and usually from a raid. Sara patiently questioned them all, creating the defences in the model.

She turned to the Captain. "Can you send a boat here," she pointed out a spot on the chart remote from the enemy village, "the pinnace, drop off Grey Fox, Pat and Mot in the evening, pick them up in the morning and meet with the Queen on her way?"

He nodded and she turned to Corporal Strachan. "Corporal, take four men, bowmen or crossbows, and create a secure outpost at the drop off point to cover them in case they need to come back in a hurry. Make sure the post is invisible to anyone, even from a metre away. Full camouflage. You come back to the ship, with Grey Fox when he reports. Pat, Grey Fox, take your time, memorise this model. We will take it with us on the ship, you must update it with as much information as you can. Do you want to take Mot, Pat?"

Pat nodded and looked at the model intently.

"Mactravis," went on Sara, "I think we are best landing the troops on the beach front by boat, in silence before dawn. The Queen Rose will signal the attack with the ballistas. A few bolts will keep their heads down. Then a shield wall, three deep, advance up the main road to the gate. We don't know the depth of the sea so we will assume the Queen Rose is unable to knock the gate down or bottle them inside."

She looked up at the Ratu, for whom Suzanne translated the conversation while his leading warriors listened.

"Ratu, I assume the enemy will attack when they see only 100 warriors on the beach, even with the shields which they won't have seen before?"

The Ratu answered, "They will attack for sure. They see shields before, many try them, but not as strong as these. They will expect to break them."

"Good. Mactravis, you take half your lads up the left, Sergeant Russell takes half up the right, divide any other archers from the ship between you. There is a small hillock here from which you can take them in enfilade. Russell, you will need most of the crossbow men as there is no cover closer than these trees." She pointed at the model which showed Russell would be firing from over 150 paces.

"Pat, you and Grey Fox are detached, take Rat with you. Your job is to make sure the rear gate is open when we arrive and to cut off escape to the interior."

"Janis, I want the Spakka as the reserve, ready to be thrown in as needed. Also I need ten fast runners to take commands. Hinatea, that's your girls." They nodded, looking at the map.

"Questions anyone?"

Pat thought a moment, then spoke. "Perryn. Need him."

Sara raised an eyebrow.

"Water fire," said Pat. "He can make it. Will use some of the yellow flowers."

"You've got him, good thought," said Sara, while Suzanne explained to the astonished kai Viti that water fire was a chemical fire which burnt underwater and could not be put out.

"Where will you be?" Mactravis asked and everyone looked at her.

"Leading the shield wall," said Sara flatly.

For the first time there was dissent, everyone speaking at once.

Lieutenant Mactravis cut through the argument, speaking plainly. "Ma'am, you must command from behind the shield wall. Place the runners and your personal guard around you. You would be a weak link in the wall, without the physical strength of these people. You would get men killed."

Sara's eyes narrowed and she shuffled in anger.

"I lead Shield Wall" the Ratu stated. "Then they attack for sure." He smiled. "New axes will be fun."

For the first time Sara looked worried, and Suzanne knew why. The shield wall needed discipline and she didn't think the Ratu possessed any.

The Ratu's eyes twinkled. "Not to worry. I do what you say. You War Ratu, you in charge." He laughed. "You forget I am the Great Ratu of the Islands, instead I am best axeman in Shield Wall!"

A roar went up from the Kai Viti, some acclamation but most disagreeing and pointing out that in fact they themselves were without question the best axeman in the wall.

"Very well," said Sara. "If no further questions, scouts off, and load the ship. We sail in 30 minutes."

Pat spoke again. "I want Wiwik and Mara too."

"Your friends?"

"Yes. Trackers. They are good at night, good fighters." Pat still didn't believe in words.

"Fine by me. Ratu, do you agree?"

He looked at Pat. "Why you choose them?"

"They are your best night fighters," answered Pat without hesitation.

The Ratu smiled. "Mara my son. Good, you take them."

People went in all directions, leaving Sara and Mactravis. He looked at her and smiled. "Just like your father, always want to be in the thick of battle. You know damn well you shouldn't be in the shield wall."

She stared at him. "You knew damn well I wanted to be. That's why you asked." He nodded. "How did you guess."

He smiled. "You look like your father and act like him. He saved my life once. You fight like him too. Same mannerisms in your sword play, though I would judge you to be considerably better, which is saying something. The way you give orders. The way you outfit yourself and clean your weapons, pure Kingdom Royal Horse. All just like your father. And he would throw a strop when we would stop him from playing silly buggers."

"Don't remember your record showing you spent any time at court to develop this courtier diplomat double talk."

"Had to wet nurse a few of your relatives over the years."

They walked down to the ship together.

The Bosun peered into the darkness, ready to move at the slightest noise. She could make out the beach, and hear the quiet hissing as the small waves ran up it. She couldn't see any sign of the scouts.

"Where the hell are they?" she whispered to her mate, crouched beside her and also peering into the night. "Do you think they made it?"

"No bloody idea," he whispered back. "Bet they can hear us whispering though."

"I guess," said the Bosun. "I didn't hear a bloody thing, not even the dog shaking itself."

A hundred yards away, Pat smiled in the dark. The whispers did carry over the sea at night, and he appreciated the Bosun's concern. Mot had swum ashore and gone into the brush without shaking herself - he knew she wouldn't till she finished searching the area. Pat stretched out naked on a rock, letting the worst of the water dry off. He scraped himself with a strigil he carried for the purpose - a small curved metal knife which picked up the water and removed it as he stroked the strigil over his flesh. Dry, or as dry as he could get, he slipped into his fighting garb.

Leather moccasins, thin and sensitive, he could feel tracks in the ground through them and they let him never, ever tread on a stick or even a dry leaf. Leather knee protectors, for when he crawled, with matching elbow protectors. On his left arm, the leather projected down his forearm as protection from his bowstring. He wore a leather belt that supported a leather loin cloth and kept his groin protected and secure. Nothing else, for Pat hated cloth when stalking - it brushed against leaves and made one hell of noise. Skin did not give the same result. But it did gleam, and he applied an ointment to darken his skin, removing all shine. He had mixed in some pigshit, giving him a slight odour, to Mot's delight.

Mot returned and thumped her tail. He ruffled her hair, and let out a noise like a sleepy seabird, a noise he and the kai Viti settled on after much debate and practise.

The others drifted up to join him like so many ghosts. More than he intended, because Hinatea, Silmatea and Trieste refused to be left behind. They checked each other's ointment with exquisite care, including the kai Viti whose dark skin otherwise shone in the starlight. Grey Fox refused the pigshit, and instead used his own from some roots he unearthed, giving him a rather piney odour. Pat found he could tell each apart by the smell as much as anything else.

Pat held his hand out, thumb up, and the others touched it, all together. Pat nodded, clicked his fingers at Mot and headed out, down a trail from the beach. Mot ranged ahead and he went swiftly, trusting in her nose. The others followed fifty paces apart, Grey Fox bringing up the rear. Corporal Strachan and his four soldiers set about finding the ideal location for the safety outpost and setting up.

The night was quiet, a gentle breeze sloughing through the few trees, with the noise of cicadas buzzing constantly. Pat registered all these noises, following the route of a nearby stream by the frog calls, cataloguing them and listening for the pockets of silence that meant men. It was warm, and he noticed one distinct advantage from his ointment - no mosquitoes.

Coconut trees sky lined themselves against the starry night sky, about two miles away. Pat thought this would be the village, a thought confirmed in his mind as he realised the path led through cultivated fields. He noted a rat scuttling off the path at his approach and smelt something rank which he didn't recognise.

The path was sand, with a coarse grass at the edges and he picked up speed to a dog trot, still moving without a sound. He scanned the fields as he went, worried a farmer might be sleeping by his crops to protect it from the rats. Seeing a little hut just off the path, a dark shape in the moonless night, he stopped and slipped to the ground, making the chirruping sound of a cicada as he moved silently and slowly along the ground. Mot responded to his call and shoved him with her nose. He waved at the hut and she was away, Pat following at half pace.

Mot disappeared into the hut, he could hear a slight scuffling and scratching, and she reappeared swallowing something. Pat frowned, annoyed, guessing it was poi, left by a farmer for his meal tomorrow. Mot shot off down the path, waving her tail to show she knew perfectly well he was annoyed with her and didn't give a damn.

He kept her in sight as they approached the village and scanned for a base point, deciding on a tall palm near the path, a good five hundred yards short of the village, with a depression behind the roots. He ducked in and waited for the others to join him, lying on the raised lip of the depression, formed where another palm had fallen over and pushed the roots into the sky.

They came in one by one, and once all arrived, he leaned over, touched Wiwik and Mara's shoulders, pointed to the right, indicating the left to Grey Fox and Rat. Hinatea and the girls he nodded to - their agreed duty to keep watch from a circle further out. He pointed to a bright star, moved his hand a span to indicate two hours, then pointed to the hollow. The others all nodded and he snaked out of the hollow, moving straight towards the village.

Moving with even more care, his eyes constantly moving to

avoid after images, Pat eased towards the dark boundary of the village which he guessed to be the wall. Mot slipped back to touch his hand in reassurance. Knowing this meant no guard, Pat glided up to the gap in the wall, his feet feeling for branches before putting his weight on them. A rough door lay inside the compound where it could be pulled across the gap if required. The nearest hut was thirty yards away, a stuttering snore coming from inside.

At this point Pat realised, despite all his caution, he was discovered. An angry eye glared at him, while its owner snuffled in his direction and a boar came through some bushes with an angry squeal, to stand in the path looking round in fury, snuffling in the sand.

Pat faded into the wall, ready to shin up if necessary, and grinned to himself, realising this boar had detected the musk of a rival boar in his ointment.

The boar's angry grunting cut off abruptly as he found himself snout to snout with Mot, a Mot with her hackles up. Now, a boar will see off most dogs, but Mot wasn't most dogs and knew just what pigs could and could not do. The boar looked at Mot uncertainly, snarled to expose his tusks, and slowly backed up, retreating under the house from whence came a loud squealing as the boar took out his frustration on a junior boar. Pat realised a lot of pigs lived under the house, all stirring about now.

An angry, sleepy shout came from the hut above and somebody emptied a bucket of water through the floor slats on to the pigs, causing more squeals and angry shouts now from the next huts.

Pat decided he had looked enough and faded back out of the entrance, keeping close enough to record what happened in the village.

A gentle thunk wafted up from the darkness below the boarding rail announced the return of the pinnace and Grey Fox came up a rope ladder as if walking a road, Corporal Strachan following considerably more gingerly. He knocked on the Captain's cabin.

"Come in," came a rumble from inside and he slipped inside. The Captain sat at his desk, talking with the Ratu, Lieutenant Mactravis and Sara.

"Ah, well done that man," said the Captain. "All sorted?"

"Sir," replied Grey Fox, "I need to make some slight changes to the model."

Mactravis nodded assent, pushed back his chair and went to watch Grey Fox make his adjustments, followed by the others. He smiled at Sara. "Grey Fox is the only person on board who speaks less than Pat!"

Grey Fox looked at him reproachfully and made minute adjustments to the beach, then remodelled the wall at the rear of the village, showing the gate and the paths. While he worked, the Captain's servant came up and placed a glass of fruit juice beside him. He nodded his thanks and continued, placing the carvings of huts in various positions, changed a few round for size, and indicated the one by the gate. "Pigs."

Mactravis rolled his eyes. "What do you mean, Grey Fox?"

"Pat found lots of pigs here, under hut."

"Ready for the victory feast," interjected the Ratu. "Instead we will eat them tomorrow!"

"Can we make use of them?" asked Sara. "Are they locked up?"

"No," replied Grey Fox. "Pat plans to drive them through the village."

"Perfect," breathed Sara; she looked up at him. "Does Pat need a signal?"

Grey Fox just looked at her, his head giving the tiniest shake.

The Ratu studied the model with great interest. "This very good," he declared. "I will use this again."

"I am glad you like it, Ratu," said Sara who turned to Grey Fox. "Thank you Grey Fox, good work by the team." She smiled at him, while he returned her look without expression. "Fine, get your gear, collect Perryn and go. Take the outpost people with you." She turned back to the Ratu as Grey Fox left, the door closing without a sound.

"Ratu, we will teach you how to make them, but first we will show you the entire attack planning method. Now we can make our final plans, which we will tell the team leaders, and they will borrow the model to pass their own orders on to their teams."

"Hurr, I understand. Is good. Then I keep?"

"We'll bring it back to your town for you. Mactravis, how in the wide world do you make Grey Fox happy? Must be the only soldier

I ever saw who didn't appreciate me telling him he had done well."

"Oh, he liked it. He will tell Pat and the others what you said, word for word. He will even get the inflection of your voice perfectly. He just never lets his feelings show in his face."

For Perryn, the following few hours would enshrine themselves in his nightmares. Sitting in the pinnace, it was surprisingly cold, especially as he slowly became soaking wet from the spray. The unfamiliar small boat movement jostled him and for some reason he felt intensely seasick. Normally he knew enough mind tricks to sort out problems of this kind, but with the impending action he couldn't concentrate, so just sat on the bench, smelling the brine, the nauseating odour coming from Grey Fox's ointment and what resembled pigshit for some reason.

The boat slowed down, and came to a halt. He raised his head, hopelessly, unable to see a thing in the pitch dark and opened his mouth to ask a question. Immediately a strong, smelly hand came across his face and he gagged, unable to even wonder how Grey Fox had known he was about to speak. Belatedly, he remembered being told not to make any noise at all.

At the insistent pulling, he rose to a crouch, and tried to squeal as Grey Fox ripped his robe off him, the hand again cutting off his cry of alarm. His hands automatically went to cover his groin, and he felt physically sick as a horrible memory from his early years boarding in the monastery came back to him. Numbly, he crawled over the side, convinced he would drown and rather looking forward to meeting his God. He eased into the water, paddling quietly as he vaguely remembered his instructions and panicked as he noticed the disappearance of the pinnace, nor had the slightest idea where the shore lay.

A strong hand grabbed him, turned him and he swam in the direction indicated. He tended to drift off to one side, he realised, as the hand kept coming out of nowhere and adjusting his direction.

The hand gripped his shoulder and pulled back. Startled, he stopped swimming and tried to tread water, to feel sand under his feet. His toe knuckles hit something and it hurt! Miserable, he started out of the sea, shivering with the cold. Hands grasped him, pulled him along most un-gently. He couldn't see a thing, except a vague sparkling from the stars. A large, fearsome shadow loomed out of the dark and he flinched before recognising a bush. The hands manoeuvred him into a space and he felt a cloth being run over him. Warmth came from it, and he began to feel a little better.

"Where's my robe?" He whispered, as quietly as he could.

Cloth was shoved into his hands, and he hastily donned it, then squawked a protest as he realised it was a LOT shorter than expected and hands were now roughly applying the pigshit to HIS body!!!! Ineffectually, he tried to push them off.

"For fuck's sake Perryn!" Pat hissed in his ear. "Stop playing the fool!"

Perryn had never heard anger in Pat's voice before, and he had never heard him swear either, and the anger rattled him more than anything else. This served to steady him, and he stood quietly while they performed shitty indignities to his body. His briefing came back to him, and he remembered the ointment to stop him shining. Ointment! He thought angrily, it's bloody pigshit!

His anger brought him back to himself and he took stock, doing a mental audit. Ah, this was the problem, fear, getting in the way. Deliberately, he recited a mantra, while helping apply the last of the ointment, and felt the fear recede to the depths of his mind. Once out of the way, he could bring his mental faculties back into line and cast about, feeling for the magnetic force he could use for power, and sensing for other wizards and people. All the time cursing himself as a fool for not doing this earlier.

He felt the tension in the person beside him, and realised the others had gone. He ran his hands around the ground, feeling for his bag, before remembering Pat was carrying it for him. He put out a hand as he stood and felt a breast. In shock, he recognised Trieste, and he blushed as he remembered how she had applied the pigshit to him. She pulled his arm and reluctantly he followed her down the path. He trod on a stone, which hurt, and he wished for his sandals, remembering Pat instructing him to go barefoot. Fortunately there weren't any more stones, Pat had said it was a soft dusty path and he wouldn't need sandals. Well, he thought, maybe not, if we were walking, but, damn it, running is something else! His toes hurt at the unaccustomed exercise, but every time he slowed, the bloody girl kicked him up the arse. She hadn't at first, but was getting annoyed at Perryn's slowness.

It went on forever, it seemed; he couldn't believe the night could last so long and it turned into a mind numbing journey of pain, as his legs turned to jelly, his feet surely bleeding with no skin left and his robe rubbing him raw wherever it touched, while his balls had shrunk up into his body to get away from the raging agony where his thighs rubbed together as he stumbled along. It was pitch dark, he couldn't see the path and Trieste kept prodding him to keep him straight, while he could hear all manner of horrible noises from either side, all of which were clearly vicious and bloodthirsty animals. One horrific bokking noise came from right beside the path and he started to jump away, but Trieste caught him and hurried him on.

Finally it ended, and she dropped him into a hollow where he was allowed to curl up in his misery.

The Bosun took a jolly boat and went to plumb the sea approaches. She eased the Queen Rose into position off the beach in front of the village. Sergeant Russell dug in his trees, creating a defensive position in less than 15 minutes while Lieutenant Mactravis' team took a boat to shore and moved on to the hill.

Sara breathed a sigh of relief to see the professionals in position to cover the landing of the kai Viti which she feared would be noisy. She listened in amazement and heard nothing as they went ashore in several boats. Not one showed any disquiet at being on the Queen Rose and they took orders superbly, forming up into a perfect shield wall on the beach as she landed with her runners and the crew coming behind her. She noticed these supposed professionals made more noise than the kai Viti.

One of the runners produced a fish oil shuttered lantern which on command she used to flash the Queen Rose. The sound of the ballistas firing was a series of thunks across the sea, and the huge bolts flew over the gap in the shield wall and thumped into the village, a couple smashing into the wall. As they landed the kai Viti let out a ferocious war cry and started to move up the beach, closing the gap with only a few stumbles. From the back of the village came awful cries, wild howling from Mot and screaming pigs. Villagers poured out of the huts, took one look at the beach and the screaming pigs milling around the village and took to their heels. A hut at the far side of the village burst into flame followed by a second, causing them to turn and run back for the beach.

The shield wall advanced at a steady pace.

A man appeared in the middle of the village, visible through the open gates, trying to stop and organise the fleeing villagers. A deep angry "Hau!" went up from the Kai Viti and Sara reckoned this was the chief. A steady stream of villagers came out of the gate, turned left and ran round the wall and off into the fields and trees in every direction. Another hut went up in flames, and the small group of villagers around the chief turned and moved towards the gate. Their numbers swelled, more joining all the time.

The shield wall came to within fifty feet of the gate and Sara started barking orders.

"Ratu! Stand firm, call them on to you!"

"Indeed War Ratu!" he cried joyfully, barked at his troops and they stopped instantly. He opened his mouth and started to sing, the shield wall crashing in with the chorus. The song was clearly deeply abusive as the villagers roared in anger and started to run at them in a massed charge. A huge fellow bounded into the lead, his face contorted with rage. He leapt high into the air, and crashed his wooden club disdainfully down on to a shield. The club smashed and the Ratu himself leaned over the wall and clinically cut deep into the unprotected shoulder, wrenching the axe out and back into position while the attacker fell to the ground without a sound, his shoulder cleaved right through with the axe reaching the heart.

All along the wall this was repeated, as men crashed into it, the shield holders, braced by five men behind them, did not move, while the second row man behind the shield holder's right leant over to the attacker's unprotected left side and cut him down.

In seconds half the villagers died and Sara was conscious of the lack of sound - only a few groans, the shouts of the villagers fading to nothing allowing the thunk of axe into flesh to be distinctly heard. The typical smell of the battlefield drifted back to her, showing some of the axe blows were going through into the guts of the attackers.

The surviving slower attackers wavered and stopped, some twenty feet short of the shield wall. Checking first that the Ratu had them under control, Sara dropped her hand to Russell and Mactravis. Crossbow bolts lanced into the villagers. Judging the moment, she called out: "Ratu! Steady and slow advance!"

He bellowed a command and the shield wall shuddered and took a step forward, the Kai Viti crashing the shields into the ground and drumming on them with the axes as they took a step, while they let out their fearsome "Hau!"

It was too much for the remaining villagers, who turned and ran.

Sara called again. "Ratu! Fast forward, into the village, keep them in squads, take prisoners!"

The Ratu shouted again and the shield wall opened, allowing the back rows to run through, unencumbered by the shields, sprinting fast up the beach and into the village, separating into squads who leapt into the huts.

Perryn was still miserable. When the dawn came, he realised he had somehow slept, and been deserted by his companions. Panicky, he started to sit up and was startled when a hand came out of nowhere and pulled him down. Pat came into focus, he couldn't understand how he hadn't seen him, he was right beside him though he seemed to blend into the ground and he begrudgingly admitted to himself the pigshit was pretty effective.

A tree wobbled in the half light, and Grey Fox materialised. The ground seemed to wobble, and Pat's scouts appeared from the bare ground, so it seemed to Perryn. Pat pulled him to his feet and they seemed to float towards the village wall. To Perryn's horror, the others promptly went in through the gate. To his relief, Pat took him to one side and up a little hill where he placed him close behind two huts, the other side of the wall. Pat somehow pushed him into the middle of a bush and pointed to two huts.

"When the pigs squeal." He breathed into Perryn's ear, pressed a sack into his hands, turned and went to the gate. From his vantage point, Perryn could see into the village, but could see nothing of Pat or his scouts. He looked around, opened the sack and checked on the contents. Yes, his bottles of firewater were there, four of them. He laid them out on the ground in front of him, taking care not to spill, and removing the sacking which kept them quiet and safe.

A thrumming sound filled the air, something made a loud sigh and he saw a hut shake. Ballista, he thought. Mot was barking, there was a weird ululating cry, lots of whistles and the pigs went mad, streaming out from under the hut, squealing as if the devils of all the hells were roasting them already. Hurriedly, Perryn threw his first bottle at the nearest hut, and watched it bounce harmlessly off the roof without breaking or spilling any liquid.

Cursing, he pulled the cork out of the second and threw it, seeing it spilling the firewater satisfactorily over the thatch, and sent a firebolt after it to set the hut ablaze. Quickly he threw the third and fourth bottles, the last with less care and he didn't notice some spill on to his arm and shoulder. Until he ignited it, whereupon he earned his first Firemage scars. Rolling on the ground didn't put it out, nor did the sacking, and he had to quench down on the searing agony and fear in his mind, take off his robe and use a stick to scrape the liquid off his flesh where it stuck to his arm. A lot of skin and flesh came with it, but the fire went out and he spent all his concentration on blotting out the pain, till he passed out.

Pat was pleased. The pigs bolted beautifully, made it to the front of the village, ran away from the shield wall, come back to the rear exit, spooked further by the fires and turned to run back through the village for a third time, this last being the best as by now people were coming out of huts and being bowled over by maddened swine. He saw a couple of warriors stand up to them and get gored, all to the good.

He strung his bow, knocked a broadhead and waited, standing in front of a palm tree where in the half-light his broken outline and smeared skin made him all but invisible.

Women and children ran past, screaming in terror. He saw a woman come back for a toddler, who was shitting himself as he tried to run, mouth open in a constant scream. He made no move to stop them, glad they were going. All his fighting had been against men, with no women or children anywhere near, and he was uncomfortable with the idea they might get hurt. He hoped Hinatea's crew in the woods would not hurt them, but feared they would.

He watched the villagers attack the shield wall, impressed by the discipline and effectiveness. The village warriors died in droves, till finally they broke, running back to the rear exit and Pat. Last came the chief, looking over his shoulder and cursing.

"Now!" Pat called, "Prisoners!" His arrow went with his voice and took the chief through the thigh, causing him to fall backwards shouting rather than screaming to the ground, where he froze for the simple reason Mot was standing on his chest, her jaws resting gently on his throat.

Arrows and clubs took down the other warriors in short order, not difficult as they had already broken and dropped their weapons, seeking only to escape.

Pat walked up to the chief, and looked over at Mara.

"Isn't your hair sacred? Nobody allowed to touch it if you are royal?"

Mara wandered over and kicked the chief in the kidneys. "This one not royal," he leant down and yanked his hair. "I piss on his hair!"

"Here's an idea," said Pat and pulled his knife out.

Mara began to laugh.

Prisoners were brought out to the crew, though Sara noticed they were all female or children. They found Bart in the third hut, together with the other fishermen. But the men had fled. There was a rear gate. The Ratu was beside himself with anger at the cowardice of the enemy. He rooted about in his rival's house, inspecting the booty when a loud shout brought him to the door.

A bedraggled figure staggered down the main street, along a corridor forming of grinning kai Viti drumming their axe heads on to their shields and crying, "Hau! Hau!" An arrow protruded from his thigh, a broadhead straight through the fleshy part without breaking the bone. His sacred hair was missing from the top, a raw and bleeding circular wound in its place, and if he slowed Mot bit his ankles which dripped gore. He was more terrified of the dog than anything in his life.

Pat strolled along behind, swinging the scalp from his hand, his bow over his shoulder. He looked seriously at Sara who brandished Lady Strike despite the annoying lack of need. "I thought you would like the chief. He was trying to escape." He spoke in Belada and smiled shyly at the Ratu. Grey Fox, Mara, Wiwik and some of the girls were beside him, all grinning.

The Ratu shouted in ecstasy, jumped to the street, and kicked his rival into the dirt where Mot pounced and stood over him. He swept up Pat into a massive bear hug.

"Ha! Great warrior! Hero! You are a true kai Viti!" He grabbed the hair from Pat's hand, shook it and bellowed laughter to the hills. He barked a question at Mara who replied through bursts of laughter.

"This good custom," boomed the Ratu. "I make collection of the hair of all my enemy chiefs!" He still held Pat with one arm, and Pat's feet waved despairingly in the air. Sara started to giggle at the expression on his face.

The Ratu turned to Sara and bowed, releasing Pat first. "Great War Ratu! I salute you. You have done what we failed to do in many years. Take up your axe; let us conquer all the islands!"

She dimpled and curtsied in return, bringing Lady Strike up in salute as she did so. "Should we not administer - ah, sort out this village first, Great Ratu? There are warriors in the hills."

"Pah! Without this pigshit they are nothing!" He kicked the erstwhile chief in the head with his bare foot, sending it cracking around. Mot jumped but managed to keep eye contact with the moving head.

He bellowed again in Vituan, and several women were dragged forward and pushed in front of him. They grovelled while he spoke to them, crawled forward and lifted his feet to put on their heads. He spoke to them briefly and sharply, gestured to his army surrounding them. They looked about fearfully and nodded, and two got up and ran off out of the village.

The Ratu answered Sara's questioning look. "They get the villagers back. They take me as their Ratu, the others will too. Tonight we feast, and when I eat his heart, they all accept me as Ratu. But I share it with you, and you!" he pointed at Pat.

He laughed at her horrified face and strode off, leaving her deeply shaken. She had forgotten about Hinatea's warning of cannibals, and she wasn't best pleased about Pat scalping the enemy chief. She might have known he would revert to Elvish customs at the first opportunity and didn't appreciate his sharing this with the kai Viti.

She turned to Maciu, who had not left her side during the short engagement, and told him to get her a casualty report. It took a moment for him to understand what she wanted, and off he went. The Ratu came back to her as he returned and reported to them both.

No kai Viti hurt in the wall, but several received cuts and blows in clearing the huts and one had broken his arm. No Harrheinians were badly hurt, though Perryn had burnt his arm with his fire.

"Your plans good. Fight very good. Never before do we fight and so few die. Now we conquer all the islands!" The Ratu was pleased, the lessons of discipline and mutual support well learnt. Sara experienced a horrific prescience, a vision of the Ratu leading his fearsome warriors off his islands in an orgy of war, conquest, rape and pillage. She must ensure it did not happen.

At least the villagers were being treated quite well. The Ratu's warriors had done little damage to the village, most of the damage caused by Perryn and the ballistas.

Pat was mortified. He sat in the place of honour to the Ratu's right, on a dais raised over the feasting ground. He was not allowed to feed himself, or take a drink - two girls waited for every opportunity to cram something into his mouth. In addition he looked ridiculous. His short hair bristled in as much of a fuzz as possible and he wore a grass skirt with a huge whale's tooth as a pendant on his chest. Apparently this was a mark of honour, the equivalent of a medal. It fascinated him, and he wanted to know how they caught the whales. It was disappointing to discover the kai Viti collected them from carcasses washed up on the beach and in this case, more than a century ago, but some were much older.

Sara was in equal regalia on the Ratu's left, though her hair made a more satisfactory fuzz, and she insisted on a halter under her necklaces, to the Ratu's frequently voiced irritation. However she loved it, in Pat's darkly felt opinion. Suzanne was relegated to a lower seat, which also irritated the Ratu for she carried on an animated conversation with the warriors surrounding and lionising her.

The warriors took it in turn to stand, orate, drink kava and cause everyone to shout at the top of their voices. Kai Viti didn't seem to have another level. Wiwik stood next, but instead of Vituan, he spoke in Belada.

"As the Great Scout" - Pat tried to shrink at this name - "and the Brave Prince" - Mara preened - "captured the leader of the pigs, with the help of the Devil Dog," he bowed to Mot, sat beside Mara in a place of honour, who barked when he looked at her. "My duty was to guard the gate. We let the women and children through before I went to find the Magnificent Magician." Perryn, doped up on herbs and barely conscious, sat near the dais. His eyes widened and he looked worried on being singled out.

"Wah!" Wiwik exclaimed, his voice rising and reverberating off the huts. "His magic was strong! He made two huts burst into flame! But he used too much magic, not realising how poorly they made huts here. He had only seen our houses and thought these as strong. The extra magic started to consume him."

Everyone looked at Perryn , who tried to fit Wiwik's description into what had actually happened.

"The Magnificent Magician is powerful! He gave the magic his robe and sucked it back into his body quickly, so it only took a bit of skin on the way, leaving him standing naked and magnificent in the sunlight. At this moment, the women and children of the village came fleeing the wrath of the Great Ratu, running and screaming in terror. The sight of the Magnificent Magician, his priestly member waving in the sun, was too much! Their legs gave way, they fell on their knees before him and begged his protection. Not only did the Magnificent Magician rip the heart out of the pig by burning his home, but also he caught all the women and children without hurting them as they tried to escape! Bula!" Wiwik clapped his hands, drank, clapped them three times and shouted "Mat hey!" Warriors pushed Perryn to his feet, as he turned bright red. He vaguely remembered some women and children stopping at the sight of him only to be captured by Hinatea's crew.

"I thought I could do magic," Perryn began as he realised he was required to speak. "Today I realised my magic is nothing compared to the concealment magic of Patraigh Connorson." Perryn's training in giving sermons came to the fore as he started to speak automatically, while Pat looked desperately for escape. "Last night we travelled to the back of the village. I fell asleep with the scouts. When I woke in the dawn, I was alone! All the scouts had gone! I was scared and started to stand, when I felt a hand on my wrist. It was Pat. He said a word, and the other scouts appeared. I was reassured, and he made them invisible again and sent them off to war. I have never even heard of a magician who can make people disappear so completely. To Pat," he cried. "Bula!" He clapped, drank the kava, clapped three times, shouted "Mat hey!" and passed a shell of kava to Pat whose evil look promised later retribution.

Pat struggled to his feet with no idea what to say. The sea of faces looking up at him confused him further, so he just drank and tried to sit down. Mara grabbed him firmly and told him to do it properly, and it took three attempts before he managed the ritual to everyone's satisfaction, by which time the tears of mirth rolled down the Ratu's face

The women laboured over the fire pits, offering up a fantastic smell of roast meat, to Pat's interest as he expected it to smell somehow different. The first morsel was retrieved, carried over on a banana leaf and placed in front of the Ratu - the forearm of the dead chief. The arm was a delicacy, the Ratu explained to him. Would he like to try it?

The soldiers and Spakka were interspersed with the warriors, while the sailors stayed in a group. There was a marked contrast between the two groups, as the sailors looked nervous, while the soldiers weren't going to let a little thing like cannibalism get in the way of a good party. Indeed, Pat could see Little using his teeth to rip meat from what was clearly a humerus. Angry shouts came from the Spakka, causing concern to Sara. Pat went to check for her, returning quickly.

"No problem," he whispered in her ear. "Stiphleek is trying to get Boersma to eat some man meat to pay some sort of debt. Usual scrabble, Janis and Esbech will sort it."

Sara nodded and he used his chin to point to where the crew girls were looking upset as some warriors teased them with a leg, from which they sliced slivers, chewing them ostentatiously.

"Think Rosie and Terri are regretting trying kai Viti boyfriends. I'll have a word with Maciu for you."

He left, leaving Sara disturbed. He wasn't supposed to be so bloody reasonable, she wanted jealousy and bit into a chunk of roasted breadfruit with savage abandon, almost taking a chunk of meat by mistake. She noted him whisper in Maciu's ear, who laughed and shook his handsome head. Sara swore internally, wondering if she could not persuade both of them to stay with her, after all a princess should come with benefits. Hinatea caught her eye, sitting tall and regal across the fires, not moving as Pat sat down beside her. Hinatea nodded slowly, before turning and kissing Pat with slow deliberation.

A tall and dignified woman came from the fire, bearing something on a banana leaf platter. She bowed before the Ratu and stayed down while a hush fell on the feast. The Ratu stood and murmured to her. She stood erect and spoke loudly and clearly into the silence.

Mara, sitting beside Pat, translated to Belada for him. "She welcomes the Great Ratu to the village. Swears fealty to him, offers him the old chief's heart as a symbol. When he eats it, he takes on the spiritual path of the village, so is linked to its past. Then all stays the same, just change of leader but the spirits and Kadavu are happy they still present."

Pat thought he understood this, and watched in fascination as the Ratu held aloft a couple of small slices, perfectly cut with one of the amazing new steel knives. He spoke, accepting the responsibilities.

All the remaining villagers came forward and took it in turn to lift the Ratu's foot and place it on their heads. Women, older children and a few old men.

Pat whispered to Mara, "Where are the men?"

"In the fire."

At the conclusion of the fealty ceremony, the women of the village came out with the bamboo instruments and started a slow, graceful melody. The warriors, led by the Ratu, sent a slow, sad song echoing down the beach with their melodious tenors. Mara explained to Pat it was a farewell to the warriors. Deep regret they were no longer there to fight and a promise they would live on in the live warriors' deeds. The live warriors felt strengthened by their death and thanked their spirits for their gift of life.

Pat mused on this as he watched, noting the similarity to the beliefs of the wild men in the north, and the elves reaction to game they killed. He saw the Spakka nodding, and realised they were very much in tune with this as well. Stiphleek's eye glinted through swelling, while Boersma flinched every time a dish passed around. He noted Sara and Suzanne's eyes shine with unshed tears, while most of the women from the crew wept openly. Hinatea's thigh pressed into him, her body very still. She would not tell Pat about her night with Kaduvu's vicar, and he felt the presence of the God now. He placed an arm protectively around her, and she pressed against him.

There was silence as the song died away, the Ratu's voice the last to tremble into the dark. The warriors sat down, one by one. Pat was deep in trance and meditation, when a loud clap and "Bula!" from the Ratu made him jump, echoed by all the other warriors and he hastily followed suit with a shell thrust to his lips.

Pat heard the Ratu whisper to Sara. "Please tell the Yellow Queen she must sleep on the ship tonight. I have my duty to perform still." He grinned, realising the Ratu was avoiding the task himself and had not explained all of his duties to Suzanne.

As the Ratu arose, Mara touched his arm. "Come, we must replenish the warriors of the village with a stronger strain." Pat followed Mara who followed Maciu and his father. Sara watched him go grimly, her lips a firm line which firmed even further as she saw Mactravis also in the lines of warriors leaving. The Spakka stayed seated, having explained at length about honour with the Ratu earlier to gain permission to miss the ceremony. Irritably, she went to pass on the message to Suzanne and join her on the Queen Rose for the night, noting Hinatea and the Pahippians join them.

Hinatea looked at her with wide eyes. "Tonight I sleep with all the girls, all together. In numbers we are safe from Kaduvu's vicar and my Fire God will protect us. I will invoke the protection and raise the barrier. You should sleep with us lest he samples you."

Sara wasn't sure whether to be more astonished at this care for her safety or the mystical beliefs revealed.

The incorporation of the village and its small island into the Ratu's empire proceeded very quickly and word spread through the islands. Several other villages came and swore fealty to him in the following week. Every day warriors would arrive, wanting to join the Ratu's army and learn the new tactics.

Pat received official promotion to Midshipman, acknowledging his leadership of the scouts, for whom he found plenty of recruits, as Perryn's tale of invisibility spread. Pat tried to tell people it was simple training and discipline, with a bit of misdirection, but Little did not help by claiming he was the most skilled wizard he had ever seen when it came to camouflage and he and Grey Fox could teleport, which was why they were so good.

The Ratu was annoyed, as he rapidly ran out of enemies to fight and took to consulting Walters and Taufik on other islands in the area. Sara and Suzanne told him directly he could not invade Pahipi, which put him into a bad mood for a day, an incredibly long time for him. Even making him their protector did not mollify him.

Sara solved the issue. She asked him to train up an army for her, which she would use as a mercenary army on her northern frontier. She and Lieutenant Mactravis agreed they had never seen such natural, skilled fighters, who took discipline better than any soldiers they had trained. As long as they were offered the chance of a fight.

The Ratu was annoyed at the lack of imminent war to which they could immediately sail. Suzanne revealed to him Sara's status as the heir to a huge kingdom and he understood the situation, embracing her and nearly choking her. The kai Viti were not a particularly demonstrative people, but the Ratu didn't give a damn what anybody thought.

Another peculiar friendship developed between the kai Viti and the dwarves. Having set up their kilns, the dwarves invested them with ceremony, which involved a lot of drinking and singing, something in which the kai Viti participated with enthusiasm. One of the dwarfs agreed to stay on the island and run the kiln. Naturally, this required another ceremony to invest the now bald Waru as a master and his assistants as apprentices. Pat reckoned it was the first time in history the dwarfs shared their ceremony, though it changed somewhat. It was not usual for an entire village to take part, normally being secretive and held underground. He discussed this with the master in dwarvish to the delight of the kai Viti who understood perfectly that a fight was not happening, while the Harrheinians fingered their knives. The Ratu declared dwarvish the sacred language of steel, which all smiths and apprentices must learn. The master smith told Sara she had better not upset the dwarves, as the kai Viti were natural allies for them - the shortest people and the tallest people in the world had to look after each other.

Sara needed more diplomacy when she discussed the terms for the army. It took some time for the Ratu to understand she wanted to pay the soldiers, and he refused point blank, deeply offended at the concept. He insisted she took her guard with her and agreed to train an army, promising her a thousand trained men within six months. They decided to leave Corporal Strachan behind to oversee the training, Little volunteering to help him but Lieutenant Mactravis would not hear of it, fearing the sort of training he would give them. Captain Larroche, now fully recovered, agreed to leave behind an experienced shipwright to build ships and teach the kai Viti how to sail them.

Sara and the Ratu signed an agreement of mutual aid and free trade between the Kingdoms. He listened to her warning for him to train up a reliable Prime Minister if he led the army himself, or he would return to find he was no longer the Ratu. They agreed to send him a team of administrators, farming experts and more military trainers on the Queen Rose when she returned, expected to be within six months. A core of Kingdom trained officers would keep him safe, and she and Lieutenant Mactravis interviewed over 100 boys, before selecting twenty for enrolment in the Officers Academy in Praesidium. They would learn Harrheinian on the way.

The day of departure dawned, without a soul in sight. Pat emerged on to the beach, judging the sun to have been up for at least three hours. His head ached as he remembered the previous night's party, and the fabulous dance Suzanne orchestrated. At one point every single person present, including aged greybeards and young children, had been either playing an instrument or dancing. Suzanne had composed a score for the dance combining the ships fiddlers and pipers with the drums of the kai Viti, the dwarven horns, Stiphleek with his bagpipes and a bugler from the soldiers whom nobody had suspected existed.

He swam in the lagoon, welcomed by the small fish swarming around him and sucking at his toes. Diving down to look at the coral, he wondered again, what they were. Rocks that grew? Amazing. Something dark flashed down beneath him and he started, then realised it was Hinatea, who came up with a shellfish which she gave him with a smile and not a word.

His headache gone and feeling refreshed and a little tired, he emerged from the sea where Mot slept on his clothes, to see something dark on the horizon. Recognizing it as people, coming down the trail to the town, he wondered if he should call the alarm.

Surely all the islands were now part of the Ratu's empire? Mara appeared, yawning, came down to the beach and clasped arms with him. Pat nodded down the trail, Mara looked and answered the unspoken question.

"The other villages come to say goodbye."

And indeed they did. Not just by walking, as the canoes started to come until they were black on the water, the rowers singing as they came and full of flower-garlanded girls.

The entire crew started to draw up on the beach on parade, the soldiers beginning to form up earlier than anyone else, something Pat understood when Little was nowhere to be found. Grey Fox went searching and he appeared moments before the sailors started to form up, his uniform looking surprisingly good despite his bloodshot eyes and white face, his short hair still dripping where Grey Fox had persuaded half a dozen kai Viti to throw him in the sea to wake him up.

Pat put on his uniform, looking smarter than ever before as kai Viti girls insisted on looking after him, something he was very uncomfortable with but unable to stop. The girls had washed and cleaned his uniform and insisted on dressing him in it, which took longer than usual as they kept putting bits on the wrong place. Hinatea did not help by laughing all the way through the operation. Domestic duties were not part of her skill set. Her uniform was a brief tunic which she would pull off at the first opportunity.

As he ran up the beach towards the crew, he realised his coat was buttoned up wrong and he slowed to sort it out, and felt the sweat streaming down his body.

"Where the hell have you been?" Sara snapped at him, glaring. "Go and get the second watch sorted."

"Second watch? That's Suzanne's. I've got the archers."

"There's no sign of Suzanne. The Captain is worried she is going to stay behind. Rat's looking after the archers."

Pat closed his mouth, and went uncertainly towards the second watch. No wonder Sara was mad, perhaps it's not me she is mad at, he thought. He looked at the second watch and wondered if they were correct on parade. Panic rose in him for no good reason and the Bosun strolled up.

"All in order, laddie. Just inspect them, make sure they are correctly turned out."

He nodded and she went off. He walked slowly down the rank, looking at each person's uniform and kit. Remembering what normally happened, he asked Billy to show him his knife and looked at it. Immaculate. The next sailor was Rosie, and as he started to look at her, he noticed her tunic was undone. He hadn't realised her bust was so big, and told her to do up her buttons.

"But it's so hot, sir, and don't I look better with them undone?" She looked at him directly out of big eyes and he felt himself blushing to the roots of his hair. He realised she was sticking her chest out and was conscious of a slight movement down the ranks.

"Regulations say to do them up, so do them up." He spoke with difficulty and hurried on to the next sailor who was not so difficult, but getting to the next caused his colour to rise again, and he saw all the girls in the front row had undone their buttons and were sticking out their chests, all trying hard not to laugh.

Bitterly, he knew he was going to be held responsible, and wished he knew what to say. Why wasn't Rat in charge? He would say something. Turning hurriedly into the second row, he stopped short, as the girls here had all undone their buttons further, pulled their tops down and exposed more of their breasts. He saw Hinatea and her girls were in the line, having joined his watch as soon as he was appointed. As he goggled at them, the whole line turned to him, bent forward and smiled. The nearest, Katie, said, "This is better, isn't it Lieutenant? Perfect for this climate!"

"Umm, I'm not a Lieutenant," he said, and heard Brian call out to him. "Carry on Edgar," he cried to the Boatswains Mate, the person really in charge of the watch and fled to Brian with a burst of laughter chasing him.

Brian glared at him. "The Captain's on his way. Is your watch ready?"

"I think so, sir."

"Why are they laughing?"

"Err, they're teasing me sir. I don't think I am suited for this, Mr Michaels."

"Neither do I, Connorson, if this is the best you can do. For God's sake man, get Edgar to sort them out and stand in front of them. Stay away from them or you'll ruin the whole thing and the Captain will hold me responsible! Where is the damn woman anyway?"

Recognising a rhetorical question, Pat fled back to the watch where Edgar told him they were all present and correct. Pat made the mistake of looking at them, and the girls in the back row shrugged their shoulders so their breasts popped out again. Quickly, he turned and took up position in front. Immediately, he felt a hand on his bottom, squeezing. Realising his mistake, he took three fast steps forward and stood at attention, or what he thought was attention, and adjusted his stance as he looked at the soldiers. He ignored the giggles behind him and dreaded what they would do next.

Captain Larroche arrived and started inspecting the soldiers. Brian led him on to Sara's immaculate watch, then Stephen's, finally to his. He turned to the Captain, knuckled his forehead and reported.

"Second Watch all present and correct, Sir! Would you care to inspect them?"

"Not quite present, I believe Midshipman, or should I say Lieutenant now? Congratulations on your sudden promotion."

Pat blushed again. "No sir. Thank you, sir. I don't really want it, sir."

"We all do things we don't want, young man. Now, show me your watch."

Pat turned and led the Captain to the front row, seeing with relief the girls were modest again and looking impeccable. The Captain went down the row half-heartedly, nodded to Pat and walked on to inspect the Bosun's people before going out to take up a position in front of the three watches, accompanied by Brian and a Boatswains Mate with pipes. The soldiers arrayed to his left, with the Spakka resplendent in kilts on the far side of them and the various other departments under the Bosun to the right. Pat noticed for the first time Sam was there with his boar, impeccably clean and garlanded in flowers. Mot laughed at him from beside them, also with flowers, her tongue hanging out. She was noticeably fat, he thought as they waited. Exactly the same as Pahipi, the kai Viti had overcome their initial fear and fallen in love with her, feeding her constantly wherever she went and the children were always playing with her.

On either side of the Harrheinians the beach filled up with kai Viti, women and children. They left a broad pathway down from the town, at least a hundred yards wide. As Captain Larroche took up his position, there was a loud "Hau! Hau!" and a shield wall ninety yards wide strode out of the village, perfectly aligned. It stopped at the top of the beach, the warriors thumped their shields on the ground and slammed their axes against the shields, raising a wall of sound that crashed down the beach and sent the seabirds screaming into the air in a whirling cloud.

The warriors started to sing, the farewell song, of the paddlers fatigue as they sailed into the setting sun. They advanced slowly, using the song to keep in step and the shields as drums, thumping them into the ground. As the song came to a mournful end, the shield wall stopped in front of the Captain. It parted and the Great Ratu strode forth, bedecked in his finest regalia and towering high over the Captain.

As he approached the Captain, his eyes flicked to Pat, and he missed step as he realised Suzanne wasn't there. Pat was close enough to see the question in his eyes, and the way his eyes scanned the crew. Pat knew damn well Suzanne had created the protocol for the farewell and dictated what was going to happen, so prepared himself for a surprise. He was fascinated to realise the Ratu had no idea what was happening.

Captain Larroche started speaking, in Belada, thanking the Great Ratu for his hospitality, to which the Ratu replied in kind, and then presented him with a Royal Guard, who strode out of the village, marched down and through the gap in the shield wall and took up position beside the soldiers.

As the Great Ratu and Captain Larroche turned back to each other, both hesitated, not certain what was supposed to happen now as it was Suzanne's turn to speak. Pat knew that and saw Sara take a step forward, clearly intending to take Suzanne's place.

As she did so, a shriek rose from a hut some way to one side of the pathway. Immediately, every woman in the crowd started screaming and wailing and pulling at their hair. Everyone stared in astonishment, this was unexpected and only Sara and Mactravis had the court experience to continue as if nothing was happening - however Sara did stop her step.

A ghostly white figure appeared from the hut, and an unearthly scream came from it. The women continued to ululate and rend their hair, the children adding to the noise by screaming with laughter and excitement. Pat noticed the Ratu take an involuntary step back, and the shield wall lose its discipline. Not surprising, this figure appeared to be some ghastly spectre, some unknown god of the island, or the ghost of somebody eaten long ago.

A path appeared between the women as they moved aside, leading straight up to the Great Ratu. The figure started down the path, and Pat's keen eyes saw it was female, with huge breasts and his eyes focused on the face and he smiled.

She was stark naked, and a ghastly white, the colour of mourning and death, even her hair which was done up to twice the size achieved in the past. Her lips were stained a horrible blue, like a corpse washed up from the sea, and her skin appeared to be shedding, bits trailing behind her in the wind, and pouring from her hair in a steady cloud. Her eyes were black pits, huge, staring and quite terrifying. She swayed down the path, moaning, gibbering and letting out an occasional unearthly scream.

Pat looked around; he was the only one to recognise her. Many of the warriors looked on the point of fleeing. Every pair of eyes locked on the spectre as she undulated down the path, coming closer and closer to the Ratu. He recognised Suzanne at the last moment, and appeared to think she had been murdered in the night. The supernatural was one thing he wasn't prepared to face.

Suzanne timed it with perfection. Another step and he would have broken, leading the warriors in a race for the middle distance.

She stopped and her voice rose, soaring over the multitudes on the beach, speaking first in perfectly accented Vituan, then in Belada.

"Oh Great Ratu, see my despair and grief at this parting! You are my world, my star and my hero, leaving you turns this life to ashes. You are the mighty one, who conquers all the islands and my love for you is as wide as the great sea. Aaaaaah!" She cried again, despair and agony echoing with the scream, and the whole crowd, entranced, moaned with her.

"Duty! What a cruel burden that drags me from your side, for today I must go! My place is beside my Princess."

The Ratu recovered brilliantly and leapt into the drama with both feet. He ripped off his headdress, throwing it dramatically to the floor, the other hand going to his necklaces which broke, scattering shells and flowers in all directions. Suzanne watched him, eyes bright with anticipation. He bellowed like a wounded leviathan as he stripped his grass skirt away to leave himself equally naked and jumped forward to scoop her up, high in the air and turned in a circle that spread ashes over the nearest warriors, then hugged her to his chest.

"Ah, my Golden Queen! How will I survive without you by my side! Your beauty is without equal, you give me the will and strength to rule and conquer. NO! I cannot let you go!"

There was a surge from the women, who rose up, led by his seven wives, and gently but firmly pried his arms from around her and pulled them apart. The Ratu made no struggle, but fell to his knees, spread his arms apart and watched events mutely and whitely as the ashes from Suzanne's body now covered him as well.

The women lifted Suzanne to their heads and held her above them as they walked slowly to the sea, Suzanne lying flat like a stranded starfish with her head trailing down, looking back at the Ratu. Now the women sang their own farewell song, remembering the dead, and the women left alone by the fire pit. They took her down to the jolly boat and placed her in the end.

The Bosun snapped an order as soon as she saw the direction in which they headed, and was waiting in the bow, 6 female sailors at the oars, six brawny men ready to push the boat out, which they did while Suzanne stood in the stern, arms raised to the heavens. The boat rowed terribly slowly out to sea.

Pat thought fast and spoke sharply. "Edgar! Get them in the boats. We must make the ship before her!" In a trice the Second Watch were afloat and rowing fast back to the ship. The rest of the crew flowed after them and it seemed the entire Vitu Nation took to the canoes and followed until the water was black and seething from the paddle strokes.

Pat's keen eye noted the Ratu's wives produce a container and empty it over the Ratu, more ashes, so he was also white as he climbed into the Royal Barge. He wasn't alone, as many of the women, accomplices all, brought their own ash and now covered themselves as well, while the soldiers did their best, scooping up white sand and pouring it into their hair so it streamed down steadily as they rowed.

Brian was proud of the speed with which the crew vacated the beach and climbed aboard, stowing the boats rapidly. The only one to give trouble was the pig, and Mot soon had him under control, though he squealed loudly all the way to the ship.

The capstan turned, pulling the ship slowly towards the open sea, while the sails shook out and the canoes raced about in front of them, laying a fragrant carpet of hibiscus and frangipani flowers through which she sailed majestically. A massed choir of over a thousand kai Viti in their canoes sang battle hymns as the Queen Rose sailed away from the sunset.

Sung

Ship life went back to normal as they sailed north east. The kai Viti fitted in, sharing a large cabin with the Spakka and the laughter level on the ship lifted, while the sea shanties sung in the evening improved beyond measure. They even started adding verses in Harrheinian, pretty poor at first. They were an excellent influence on the Spakka, who at last started to become part of the community. Stiphleek in particular spent time with them for these brother axemen would let him sing, even encourage him and join in. Esbech struck up a firm friendship with Wiwik after a vicious fight ended in a draw, both laid unconscious by the Bosun to the loud protestations of the onlookers. The Bosun actually broke a marlinspike in the process.

A week's voyage with the prevailing winds brought them to a string of small islands, coral atolls, most of which were inhabited. The occasional inhabitants fled at the sight of the Queen Rose and Captain Larroche didn't stop.

Another four days brought them to a larger island, still tiny compared to Vitu Levu, and something about the haze of the island caused Captain Larroche to send Pat up the mast with Nils. They sat in the crow's nest and discussed what they could see, Nils explaining to Pat how to compensate for the haze and see through it, not an easy trick. To make it more difficult, the sea-birds swirled around the island and the distance made them appear as a moving cloud.

"That's no mountain," grunted Nils.

"Village on fire," said Pat. "Under attack."

"Not kai Viti," said Nils. "They wouldn't fire a village, they'd take it over."

"Pirates?"

"Well, it's the sort of thing the Spakkas do. Come on, we'll learn nothing more till we get round the point. Let's tell the Captain."

They slipped down the ropes to the mainsail spar, slid down the mainsail to the main deck and trotted up to the poop where the Captain waited. He listened to the report, and called for his officers. Aware Pat was showing his youth by his excitement and eagerness, he took care to project steadiness and calm to quieten the lad.

"When we come round the point we will find at least one pirate ship. I have no idea whether it will be a galley or a sailing ship, but there will be a number of fighters, for sure. We will sail to the windward of them, and as we go past, Nils, you will fire the ballistas on my order. Pat, the archers can start firing as they come in range. On my order, we will come about and close with them. Lieutenant Mactravis, you make the decision and lead a boarding party of soldiers, Spakka and kai Viti aboard the largest ship as the hulls touch. Repeat for each ship, Brian. Any sailors you want in the parties?"

"No sir, keep them in reserve."

"Princess," continued the Captain, emphasizing the title, "kindly prepare the kai Viti and Spakka but you are NOT to accompany them, which is an order." Sara's lips tightened, but she nodded.

"Brian, when Mactravis has the situation under control, lead a boarding party and take control of the main ship. Make four parties ready, for other ships, to be led by Delarosa, Stevens, Starr and the Bosun. Go by boat, the pinnace for the largest ship. Any questions?"

There were none and the officers went to brief their crews.

As they rounded the point, Else stood in the rigging with most of the girls to operate the sails if required. Coming about, the deck crew would handle by the timing of turning the rudder and pulling on the stays, but the sails would need to come down as they closed with the enemy. Pat led a band of archers on the foredeck while Little commanded the crossbow men on the poop deck. They found a bay with a village by the usual small stream. Flames licked from the rooftops and some white robed people were taking naked villagers in chains to a ship in the bay. The ship was a long low shape, with a small cabin area at the stern and a single mast near the bows, from which came out a long spar running low above the deck. A dirty white sail fell roughly around the long spar running down the centre of the deck and the ship seemed to have stripes down the side.

"What is it, sir?" Suzanne asked.

"It's a dhow," answered Taufik before the Captain could speak. "Umayyads."

"Why have they painted stripes on it?" Sara asked innocently.

"That's shit," said Taufik. Sara looked again with distaste. The whole ship was filthy.

The appearance of the Queen Rose caused consternation on the dhow, while the sight of the slavers caused a growl amongst the crew.

The slavers on the beach left the slaves in chains and ran for their boats, climbing in with desperation and causing a confused commotion as they tried to row without being in time. The one full boat at sea raced to the dhow and was hauled aboard, slaves and all, to be dumped on the deck and ignored while an empty boat, going back to the beach for more slaves, turned for the dhow.

The Queen Rose laid a course to block the dhow; Pat judged it would take them twenty minutes, as they tacked across the wind to gain the weather gage, the advantage of coming down the wind. Navigation lessons made a great deal of sense as he realised the ship was moving sideways almost as fast as forward, and he finally understood what Brian meant when he explained about the slippage when they tacked. The Captain demonstrated an awe inspiring level of skill to manoeuvre the ship. Pat felt he could never become a real officer. He noticed Brian, Suzanne, Sara and Stevens watching intently, doing their own calculations. He switched to studying the slavers, wondering if they were Umayyads. He catalogued them with care, choosing targets. He nudged Grey Fox.

"Two on the helm." It was not a wheel like the Queen Rose, but a long rudder at the back, a simple arrangement, very heavy, and took two men to operate.

"Then Greybeard". Grey Fox spoke in an equally terse and laconic manner. A man with a long, matted grey beard shouted orders at the crew of the dhow, most of which seemed to create no effect.

They watched the second boat swing aboard and an argument develop over the chained slaves on the deck.

"Hey, Cap'n!" Little, always wise in the ways of the world, called from the main deck. "If'n you want to rescue them slaves, you'd better get a move on. Betcha they ditch 'em."

"Sara," called Captain Larroche, "take your boarding party and the best Pahippian divers, see if you can rescue any of them."

"Jolly boat sir?" Sara asked as she moved to the head of the stairs. He nodded and she jumped down to the deck, issuing orders and calling for Hinatea.

The slavers hauled at their anchor, till a burly man came running over and cut through the rope with a few slashes of a huge, wide sword. "Scimitar," Grey Fox murmured to Pat. "Spakka sometimes use them."

Seeing the dhow start to swing into the wind and raise the huge triangular sail, the remaining slavers in the last boat dropped their oars and dived over the side, swimming to the dhow, grabbing ropes trailing from the side, and deserting their boat. As they came aboard, one of them grabbed the nearest slave and threw him overboard. Chained together, but sensing freedom, the rest followed on, falling into the sea on top of each other.

"Little!" Pat cried, "crossbow range, let go!"

The heavy twang of the crossbows sounded and two of the crew, hauling on ropes, fell over the side.

Pat and Grey Fox waited a moment longer, nodded to each other and raised their bows. Both the men on the tiller slumped, one falling over the low side. Greybeard was next, followed by the burly man, while the rest of the crew dived into shelter. The dhow's sail shuddered, and the dhow slowly turned into the wind, coming to a halt.

Sara cast off in the jolly boat, moments before Little's crossbow men got off a second volley. Pat and Grey Fox picked off anyone who moved, then Nils let off the ballista, using a heavy bolt which crunched through the walls of the small cabin area, causing it to collapse and some of the robed slavers emerged to be skewered by Pat and Grey Fox.

Captain Larroche called out his orders, the Queen Rose swung around and fetched up along side the dhow, which banged and ground its way along the side of the ship causing the Bosun to wince and swear.

At the noise, robed men rose out of the shelter of the side of the dhow, waving swords and scimitars. The Spakka didn't hesitate. Boersma leapt first, and three swords raised, prepared to skewer him as he landed. At the last possible moment, he swung his axe in a practised motion beneath his feet, smashing all three swords to one side and going through to land feet first on the chest of one of the slavers. Stiphleek and Esbech landed moments later, either side of him, Esbech also needing to clear a couple of swords out of the way. Stiphleek landed cleanly on the balls of his feet and in one motion reversed his axe to remove the hand of the Umayyad about to skewer Boersma who recovered his balance a trifle slowly, with his axe stuck in the chest of his landing pad.

The landing point made, the first three whirled their axes into the surrounding throng while more Spakka leapt into the space created, pushing forward into the expanding area. The Umayyads appeared uncertain as to how to handle axemen, and although many stood their ground bravely, too many watched the axes gleaming in the sunshine rather than the eyes of their opponents. The Spakka revelled in their inexperience, joyfully cleaving into the defenders.

A few paces down the ship, the kai Viti betrayed their inexperience. The first to land swung at the waiting swords and collected two, but two more transfixed his legs as he dropped. He shouted in pain and fury, swinging his axe wildly to kill one slaver and cripple another, before a third stepped forward and lanced his body, only to have Maciu land on his shoulders and remove his head. More kai Viti arrived, several taking stab wounds to the legs, but once aboard they tore into the wavering defenders

Stiphleek paused, letting his bloodthirsty brethren move past him, a gleam came across his eyes and he threw back his head and started to sing, bellowing out the Saga of Stiphleek the Bold.

He expected his voice to encourage his ship mates, inspired by the Princess singing with the Royal Pathfinders.

Janis pulled back from the fray, shortly followed by Esbech.

"Where are you hurt, my brother?" Janis asked, grasping his arm and looking for blood.

Esbech was not so polite. "Fryssa fuck you, you stupid poxed up arsehole! Will you stop that bloody wailing and do your fucking job? That bastard goat fucker nearly took my arm off because you fucked off!" He swung a meaty fist into Stiphleek's midriffff. Stiphleek's song cut off in mid flow as he doubled over, swinging to one side to avoid Esbech's raised knee, which he grasped and pulled, throwing Esbech to the floor. Before he could follow up, Boersma was between them, issuing the magic words of the peacemaker.

"Battle's over boys. Let's see if there is any booze in the hold."

Indeed, the Umayyads couldn't withstand the fury of the axemen, their swords snapping when trying to parry the axes and unable to live with the speed with which both Spakka and kai Viti swung their axes. The survivors broke and ran, some for the hatches but most for the side where they jumped into the water and swam ashore.

Newly promoted Corporal Little grasped Maciu's arm and gave him orders to search below, and the kai Viti followed the Spakka into the bowels of the dhow.

This time Esbech led the way, leaping blindly into the dark hold, falling further than he expected before landing on flesh that screamed. He dropped his axe in the collision, which prevented him from slaughtering the chained slaves in the bowels of the dhow. Moments later Boersma performed an identical leap with similar results and Esbech's shout caused Stiphleek to swing from the hatch, where he swore loudly as an Umayyad stabbed his sword into his thigh, causing him to let go and land beside Esbech. That worthy blinked his eyes as they adjusted to the dark and picked his way through the shrinking slaves to the gangway where a defender waved a sword, only to drop it and fall to his knees as Esbech approached. He lifted his hands in supplication, which Esbech ignored as his measured stroke removed the head cleanly and he grunted in satisfaction.

Janis shouted from the hatch. "Esbech! No more killing. If they surrender, take them prisoner and bring them to the Princess."

Muttering, Esbech continued into the bowels of the ship followed by Boersma, while a chastened Stiphleek made for the hatch to have his wound treated. He stepped on a barrel, which tilted and sloshed, causing him to stop abruptly and check it.

Sara's jolly boat reached the chained villagers, struggling to keep afloat, the weight of chains pulling them down. The Pahippians dived overboard, Sara threw a rope out and turned the boat to row for the shore. The girls thrust rope into the hands of the chained villagers and dived looking for more. The jolly boat slowed as it took the weight, while the girls picked out the weaker ones and held them up, hanging on to the rope and being towed shoreward. Before long they touched the sand and began to walk out, still chained together. Sara left them with the girls, who worked on several, pushing at the chests to make them throw up the water. She hurried the jolly boat back to the Queen Rose.

Brian led his boarding party to the dhow, taking over the rudder and getting another anchor down. Captain Mactravis reappeared on the deck, followed by his men who dragged along four slavers. Cheerful kai Viti came up, bloodstained axes over their shoulders and chatting happily like magpies. Pat couldn't see an injury on any of them, the wounded and dead already back on the Queen Rose and in the galley. The Spakka were likewise untouched apart from Stiphleek who emerged triumphant, brandishing a barrel, Esbech behind him arguing over the possession.

Mactravis called up to Queen Rose, asking for smiths to release the slaves. Sara appeared over the rails with the same request. At the Captain's signal, the Bosun went to catalogue the dhow's goods but stopped with her foot on the rail at screams from the shore. The kai Viti, the soldiers and the Spakka raised a cheer at the scene unfolding.

The escaping Umayyad emerged dripping on the shore, fleeing towards the jungle. Racing round from their mission of mercy came the Pahippians, led by Hinatea, all stark naked in battle array. Sara thought they were unarmed and sucked in a breath, but something gleamed in Hinatea's hand and she recognised her favoured lava knife.

Taufik grunted on the poop deck, and laughed. "Their religion teaches they will be given beautiful whores when they die, if they live a good life and believe in their god. I think they know they are already dead and lived a bad life!"

Hinatea at full speed was like a cheetah, low and graceful as she swept past the first fleeing slaver, her arm swinging as she went and he collapsed in a heap, blood spurting from a leg wound gaping so wide it could be seen from the ship. Silmatea leaped full onto the back of another, pulling back his head and cutting his hamstrings once he landed on the ground, thrashing madly. Trieste and Rerata took one together, each pulling an arm while Monata slashed the back of his legs.

Hinatea lunged swift and menacing into a group who tried to bunch together for protection, scattering them to become easy prey. In moments the girls disabled all the refugees and the screams grew louder as they dragged them into nearby bushes.

"Dammit, those blasted girls have no discipline. Those are unarmed men who have surrendered," complained Captain Larroche. "Sara, you will need to round them up."

"I don't think that is possible, sir. These slavers are their traditional enemy. I think all these girls have seen loved ones die at the hands of Umayyads."

"Silmatea was raped when she was just thirteen," said Pat who had come to the poop deck for a better look. "Hinatea killed the man as he did it, with a club. They saw the rest of their families killed, killed badly, by these slavers. Trieste was beaten and at least two of the others raped. Why they are so fierce, they killed their attackers and escaped. That was five years ago. They still have nightmares, why they told me."

Silence spread across the poop deck as Boersma and Maciu dragged two surviving slavers in front of Captain Larroche.

"Lieutenant Mactravis said you wanted some, Sir," said Maciu in his careful Harrhein, while Boersma grunted. "Did you want us to kill them for you, or do you want to kill them yourself?"

Boersma helpfully pushed his captive to the ground and offered his ace to the Captain, his foot holding the man still though he squealed in terror and wet himself.

"No, no," said the Captain with some exasperation. "I need to talk to them. Hold them up against the rail."

The slavers were no longer capable of standing, with excruciating screams echoing across the water and black and white savages with axes standing over them, and collapsed into a heap.

"Do you speak Belada?" The Captain asked.

Two thin brown faces turned towards him, huge eyes wet with terror looking up at him, desperate for rescue. The Captain squelched the feelings of pity rising up inside.

"Why were you attacking this village?"

One of the slavers gulped, the other tried to throw himself on the Captain's feet, to be jerked back roughly by Boersma.

"If it pleases the Mighty Captain, they did not supply the trepang as ordered. Our trip wasted, we needed other cargo."

"What were you going to do with them?"

"It is the season for the Sung to arrive in Trincomalee, we would sell them there, those that survived the cutting."

"What do you mean, the cutting?"

The slaver was confused, and Taufik stepped forward.

"Sir, the Sung will only buy emasculated slaves to ensure they cannot breed in their country. They only buy men, eunuchs. Trincomalee is the capital of Tamila, on the southern shores of Hind. Every year the Sung come."

"Who are you people and where are you from?"

"If it pleases the Mighty Captain, we are from Ormuz in the Caliphate of Hussein ibn Al-Raisa, May He Live For Ever."

"Hmmph. Sara, do you have any questions?"

"A few Sir. Was your ship an independent trader, and who was the captain?"

The slaver shuffled his feet and ducked his head a few times, before answering. "Beautiful Pearl, the ship belongs to the Caliph and the captain is the Emir Muhammad ibn Al-Raisa."

"One of the Caliph's sons, I presume, so he won't be best pleased with us."

"The Caliph's anger will be like the mountains that explode with fire. We are dead men if we return to the Caliphate, for losing his ship and his son. Please, take us aboard as your crew, we will show you the secret trading ports and I know where the Emir of Qalhat stores his pearl, the entire seasons crop."

The second slaver managed to speak now, gabbling fast so his words were hard to understand. "Qalhat has the finest pearls in the world, Highness, even the royal Black Pearls, the store is worth a Kings ransom, we can show you where it is, the guards are weak and will flee before your mighty warriors. We are good sailors, Your Worship, we are useful," and his pleas faded into broken sobs as Boersma stirred.

"Tell me, have you ever heard of Harrhein?"

"The majesty of it is beyond compare, Great Queen, all know and sing its praises."

"What is it?"

The slavers looked at each other, groping for a reply.

"Never mind. You deal in slaves. Here you take slaves from the islands, but do you also deal in slaves from the West, ones with paler skins?"

"Never, Lady, on my honour," said one while the other nodded without thinking.

At her gesture, Maciu hauled the first one away, struggling while he second collapsed in terror.

"Tell me about them," she hissed and his robe darkened as he urinated spasmodically, his mouth open revealing blackened stumps as he stared at the Princess.

"They, they come from Havant, from the north, barbarians, big men like your axemen."

"Any others?"

"No, Lady, j-j-just the big barbarians, please Lady."

"Look what we found," said Mactravis, his voice as cold and bleak as the northern mountains. Standing beside him, Husk cradled a young woman in his arms, crying onto his shoulder. Behind him the soldiers helped a small coterie of pale skinned people out of the depths of the dhow, blinking in the unaccustomed light. Last were two boys, crying and walking bow-legged.

"You emasculated my people," Sara whispered, her voice a monotone. "Hang them."

Maciu didn't understand, and Husk set down his burden, exchanging her for the nearest slaver. "You just watch, chick, what we do to these bastards," he said. The girl fixed her eyes, narrow with hatred, on the slavers as Husk and Boersma, who knew what to do, hauled them down to the main deck where sailors set ropes from the yards. Maciu came to Mactravis and in Harrheinian, which he insisted on speaking, asked what hanging meant. Mactravis explained, and Little intervened and took Maciu off, explaining in lurid detail. He tried to interest Maciu in a wager as to which one would last longest, but to his disappointment the kai Viti, with no understanding of personal wealth, couldn't entertain the concept of gambling to possess something. He loved the experiment though, and watched as Little demonstrated how to tie a hangman's knot.

The girls and the Captain retired to his cabin, but the rest of the crew were not squeamish, and all watched with relish, raising a great cheer as the Umayyads swung out from the yards, struggling and screaming till the rope cut off their voices. An equal cheer came up from the shore, where the released villagers watched, joined by escaped villagers who appeared from the jungle.

Hinatea and her girls appeared from the bushes in time to dance happily along the sand, gory with the blood splattered all over their bodies.

"You know," said Stephens to the world in general. "I don't think I will ever get excited about the sight of a naked girl again."

What to do with the dhow made an interesting question. It wasn't capable of making the journey back to Harrhein, and taking it along with them would proclaim their actions, which the Umayyads would regard as piracy.

Not one of the crew of the Queen Rose were prepared to sail on it - the ship stank: of fear; rotting, putrid flesh and everywhere the smell of shit. It was filthy, stained and full of rats.

Sara suggested some of the kai Viti could sail it back to Vitua, where it could be set up as part of the Ratu's planned fleet. This was agreed, but it was difficult to find kai Viti ready to go. Eventually Maciu picked those injured in leaping on the dhow and detailed them to return. They enlisted the help of the released villagers and were left to clean the ship and sail it to Vitua, with the promise they could come with the army being trained by the Ratu.

A day later, as the Queen Rose picked her way through coral shoals, three dhows appeared and approached the ship. Full of savage looking people grasping the strange scimitars, they crowded the decks and stared at the Queen Rose.

Captain Larroche knew a pirate when he saw one. Or three. The ballistas were loaded, archers went to their stations, swordsmen, pikemen, Spakka and the kai Viti axemen all manned the ship, very obviously.

The pirates sheered off, sailed past and called greetings to them.

The Harrheinians stood stolidly staring at them, as did the Spakka while the kai Viti were disgusted by this display of cowardice and waved their naked bottoms at them.

A day from Trincomalee the wind failed to a gentle push. Pat was sunning himself with Mot and Perryn discussing how to ensure a lack of sharks so they could go swimming, when there came a shout from the masthead.

"Sail ho! Wide to starboard!"

Pat was up and running for the mast in a moment, while the crew stood to automatically, not waiting for the command.

Pat reached the crow's nest.

"Hi Willy, what do you make of it? Point it out."

"It's not a dhow," said young Willy, one of the few younger than Pat who looked upon him as a hero. "It seems to be very big with lots of sails."

Pat watched the ship come over the horizon with disbelief. At first he thought he saw several ships close together, or towing one another. The hull crept into his view, and he counted seven masts. Through the glass he could see an officer looking at them through a much larger telescope from high up the front mast. The crew carried on as normal, not concerned about them, but he could see the ship change course for an intercept. At the speed both ships were travelling, it would be late afternoon before they met.

Pat dropped down to the deck and made his way to the poop. He reported with care, describing the ship in as much detail as he could.

Taufik nodded. "It is a junk from the Sung. They build very big ships. Slow, but not bothered by bad weather. They will be friendly, they always are. They are fierce fighters but never start a fight, only defend if attacked." He grinned at the Captain. "They have whores on board they use to negotiate with people."

The Captain bit his tongue as he saw Suzanne's eyes narrow.

"So, worth talking with them?"

"Very much so. They will trade with us, here at sea. Means we don't need to go to Trincomalee. They will want the trepang, gold and silver while they will have silks, tea, cloves, nutmeg and other spices. It is a trading ship. If we trade here, we pay no taxes."

"I like these Sung already! What language do they speak?"

"Their own language I do not know, but their writing is chicken scratching. They write a lot. Always when buying. But they will all speak Belada. It is the trade language."

In the late afternoon the ships came within hailing distance. The Sung crowded the rails, as did the Harrheinians and both stared at each other. The Sungs were a very different looking people, with flat faces, tanned with slanted eyes. They looked tough and capable. Sara noted a few women, dressed in flowing silks and with long hair, wide hats and chalk white faces. The men were dressed in loincloths, while the officers wore colourful jackets with wide shoulders.

"Silk," said Suzanne beside her. "Those girls are wearing a fortune for everyday wear."

"I think the uniforms are silk as well," replied Sara.

A hail came from the huge ship, one of the officers shouting through what looked like a funnel. It made his voice louder. He spoke in Belada.

"What ship? Where are you from?"

Captain Larroche answered. "The Queen Rose out of Rikklaw's Port, Harrhein, in the Western ocean bound for Trincomalee."

A stir went through the other ship's crew and they started talking to each other.

"We are the Imperial Orchid, from Soochow, Minyue, also bound for Trincomalee. I am Captain Lim Hsien Tsu. You are traders?"

"We are indeed. I am Captain Larroche. May I invite you aboard, Captain, for refreshments and perhaps we can discuss trade."

Lim Hsien Tsu grinned. "Thank you. I accept. I will bring some of my officers and ladies." He turned and barked some orders in his own language. Suzanne turned to Sara.

"Come on, we need to look something special for this lot." They went to her cabin.

The Bosun put down a special ladder for the Sung, with wooden steps a good foot deep. The ship's pipers played a tune as the Sung came up the ladder from their small pinnace, led by the Captain, while Larroche and his officers waited, resplendent in their dress uniforms, blue with scarlet piping. Suzanne and Sara had worked on their uniforms so they enhanced their femininity, very much so with Suzanne.

Captain Lim Hsien Tsu smiled as he came up the ladder on to the deck and bowed to Captain Larroche, who saluted along with his officers, while the crew let out three cheers.

"It is nice to meet some cultured people here on the far frontiers,

Captain."

He introduced his staff, the most interesting of which to Sara was a tall man with long thin moustaches which fell past his chin. Captain Lim introduced him as Wu Chen Kai Lee, the Wu clearly a title. She noticed both Mage Walters and especially Perryn looking at him with interest, which Wu Chen returned.

Captain Larroche introduced his officers. Captain Lim stopped when introduced to Suzanne.

"Lieutenant Delarosa? You are an officer?" His eyebrows raised, and Suzanne was impressed he looked into her eyes.

"Indeed sir. I have won promotion on this voyage for my capability."

"And in fighting? What happens when your ship encounters pirates?

"I am an effective close quarter fighter, sir, while Lieutenant Starr is the finest swordsman on the ship, indeed one of the top five bladesmen in our Kingdom."

"Truly? How wonderful. It is so invigorating to meet people of other cultures with different customs. In our country women do not fight. Perhaps," he nodded to Sara, "you would agree to an exhibition match with one of our sword fighters? I think we have a few who would give you a match. Though none so young."

"It would be a pleasure, sir. I would be fascinated and honoured to see the styles of fighting you use," replied Sara.

"We have a fighter from Tokkaido on board. They are unusual people; you may also wish to exercise with him. His style is very unique." The Captain nodded and moved on.

Pat stood sweating at the end of the line, reluctant and he stood mute as he was introduced. Captain Lim, who explained the Sung used their family name first, followed Captain Larroche to the wardroom, where the cook and his helpers laid out refreshments. The Sung staff followed their captain, each introducing themselves down the line. Pat noticed the last, a petite girl, dressed like a doll with a belt under her breasts making her look even smaller. She hadn't been introduced, unlike the others and now did not speak. He couldn't see her face, as she held a fan in front of it, and peeped out from behind it at the staff of the Queen Rose as she went past them. As she came level with Pat, he saw her face was the whitest he had ever seen, with slanting eyes and raven dark, long hair. The fan was misleading, as the eyes were full of lively interest and they lit with pleasure when they fell on Pat. He started as she winked broadly at him from behind the fan, and stuck her tongue out when he didn't respond.

As he trailed in last behind the other officers, he found her waiting beside the only spare place having manoeuvred Stevens past her. Pat found her looking at him expectantly and went bright red.

"What this?" She asked in sweetly accented Belada, indicating the chair.

"It's a chair," said Pat stupidly. "You sit on it." He pulled it back for her, as he remembered his manners.

"No sit on cushions?" She winked at him again from behind the fan, and sat demurely on the chair as he eased it forward.

Desperately looking round for escape, Pat sat on the last chair beside her and she turned to him, ignoring Stevens on the other side.

"What this?" She indicated the bottles in front of her.

"This is wine," said Pat, "from Varn Valley in Harrhein. Let me pour you a glass." He did so and she sniffed it with grave suspicion.

"Is alcohol?"

"Err, yes," said Pat, and jumped as she put her hand on his knee.

"Not good for girl when so many big men near." The hand squeezed and Pat blushed again, looking round for help. "No tea?"

"Sure," said Pat and grabbed the nearest pot, pouring one of the herbal teas on the table into a mug.

She looked at it with distaste, tried it and wrinkled her nose. "Very big cup. Funny taste. Not tea. What is?"

"It's, err, leaves and flowers from home. Good for digestion."

This caught her attention. "You know such things? You healer?"

"I know a bit," said Pat, and found himself being drawn out on what he knew.

Meanwhile, the Captains debated the Harrheinian wines and the Sung were particularly keen on the brandy, though Wu Chen refused alcohol. Suzanne sat with the other Sung girl, their heads bent close together while they talked in a low murmur. Sara found beside her a hawk faced man, whipcord thin, who looked at her with interest.

"May I see your hands?" He asked courteously.

Sara raised an eyebrow but extended her right hand. He looked at it, raised his own and looked at her. "May I?" She nodded again and he took her hand, turning it over and looking at the calluses. Sara grinned, realising what it was about and he smiled, extending his own hand and showing his own calluses.

"You wield a heavier sword than I do," she said, measuring the calluses.

"Perhaps, or maybe I exercise more!" His eyes twinkled. "Or maybe our styles are different."

Sara looked at him, sensing the test. "I think not, sir. I think you perhaps twirl your sword in your hand, which I never do." She held back the feeling he was weaker on attacks from his right.

"Perhaps we could arrange a bout?" he asked.

"I would be delighted. Tomorrow?"

"Excellent. In the morning, before it is too hot. Do come to our ship, we have more room."

"With pleasure, I look forward to it." Indeed she did, and he wondered at the eager anticipation she made no effort to hide.

"Excuse me, you are very young. Your Captain perhaps exaggerated your skill?"

She dimpled. "I think not. I beat our champion in the semi-final of an open competition two months ago, but was disqualified" - she hesitated at his blank look - "ah, I was made the loser because I used a move outside the rules."

"A competition? For the whole country?" She nodded. "So all your fighting is from the practice floor? You have not killed your first man?"

"On the contrary, I fought for a year on our northern frontier and have killed a few. I didn't keep count." She smiled at the newly furrowed brow. "What the Captain did not say is that I am a Princess in our land, with no Princes, and my line is a fighting line. If I cannot lead men, I cannot lead our country. Some of the men here served under me on our northern frontier. They have seen me fight!"

For some time the Captains discussed trade items, then Wu Chen leaned forward. His captain nodded to him, and he spoke, "Captains, with permission, I would like to discuss with your priests. Our converse will be esoteric, I am sure, to others, so perhaps we may be excused?"

He arose from the table on the Captain's nod, and Walters and

Perryn took him to Walters' cabin. He glanced at Perryn. "I felt you for the last two days. It is a pleasure to see you at last. You have a gift, boy."

"Thank you, sir. I hope it is true."

"Where do you study?"

"We have an academy in Rikklaw's Port. I have studied there since I was a small child. Bishop Walters is a teacher there."

Wu Chen glanced at him curiously. "You have no power. How can you teach?"

Walters flushed. "The academy is not just for magicians. I am a scholar, sir, as indeed are most of the teachers and students. People with power like the boy are unusual."

"Indeed, with us as well. Why is he travelling with no teacher?"

"It is his time of testing and trial. He must travel and see the world, and discover himself. We have found boys with power do better at this stage without a guide, and indeed young Perryn has made great strides. It is time perhaps for him to return to the Academy for the next stage of his education."

"You have magicians capable of training him?"

Walters looked affronted. "We do, several."

Wu Chen's eyebrows lifted. "You have several in one place? A school. I must visit it." He turned to Perryn. "Boy, I would study your wa. May I?"

Perryn nodded, not sure what he meant but liking the man. Wu Chen leaned forward, took Perryn's hands and looked into his eyes. Perryn felt as if he were being hypnotised, and Wu Chen slipped into the surface of his mind. It was not intrusive, Perryn found himself showing the Mage around, which was the best way he could explain it to Pat later. Wu Chen looked at his ambition and loyalties, his skills and knowledge, and withdrew gracefully.

He looked at Perryn. "I wondered why I had to come on this voyage. You have great promise, boy, and you are pure. You will find in due course there are Mages, some powerful, who use the powers for their own ends rather than the good of all. You will never be one of those."

He stood. "I will return to my ship and get my things. I must come with you - I wish to see your academy and meet your wise men. And this boy needs a teacher now."

He left the cabin. Walters looked at Perryn and whistled. "I think you have found someone special, Perryn."

The meeting in the wardroom ended amicably, with both ships agreeing to hove to and discuss trade further the next day. Captain Larroche accepted an invitation to supper, and presented some trepang as a gift. Captain Lim examined it.

"This is from Harrhein?"

"Well, no," began the Captain, but Sara interrupted him.

"Yes, sir. From our Eastern Frontier!"

Captain Lim raised an eyebrow at this, and Sara continued.

"On this voyage we encountered people on the outer islands with whom we concluded trade agreements which brought them into our empire. The trepang is from there."

"The outer islands? We do not sail there. The people are very ferocious and we hear they eat people."

One of his men leaned forward and spoke in a strange tongue, with a strange modulation, going up and down.

Captain Lim looked at the Captain, tensing. "My Lieutenant says you have some of the man eaters on board. Is it your custom to eat human flesh as well?"

"It is not," said Sara, causing Captain Lim's eyebrows to rise fractionally at the interruption..

Captain Larroche leaned forward. "Lieutenant Starr is under my authority as a sailor, but she is on a learning cruise as she is the Crown Princess of Harrhein and as such she outranks me on diplomacy. I am a simple trader, she is my future Queen."

Sara continued. "We do not eat flesh, sir, but we do not impose our rule on our subject people in a manner which is distasteful to them. The people of the islands are different people. Those to whom you refer are the kai Viti, and they are a proud and warlike people. They do eat human flesh except as part of a religious ritual, a religion we do not share but we will not stop. They are not the only islanders with whom we allied."

Captain Lim watched her, his eyes never leaving hers.

"I understand you find it distasteful, Captain, as do we. But the people themselves are good and true allies. There are other customs we find distasteful, and the most important of those is slavery."

Captain Larroche hung his head and kept his face serene, while inwardly swearing at the girl.

Captain Lim was all attention as he couched his reply with care.

"You are clearly aware we practise slavery." Sara inclined her head. "You are perhaps not aware of the manner of it. I am aware of the way slavery is practised by the Umayyads and the Havantine, and ours is different. In our country, it is a way to power. I myself am a slave."

Sara's eyes widened.

"I belong personally to my Emperor, as does this ship and most aboard it. My parents sold me into slavery as a child when they saw my potential, to enable me to achieve position in the Empire."

"But I thought the Sung ..." Sara's voice trailed off.

"Yes," continued Captain Lim, "our family doctor emasculated me to allow me to be a slave. It frees me from the emotion that rules so many. Of course foreign slaves cannot rise to the levels Sung slaves can, but I trust you will understand we have a different attitude."

"Yes," said Sara, "I do indeed. Captain, we discovered the Umayyad trade in Harrheinian slaves. Are many sold to the Sung?"

For the first time Captain Lim hesitated, reluctant to give away how much he knew, but he inclined his head. "We have some. Not many."

"Captain Lim, we would trade with you. We have many things you want, as you have many things we want, and I have heard you are peaceful people. We are also peaceful people, but we can fight. One thing we do not want is our people stolen and sold to other countries. I ask you, agree not to trade in Harrheinian people as slaves, and to search out Harrheinian slaves in Sung. We will buy them all back from you."

Captain Larroche blanched, thinking of the cost and the waste, but saw the faces of the rest of his officers, shining with pride at their Princess, all other conversation ceased with everyone following each word. He saw the agreement in all the faces and groaned inwardly.

Captain Lim considered Sara. He was used to negotiating with many peoples, some exceptionally devious, and he was aware of the pitfalls in this conversation.

"The Princess should be aware I am unable to speak for all the trading ships or the entire Sung Empire. I am able to promise I will not trade in Harrheinian slaves, which I do freely, and I will act as your agent to buy back your people. For a percentage. However, you should know many of your people are happy in their new station in life, and many will not want to return."

"That is acceptable, Captain. I do understand, as many would find life very different and their position socially unacceptable back in Harrhein, but we must do what we can for our people. We will make a sole trading agreement between yourself and the Crown of Harrhein, and as such you will find your own power increases. You, alone from Sung, will be welcome to trade in Harrhein or our ships can meet you half way. This should help you to ensure the trade in Harrheinian people is significantly reduced."

Captain Lim felt lights go off in his brain. He knew from the small sample of exotic goods that these people were a key to unimaginable wealth and it was being offered to him on a platter. Sole trading agreement! Sung merchants would pay fortunes for these exotic wines, foods, liquors and fabrics, only available through his house. His future and that of his ancestors and their descendants would be secured for a hundred years! His name would live forever. Yes, the price was high, because it would mean assassination would become something to avoid on a daily basis, but this was not something to turn away. And this slip of a girl, so young, was sitting there staring at him, knowing perfectly well what she offered him. And the price he must pay. He noticed the steel and sadness deep in her eyes and felt respect rise in his body.

Showing nothing of his churning feelings on his face, he stood abruptly and bowed low from the waist, holding the bow long, making it the mark of respect to a powerful king, the greatest sign of respect the Sung made to people who were not Sung. He heard the hiss of surprise go round his staff. He rose, finding as he did so the Princess had also risen and bowed to him, the perfect level of bow to a person of status, lesser status.

"Please join us on my ship for the evening meal." He spoke directly to Sara. "Do bring your Captain and those of your staff that you will. Let us have pleasure and we can discuss matters further after the meal." He turned to Captain Larroche, saluted and left the wardroom, followed by his own staff in silence.

Back in his cabin with Brian, Captain Larroche flung his hat against the wall and swore. "That bloody wee girl has bigger balls than I do. I thought she had blown it with the slaves."

Brian chuckled. "She will be Captain before the voyage is over! Captain, you're the best negotiator I ever sailed with, but this girl has done us a deal which is going to make us very wealthy - and we couldn't have done it without her. This is opening up an entire country, and you know what Taufik said about the Sung, they're the richest and most important nation in the world. She's laid the ground work and I bet you she leaves it to you to fill in the details now." He accepted a glass.

"Indeed," said the Captain, "a good thing I suggested to the King to send her along."

Brian fell silent for a moment at this outrageous claim, before returning to the subject. "I can't get over the speed with which she concluded such a deal."

"She didn't conclude anything. I'll have to finish it off. She just opened the door."

"Which is exactly what Royalty is for. We're lucky to have her aboard."

Pat stood by the jib in the bows of the ship, looking down into the sea, flat and still like a mirror. He could see the stars reflected in it, and could feel Mot's warm body by his side. Hinatea was off sorting out a dispute between the Pahippian girls. He was thinking about the Sung, trying to concentrate on the bows he had seen at a distance and wondering at their range, though the little girl with her disconcerting eyes and warm hand kept pushing into his thoughts.

She had not attended the meal, an endless parade of tiny dishes, all delicious with the food pre cut to bite size. The Sung did not use knives and forks, but spoons and sticks. Only Suzanne managed to master the sticks, but Pat had used his as a scoop, lifting the bowl of food to his mouth, managing very well. Brian had frowned at him, but several of the Sung did the same.

He sensed warmth and felt the slight vibrations of footsteps coming his way, recognising Sara by the feel. He had seen her return from the Sung junk half an hour earlier. He smiled to himself, thinking how people accused him of being a witch because of his ability to know when somebody was close at night, when all he did was train up his senses.

Sara came up beside him and slipped her arm into his. She knew him well enough to know he had sensed her approach, so she was encouraged that he allowed her to come up to him, the first time since arriving on Pahippi.

"Poor Pat," she murmured into his hair. "I hurt you badly, didn't I?"

He turned slowly and looked at her. She looked into his eyes, and kissed him gently on the lips. Looking up at him, she murmured, "I will always love you, Pat. Thank you for being there for me. Despite everything I have done to you."

He didn't move, just looked at her. "They were our friends, Sara. I feel that we have let them down and don't know what to do."

Sara stiffened. "I'm sorry, Pat. I know it is difficult, and I feel the same, but we could not blame the Pahippians. You know Hinatea is a leader and will have killed our people?"

Pat nodded dumbly. "She killed Dan. She told me. She's sorry, but blames her priestess and gods for not stopping the attack."

"She is probably right. I still don't like her."

Pat smiled. They were so similar. "Why am I landed with girls who tell me what to do all the time? First you, now her."

For a moment Sara's heart stilled. Could she tempt him back? Then it hardened. No way would she have him back after Hinatea and somehow she didn't think he would accept Maciu. She sighed. She kissed him again, softly on the cheek, and murmured in his ear.

"You were my first love. No matter what I do, know you always hold my heart." And she was gone. Pat looked bleakly at the sea, and felt Mot lick his hand in sympathy. In the distance he heard Stiphleek's voice raised in song, in Harrheinian this time, till quelled by mutinous shouts.

The sun smote the sanded deck like a sledge hammer, even barely a quarter of the way up the sky. There was not a breath of air. Sara could feel the perspiration dripping down her back already, as she stood in her fighting leathers, barefoot to grip the deck. Chen Li He looked cool, dressed in what looked like a silk robe, belted at the middle. He gripped his sword, holding it negligently to one side. It had an extra reach of a good four inches.

The crews of both ships surrounded the fighting deck, the Sung in the rigging while the crew of the Queen Rose stood by the rails. Pat found a place to one side, with his scout crew by the corner where Lieutenant Mactravis and Little fussed over Sara's leathers. He could hear Little's whispers.

"Feel the bastard slowly, Princess. He'll be like a striking snake, and he'll leave openings for you all over the fucking place. Don't take them, that's what he wants. Look for patterns, but he's a killing swine for sure, and I don't reckon you'll see any. Don't let your own patterns last long, and don't repeat them. See what he knows, bet he don't know all the shit we do on the frontier." He talked with half his attention, lovingly greasing the leathers with a rag, oblivious of her skin.

A bell rang, and the two fighters stepped forward. It rang again, and the swords lifted. Chen Li He crashed hard at Lady Strike, applying brute force. Sara expected this; many people tried it against the poor little girl playing with men. She gasped and staggered then whipped forward with a stinging riposte as she sidestepped the lunge. Chen managed to avoid it by a hair as he aborted his lunge and parried. For a moment, Sara gained the upper hand and she pressed him hard, pushing him back along the deck while he tried to circle. The speed of the swords was so fast, that only a handful of men were able to follow the moves.

Pat was not one of them and he glanced over the crowd, looking at the reactions of people. He noted one man, different from the rest. He dressed in a different manner, and he was stockier, giving an impression of power. This was a fighting man, he thought, looking at the strange garb, for he seemed to be dressed in skirts with a shirt that swelled at the shoulders. The man sensed his eyes and looked up, directly at him across the fighting deck. Hard eyes assessed Pat in the same way, and he nodded thoughtfully at Pat, and returned his gaze to the fight.

'That,' thought Pat, 'is a dangerous man. One who would really give Sara a fight.'

He jumped as a hand slipped under his shirt, caressing his back and a little throaty chuckle came from behind him. A fan fluttered, and he wondered why he hadn't sensed her. Perhaps she was more than she appeared. No, she was definitely more than she appeared.

"Your Princess, good fighter, no?" Slanting eyes smiled at him.

Pat blushed, "Yes, she is good." He ignored Rat who was grinning and looked back at Sara. Hinatea scowled, and he was thankful she was unable to see the girl's hand.

Sara measured her man, felt his strength through his blade and followed his moves. She knew he was holding back, but watched all the flowing moves that came from him, saw the stamping foot. He was good, very good, but so far limited in what he knew. Strong, but she had beaten stronger swordsmen. Very, very fast, but she was faster, though she held her speed down and slowly drew more and more techniques from him.

Chen Li He was stunned. He knew he was a good fighter, but this girl was unbelievable. Every move he tried, she countered easily and he could tell she knew the move and even felt she knew before he did what he would try next. Her strength was so great he couldn't measure it, and he stopped thinking of her as a girl. He deliberately cleared his mind, repeating the mantra and felt for the void.

Sara sensed the change in him, and raised her game. She flowed into her moves, her mind blank, and she felt the dance begin. Time stood still for her. She had only moved into this mental state a few times and welcomed it.

Lieutenant Mactravis recognised the change, as did Little. "Fucking hell," whispered the latter.

Pat's dangerous man also saw it and his eyes narrowed with interest.

Pat knew something had happened because the hand on the small of his back tensed, seeming to grip his spine. He whipped his glance back to Sara and saw her in fighting state.

The blades blurred and danced, Sara dancing round the deck and driving Chen where she willed. It seemed to go on and on, a deadly beauty in the intricate steps. The crews murmured, even their untrained eyes knew they were seeing something special. Chen Li He's sword arced up into the air, flicked away by an untraceable movement from Lady Strike. He dropped to his knees, arms forward and bent his head backwards, exposing his throat. Lady Strike whistled as she sliced the air at her highest speed so far.

With a huge effort she stopped, inches from the vulnerable throat.

She gasped, and sagged, her eyes rolling back and a victory smile blossoming.

Silence.

The dangerous man moved first, and he was beside Sara and supporting her as she sagged.

"Steady, girl," he whispered. "Come, gently, back to this world. Here, your soul belongs here, in your body." He continued speaking softly and insistently, cursing his poor Belada and relapsing into his native tongue.

Both crews stayed silent, none understanding what they had witnessed, but all knowing it was something special. The kai Viti broke the silence, breaking into song, a melancholy song of victory none had heard before. It broke the spell, and Lieutenant Mactravis moved forward to help with Sara, while Sung people surrounded Chen.

Sara found herself. She opened her eyes and smiled beatifically. "Oh, my. That was so good."

"You were magnificent, Highness." Mactravis whispered with a note of awe in his voice.

"Fucking brilliant."

Sara smiled. "First time I have heard a note of genuine respect in your voice, Little!"

"You are a child of the void." This was a new voice, a lisping one. Sara looked at a strange man, with an aura of power, who looked back with a flat gaze. "I look forward to touching it with you, and perhaps in my own small way I can guide your advance. You have incredible potential." The man bowed slightly, turned and left.

Chen came to her. "Princess, I thank you for my life," he said formally. "I was outclassed, and you drove me into the void for the first time. I thank you, and pray you will grace me with your teachings in future."

Then to the astonishment of the Harrheinians he dropped to his knees and banged his forehead against the deck at her feet. He rose and walked away with an unsteady gait.

Taufik pushed through the crowd and whispered in her ear. "That is the Sung mark of respect, they are supposed to reserve it for their revered superiors. I have never seen it done before, never heard of it done to somebody who is not Sung."

Pat was quiet, thinking about what he had just seen. He knew what had happened to Sara, for he went into grace, as he called it from the Elvish, the zone, a peak emotional state, whenever he shot arrows. And often when he hunted. This was the first time he had seen her go into it, and he wondered at the reaction. He had used grace for so long he could not remember the first time. The others had gone, mobbing around Sara, even Hinatea forgetting all about the Sung girl.

"Come," said a voice in his ear and he realised the girl still gripped his spine, under his shirt. The slight pressure urged him aft and he went unresisting. Sara entering fighting grace had brought him to its edge, and the consequent extra vision and completeness of his awareness let him recognise the aura of this girl, the hard edges showing her ability, golden colours shot with red and black.

"I thought you one of the courtesans," he said looking down at her.

She smiled sunnily. "So kind! You mean I beautiful?"

He laughed. "So why you interested in me?"

"My job is protect. You most dangerous on board ship. Must know more about you!"

"Me? I'm not dangerous. I'm just a kid."

She dug him hard in the ribs. It hurt. "Don't lie to me. I am your other half. I know you. I know you better than you know self." She tossed her head. "Besides, I good listener, I hear your men talk. You very special archer. And you speak to animals."

Pat felt bewildered. Her conversation flowed in strange directions.

"What do you mean, other half?" He decided on the safer route of ignoring her other comments. They came to a door which she opened and they went down a passageway. "You are also dangerous, I think. Not many can sneak up on me."

"No. Only me. Because we are pair, you and I. But I trained, at monastery. You learn yourself, I think. No matter. I teach you, soon you too flow through walls."

She opened another door and pushed him through. He found himself in a large room, with a pile of cushions for a bed. An odd room, on the one hand feminine, on the other dripping with weapons. He picked up a little metal star and studied the blades, feeling the sharpness. He noted darkness on a couple of points and avoided them.

"What is the poison?"

"Can be all sorts. Depend what I can get. Sometimes plant, sometimes animal, sometime rock. You not know poison, I think."

"No, not needed. I hit what I aim at. How did you hear our men talk?"

"I swim over last night. Hide. Listen to you all talk. Learn. Heard your talk with Princess. Poor Pat. Girls not nice to you."

"That was private!"

"I know now. But I needed to know."

"How come Mot did not sense you?"

"What is mod?"

"My dog."

"The animal? Like you, I know animal. Now, come, enough talk. Take off clothes!"

Pat turned from examining the weapons to find her naked, her clothes stacked neatly on a cushion, and now she pulled at his clothes.

"What are doing!" he gasped, feeling a surge of emotions rush through his body and unable to tear his eyes from her delicate breasts.

"I tell you. We pair. Destiny. Joined. Forever. You just not understand yet. We make love, then you know and understand."

Feebly, he tried to push away her hands, but she ripped down his trousers and exposed his need.

Some hours later, Pat lay on the cushions, his head on her small breasts, feeling the muscles ripple in her body as she stroked his hair and crooned a low song. He didn't know he could get this exhausted. Their lovemaking had gone into grace, both of them, a pair of minds linked, and she had shown him how to use it in different ways. He felt they had been making love for days, weeks.

"It is special, is it not? See how many ways you can use the void. Once you can touch it, we can learn other ways. This way we call tantric. You use it for shooting and stalking, I teach you how to use it for everything." She stretched languorously as he rolled over and nibbled her breast.

"You must tell your Captain and your Princess you leave them.

I take you back to Sung, we climb the mountain and visit the monastery. You meet the Sifu. He will teach you and me together. We make great things happen, you see."

"Sung?" Pat murmured without thinking, then with some surprise, "You have still not told me your name."

"I take new name now? Pat's Shadow? Is good name?"

"No. What is your real name."

"I am Bai Ju. They don't give me family name, or maybe they call me Sung Bai Ju. Bai Ju mean white chrysanthemum. Is flower. Is flower of death!" She giggled. "But has many meanings. I like Pat's Shadow better!"

"Bai Ju. I like it, nice name. What you mean, go to Sung? I cannot."

"Why not?"

"I am protector of the princess. It is a duty."

"You slept with her." Pat yelped as Bai Ju pinched him. "Then she drop you. For other man, I bet. Yet you still want to stay with her?" She ground her thumb into his thigh and he screamed as she hit the nerve. "Or because she whisper "Ai lurve yu" in your ear! And now you see she can touch void too so you want her again!"

Pat laughed at her and caught her wrist as she moved to jab him again. He cleared his mind and slipped into the void, looking deep into her eyes and feeling her come with him. They suspended there for what seemed an eternity then slipped out again.

"You see?" he said. "We are called. Our future for now is with the Queen Rose. But I think we will go to Sung one day

Yes," she said thoughtfully. "I wondered why Sung called me to ship. We will move world, you and me, my Pat. You will be first foreigner to come to Sung uncut. For I not let them cut you. You have nice cabin like this?"

"No, very small."

"Hmmph. They not understand you important. Does dog sleep in cabin?"

"Sometimes. When she feels like it."

"From now on when I feel like it. Dog is dirty?"

"No! She is very clean."

"You sleep with dog and I get very angry, I warn you!" She giggled so he knew she was joking. "Come! Put on clothes, we go tell Captains and Princesses."

"Why do you bloody women always think you can tell me what to do?" He complained half-heartedly, but did as she said.

To Pat's astonishment the sun still rose through the sky, approaching midday. He thought it had been weeks. They found the Captains seated on cushions around a dining table, with Sara, discussing trade and treaties.

Bai Ju swept in imperiously, speaking in her broken Belada. "Lim, you send men to pack my things. I leave you now, go with this ship. Is my destiny, why I come. This man my other half. My future with him."

Captain Lim bowed low, his head almost touching the floor. "Your wish, Flower Lady."

"One day come back. I write letter for monastery. You take."

She swept out again, sucking Pat with her in her wake.

Sara felt fury boiling up within her, and saw Captain Larroche sitting with his mouth open. She looked questioningly at Captain Lim. He spoke slowly.

"The Lady Sung Bai Ju is strange. She is not part of my command but I am very happy she chose to come on my ship."

"What did she mean, other half?" Sara's eyes narrowed.

"I do not know, Princess. She is special, nobody knows much about them. They come from the mountains, from a secret monastery where nobody can go. They are great fighters, and with her on my ship I fear nobody. Her very name indicates her rank, for it means the Lady of Death, a title which is given to few of them. It is a hundred years since one with that title came out of the mountains. She is the most dangerous person on my ship. Is the boy also dangerous? His eyes betray skill and death."

"Yes," said Captain Larroche with finality. "Best archer by far I have ever seen and a scout who disappears into the landscape."

Captain Lim nodded. "They sound like a fine pair. Your worries will centre on trade with them on board to protect you. You seem to be taking half my ship, Captain Larroche! My best wizard insists on going with you, and the Tokkaidan also."

"It is disturbing," said Captain Larroche.

"Indeed. There is something in the future, rushing down on us.

You heard the Flower Lady talk of destiny. As did the wizard." He glanced at the Princess. "You are another one, Princess. A world changer. Pity us poor trading captains when ones such as you stride the world."

Sara's lips were tight, and she cried inside, '*Not another bloody woman for him! How many more? I am over him!*' She nodded stiffly, curbing her emotions. "Hinatea's reaction will be interesting. Shall we continue?"

Trade

Bai Ju issued orders to the men sent by Captain Lim, in the singing language of Sung. She oversaw them packing her things, barking out more instructions. The brawny men were terrified of her and would not touch the weapons till she packed them tenderly away.

"All done here," she said to Pat. " Let's go to your ship, I want to meet Mot properly, know she important to you. Things come later."

"Fine, I'll call a boat."

"No, we swim. More fun."

"What about sharks?"

"Even more fun!" She smiled brilliantly. "Come!" She led the way on to the deck and they went to the side away from the Queen Rose. She selected a point out of sight of anyone, and took Pat's hand. She went into grace, and Pat found himself going with her. Time stood still and they swung over the side, Pat finding from grace that the wooden planks of the sides had protruding edges he could grasp and climb down. Before they reached the sea, Bai Ju sucked in her breath and dived. Pat followed suit, opening his eyes under water. He swam after her, down and under the ship.

Deep in grace it was no distance, they came up for air periodically, breathing out before reaching the surface, taking a breath and going down again like dolphins. The clear water revealed several sharks which sheared away from them, staying at the edge of their vision. One circled round behind them and Bai Ju twisted in the water to face it, while he followed suit, and the shark sheared off from their readiness. They came to the Queen Rose in no time, dived under the boat and came up on the far side. They scaled the side just as fast, using the anchor cable, and grinned at each other as they shook the water off. They relaxed in the sun to dry, out of sight of all in a corner above the poop deck. Neither wanted wet footsteps to give them away.

Pat noted with interest the white face had gone, realising it was make up. Without it, Bai Ju looked younger, still stunningly beautiful, but her skin was a smooth, delicate colour, not far off his own, perhaps a little darker and a little burst of freckles trickled across her nose. She stuck her tongue out at him.

Going back into grace, he slipped along the deck, his feet gliding silently. He glanced round the corner and came out as nobody was there. Not running, but moving fast they went forwards and found Mot curled up asleep in the sun by the pig pen.

She started when Pat laid a hand on her head, then raised her muzzle and licked his hand. He introduced her to Bai Ju and she wagged her tail. Bai Ju went down on all fours and met her eyes for a long moment, before leaning forward and hugging her, burying her face in Mot's neck. When she came up, Pat noticed the shine of tears and hastily and wisely averted his gaze. Bai Ju pinched him anyway.

Pat led off to his tiny cabin, Bai Ju and Mot following behind. Mot delighting in falling into the old tracking pace.

Bai Ju was not impressed by the cabin and said so. She was all for going immediately to the Captain and demanding a bigger cabin. She was not happy to find out the chances of success.

"See what I sacrifice for you!"

"It was your choice." In some ways an old head sat on his shoulders, but he was still not forgiven as Bai Ju threw him down and prepared to teach him more tantric, when the door flew open to reveal a furious Hinatea.

She stalked into the room, bristling, slammed the door shut and loomed over them. Mot whined and tried to get under the bed. Pat almost followed her. Bai Ju didn't turn a hair, but turned away from Pat and sat cross legged, facing Hinatea. She said not a word, but the invitation was clear and Hinatea took it, sitting opposite her, also cross legged. The two girls studied each other, Bai Ju studying Hinatea's aura with fascination. Both girls wore brief tunics, Bai Ju's having barely dried out.

Pat gathered his thoughts, realising how he had forgotten about

Hinatea while immersed in Bai Ju's intoxicating presence. He did the bravest thing he had ever done. He spoke.

"I'm sorry," he began.

Both girls snapped in unison "Quiet!"

"This does not concern you." Hinatea spoke flatly, neither girl taking her eyes off the other.

Pat shrank down, like a mouse with two snakes over it. The girls were immobile, just looking at each other and it was wearing on his nerves. He could wait in ambush for two days without moving, but after less than five minutes, he started to move. Immediately, two hands shot out, one grabbing his arm, the other his leg. He subsided.

"Oro, my God, told me of you." Hinatea stated after an eternity. "Say you priestess of living god. Strong god. You are his vicar."

Bai Ju inclined her head. "Sung spoke of you also. He does not speak direct, let's me try to understand. We want you. We need you."

"Oro tell me not to fight you. But I not give him up."

"We must become as one. It is written. Sung say Oro his friend."

Two heads turned slowly and two pairs of black, obsidian, hard and empty eyes transfixed Pat's soul.

In the evening an interesting group gathered on the poop deck, sipping the tea they had obtained from the Sung. Perryn was sitting there with Walters and Wu Chen when the wizard stiffened and Perryn found Pat, Hinatea and Bai Ju sitting cross-legged beside them.

"Oh, damn you, Pat," said Perryn. "Will you stop creeping up on people? It's damn annoying."

"Good tea," said Pat without expression.

Wu Chen bowed low from his sitting position towards Bai Ju. "Lady, we are honoured." He spoke with care.

"Are you going to introduce your friend?" Walters asked.

"Sure," said Pat. "Guys, this is Bai Ju. She is sailing with us now. Bai, this is Perryn and Bishop Walters. They are priests and Perryn knows some tricks."

Walters smiled and nodded, while Perryn, irritated at the introduction, extended his mind towards her, testing her aura and sensing a stillness he had not experienced before, though there was a similarity in Wu Chen. Wu Chen started to speak and put a hand on his arm, there was a blinding pain in his skull and he rocked back on his haunches, stunned.

Bai Ju glared at him. "Is not polite."

Wu Chen's nervousness became apparent. "Please, Lady, he is young, he does not know. I will teach him. My apologies for my student."

Bai Ju smiled serenely. "Accepted. You take responsibility, wizard. He strong and unschooled. Train fast."

Pat and Walters wondered what had happened, Hinatea just smiled. Sara, Maciu and Suzanne came up and joined them, followed by the Tokkaidan. Sara sat beside Bai Ju, determined to make friends, while Suzanne put her hands on Perryn's head, massaging it and looking thoughtfully at Bai Ju.

"This is Takeo," Sara indicated the Tokkaidan and introduced the others while Bai Ju was introduced to her and Maciu. Sara could sense the discomfort of the wizard and Takeo at Bai Ju's presence and wondered what to say.

Suzanne inspected the two girls arrayed beside Pat. "So, you met Hinatea," she began. "No blood. Little is offering good odds you kill each other."

Hinatea's eyes went cold and black, causing a shudder to run down Suzanne's spine. It was Bai Ju who answered.

"We Triad. Is good."

"Oh, the Captain will love this," Suzanne smiled with enthusiasm. "We love ménage à trois in Galicia, quite a few. It can be so special."

Wu Chen coughed. "In Sung, Lady, a Triad is something else. It is a fighting unit of myth, extremely powerful and dangerous. Bandits call their gangs after the Triad to make themselves more fearsome." He was inspecting the three with care, his brows drawn together.

"Not trained yet," nodded Bai Ju. "Strong later."

As the mutters died away, Bai Ju changed the conversation.

"Bishop, it is title, yes?" she asked Walters. "What it mean?"

"Uh, it means I am responsible for the spiritual guidance of a town, but in my case I earned the rank as a scholar and teacher more than a priest."

"A scholar?"

"One who studies and learns. My main interest is in cartography, map making, and what is in the world."

"Is good. You know are men like you on Impe'ial Orchid?"

"Really? I am not surprised, but hope to meet them. I would appreciate talking and sharing information with them."

Bai had not finished. "You here for reason too. You study so can write, is so?"

"Yes, of course."

"I think you not map maker now. You here to record what happens." She had everyone's attention now.

"What happens?" Walters whispered. He had a sinking feeling he wasn't going to like where this conversation went.

"These people," Bai Ju went on with a gesture encompassing them all. "Strong people. All different. On own become leaders, rulers, scare people. Now we together. What mean?"

Sara spoke slowly, "Captain Lim says we are world changers."

"Good name. I think yes. So, what are our duties, neh? We, Pat, Hinatea and me, we the knife, the knife of the Old Gods. You, Perryn and Chen, you the umbrella. You speak to the New Gods." Perryn started at the lack of honorific for Chen and cold fingers stroked down his spine. Bai Ju went on, looking at Sara. "You the flame, the beacon, leads men. Takeo, he the smith, beat flame to steel. And keeps it white hot." She considered Suzanne.

"You I not know. Think important. Think you keep her human."

She returned to Sara with troubled eyes.

"Be careful, girl. Men follow you. People follow you. Countries follow you. You take them to flames and death, make desert, or you their light, who bring rice and freedom? This one," she indicated Suzanne, "she keep you straight. Or the world ends in darkness."

There was silence as her words echoed in the dark, and Bai Ju sipped her tea serenely. Mot broke the silence, thumping her tail to the deck, causing Bai Ju to smile.

"Dog clever. She happy, she not worry about death, she think only of good things. We must be same. Concentrate, focus on good result not bad."

"What about me?" asked Maciu.

Bai Ju smiled sweetly at him. Only the perceptive Suzanne caught the sadness and compassion in Bai Ju's eyes. "You good man. You give her love, she needs this. You shield and rock for her. When she angry, she hit you, you not mind. Is good. You take anger from her."

Sara groped for words, anger boiling up in her. *'Brazen little hussy! How dare she suggest such things?'* Maciu put an arm around her shoulders and she stilled the words. But it was Pat who changed the subject, to Sara's surprise. "You did well today, Sara. You found fighting grace today, first time I think. Right in the zone."

Takeo responded with quick interest. "Zone? Grace? This I not know. She touched the void and entered it."

"Void? Yeah, good name. I call it grace."

"Grace? What you mean, grace?" asked Bai Ju.

Pat struggled for words. "When you do things, you are in different mental states, emotional states. It's a word I use to describe being complete, feeling one thing only and losing other feelings. When you do it right, time slows down, everything is easy. I learnt it from the Elves for running and archery. They call it the state of grace. I found it can be used for other things, like learning. We used it to swim over this afternoon, and, uh, other things."

Suzanne instantly knew what other things were and smiled faintly for the first time. But Pat's description hit a chord with her, and she understood what he meant for she used it for sex and hadn't understood void.

Takeo, Wu Chen and Bai Ju were fascinated by Pat's words, leant forward and spoke at the same time, then, embarrassed, leant back. Wu Chen checked with the others and spoke first.

"Young man, this is wonderful. A difference in approach from East and West. Tell me, how do you learn to enter 'grace'?"

"Practice," said Pat with finality. "I try to remember how I was feeling the last time I did something well, and put myself so I am feeling the same - hold my body the same, breathe the same, take the same steps or sit the same way, think the same things, empty my mind of everything else, and I find myself in the same state of grace. If I work on it, each time it gets a bit better."

"Do you not practice exercises?"

"Not sure what you mean. I am always exercising, running, shooting, riding."

"I meant more mental exercises. Words you repeat?"

"No, I don't think so. For me it is actions. The mind thinks differently depending on what the body is doing."

"Yes, we seek the void by making the body still and exercising the mind. Your way is interesting. I think we could combine techniques for good results."

"It lets us dive deeper," said Hinatea. "My grandmother teach me. We use breathing to get there."

"I think," spoke Takeo deliberately into the following silence, "the boy's methods are good for swordplay. They would work well - we practise moves constantly so they are automatic. At this stage we are not seeking the void, we do later. Perhaps to combine the two. But I do not think his grace and our void are the same. Similar, yes, but not the same."

"I not agree." Bai Ju spoke slowly. "I see him go into grace. It is void. Same thing. Different route. Our training different to yours, Takeo, we use his grace. There are many routes to void. See his aura. Only one touched by void with aura like him. These five only ones on ship to have it, like us three only ones of us. I never see aura like yours, girl. Where you find void?" She spoke to Suzanne.

For the first time Suzanne was unsure of what to say. She was slightly out of her depth and wasn't used to it. Sara spoke up for her.

"Suzanne is the most beautiful woman in Harrhein. She is the most accomplished courtesan, men pay fortunes for her time. Her coaching of the men and women on our ship ensures no fights over partners. Her coaching makes everyone happy."

The aesthetic Wu Chen appeared blank, while Takeo showed a glimmering of understanding, but Bai Ju understood the implications.

"Oooh! You tantric master! Very good!" She clapped her hands with pleasure. "You share night with us, please? I only poor student, happy to learn more from you!"

Wu Chen was horrified. "You claim to touch the void with pleasure! Ridiculous! It is only through abstinence you can achieve the ethereal heights and mental stimulation of the void. It is impossible to use the low drives of the body."

"If you strong enough, it makes you better not weaker. Very strong power comes from sex." Bai Ju spoke with authority. "Big mistake in your teachings, wizard." She contemplated Perryn who shifted his weight, unsettled. "You no listen to him about sex, boy.

Tantric master can make you stronger, but careful of witches. They drain your power. His lot think all women witches." She pealed with laughter at Wu Chen"s face.

Wu Chen was angry now. "Witch! Good name for you! Speak with more respect, or you will feel my anger!"

"I know your ability and fear not your anger, wizard. I listen inside your walls while you teach. Try me not, or shuriken will feel your throat."

"Enough! Both of you!" Suzanne was angry. "Bai Ju, never hurt a man's pride. Wu Chen, accept we are all able to learn from others and some of which we take for truth is not. But both of you remember we are together on the same team, or our in-fighting will bring on the darkness before time!"

Bai Ju responded immediately. "Yes Master." She leant forward, amazingly supple and knocked her forehead on the deck at Wu Chen. "Wu Chen, I most humbly apologise for my rudeness. I promise to help you where I can and learn from you too."

Wu Chen rallied magnificently, through the confusion written on his face. He made a brave attempt at reaching the deck with his forehead but was unable to reach it, lacking suppleness. "Bai Ju, I acknowledge your abilities as supreme in your area. Long have we feared you studied us. I look forward to learning from you, and teaching you what little I can." Concern spread across his face. "But I am too old for sex."

"I think I will change your mind," drawled Suzanne, "but plenty of time."

Sara awoke early the next morning, still thinking about the conversation of the previous night. Bai Ju's words echoed uncomfortably from her dreams, full of ravening hordes rampaging over countries, leaving deserts and burning towns in their wake while she laughed over the carnage. Getting herself some porridge and tea from the galley, she heard indistinct but shrill cries outside and went on deck. Half the crew were there, looking up.

Pat raced along a spar high up the mainmast, closely followed by Hinatea, and as she watched they jumped, caught a rope and swung down to the next spar in an amazing feat of agility she would never dare emulate. They ran back along the spar, dodging as Bai Ju tracked them from above, a long stick prodding at them.

It was Bai Ju who was crying out.

"Keep arms in! Not need! Use wa! Feel it! Shut eyes! Faster! You can go faster!"

She kept up a constant stream of words, and Sara couldn't work out whether it was encouragement or criticism, eventually concluding it was both.

Nils came up to her. "What are they doing? They will kill themselves."

"They are training." Takeo appeared from nowhere. "You privileged. Not many see ninja train."

"Nin-ger?" asked Sara. "What is that?"

"What we call them in our country. Secret society of assassins. She is same, I think. She train them."

"Is she making them run with their eyes shut?" asked Nils.

"I think so. Ninja work at night, other senses more important than sight."

The spectators watched entranced as they ran about for a good half an hour, before both jumped into a sail and slid to the deck, followed by Bai Ju. Pat was dripping with sweat, Hinatea exhausted. Bai Ju was cool and fresh, immaculately turned out but without the white face. Crew members surrounded them and Sara could hear the questions. What were they doing, who was Bai Ju, could they learn, had he really had his eyes shut.

Pat waved them off, saying to let him clean himself first, and went to the rail where he dived over, followed by the two girls. A cry of "Sharks!" went up and everyone rushed to the rail, to see them climbing up the side of the ship like lizards.

The Bosun was waiting. "What the fuck do you think you are doing Pat? Trying to kill yourself."

"Is training," said Bai Ju. "Must be hard or no good."

"Who the hell are you?"

"She's our trainer," said Pat.

"Sifu!" said Bai Ju.

"What the fuck are you training them to do?"

"Kill," said Bai Ju succinctly.

"Well, they're already pretty fucking good killers!"

"I know. Soon best in world. Even better than me and I best in

East."

Bai Ju said this in such a matter of fact manner it did not seem preposterous coming from this tiny girl. It rather took the wind out of the Bosun's sails.

Two kai Viti came up and threw themselves prostrate on the floor in front of Bai Ju. One reached out and took her foot, placing it on his head. Silmatea was with them.

"Pat is our leader." Mara spoke. "Where he goes, we follow. Please, teach us too. We must fight with him, help protect him." Wiwik and Silmatea nodded, the other Pahippian girls coming up, and looking as if they were going to join them.

Bai Ju carefully and respectfully removed her foot, looking closely at the men. Pat knew now she was looked at their auras.

"Maybe. This afternoon we test. Test anyone who want to learn."

"Run along a spar with your eyes closed? Fuck that!" said Pete with feeling.

Rat pushed himself forward. "I'm game." He took a deep breath, and looked at Pat. "I can do this, Pat. I am not far off you."

Pat nodded gently. "I think you can, Rat."

Bai Ju grinned in delight. She looked up at the poop deck to where Sara stood watching. "Soon, Princess, soon we have whole pack of night stalkers for you!" She looked at the crew.

"I impressed. On Sung ship all scared. Here we have six quick-quick!" To the delight of the crew, she turned and waggled her little bottom at the Imperial Orchid. "Now we rest, and soon you show me your ar-cher-ry. See if you shoot better than me!"

Takeo spoke to Sara. "You are interesting people. The Imperial Orchid sailed for two months to get here. I saw her maybe five times, and did not hear her speak. I never heard of ninja boasting before. Or talking. Now on your ship, look at her."

"How about you, Takeo? I think you didn't speak much either."

"You are right." His eyes twinkled. "Like I say, interesting people. No respect for others, but lots of friendship. Different. I think I like. Now, I think I will join in the archery. This very brave of me, because I think I am very good, but I know the ninja will be better and I think your Pat will be too."

"I will join in too. Only Pat and Grey Fox on this ship are better than I am, so it will be a challenge between us, perhaps?"

There was a long debate on where to set up the archery range. Bai Ju thought there was room on the Imperial Orchid, but Pat's view prevailed and they towed a barrel behind the Queen Rose. After the swordsmanship exhibited the previous day, none of the Sung entered, but all wanted to watch. The Bosun took charge of the barrel, and all the ship boats were arrayed around it, with the staff of both ships on the poop deck of the Queen Rose, looking over the fighting deck where the participants and the Bosun stood. The rigging creaked with the weight of crewmen.

First came the speed test, with the barrel floated fifty yards behind the ship. Bai Ju went first, and in a minute by the hourglass sent an incredible fourteen of her black, red fletched arrows into the barrel, missing none. She had the smallest bow, made of bamboo and horn glued together and recurved. Takeo's bow was similar, perhaps a hand longer and he sent nine arrows, missing with two which glanced off the barrel.

Sara, with her longer bow, matched him for speed but only missed one. Grey Fox struggled, launching eight arrows and missing none. Pat's bow impressed the Sung with its size and Bai Ju laughed in delight when she struggled to pull it three quarters of the way back. Pat sent nine arrows, missing with none, only part drawing his bow.

The distance competition saw the barrel sent out a hundred yards, with each competitor sending five arrows, and the distance increased by fifty yards for a tie. Sara missed with two arrows, Takeo with one, while the others hit it every time though Bai Ju took longer.

At 150 yards, Bai Ju missed with one arrow then Pat and Grey Fox went neck and neck till Grey Fox missed one at 250 yards. He swore it was a rogue wave and laughed with Pat about it.

Pat grinned and smashed the barrel with one of his boat sinker arrows.

On the poop deck, Captain Lim commented to Captain Larroche he understood now why they weren't bothered by pirates and offered to buy Grey Fox.

As the Sung went back to their ship, Bai Ju collected Suzanne and Walters, saying she would make the introductions they needed and took them over to the Imperial Orchid. She led them down to a cabin which she opened without knocking.

Inside were a startled looking group of men, grey haired, working over scrolls. Bai Ju started to speak and the men fell to their knees, knocking their foreheads on the floor. Bai Ju snapped at them in Sung and they leapt to their feet. The leader listened to her and nodded. She turned to Walters.

"I tell them what you are and they will help you. Enjoy." She nodded and went out of the door with Suzanne in tow before he could speak.

Walters looked at the men, wondering at their white faces. The oldest collapsed into a chair. One came towards him.

"You are our honoured guest. The Flower Lady says we must show you our maps, even the secret ones." He shook his head in amazement.

"Well, that would be very kind of you," replied Walters. "I have brought some of my own maps to show you." And he spread some scrolls on an empty desk. All the men came over and peered at them.

"Ah, yes, the island chain." The apparent leader smiled his delight. "A detailed map. Very fine work. What does this symbol mean?" All thoughts of introductions left the heads of the scholars as they delved into the work and started to argue about it.

Bai Ju led Suzanne back to another area of the ship, where there was a large superstructure on the main deck. She went into this, revealing an airy room covered in cushions, full of girls who were busy doing their hair, applying make up, sewing clothes and even a few practising on musical instruments. The chatter ceased as they came in, stillness spreading across the room.

Bai Ju looked around the room, and snapped something in Sung. One of the girls jumped up and ran to a door at the back, reappearing moments later behind an older woman, fresh from sleep. Her eyes were wide with apprehension.

"Heya, Old Mother," said Bai Ju in Belada. "I bring you someone special, this Suzanne, she best courtesan in Harrhein. Also, she Tantric Master."

There was a slight murmur at this, but the girls all looked at Bai Ju, transfixed like rabbits watching a snake. The older woman prostrated herself at Bai Ju's feet and tried to kiss them. Bai Ju dodged the slobber and kicked the woman in the side.

"Get up, old mother. Never mind me, talk to Suzanne." The woman began to weep, and started calling out in Sung. Bai Ju looked disgusted.

"These ship's courtesans. Captain use them to help trading with new peoples we meet. I cannot stay. This too frightened. Will not help you while I here." She turned and left the room. There was silence in the room except for the woman, weeping in heavy, gusting sobs. The girls came and clustered around her, helping her up and seating her on a cushion. One brought her a cup of tea and another fanned her. They murmured to her in Sung, and one or two dashed a glance at Suzanne.

After a few minutes and as her heaving bosom subsided, the woman looked over at her, and said something in Sung. Another replied and the woman's eyes sharpened. She barked an order and one of the girls brought Suzanne a cup of tea.

"A thousand apologies, beauteous one, the White Flower frightens us, we thought we were going to die. Please, sit down. Here beside me. Tell me your name and what you are doing here."

In the afternoon Bai Ju held her trials.

All the kai Viti volunteered, as did about fifteen of the crew and of course Hinatea's girls. Esbech and Stiphleek surprised themselves by entering, though from their faces Sara thought they had gone along with their kai Viti friends without realising what was happening.

For the first hour it was simple exercise - running round the ship carrying sacks, climbing the rigging, performing exercise routines. Bai Ju monitored them, dropping the occasional observation in a low tone to Hinatea and Pat, telling them what she was looking for.

She pulled one of the crew girls out of the exercise routine, gave her a small wooden ball and told her to balance it on her head while standing on one foot. The girl looked blank, but made a game try, though she looked nervously at Bai Ju as she did, the ball falling off all the time. Bai Ju studied her, and shook her head, gently excusing the girl.

She selected Esbech next. He caught the ball as it fell without looking at it and tucked it into his beard. Bai Ju laughed and kept him.

Testing continued and the group winnowed down.

Silmatea was chosen and given the ball. She didn't look at it, held it in her hand and Pat could see her clear her mind, fluidly extend her foot for balance and raise the ball to her head without looking at it. She was in grace, even though the ball rolled off. She shook herself, and lowered herself to retrieve it, but Bai Ju stopped her.

"Good. You start. What your name?"

"Silmatea, mistress."

"You strong, girl. Stay and watch, tell me when you know what I look for."

"You look for the god-touched, mistress, those who can slow time. And can do it when tired, I think."

"Good girl. Don't tell the others!"

The afternoon passed and most of the audience lost interest. Rat was chosen, as were half a dozen of the Kai Viti, three more of the Harrheinian boys, two of the crew girls and all four of Hinatea's wild girls, though none of the other Pahippians. Both Esbech and Stiphleek made it through. Bai Ju called the survivors together and spoke to them.

"Well done. You did good. You selected. Now it gets tough. Some of you pass easy, some just make it. Now we see how you do. Not all make training. Can stop anytime. If not make it, you still better soldier, hunter, than anyone else. Rest now, come back here at midnight and we give you exercise."

The group broke up, going off too exhausted to talk much, high on the euphoria success gives. Brian came over, looking warily at Bai Ju.

"I think we need to talk. You have chosen these people, which is fine, but the training you give them must be outside their normal work hours. They still have work to do."

"But I choose them." Bai Ju was puzzled. Wu Chen came over, with Sara.

"Honoured Sister, these peoples' ways are different from ours," Wu Chen began. "They do not understand what you are; they do not have people like you in their country. We must fit in They know nothing of what you are or what you can do. The special status you receive in Sung has still to be earned in Harrhein."

"Oh, think I understand." She looked at Brian. "Cannot have all time for training?"

"We may be able to come to some agreement," said Brian, as he took in the meaning of Wu Chen's words. "I need these people to sail the ship and to keep it clean. When the weather is fine, like now, and steady, I do not need them and any work I give them is to keep them busy, or to train them for when they are needed. But in bad weather, especially when the wind changes or we are close to shore, I need all the hands to change sails quickly."

"So if training includes changing sails quickly, I can train all time and give to you in bad weather, better trained?"

"Yes, that would be fine," said Brian, unable to perceive a trap in her words.

"When can practise changing sail?"

"Ask, and I will tell you."

"Is good. I go now, need bath!" She smiled at him and went off to the rails.

Brian looked at Wu Chen. "What the hell is she, Wu Chen?"

"She is very special in Sung, Mate Brian. A trained killer from the secret temples. Even the Emperor is wary of her, for her people consider him to be their vicar to the people. They hold themselves apart and chosen by the Gods. In Sung, she can go where she wills and take what she wants, and nobody will say anything. I had to ask Captain Lim for permission to come on this voyage, with a letter from the Emperor. She appeared and chose herself a cabin, told him she was coming along on the journey."

"You were right, we have nothing like her in Harrhein." Brian thought for a moment. "Well, maybe the princess. I can see the Captain is going to be over the moon with delight at another pushy woman on board."

"She has chosen sixteen people, I think. When she has finished training them, no army can stand before you." Wu Chen did not understand Brian's comment, so continued. "I met her once. The city where I lived was plagued by bandits. They were strong. I was in the throne room discussing with the Hand of the Emperor how to deal with the situation, when the doors swung open and this one came in, followed by four of the bandits carrying baskets. She waved to the bandits, and they opened the baskets. They contained heads, the bandit leaders. And she left, all without speaking. The bandits she left behind for the Hand to do what he willed. There was no more bandit problem."

"Are there many of them in Sung?" Brian spoke into an echoing silence.

"No. Nobody knows how many. When the horse riders came in from the steppes a hundred years ago, fifty came out to help us. Old, young and children. In the last ten years, she is the only one we have seen, that we know about. She appeared for the first time two years ago. In the Emperor's court. Told him there was too much banditry in the Empire and he must clean it up. Said the people were suffering. Nobody tells the Emperor what to do. She did."

He looked bleakly at Brian.

"All my life I have feared them. They are the only ones we magicians fear. We think they are the servants of death himself. Now this one appears and talks! She laughs! She is human. She looks like a young girl and which makes her all the more dangerous. It is passing strange. And now I am on board a ship with this changeling, with destiny calling me to train the most powerful novice I have seen. We live in interesting times, Brian."

"We do indeed. Well, we must make the most of it."

"Brian, in Sung, this is a curse. May you live in interesting times. People die in interesting times"

Captain Larroche grinned at his coxswain as he climbed into the jolly boat. "A good days trading today, Ben. You'll have your work cut out tomorrow."

"That'll be fine, surr. What'll we have to do?"

"We're going to lash the two ships together so we can transfer cargo."

The cox'n mulled this over.

"Us'n 'll check the fenders tonight, surr."

The Captain smiled as he went up the ladder to the main deck and continued up to the poop. He stopped for a moment, at the sight of Sara sitting cross-legged opposite Takeo, with her eyes closed. Her right arm was outstretched, balancing a ball in the palm of her hand. He raised an eyebrow to Brian, and went up to him.

"Brian, tonight I feel like celebrating. We will have a full dinner in the ward room. Tell the cook. All the officers and the craft masters to attend."

"Good idea, sir. Are we inviting any of the Sung?"

"No, only our complement. The Sung are doing the same."

"You are aware we have three more, ah, craft masters, sir?"

"Three? What, the wizard, Sara's swordsman and... not the little girl with Pat? What's she a master of?"

"Killing, sir. Yeah, I know. There's a lot I have found out about her, sir, which I will tell you, but the bottom line is we don't have to worry about being attacked. I think we should have Hinatea as well, as the leader of the Pahippians."

"Sara won't have her in the same room."

"I don't think we have to worry about those two any more, sir."

Pat received the news of the wardroom dinner with some trepidation. He had only attended one since his elevation to the ranks of officers, in which he had received some pointed instructions as to table manners from the First Mate, after which Sara had whispered instructions to him. Somehow he knew she wasn't going to help him this time, and he dreaded to think what Bai Ju's table manners were like. He didn't think Hinatea's invitation was at all a good idea. She disdained using forks and spoons.

"What this wardroom dinner?" Bai Ju sat cross-legged on the bunk, with Hinatea opposite her. Both girls had their eyes closed and were holding hands.

"All the officers and craft masters will attend and eat together. It is important to have good table manners and we must be dressed in our court uniforms."

"Ah so. Court manners, neh?"

"Yes, that's right," he said, heartened.

"So must make noise like this when eating soup," she made a dreadful sucking noise. "Belch to show food is good and spit on floor when food arrives."

She pealed with laughter at the horrified look on his face, and rolled on the bed in a paroxysm of glee, while Hinatea grinned and mimed scratching intimate places. The girls were getting on well.

"Is alright," she choked through the giggles, "we make fun of you! You so funny sometimes."

"Well, the trouble is, I don't know what the manners are supposed to be, so how am I supposed to tell you?" He grumbled. "I am sure to get the blame when you two do something wrong."

"Poor Patty," she stopped laughing instantly and started to stroke his hair.

"And don't call me Patty!" he snapped.

Smiling, she stopped. "What you want me to wear? Sung court dress?"

He looked at her with deep suspicion. "You have it? Is it decent?"

"Of course, I have everything." She gestured at the wooden chests filling up the tiny cabin. "What you mean, decent?"

"Your bosoms are covered up, and legs not showing," he said going red again.

"Bosoms? What are bosoms?" she said with a wicked grin.

Hinatea broke in with a smile. "I have my ceremonial dress. It is very beautiful."

"What is?" Bai Ju wanted to know. "Is pretty?"

"No!" said Pat in horror. "You can't wear Pahippian clothes to a dinner!"

Hinatea pulled a grass skirt and some shells out from her chest. "See, very pretty. No wear anything else, very good."

"You are not wearing a couple of leaves," said Pat firmly. "Ask the Bosun for a proper uniform."

Both girls spoke at once, proclaiming how beautiful grass skirts were and Bai Ju could borrow one as well.

Pat ignored them, and started getting out his court uniform. He had only worn it once, after he had been given it from ship's stores, and he started worrying over the creases and a nasty looking stain. Bai Ju was fascinated by it and took it away from him.

"Nasty thing! The cloth is so hard. What this thing for?"

"This is an epaulet, it shows my rank as a junior officer. Come on, give it back. I have to get the wrinkles out of it and clean the stain."

"How you do?" she asked, ignoring his hand and still studying the uniform.

"I'll take it to the galley and steam the creases out. Maybe the cook can get rid of the stain. Come on, give it to me."

She sniffed. "Cook! Ha! Leave to me, I sort. You need new rank now, to show what you become."

"NO!" he cried in horror, visions of a gaudy monstrosity sitting on each shoulder.

"Yes," she said with finality. "You go wash, you smell bad. Wipe salt off, not hurt clothes."

"Please, Bai Ju, this is important. I must do things correctly according to our customs. You cannot know what is right."

"Ha!" she turned on him in mock outrage, eyes flashing. "You think I stupid whore? I know what you need. I fix. Go!" She pushed him out the door. He bumped into Suzanne in the corridor, who saw him ejected and smiled.

"Hi," he said, a picture of misery and attempted to get past her. She moved to cut him off.

"And why do you have a face like the world is about to end? I thought all was well in Pat land, with your clever little girl taking charge of you and Hinatea?" Suzanne delighted in Pat's triad, particularly in the outrage engendered amongst the more conservative in the crew.

"She's decided she knows more about Harrhein court uniform than I do and she's getting it ready for me. I hate to think what it is going to look like."

"She's probably right," said Suzanne, "as you know what to wear on a horse but you know absolutely nothing about court. Don't worry, Pat. She wants to be proud of you, so she will do it. Go on now, and don't worry." She watched him disappear, and thought to herself, all the same, it might be an idea to proffer some advice. She knocked on Pat's door.

Rat was washing when Pat climbed down to the platform, and became the surprised recipient of Pat's woes. He had never heard Pat say so many words, and with endearing male sensitivity roared with laughter.

"Ah, Pat, thanks mate, I needed a good laugh. Been feeling a bit down! Seriously, mate, you go and buy a beer for any of the married men and ask them about married life and they'll bend your ear for hours. Get used to it, 'cos those two have you well under the thumb! When have you got to report back?"

Pat glowered at him. "She didn't say."

"Well, come down to the fo'c'sle and have a beer. Tell the Bosun all about it, she'll put you right."

"If you so much as hint at this to the Bosun, I swear I'll kill you!"

"Well, you'd better come along and make sure I don't! Come on, you're clean enough and you've got no whiskers to shave anyway!"

Over the next hour, with Rat's help, he worked out what he was going to say to Bai Ju and felt much better. He strode down the corridor to his cabin, when Bai Ju came out of Suzanne's open door.

"Ah, good, there you are! Come here, quick, quick!" She dragged him into Suzanne's room which was packed with women. "Now, stand still, don't move." And she began to strip his clothes off.

"Hey! Wait! What are you doing?"

"I said don't move!" Looking around, he saw Sara, Maciu, Hinatea and Suzanne, equally naked, standing upright. Each had two Sung girls chittering away on either side of them, offering up bits of cloth and somehow fixing them around them. Two more girls descended on Pat, helping Bai Ju to take the last of his clothes off and subjecting him to the indignity of being measured.

"What's going on?" he asked faintly.

Suzanne answered. "Your clever girl told me she wouldn't be seen dead in the cloth they make the uniforms from, and said she would make them in silk for you. I asked for one too, and she is doing one for Sara as well. We are creating new unifomrs for Maciu and Hinatea. I designed them! Bai Ju sent to the Orchid for some seamstresses and cloth, and they will all be ready in time for supper!"

"We've only got an hour!"

"I know! Brilliant isn't it - look at those girls go!"

Indeed the Sung seamstresses were already trying a uniform on Suzanne and checking it. Even Pat could see it looked better than her previous uniform.

Hinatea grinned at him as her uniform, a long dress, was held up to her. "Look, Pat! Isn't it pretty. The same colour as the sea after a big storm. Very beautiful. Do I look beautiful?"

She did, and Pat was tongue tied looking at all the girls, while being dressed himself.

"Look at him!" said Sara to Suzanne in Harrheinian. "Doesn't he look just like a dog being given a bath?"

Both Suzanne and Bai Ju laughed, which Suzanne cut off and stared at Bai Ju.

"You understood what she said?"

"Sure, I speak Harrhein perfectly. It's Belada I have a bit of a problem with," Bai Ju smiled. "The reason I came on this trip was to try and find out more about you people, and I learnt the language from some slaves before leaving. Come on, let's get these uniforms finished."

"But why didn't you tell us?"

"I was still finding out about you. No time now, let's get these uniforms finished and you will want to get your hair done as well. This one is a good with hair, let her do yours." She indicated one of the seamstresses and diverted attention.

Captain Larroche looked up at the knock on the door. Brian stuck his head in.

"All present and ready for you, Sir."

"Fine, I'll be right there."

Brian led him to the wardroom, and the opening door caused conversation within to come to a halt, and all came to their version of attention. A varied chorus along the lines of "Good Evening, Captain," came from most of them, though the dwarf smith's sounded more like a gargle.

"Yes, indeed, thank you all, delighted to see everyone here. Carry on, carry on, what wine do we have today, Sara?"

Sara had been appointed wine officer shortly after she became an officer, a duty she enjoyed immensely.

"I am afraid we have finished the red you liked, sir, but I found another I think you will appreciate. It's from the same area and has a very similar taste." She passed him a glass.

"Finished it? Shame - still, better than trading it away! Yes," he tasted the wine and smacked his lips. "Excellent indeed! Why, I think it is better than the other one. Sara, when we get back to Port, I shall have you select the wines."

"Thank you sir. Plenty of water to go under the bows, I think."

"Maybe not so long after all. But come, take your places, Ladies and Gentlemen, and I shall explain. Good God! Pat, what are you wearing and where did you get it?"

"Oh, sorry sir, I knew it was wrong, but thought it would pass." Pat reddened and desperately tried to straighten his immaculate uniform.

"Pass? It's fantastic! First time I have seen you looking correct! Can't be a ship's uniform, fits you too well. Come here, lad."

Blushing, Pat went over to the Captain who inspected him, feeling the material.

"Damn me, this is silk! Must be wonderfully cool in this heat! Where in the world did you get it?"

Seeing Pat was his usual self, incapable of speech when the centre of senior attention, Suzanne interjected.

"Sifu Sung Bai Ju was able to help, sir. She brought some seamstresses and silk over and made uniforms for herself and for us. Sara and I helped her with the correct design."

"Damn good job. Don't suppose there is any silk left over, is there?" Captain Larroche wondered at the uniforms on display, seriously impressed, both at the cut and the tailoring. "Best damn tailoring I ever saw."

"I will bring the seamstresses to you in the morning, sir." Bai Ju spoke in perfect Harrhein, causing stares from several of those present, but the Captain was too interested in the uniforms to notice.

"Capital! Capital! Very kind. Now, everyone take your seats please." The Captain sat down, followed by everyone else. Brian had laid out the seating plan so the older and more senior were at one end, the junior at the far end, which included Pat, Hinatea and Bai Ju, to her disgust. She spotted the slight straight away. Now she was inspecting the cutlery, which was good silver. She was particularly taken by the engraving of the royal crest on each item. Pat prayed she wouldn't test the quality by biting the handle. She did.

Brian tapped his glass with his knife, and everyone looked to the head of the table, where Captain Larroche stood.

"I am very pleased to report we have concluded our negotiations with the Sung, and we are mutually very pleased. Tomorrow we shall lash the two ships together and we will exchange our cargoes here at sea - which saves us harbour charges and rapacious taxation, you will be glad to hear." He waited for the buzz of comment to die down.

"The trepang is to be exchanged for a cargo of tea, pepper and a new herb called clove. The trepang from Pahipi and Vitu Levu is far superior to any they have seen for several years, as the dhows trading practices are not very good at producing quality. We have done very well on this exchange, I think. They are also interested in the artefacts we have brought along. Harrheinian silver is in demand, and they want some of the bows and crossbows. But what excites them most is the pigs! They have their own pigs, smaller, more layers of fat and an inferior flavour, so we are trading all our pigs. They want us to bring as many boars as we can next time.

"Next time, I said. Because we have agreed to meet here again in six months. Bishop Walters agrees we shall be able to sail home and return here in four months, so this affords you all six weeks of shore leave, enough to go home and visit your families."

This caused a stir of conversation and he looked round the table. Everyone was looking excited and talking about this, except for Sara who looked grim. He saw Pat whisper to her, and she shook her head.

"Damn," he thought, "it is too soon for her to go back. That is a problem we need to sort."

He tapped his glass again and the room fell quiet.

"So I give you a toast, to a successful voyage, shorter than expected, which makes us all rich!"

A cheer went up round the table and everyone drank, though the Captain noted Lieutenant Mactravis and Suzanne looking less than festive and throwing glances at Sara.

"Brian, you can tell the cook to start serving the meal."

The food started to come through, and Wu Chen took the opportunity to ask a question down the table.

"Honoured Lady," he spoke to Bai Ju in Belada. "I could not help but notice you spoke in the language of this ship earlier. How is it you are able to speak it so fast? Even with drugs, we magicians cannot learn a language so quickly."

"So sorry, not so good in Belada. I come on this voyage on mission to find out more about the new slaves coming into the Empire. My Master was concerned. So I learn Harrhein before I leave. Have to learn Belada on Imperial Orchid."

All eyes turned to her, and she smiled sweetly. Wu Chen was silenced by the words, '*My Master*'. This revealed more about her than his school had discovered in five hundred years.

"You speak Harrhein very well," said Sara, "but what interests me is why you have chosen to reveal your ability to us, and tell us you came to spy on us."

"Excuse please," she said to Wu Chen, "I need reply in Harrhein." She turned to Sara. "It is because of you, Princess. When you offered to buy back the slaves from Sung, rather than make empty threats, I knew you were a civilised person and your country would not be a threat to us. Also, I understood from Bishop Walters the distance between our countries is so vast there is nothing to worry about."

Walters spluttered. "I never said anything to you! We have not spoken!"

"No, we have not," she smiled at him. "I listened when you spoke with the cartographers."

"But you weren't there!"

"Oh, I was, but I am very good at coming and going without being seen."

Suzanne decided this was enough, she could sense Bai Ju beginning to go defensive and didn't want her back in her shell. She spoke to Takeo in Belada.

"I have heard the Sung refer to you as a Tokkaidan, Takeo. I take it Tokkaido is another country?"

"Yes," he replied. "A small country, north of Sung and Cathay, islands. We are known as warriors."

"Very good warriors," affirmed Bai Ju. "Master smith, you should see his sword. Special way of making, you interest I think."

The dwarf looked up from his meat which was disappearing at high speed. "Special way? Steel, huh? What is special about it?"

Takeo answered. "I pleased to show sword. Steel heated, beaten and folded one thousand times. Very hard. Cut through Sung swords. Very sharp. Carry two, short one and long one."

"A thousand times? Must be more to it. Would be pleased to see your sword, please come to the forge tomorrow." He returned to his food and called for more beer.

Sara called down the table. "Sir, will we be going directly back to Harrhein, or do you plan to stop anywhere on the way back?" The conversation stopped while the Captain took a moment to respond.

"The final leg of the voyage will be past the pearl islands of the Umayyad and of course Spakka, as well as other countries like Havant which are likely to be equally unfriendly. I wish to avoid them, and get the cargo home as quickly as possible So we shall go up the side of Hind, calling at the ports on the way, possibly do a little trading, and at the last city of Hind we shall put out to sea and sail home, far from shore and out of sight. We need to see what cargoes we can pick up in Hind, but we can go no further north than a city called Kadwad, after which there is a Havant trading station."

"Thank you, sir."

He considered her expression. "Is it too soon for you to return, Princess?"

"I don't know sir, it is impossible to get news. But I am concerned about the situation in Harrhein, and my advisors told me to stay away for at least six months."

"Hmmph. Would a trip away of nine months make more sense?"

"I would be happier, sir."

"Well, pity Sung doesn't have a city here. We'll see if any of the countries in Hind are civilised, and, if so, you can stay and build an embassy and trading post. How does that sound?"

"Perfect, sir, and you would have news for me on your return."

"Exactly. I am sure we can find a few crew to stay with you."

"Never mind the crew, you will need a load more officers," said Suzanne.

"The army will stay with the Princess," said Lieutenant Mactravis flatly.

"Yes, I'm sure you will," said Captain Larroche. "We'll need to train up some more officers, and I'm sure the kai Viti and Spakka will stay with you, Princess, apart from the academy kids. You will have enough to keep you safe. Any thoughts on who should be promoted?"

"Why not Nils?" asked Pat, who was still irked at being promoted ahead of him.

"Not an option, Nils is a topsailsman and that's all. Brilliant there, but nowhere else." Brian spoke with confidence. "Josh has been with us long enough, sir, I'd like him to step up. Perhaps young Phil as well."

"You will be without any female officers," said Suzanne. "Shouldn't you have at least one? Mattie is very capable and been a Bosun's mate long enough."

"Sure you don't want to get back to the bright lights, Suzanne?" asked the Captain.

"My duty is with the Princess, sir," said Suzanne.

"I will need all my recruits, their training has only just started," said Bai Ju. "It would be dangerous for them to stop now."

Brian looked at her and Pat. "So you will stay with the Princess, too, young Pat?"

"Hadn't occurred to me not to, sir," said Pat.

"I think, Princess," said Bai Ju, "I will ask Captain Lim if I can have a couple of those girls, particularly the one who is good with hair. If we are going to be in a hot country for several months, it will be useful to have servants who understand civilised behaviour."

"Brilliant idea, Bai," said Suzanne with feeling. "The courtesans have a young man - do you think I could borrow him?"

"Do you mean Taman?" said Bai Ju with a smile.

"Yes, I think that is his name."

Bai Ju laughed. "He is very special. I do not think you can persuade the Old Mother to let you have him!"

To Sara's surprise, Suzanne turned slightly pink. She had never seen Suzanne show any embarrassment before, and was fascinated. She wasn't the only one to notice, as Lieutenant Mactravis leaned forward with interest.

"What's special about this Taman, then?"

"Oh, nothing really," said Suzanne, to no avail, as Bai Ju answered with enthusiasm.

"He is from the south eastern tip of this continent, a place called Perak. They are very nice people there, live well, and don't work too hard. Very much like sex. They take gold beads, small, hollow and with a grain of sand inside them so they rattle. With a special knife, they make a small incision in the skin at the head of the penis and insert the beads. This Taman has them all around the head of his penis, in a ring." Bai Ju was talking to Mactravis with great pleasure, totally oblivious of Captain Larroche's increasing horror. "It makes a noise when he makes love and is supposed to be very pleasurable for the ladies. Is this true, Suzanne?" She smiled demurely across the table.

"Yes, it is," said Suzanne, not looking at the Captain.

"I don't think Old Mother will give up Taman for anything, but I am sure she will let you have some gold beads and perhaps some of the men will have them fitted. Will you volunteer, Lieutenant Mactravis?"

Mactravis had been smiling broadly, but this wiped it off his face. "Ah, perhaps not, but I am sure Little would delight in being a test case."

"No thank you," said Suzanne. "Nothing could make up for his other habits!"

Everyone laughed at this, but Pat's laugh was cut off when Bai Ju started looking at him contemplatively.

"Perhaps I'll get Pat done. Might be fun if Tantric Master Suzanne recommends it." She smiled innocently.

Hind

Lashing the ships together was a ticklish task, which had the Bosun bellowing. The capstans did the work of pulling the ships together, sweating sailors on each ship turning them, while the Bosun shouted at them to stop and start depending on the slack. The Sung had an equivalent of a Bosun doing the same job on the Imperial Orchid, almost identical to the Bosun, apart from the eyes, dark hair and an elaborate moustache. Sara and Suzanne had a fit of giggles, till quelled by a suspicious glare from the Bosun.

The Bosun did not allow anyone else to be involved, with her mates plus Nils and Pat overseeing sailors tying fenders along the side of the ship. These were big balls of old rope designed to stop the two ships from damaging each other. The Sung used identical fenders, perhaps slightly different tying of the balls, and Sara overhead Walters telling Perryn it was a remarkable example of how different cultures found identical solutions to a common problem. Taufik, standing by the wheel, remarked they had been around long enough for the idea to spread across the world from the Sung. Walters ignored him.

The ships came together with a creaking groan, and the sailors from each ship exchanged ropes and tied them off, while the Bosun oversaw a sweating group of sailors manhandle a wide gangplank, hastily assembled overnight by the carpenters out of several planks, across the short remaining gap. Both ships were fatter below deck, so they needed to bridge more than ten feet. There was a slight difference in height, the junk being much larger.

The various cargoes were brought up from the holds, each ship using their own methods. The Harrheinians used a crane, the cargo being put into a net which was hauled up to a yard using a block and tackle, whereupon the yard was swung round over the Imperial Orchid to lower the cargo to the deck.

The Sung, on the other hand, used labour, each bale being manhandled to the deck and carried on the head of a coolie; stocky, grinning little men who worked tirelessly, chattering to each other in their own language which Suzanne's trained ear noted as being different from that spoken by the Sung. Chen Li He confirmed to her they were a different people, who lived on boats. They spent their whole lives afloat and never went ashore. They made excellent sailors provided your officers understood them.

Each bale was checked and graded, the price for the grades pre-determined. This caused the trading masters to argue. Sara, watching from the poop, explained to Pat, Suzanne and Bai Ju that the grading was where the money was made, the better seller pushing a bale up a grade here and there, the better buyer pushing it down.

Eventually the exchange was complete, and the two ships made their farewells. Bai Ju's two little girls were on board, looking confused. Suzanne took charge of them, as they were terrified of Bai Ju, and bedded them down in her cabin, threatening castration on anyone who molested them.

Early the next morning Sara and Takeo met on the main deck. The ship scudded on the main sail only, with most of the crew off watch. Suzanne had the dawn watch and she nodded at them from beside the wheel.

Moving to a position out of direct line of sight, Sara drew Lady Strike and saluted Takeo who gripped his own sharkskin handled blade, thicker with less reach.

"Princess, we shall practise the form I taught you. We shall make the first twenty moves and stop. You will tell me which form we follow."

Sara nodded and Takeo cut at her foot, a blow she blocked, turning the parry into a riposte to his arm, remembering the rigid pattern of moves he taught her. Already she thought she knew and a few more low strikes confirmed her suspicion.

"The Crane in the Morning Mist," she said, disdaining to stop and continuing the form.

"Excellent," cried Takeo, increasing the speed of the dance.

Sara tried to remember the moves several steps ahead, but found it much harder with speed. They reached the end of the series and she wondered what to do.

"Continue," said Takeo, "guess the right move. See how long you last."

Sara slipped into the void, finding it easier now she entered daily. Time slowed, the pattern became obvious and she stopped following the pattern and started to create her own, forcing Takeo into certain moves as the only response to her own swordplay. She cut at his wrist, spun to force him outwards to belatedly see him flow into his own spin, coming round out of reach to smack the flat of his blade against her ribs.

Takeo laughed, for Lady Strike dug into his throat. Sara smiled and started to bow, to go rigid with tension as she realised they were not alone.

Perched on the ship's rail, with some in the rigging, were Pat, Hinatea, Sung Bai Ju and the entire group under training, level eyes watching them with no expression.

Sara wondered at her inability to sense their arrival, knowing from Takeo's tension he had missed their appearance as well.

"Your pardon, Sifu Takeo," said Bai Ju. "My children must learn swordplay. May we learn from observing you?"

Takeo bowed stiffly in acquiescence.

Bai Ju smiled. "May I speak to explain what you do?"

Takeo bowed again, turned back to Sara and spoke, his voice a little cracked and rough. "You did well Princess in creating your own pattern. This is how the great patterns were created. Of course we all learn the counters to each pattern and the counter to the pattern. Now I will show you The Counter of the Frog, which sticks in the throat of the Crane."

Sara proceeded to lead the Crane in the Morning Mist while Takeo began to force a different response.

Bai Ju's voice rose to annoy their senses and prevent the entry into the void. "The Tokkaidans are masters of the sword, they learn precise ways of winning, very formal. They hold the blade and make the stroke while placing the body in a particular way and moving in a special direction. This forces the opponent to respond in a way he expects. So the blademaster can lead his opponent to where he wants, and cause him to expose part of his body for the killing blow. If his opponent not know the form, he is dead. If he knows the form, he must follow it and lead the right response. This is what he shows her now, a counter to beat the form. The great masters must learn over one thousand patterns."

Sara could feel Takeo's indignation and annoyance through his blade, while at the same time marvelling at the precision of Bai Ju's description which gave her a fuller understanding of Takeo's teaching.

"Watch now," Bai Ju continued, "and later you tell me how you will take an expert swordsman."

Sara sensed Takeo listening, as he missed a cut. She switched to a new form, Takeo went the wrong way and exposed himself to her lunge, which she pulled at the last moment. Takeo considered her, his face a mask. He bowed and she followed suit. When they came up, their audience had evaporated.

"My apologies, Princess," he said. "It is a good lesson for me, I must learn to control my pride. The ninja, she knows where to push me. "

"With respect, Sensei, I think she cares not and you create this in your mind. Do you know why?"

Takeo took a moment before he replied, eyes downcast. "I fear her. I am sorry. To nobody else would I admit this, Princess." He pulled back his silk jacket with a violent motion, exposing a chiselled chest and a nasty scar drifting down from the left nipple to the waist. "In Tokkaido a ninja in the employ of a Daimyo gave me this as a warning. I was a child to his skill. I feel the power in this one, and it is greater." He let his head fall forward and kept the abject bow. Sara became alarmed.

"Takeo, my friend, she is not a ninja. She is a monk. In her country they do not have ninja."

"She is same thing." His voice sounded muffled.

"She is on our side. She is my tool to use. She will not harm you." Sara hoped this was true.

High in the rigging Pat's Elite Royal Scouts, as Suzanne had dubbed them to his annoyance, gathered in their favourite aerial formation. A ball, with their sifu, their trainer, in the middle so all could hear her words.

"So, who will tell me how to take a samurai?"

Hinatea shifted imperceptibly, enough for all to turn their eyes to her. "He was distracted by your words. This gave Sara the opening. So I would distract him."

"How?"

"Must be unexpected. So I fight with clothes on. Then when sword come close, I stagger and tit fall out. Then he look and I kill him. One movement. Tit out, blade in."

"Make sure he not too good or you dead. If he in the void, he not see tit. Don't let him in void. You must become much better with sword before works. Who else? Maru?"

"We work as team," said Maru, his voice deep and thoughtful. "We never get good enough with sword to kill samurai. But I can defend, better than Wiwik. I keep his attention, Wiwik go round behind, when he ready I start form that Samurai knows will expose me. " He stopped and Wiwik picked up the narrative.

"I know the form, so I watch his muscles. When he starts the movement to kill Maru, I strike. He cannot stop his movement to save himself, not see me."

"Good! Will work, but not if he is in void. Not let him in void first. Which form you use?"

Both boys were silent, then Maru suggested, "The Mouse that Roars?"

"Later I show you variation. Good. Who else?"

"Why fight him?" asked Rat. "I would throw a knife or shuriken at him, or have Pat shoot him with his bow."

"Samurai very, very fast. Especially if in void. Knife or shuriken too slow, he can hit away with his sword. If not in void, Pat can kill him with arrow."

"So we distract him, either with Maru or one of the girls, and kill him from behind."

"Stiphleek starts singing, and I kill him with my axe while he covers his ears," offered Esbech without the slightest hint of a smile.

"Let Esbech get close, he will die from the smell," countered Stiphleek.

"You make fun, but truth in your words. We use many senses, and we can distract with all of them. Wilhelm sings, Andreas smells, Hinatea take tit out, Ratty throw knife, Pat shoots arrow, Maru defends, Wiwik attacks, he very distracted for sure, cannot enter void."

Pat smiled at the conversation. Once Rat would have hesitated at the idea of killing from behind. He felt his Scouts were ready now, though he knew battle would refine their skills. The quicker the enemy died, the less of his own would die.

The Queen Rose sailed to the north, where a great mass loomed off the starboard bow. They passed a vast land, full of people, but all small villages which on Taufik's advice they ignored. Fish traps were everywhere, great square structures of bamboo dotting the ocean, sometimes with a fisherman squatting curiously on the top, gazing at the ship and ignoring the waves of the sailors.

Sails constantly appeared now, the largest no more than half the size of the Queen Rose. They followed these into a river mouth, which opened up into a huge bay as five rivers flowed into it, three from the north and two from the south. Slow, turgid rivers, with a mass of small boats going every which way, crammed with people all staring at the Queen Rose. These ones waved happily. This was the Malabar Coast, and up this river should be Kochin, according to Taufik.

A small boat came along side and a dark brown man scrambled up the rope ladder, grinning toothily, dressed in a dirty white robe. Taufik went to meet him, and haggle over harbour fees and where they could anchor. Captain Larroche refused the opportunity to tie up at a wharf.

The pilot guided them up the southern, inland river to a sheltered point where they anchored. Taufik questioned him at length, before he boarded his boat and left them.

It was early afternoon, and Captain Larroche noticed many of his crew looking shorewards with anticipation. As the ship swung at anchor, the slight wind dropped and the heat became oppressive. He noticed the wash raft being hauled up from the hold and called the Bosun over.

"Bosun, ensure everyone knows this river is polluted. This river flows through a city of a good 20,000 souls who all shit in it. Touch that water and you are touching shit."

"Beg pardon, Captain, but I fear you are wrong." Taufik spoke loudly. "There must be 50,000 people in the city."

The men pulling up the wash raft glanced at each other, and started to put it back.

"I trust we have plenty of good clean water in the barrels, Bosun?"

"Aye, aye Sir. No worries.

"Brian! Keep everyone occupied, nobody allowed aboard and nobody on shore without special leave. Send Lieutenant Starr to my cabin, Delarosa as well. Taufik, come with me."

When they came in, Captain Larroche was considering his drinks cabinet, morosely deciding it was not a good idea to drink brandy in this temperature. The cabin was sweltering. Thank heavens for the silk uniforms, he thought to himself.

"Ah, Sara. Have you decided what you want to do yet?"

"After hearing Taufik's report on Kochin, I have little confidence there is anything here for us, in trade or anything."

"There is pepper," Taufik nodded sadly. "It may be they have resolved their problems with Kalicut."

"Even so, I think it would be good practice for us to contact the Sultan."

"I think it is vital, and we must make a serious impression," contributed Suzanne. "You can be sure the story of what happens in the next few days will be up and down the coast in no time."

"Do you want to be the Princess?" asked the Captain of Sara. "How much influence will the Spakka and Havant have here? They will capture you if they can."

"The Spakka are not known here, sir," said Taufik. "But the Umayyad and Havant are important. They are major traders in the area and take much of the exports. The Sultan likes them for the money they bring, but he doesn't like their religions. Do not trust the Umayyad. They will catch you if they can, and sell you to the Spakka. Here in Kochin the Sultan may try and sell you to them."

"That will take time to organise, so let's make sure we don't stay here too long. How do I get to see the Sultan, Taufik?"

"I am sorry, Lieutenant Starr, but I do not know. I was a simple seaman, these people live their lives in their palaces and there is no way I would ever see them. Merchants, I met and dealt with. Royalty, never." He hesitated.

"What is it, Taufik? You want to say something? Come on, I won't be offended."

"Mistress Sara, you were clever with the Pahippians and the kai Viti, but these people are different. I mean no disrespect to the islanders, but this city existed here for longer than man has memory, thousands of years."

"There is something you are not saying. What? Are you saying not to trust them?"

"It is not for me to say, but when we are trading, we agree a deal and know they will not send what we agreed, and we will have to turn away the goods they send to us, and not give them our goods till after we have seen and have checked theirs. Eventually we will get what we agreed, but it is like a game with them, to try and get the better of the deal. They need to try, it seems, and are not bothered what you think of them."

"Tell me what you know of the Sultans, do they dress well, do they like ceremony? Are they fat, and eat a lot? Or do they fight and hunt?"

"Both, all are different. They dress well, and like to show off their wealth. Always they are covered in jewels. When they fight, they dress like a peacock and parade with all their troops, and like the troops which look the best. Usually they shout insults and there is not much fighting, perhaps a few heroes fight in front of the armies. I have not seen, you understand, just what I hear."

Sara thought about this for a moment.

"What's a peacock?" asked Suzanne.

"So sorry, it is a big chicken, with a bright blue front, a headdress and a huge tail, maybe ten paces across, with lots of fake eyes in it. It holds it up like a fan and looks very fine. You will see tame ones in their gardens, they like to keep animals. You will understand what I mean when you see one."

"So they like drama, here?"

"Drama? I don't understand."

"Theatre, acting like your peacock, making ourselves look important and rich."

"Ah, yes, very much so. What you look like is very important to them. You must have lots of jewels or you are nothing."

"So, when the Sultan and his ladies go through the streets, how do they travel? Do they walk? Ride horses? Have a carriage?"

"Sometimes they will ride an elephant, or they are carried in a, a, I do not know the word, it is like a box with a chair in it and poles so men can carry it."

"I don't think I know a word for that either," muttered Captain Larroche. "And what in the bright blue sea is a damn elephant?"

"It is like a very big cow, very, very big, maybe three times as high as a big one, and it has a long nose that reaches to the ground and it can use it like a hand. It has no fur, but grey skin. The Sultans put chairs on their backs. They use them for war, as they have long teeth that stick out like a pig and they are very fierce."

The three of them stared at him.

"You've seen this, this giant cow?" asked Sara, frankly disbelieving.

"Yes, I have seen. There are many here. I have not seen them fight, but sometimes they go mad and run around killing people."

"Can we hire one?" asked Suzanne, her eyes sparkling. "We could make a procession."

"I am not getting on a bloody great cow with a hand for a nose," said Sara with finality.

The following morning the Archan was reading reports in the palace when a servant came to him, warning him there was a procession coming to the palace.

"What sort of procession?" said the Archan, without looking up.

"From the big foreign ship, Lord," said the servant, "it is ...different."

Something in his tone caused the Archan to look up; sweat beaded the servants brow and he realised the man was worried.

"Show me."

The servant led him to a window where he could see down the Royal Parade, the main road leading to the palace, lined with magnificent Royal Palm trees whose white trunks soared high overhead. Coming up the road from the harbour was indeed a procession, and the Archan saw what concerned the servant. He suspected the guard commander had sent the man.

For the procession was led by four huge savages, cannibals from the islands, monsters of men with their frizzy hair ballooning out from their heads, dressed in grass skirts and shells, but over their shoulders not the crooked wooden clubs he would expect, but monstrous, gleaming steel axes, sparkling in the sun. Wonder of wonders, the cannibals were marching in time! He barely noticed the palanquin swaying behind them, as his eyes were drawn instead to the two men marching behind the palanquin.

Each was dressed in bright white clothing, not wrapped around them, but rather following the body. The legs were separated into trousers. Each had some sort of stick over their shoulder, and while small compared to the giant savages, were far bigger than the eight coolies who carried the palanquin.

The Archan smiled. Today was going to be different, he could see, and promised to be far more interesting than the reports he had been reading. Protocol be damned, he decided, he would meet this procession himself. Besides, he didn't trust the guards not to panic at the sight of the cannibals.

"Get my second court jacket and meet me at the gates," he snapped at the servant and headed off to ensure the guard did nothing stupid.

His arrival at the gates was opportune, not to prevent stupidity but to stiffen the backbone of the guards, who were young men. They had clearly been regaled on tales of savage cannibals, and were ready to run.

They were dressed in the Royal Kochin Infantry uniform, baggy white knee-length trousers, with a red jacket and yellow surcoat, armed with long spears.

"Steady lads," said the Archan kindly, "remember your duty. They won't hurt you."

The two guards stiffened a little, standing at ramrod attention, remembering their drill sufficiently to stamp their feet and cross their spears in front of the gate.

One of them called out, "Welcome to the Palace of his Royal Highness, Ravi Varma, Gangadhara Kovil Adhikaarikal of Perumpadapu Swaroopam. Who seeks entry?"

The Archan watched enchanted as the savages came up, showing wonderful, perfect timing, stopping in unison with a stamping of feet in front of the guards who quivered.

The largest one opened his mouth and spoke in Belada, "We bear a message for the Sultan. Summon one who can receive it." He clearly bit down on some sort of insult at the end of this, looking down on the quivering guards.

The Archan realised it was probable the guards could not speak Belada, and made a mental note to ensure that was a future requirement. He stepped forwards.

"I have the honour to be the Archan to the Maharajah of Kochin, Ravi Varma. I will bear your message to the Maharajah and discuss it with him."

The savages said not a word, eyes fixed straight ahead. The Archan noticed a good crowd gathering, at least five hundred people lining the road, even a few hawkers selling things.

The moment dragged out, the palanquin shook and out slid a lithe island girl, to his shock and that of the crowd, virtually naked, a tiny grass skirt and some shells across her small breasts preserving her modesty. Ignoring him, she raised a parasol made of bamboo and gaily painted. He recognised it as a Sung artefact and wondered. She held it high over the door of the palanquin. A long leg came out. He could see the ankles, and blinked. It was not the femininity that astonished him, but the colour. It was white. Not the glorious ivory white of the high born Brahmin, but more the lustrous gleam of cream on the top of a cool pail of rich milk.. The leg was followed by silks, and a figure emerged from the palanquin, causing shouts of astonishment and consternation from the watching crowd. From her head fell a mane of glorious, shiny, lustrous hair.

It was yellow.

Her face was veiled, but above the veil were two eyes, eyes of a Goddess perhaps, for they were a vivid blue, piercing eyes that surely saw through to the depths of his soul.

For a moment, the Archan was unsure and taken aback, the first time he could recall. He recovered and fell back on protocol, bowing low and bending his knee.

"Madam," he whispered, then repeated it loud enough to be heard. "Madam, welcome to our Palace."

"Thank you." Her voice was like music, low and melodious. "I apologise we do not possess an interpreter on board our ship that speaks your language, never having encountered your people before. Rather than use a local interpreter, who may not pass on our exact meaning, we beg your leave to converse in Belada which we have learnt to allow us to speak with you."

'*Where is she from,*' he thought to himself, '*never having encountered any of us before!*' He composed himself mentally, before responding. "Your voice is beautiful in Belada and it gives me great pleasure to hear you speak it. I await the day you speak to me in my own language, and shall endeavour to reply in your language, my Lady. Would you care to come in?"

"Thank you, that will not be necessary. I am here simply to bear a message."

The Archan nodded, inwardly regretful.

"My name is the Lady Suzanne Delarosa, second officer on the Royal Ship, Queen Rose, out of Rikklaw's Port in Harrhein. On board we have the Crown Princess Asmara of the Starr Line, Lady of High Reaches and Commander of the Royal Horse. We sailed across the Great Southern Ocean and are visiting our neighbours here on the far side.

"The Princess sends her greetings to her Royal Cousin, Ravi Varma, and begs leave to visit him on the morrow. She bears gifts for him and wishes to establish friendly relations between our two noble countries."

Suzanne inspected the Archan, seeing a tall, aquiline man with a thin moustache and eyes with laughter lines around them, offsetting the creased brow.

"I am expecting to receive a response from you later, to the ship. May I suggest you send with the response a protocol officer, so we can discuss the correct procedures?"

"Good Lady, I shall do no such thing. I shall come myself to discuss with you, as I have no faith in any of our protocol officers to do justice to this monumental meeting."

"In that case, sir, please do me the honour of taking refreshment with me on board ship an hour before sunset, in the cool of the evening."

"I shall speak with the Maharajah over luncheon and anticipate our renewed acquaintance with pleasure."

The blue eyes sparkled. "In my country, sir, on the conclusion of a mutually satisfactory and enjoyable conversation such as this, it is the custom for the lady of quality to offer her hand to the gentleman, like this, and for him to raise it to his lips in farewell."

"A custom I am delighted to discover," he replied, bending down slightly to kiss her hand.

The eyes sparkled again, and she turned and climbed gracefully into the palanquin, followed by the island girl, with a twitch exposing a shapely buttock. The Archan smiled deeply, then checked as he caught the eye of one of the men behind the palanquin, and a chill went through him. This was a killer. The girl was well protected indeed - savages in front and, unless he missed his guess, an even bigger savage behind. Though this one was a more usual colour, if considerably lighter than normal. The stick he now saw was a massive war bow, three times the size of the bows carried by his own soldiers. Indeed, judging by the quiver, the arrows were as long as the bows his soldiers carried. He surmised they would go clean through the leather armour of his soldiers as if through paper. Sex and violence, he mused, these are a clever people. Harrhein? Never heard of it. He watched the procession depart, and went straight to the library to confer with the geographers.

Sweat trickled down his spine, causing Pat to wonder if his scent would give him away. He stood in plain sight, his nondescript trousers and shirt blending in with the cabin wall where he stood feet from the door from which the Archan and Suzanne emerged, occupying a scrap of shadow. Suzanne's behaviour fascinated him, able to see her wiles with the extra perception he was learning as part of his studies. He noted the deeper breathing, the tiny pressure of her hands, the way she curved her body, just sufficient for her bodice to gape, and the angle at which she stood. The Archan was taken by her, wily old bird though he might be. He took longer this time in kissing Suzanne's hand, possibly because she held it closer to her chest. Pat tracked his progress back to the dock, smiling at the bounce in his step as he climbed on to the dock and headed back to the Palace.

He was prepared to go and find Hinatea, who should be back from some ceremony the girls wished to conduct, when Boersma emerged from the Spakka quarters and rushed up to the heads, the rigging suspended from the side of the bows they used as a toilet. Pat smiled at his urgency but paused as the sound of liquid spattering floated up. A second and third Spakka emerged, and Pat became concerned. He slipped into their cabin and found the rest of them prostrate in their hammocks, sweating profusely. A strange odour in the cabin led him to some plates with an indeterminate substance congealed in smears.

Pat debated with himself briefly before electing to report the matter before calling Walters. He thought the priest's remedies ideal for this, as retribution if nothing else. He swung up the steps to the poop.

"Sir," he said to Brian, "the Spakka are all down with the flux. Looks like they smuggled some local food in to their cabin. No idea how. Shall I report it to Walters?"

"Very well, Pat. Why don't you know? Thought you three knew everything."

"Oh, do you want us to monitor the crew, sir? Can do, no problem."

"Oh don't be so blasted eager, boy. I was just pulling your hawser. Go and tell Walters, but first get me Starr."

"So, Lieutenant Starr, can you explain how members of your watch managed to obtain local food?" Captain Larroche spoke in a low level tone, but Sara was not misled, and knew he was furious. So was she.

"Sir, they purchased it from a little boat." Sara sat opposite the Captain, although she would prefer to stand at attention for the chewing out.

"And where did they get the money?"

"Sir, they traded a dagger. An old dagger."

"Bosun, explain to me why you allowed the boat close to my ship."

"It was my watch, sir, and I am afraid I did not foresee the problem in the crew talking with the locals," Stevens interjected. "It won't happen again."

"Don't try and take the blame, laddie," said the Bosun. "I guess we should have learnt the lesson from Pahipi, when the girls came aboard. Sorry, boss, but it's something new for us to learn. Different ways we need to get used to and prepare for them. There are so many people. We are used to boats being impossible to get out to the ship, while here you can't keep the bastards away. Everybody trying to sell you something." She decided the Captain didn't need to know about the girl Little smuggled up from one of the boats.

Brian came into the Captain's cabin, face drawn and grave. "There is worse, sir. All the Pahippians and some of the kai Viti are down sick. Pat and Suzanne are with them now. It seems one of the bum boats sold fruit and they couldn't resist it."

The Captain ran his hand through his hair. "They don't even understand money. How in hell did they pay for it?"

"Ah, they dived for them, sir," said Brian trying to be circumspect.

"Dived for them? From the ship? Well, so what? How did they pay for them?"

"Ah, you know how the girls swim, sir. The locals appreciated them and kept throwing the fruit to see them. The girls shared them with the kai Viti. It seems it was a popular entertainment this morning."

"The Captain processed this information, his brow furrowed trying to work out why the locals wanted to see the island girls dive. Finally he realised what they would wear.

"Oh. Brian, Bosun, new orders for the crew. Nothing to be purchased from these boats and they are to be kept well clear. Use the jolly boat to patrol if you have to, Brian and I don't care if you sink a couple of the bastards. Keep them and their filthy produce away from my ship."

The wardroom was transformed into a makeshift hospital, full of sweaty, moaning islanders as the flux ran its course through their guts. Unused to such problems, they were poor patients, unlike the stoical Spakka who endured. Hinatea retained a death's grip on Pat's hand while he gently washed her repeatedly. She moaned in pain and terror, never taking her eyes from his face, one hand on her stomach as it roiled and cramped.

Beside them, Silmatea squealed in pain as she voided herself again and Rat cleaned her patiently. One of the benefits of the partner system on the ship, reflected Suzanne as she considered the scene, was they all had nurses. She thought this might pull them through, as the islanders were convinced they were about to die. Maciu came in with more water, and with several of the kai Viti emptied the slop buckets. Suzanne considered again banning them from the sick room, concerned they would pick up the illness, but thought their presence gave heart to the invalids.

Bai Ju slipped into the room, bearing a tray with mugs of hot tea. Pat snagged one, lifting it to Hinatea's face. She tried to push it away with her chin, sticking her tongue out and grimacing, knowing the taste would be bitter. The Sung didn't believe a medicine would work unless it tasted bad. Pat simply took a sip into his mouth, bent forward and pushed the liquid into hers, holding her lips till he felt her swallow. Hinatea glared at him and her stomach heaved and squelched. Bai Ju sat beside them, after distributing the teas, and started to gently massage her feet. Hinatea screamed and tried to pull them away. Bai Ju yanked them back, concentrating on one.

"Silly girl. Stop it, this good for you. It hurts because I massage your stomach area on your feet. Soon better."

Suzanne came to watch and saw her run her thumbs through the middle of the foot. It didn't appear any different to anywhere else, but it certainly hurt Hinatea. She tried it on Silmatea, and was rewarded with a scream of pain. She couldn't feel anything in the foot but she persisted as Hinatea relaxed under the ministrations. Soon Silmatea relaxed as well, and Suzanne set up a team rubbing the feet, filing the information away in her mental library.

A sweating Suzanne sat down heavily opposite Captain Larroche. "We're over the worst of it, sir"

The Captain tried to prevent his nose from wrinkling, as a distinct smell emanated from Suzanne, a dirty, exhausted Suzanne. He began to rue the instruction for her to attend him immediately.

"It is not a dangerous illness, just new for the Pahippians. A few of the Harrheinians are a bit queasy, and the kai Viti took it quite well. The Spakka are fine, used to eating rotten food it seems. I am told a rotting bird is a delicacy to them. I expect the girls will be stronger in future but it underlines Taufik's warning about the water. Sung Bai Ju proved her worth, and so did her serving girls. They knew the illness and the right herbs to treat it, making teas. I took heart from them, as at no stage were they worried. I prepared samples of the herbs so we can buy more, I think we shall need a lot and it will also prove a hit at home."

Captain Larroche peered at her through the lamplight. This was the first time she appeared dishevelled which interested him. He thought it made her appearance far more human and attractive.

"Well done, Suzanne, I'm pleased with you. Nursing agrees with you. Take to your bed now, that's an order, you have a busy day of diplomacy tomorrow which will present more challenges. Do you think Sara will be fit?"

Suzanne snorted in unladylike fashion. "She'll be fine. First time I have seen Maciu strong with her. Wouldn't let her anywhere near the sick bay. Not that she tried very hard. Good night, sir." Suzanne staggered a little as she pulled herself up and made her way to her cabin.

Pat stared at the elephant in delight, oblivious to the disbelief coming from those around him. He was sitting on a stand of benches beside Bai Ju, with Grey Fox on the other side of him. They were watching a procession laid on for their benefit by the Maharajah, who was entranced by Sara and was keenly showing off the might of his country in an effort to win a trading post from Harrhein. The Pahippian girls still recovered aboard ship and missed the excursion.

The elephant was leading a procession of a dozen other elephants, richly dressed with a tapestry over its back and head, coming down to a point over its trunk. On its back was the box Taufik had described, which he learnt was called a howdah, and contained some half a dozen archers. Richly dressed, but the bows were puny in his opinion. The elephant was something else. Little rheumy eyes, that long trunk and long white spears growing from its mouth, it exuded menace and danger, to his knowledgeable eyes.

Little moved along the bench behind and above him, pushing some of his trainees out of the way to sit behind Pat.

"Wot you think, then mate. How'd you kill one of those buggers?"

Pat examined it, as did Grey Fox.

"Lots of meat, probably fat as well. Those bones are heavy and strong. You would have to know where to put an arrow." Grey Fox answered first.

"Look at the legs," said Pat. "See how the tendons stick out. Reckon you could snap those with a broadhead? Then it wouldn't move so fast."

"They do quite well on three legs," said Bai Ju quietly. "You would need to take two legs. I have read reports of fighting them. It is best to hurt them, then they attack whoever is nearby, including their own people. Very dangerous."

"So a crossbow bolt up its arse would be just the thing," said Little, "if you can get round" Pat was interested to see him thinking so deeply.

"See the horse," said Bai Ju, looking behind the elephants. "That is their strength. Very good horsemen."

The cavalry was marching behind the elephants, five hundred strong with beautifully matched, lithe, strong horses.

"Light stuff," said Little, "no heavy horse. Pat and Foxy would sort them in no time."

"Yes, but I think the kai Viti might have more trouble." said Bai Ju.

Sara was sitting in the place of honour a few rows down, with Suzanne on one side and Captain Larroche on the other. She had clearly been following the conversation, as she now turned.

"Little, when we leave here, I want you to teach the kai Viti how to deal with cavalry charges."

"No worries. Reckon they can handle a pike twice the bloody size of normal."

"Oh my!" Pat's long distance vision was fixed on something behind the cavalry.

Grey Fox could also see something, and stiffened. Their reactions caught the attention of everyone, who strained to see behind the cavalry. It was possible to see infantry marching, and in front were two soldiers with something beside them like large dogs.

"What is it, Pat?" asked Bai Ju.

"You see those animals in front of the soldiers?" he answered. She nodded. "They're cats. Huge cats, with stripes."

"Don't be bleeding stupid," said Little, "look at the size of the things! They must be dogs."

Pat didn't answer, he wore a half smile on his face as he watched them come closer. They all fell silent at the sight of the cats, which walked beside soldiers on chain leads. They seemed a little unsettled, heads turning constantly towards the crowds on either side.

"Bloody hell," breathed Little, "giant cows, monster cats, I'll be bloody careful next time I need a shit in the night 'cos the rats might be bigger than your bloody dog!"

"It's a tiger," said Bai Ju, "we have them at home. Often there is trouble in the villages as they eat people. The Emperor has them as pets, I have never heard of them being used for war.

The Archan sat beside Suzanne, pointing out items of interest - the Maharajah rode in splendour on the largest elephant. He was aware they were discussing the parade and could see the reaction to the tigers. He turned with a smile, and spoke to them in Belada.

"These are our best regiments. The first is the Tigers, and they are followed by the Leopards."

Pat leaned forward. "Thank you, sir. Would it be possible to visit the regiments and meet these animals?"

The Archan gaped momentarily at being spoken to by an inferior, but he smiled. "Certainly, I will arrange it after the parade."

Everyone wanted to come with him, and numbers had to be limited. Sara and Suzanne were not going to be left behind, so the Archan came with them. They went to the elephant barracks first which was in the charge of a wizened little old man with limited Belada. He was delighted with his visitors, though completely unaware of who or what they were. He led them to the first stall.

"This is Puthupally Keshavan. She very nice elephant, very friendly. Like peanut."

They had been armed with peanuts on arrival, but the sight of the elephant was intimidating. Nobody had realised quite how big they were, and Puthupally was twice the height of Grey Fox, never mind anyone else. Sara stopped abruptly as the elephant peered at them and raised its pale trunk in their direction.

Pat pushed passed her and went up to the elephant, a smile on his face. He stopped a trunk's length from her, and stood patiently while the elephant's trunk snuffled over his face before offering her some peanuts. After tweaking at his head, inhaling his scent, the elephant curled up her trunk and blew it into her mouth. Pat could see red marks flare on the back of her throat as she did so and wondered, but recognised the scenting behaviour of an animal. These must be the scent glands of the elephant, and she was blowing his scent on to them. Noting the tiny eyes, he asked the little old man, "I think her eyes are bad? She likes to smell things?"

"Yes, yes, just so! See, come here and scratch behind her ear -

you can climb on wood here. She like!"

Pat did as he was bid, scrambling up the side of the stall and scratched hard behind the elephant's ear, where the skin was pink and tender. The elephant made a little hiccoughing sound, quite ridiculous in such a large animal, leant against the side of the stall, closed her eyes and started to run her trunk up and down Pat's side as she blissed out, making a little crooning noise.

The others watched in silence from well out of trunk range. Little stepped forward slowly, proffering some peanuts in his hand.

"Not good idea for you, Steven! She hunt by smell!" Maru called out, and the brittle laughter caused the elephant to open her eyes, lean forward and inspect Little with her trunk. She accepted the peanuts, then ignored him and went back to stroking Pat.

Sara was the next to brave the elephant, and climbed up beside Pat, but nobody else was prepared to get close, though Bai Ju and Grey Fox were going down the lines looking at the other elephants from a safe distance. Pat left the ear scratching to Sara and started to examine the animal more closely, running his hands over the skin, feeling the ribs and examining the various parts closely. Reluctantly, he left her when Sara called him away, the Archan having grown impatient and it was some distance to the barracks of the Tigers.

Puthupally watched him go sadly, a tear dribbling down her cheek, and trumpeted loudly after him, which set several other elephants trumpeting as well.

"She really fell for you, that elephant," said Suzanne in wondering tones. "Look, do you see? She is crying because you are leaving!"

"I don't think so," said Pat. "See there is a regular line down her cheek - the eyes of all the elephants weep a lot, I think. Probably to clean the eye of dust."

"You're so romantic." She punched him lightly on the shoulder.

"Aie! I have to be careful," cried Bai Ju, "I have a rival for Pat's love! Maybe I should eat more to be the same size!"

Suzanne climbed into the palanquin with the Archan, but Sara elected to walk with the others, to the shock of the Archan who worried about the heat. Sara insisted she needed the exercise. In fact, she wanted to talk to Lieutenant Mactravis, as well as the others.

"Well, Jim," she said as the palanquin pulled out of earshot, "what do you think?"

The lieutenant pulled at his ear and replied thoughtfully. "Hard to stop. Very big. They don't look very fast, though."

"They can run fast," interjected Bai Ju. "Not as fast as a horse, but almost as fast. Can run a long way too."

"You know a bit about them, Bai Ju?"

"I am always interested in war and threats to the safety of the Imperial City. I have read accounts of all the invasions to Sung over the centuries, which included first-hand accounts of being attacked by elephants."

Everyone was looking at her. "Tell us about them," asked Sara.

"The first time they attacked was seven hundred years ago, when they brought sixteen elephants over the passes into Sung. They were met with infantry, a force more than ten times their size. They charged the infantry with the elephants in the middle and horse either side. Each elephant had one rider."

"Did you say seven hundred years ago?" Mactravis asked. "Do we even have records from that long ago?"

Sara shook her head.

"Our written records go back three thousand years, we are an old Kingdom, thanks to Sung," said Bai Ju before continuing. "They cut through the infantry as if it wasn't there, a great slaughter. No elephants were hurt in the battle, and not many horse."

"But they were beaten back eventually?" Sara asked.

"The elephants died. Some sickness from the passes, wrong food, who knows. The horses were fine, but they could not attack cities with them and after the elephants died they retreated. It was fifty years before they came again.

"This time they were met by the Eunuch General Sun Chai Yen. When the elephants charged, his men retreated before them, behind pits they dug and lined with sharp bamboo. The elephants fell into pits and could not get out, or turned aside. They could not cross. The horse too. Then our infantry crossed the pits and slaughtered them. They not come again for war, but sometimes one or two for carrying goods. I think not good as eat too much."

"Yes," said Sara. "The Archan was complaining about the cost of them."

"We shouldn't think about how to defend against them," said Pat. "We should instead think of ways to use them."

"Ha! Want some for yourself do ya?" Little was in quickly. "You ain't getting me on one of those buggers."

Pat looked at him. "It is the best way to know what they may do with them."

"So how would you use them, Pat?" Sara asked.

"Their big advantage is the fear they inspire. So you can use them as shock troops, to break up an established position. They would be good at knocking down defences, I think. They are strong, so you could armour them against the Hind bow. I have not seen a crossbow here."

"I like the idea of using them as cavalry," said Lieutenant Mactravis. "Not all infantry will be capable of digging pits, and once you know about it you can avoid it. Go round the pits - they can't dig them everywhere. Make sure you choose the fighting ground."

"Wonder what they think of fire?" Little asked. "Either they don't mind, or it is a good defence against them. You can use them to pull catapults bigger than usual too, and maybe they could push a ram against gates."

"I think you have something there, Little," said Sara. "The Archan said they are used to haul and push logs in the hills, so they would be used to pushing."

They arrived at the barracks of the Tigers, where two guards stood outside the entrance, which had a wooden pole on a pivot across it. They saluted the Archan and raised the pole for them to enter. Waiting inside was an honour guard, who came to attention as the Archan dismounted from the palanquin, followed by Suzanne. The Colonel of the Regiment was waiting, and came up proudly to show them round. Sara left the men and went to join them. After a brief exchange, the Colonel called to a nearby officer and gave him instructions. He came over to the others.

"Which of you is Lieutenant Connorson?" He spoke in Belada.

"I am."

"My name is Lieutenant Ranjit. I am instructed to show you our mascots. Please come this way."

"Thanks. Are you in charge of them?"

"No, I am the Duty Officer. The tigers are in the care of a sergeant and his team." He looked at Pat's build. "You are a soldier?" There was a tone of doubt in his voice.

"I lead Her Majesty's Scouts. This is my Lieutenant," he indicated Bai Ju who smiled, "and some of my men." He noticed Grey Fox and Little were with them, while Lieutenant Mactravis had gone with Sara. "These two are Royal Harrheinian Pathfinders."

"Unusual. We do not have specific regiments of scouts, or pathfinders. We send out cavalry when required." The young officer showed a great deal of interest and stared at Bai Ju. Pat liked him. "Have you seen a lot of action?"

"Here and there." Pat smiled lazily.

Ranjit smiled. "I envy you. I think you are younger than I, but I have yet to see action. Maybe it will happen soon, as the Kalikut whoreson is rattling his sabre. I lead a troop of 50 men when we ride to war."

"How do you train?" asked Little.

Ranjit looked surprised at being addressed by him, but answered readily. "I listen to my senior officers, who tell me what to do. They are happy to share their experience with me."

"When do you work with your soldiers?"

"The soldiers? Why would I work with them?"

"We do things a little differently, I think," murmured Pat. "Is this the tiger quarters?"

"Yes. Havildar! Our guests would like to see the tigers."

A soldier came rushing out of the building in front of them. "Yes sahib. Rani is in a good mood. This way please, gracious sirs."

They went through the door of the low whitewashed building and found themselves in a cool corridor, also whitewashed. The right side of the corridor was lined with iron bars about six inches apart, and there were several rooms on the other side of the bars. In the first was a large tiger, lying on a pile of straw. Pat noticed there was a low open door leading outside where the sunlight shone in. The tiger raised her head and considered them.

Pat went forward and squatted down by the bars.

"Careful, honoured sir. She can reach easily through the bars." The others backed away at this, but Pat stayed where he was, looking at the tiger who looked straight back at him. There was a snarl from the next cage, where a tiger had come up to the bars and was glaring at them fiercely, one paw already through the bars. The size of him close up was astonishing, at least twice the size of Mot who was a big dog.

Pat spoke quietly to the Havildar, without taking his eyes of Rani. "Are their habits the same as ordinary cats?" He had to fumble for the word in Belada.

"Yes, sahib, except the tiger likes to swim."

"Seeing her now, she is content and happy to lie there."

"This is true, sahib."

"I think she would like her ears rubbed." Pat turned to the Havildar.

"Indeed, sahib, it is something she likes." The Havildar considered him with interest. "Would the sahib like to rub her ears?"

Pat thought for a moment, and nodded. The Havildar went up to the cage door and opened it, holding it for Pat. There was devilment in his smile. Bai Ju grabbed Pat's arm for a moment, and released it. Pat walked into the cage and the Havildar closed the door behind him. Rani raised her head and the tip of her tail twitched. Pat stopped and crouched down, with his head at the same height as Rani. She stared at him for a moment, turning her head slightly, still watching him.

Pat moved closer, still crouching down, and stopped six feet from her. He started to talk quietly to her in Harrheinian, low so all the others could hear was a murmur. She looked at him again. He leaned forward and proffered his hand to her. She smelled it, from a distance, then leaned forward and took his hand in her mouth, her eyes not leaving his.

Pat kept talking, never changing his tone, leaned further forward and started to scratch her ears. A deep rumbling sound came from her, and he realised she was purring. He smiled. She released his hand and licked it, the warm scratchy feeling making him laugh.

He heard the door open again, and the Havildar came in. He walked up to Rani and also started to stroke her but looked at Pat while he did so.

"You know animals, I think Sahib. Would you like to meet Rajah now?"

"Him in the next cage?"

"Uhuh."

"Thank you, I think not..."

The Havildar smiled again. "You are welcome to come and visit the tigers whenever you wish, sahib."

In the Captain's cabin, they sat around the table. Sara was presiding.

"OK, Suzanne, can you recap your thoughts please. You seem to have got on well with the Archan."

"Yes, Princess. He would like to be allied with us for a simple reason: Kochin needs allies. They will be at war with Kalikut before long."

Pat stirred, and the girls looked at him. He blushed.

"The Duty Officer expects to be at war with Kalikut shortly. He looks forward to it."

"Bloody fool," said Suzanne. "They don't have the resources. The Archan knows this, but the Maharajah is conscious of every slight and there are many. Kochin will be a vassal state of Kalikut within a year, I think."

"Resources can be overcome, if the army is good enough," said Sara, slowly. "What do you make of the Army, Mactravis?"

"I can't tell you about the soldiers. Oh, they look very pretty and have discipline on the parade ground, but in war, who knows. But the officers are poor. There is no affection with the troops, and no training together. I suspect it is a show army, not much good when it comes down to it."

"What will happen if Kalikut takes over?"

Suzanne shrugged. "Either the Maharajah bends his knee, which the Archan doesn't expect, or he will be trampled by elephants in a large parade and a nephew of the Kalikut Maharajah will take his place, while the Archan will keep on running things."

"How would this affect trade?"

"Should be good prices when they are desperate, if surrounded, but in the long run it won't make much difference. Kalikut will tell us not to trade with them while they are attacking."

"Is this a good port to have a base in, Captain?"

"The harbour is excellent, but the port authorities are thieves who line their own pockets."

"That is the same everywhere," interjected Taufik.

Captain Larroche glared at him and went on. "There are plenty of unused facilities near the docks we could hire. I noticed one disused wharf with its own warehouses. Rent the whole thing and get a licence from the Archan to handle your own port charges. Bet we could charge lower prices and still pay more to the crown."

"That's a good idea," mused Sara, "and this is a pleasant place. If the war won't affect us..." She checked their faces. Pat looked worried. "Come on Pat, don't be shy. You have something to say."

"If we stay here, at least half of us will be dead within six months." He shrank back in his chair beneath the astonished stares.

"Why Pat?" Sara was sharper than usual.

"This is a city of disease. They shit in the river and drink the water. Downtown, away from the palace, it is teeming. I cannot believe how many people there are. There is sickness everywhere, and in this heat our people do not know how to prepare food or look after themselves. All the men have heat rashes, sores, we have two with boiled heads and already six with the flux, never mind the islanders who are recovering slowly."

"What are you talking about?" Walters spoke warily, having lost previous health talks with Pat. "Boiled heads?"

"Boiled heads are people who walk in the full sun with no covering. Their head gets too hot. If the head gets hot people go crazy. They have to be cooled down and it takes a few weeks for them to get right. The flux comes from drinking water with shit in it. If the men drink clean water, they do not get sick. The islanders ate fruit washed in the river."

Walters started to protest, but Taufik leaned forward first.

"This is true. In Hind everyone drinks tea, which is made with boiled water. When the water is boiled, it is safe to drink. Here we know this."

"This is true," Bai Ju joined in. "We have many people in Sung as well, and the same problems. We boil our water too, and also drink tea. Nobody drinks water, it is not safe. These are habits learnt from childhood. I think your Harrhein does not have so many people?"

"Nothing like here, that's for sure," answered Sara. "I take your point, and I think our people would have difficulty adjusting, while the kai Viti would find it hard and the Pahippians would simply die. Fine, so it is the water for the flux, head coverings for boiled heads, what about the rashes? Are they incapacitating? I have rashes myself, but not bad."

"Wash," said Bai Ju succinctly. "It is where the sweat gathers that it gets bad, the skin cannot get dry. Wash three times a day or more, and dry carefully."

"Wash three times a day?" Walters demanded. "They will get the vapours and die. It is dangerous to wash more than once a week."

Mactravis showed his interest. "We have a similar problem on the northern frontier, not from heat but from campaigning in the marshes. We also have to ensure the men keep dry. Half the reason an officer is successful is because he keeps his troops healthy. He does that by making them ignore the priests and wash daily."

Walters subsided with an unhappy expression.

"Very well, I accept these arguments, but surely they will affect us everywhere in Hind? Does this mean we cannot establish an outpost here?"

"Princess, to the north there are mountains that come down to the sea. In the mountains it is cool, and the people in the region are not so numerous. Above Kalikut there is another kingdom, a larger kingdom with much agriculture, then there are mountains for many days. Amongst these mountains are many small kingdoms, and I am thinking of one with a good harbour, some of which backs onto the mountain. There are streams coming off the mountain that are safe to drink.

"It is a small kingdom, Vijaya, with little going for it, but it has trade routes to the larger kingdoms, and the people are healthy. In Hind there are always plagues, but they attack the masses in the big cities, never in the little kingdoms."

"And further north?"

"As you go up the coast, you come to larger kingdoms, Sind, Guja and others, and then to the Mother River where man has been since time began. There are more people."

"Wealthier people? Better trading?" Captain Larroche asked.

"Yes Captain, there is much trade there to Sung and to Havant."

"Havant, we need to keep out of their way."

"Yes Captain. They do not like other peoples trading where they trade."

"Enough," said Sara. "Taufik, I am convinced enough that I want to see your little kingdom, and we should see others. Let's sail to Kalikut and the other city, then have a look at the mountains. If we find something good there, we can establish a trading post where the Havantines can't interfere."

"They claim the whole coast, Princess. They will find you, and they have a large trading post to the north where they have taken control of a kingdom with much crucifixion. They are hard, cruel people."

"Crucifixion?" Mactravis asked.

"They tie the people to wood in the shape of a cross and leave them in the sun till they die. Not nice."

"We will take that on board and make preparations." Sara didn't seem particularly bothered. "Right, if there are no further thoughts, let us take our leave of Kochin tomorrow and sail for Kalikut and the mountains." A thought struck her. "Taufik, just how many kingdoms are there in Hind?"

"Who can count, Princess? More than a hundred, with a certainty. Maybe two hundred, but they change all the time. There are a few different peoples, and a few different religions, all divided into many kingdoms, often into empires. They rise and fall."

"Are there many as big as Harrhein?"

Taufik showed his embarrassment. "Hind is huge, Princess. Most of them are bigger, some much bigger. I am sorry."

"Never apologise for telling the truth."

"This I have learnt. But in Kalikut I would be impaled!" His eyes twinkled.

Kalikut

The pilot waited by the wheel for a decision. Captain Larroche convened his officers, Sara amongst the last to arrive.

"Ladies and Gentlemen, your opinions please. The pilot says that it is not possible to anchor in the main current of the river, but we must tie up to wharf. He wants to charge us two tarens to go in or out of port and another two tarens for a week, just to tie up. Taufik, what's a taren?"

"Tarens are part of the currency here, Captain. Sixteen silver tarens to one gold fanam and sixteen copper kasu to a taren. It is not very big, but it is still silver." He shrugged. "If he asks for two tarens, then he probably has to pay one kasu to the government and the rest he keeps. Offer him one kasu for a week, and settle for three if we get a good place to tie up. A place that is secure and not too much traffic going past. Pay whatever is reasonable to be get in or out."

"It's actually reasonable to tie up here, sir," said Brian, looking at the river. "There aren't any suitable anchorages. Lot of movement." Indeed, ships of all sizes were coming and going.

"It's not a problem to guard the ship and stop anyone coming aboard," Pat shocked everyone by volunteering an opinion. Clearly he was gaining confidence from his training.

"How quickly would we be able to depart?" Sara asked, looking at the wharves.

"That's the question, isn't it? The wind seems to be pretty steady down the main channel of the river, but we would still need a tow into it and the current. Taufik, are you sure we should come here?"

"Kalikut is known as the City of Spices, sir," said Taufik, with the long suffering air of one who has made his point many times.

"Here you will find all the spices available in Hind, and you will find wealthy merchants and all the information you could require."

Captain Larroche sighed. "On your head be it, Taufik. Go and negotiate with him, see if you can get that spot there," he pointed, "which is a little bit separate."

He examined the shoreline, trying to see past the warehouses besides the wharfs. Seemed to be lots of onions, for there were lots of buildings with cupolas, onion shaped roofs. Masses of people again, and the water was filthy. People swarmed over the wharfs, loading and unloading ships and just coming and going. Despite the filthy water, kids were jumping off the wharfs and swimming in several places.

Taufik completed the transaction, the pilot shouting at the boat that brought him out, and Taufik told the Bosun to throw them a line. Shortly, they were being towed infinitely slowly towards a wharf, not the one that the Captain had wanted. Apparently that belonged to one of the factors who ran the harbour.

They moored the Queen Rose to several stone pillars on the wharf, with the Bosun personally checking each fender as it was positioned. As the ship docked, Pat and his Elite Royal Scouts dropped on to the wharf and spread out, going through the immediate area with care. Lieutenant Mactravis stationed Stiphleek and Boersma at the bottom of the gangplank, each armed with axes, just in time to deter an army of beggars that swept toward the ship like an inrushing tide. Wiwik grasped one by the arm, felt the muscle and shouted to Maru, in Belada.

"We will eat well here. This one feels tender, and so many of them, they won't be missed."

"Not now, wait till dark, but we can choose the best now," replied Maru with a straight face.

The beggars melted away. Within five minutes the Queen Rose was the only ship in the docks without a besieging army as the word spread.

Before long, a local man, dressed in clean white robes and with a neat, white turban, approached the Spakka and spoke to them. Stiphleek came up the gangplank and called that a trader wished to speak with the Captain. Accordingly, he was ushered aboard and up to the poop deck, where he introduced himself as Mohammed

Ashrafin, representing the Ashrafin house, Mappila traders and specialists in spices. Sara went to listen into the trade talk, to see if she could pick up any other information about the city.

The conversation was extremely long winded, without a mention of spice or trade, but Mohammed was happy to tell them all about himself and his family, while enquiring about Harrhein and their families. Captain Larroche did try offering some wines, but Mohammed explained he was a Mussulman, and could not drink alcohol. This required some explaining, and it transpired that he and his fellow traders had accepted the religion of one of their principle trading partners many years previously. No, this was not the Umayyads, though they were of course traders, but similar peoples like the Abbasid and especially the Sufi. Highly educated and civilised people, apparently. Mohammed pursed his lips and said nothing at the mention of Umayyads. Bishop Walters was called, who was delighted and fascinated by Mohammed's description of his religion. He proclaimed it to be a branch of his own, which met strong disapproval from Mohammed, who explained that Walters' religion was the same, but based on a prophet. Wicked priests proclaimed him the son of God, though actually he was just one of a line of prophets. The latest prophet, Mohammed, in whose honour he was named, had come to rectify this and ensure the purity of the religion. Mohammed would be pleased to take Walters to prayer and learn the errors of his way. Walters exploded with anger and was taken off to calm down by Perryn at the Captain's intervention.

Sara asked about the rulers of Kalikut, and was told that he was called the Saamoothiri. He was not interested in trade, except for the taxes he levied, but more concerned with expanding his kingdom. Sara detected something odd about the way Mohammed spoke to her, but it wasn't until he was unable to hide his distaste when Suzanne joined them that she realised he was reacting to their being women. Grasping the situation rapidly, she took Suzanne's arm and led her away. Suzanne was quite put out.

Mohammed invited the Captain to his factory to view the spices there, making it very clear that the women were not invited. The Captain went with him, taking Taufik and Brian. Sara and Suzanne discussed the situation with Walters, who thought Mohammed's reaction to women was something to do with his religion. This bothered the girls, and they went down the ladder to the main deck.

"We're not going to stay somewhere they virtually ignore women," said Sara disdainfully.

"We don't know enough about this place," mused Suzanne. "Why don't we go for a walk? Let's go shopping!"

"Ooh, yes! We need some money though. I'll get some silver."

"Will it be any good here? Won't we need some local money? Tarns, or whatever they were."

"I don't know, but I bet Bai has some ideas. There she is, let's see what she thinks. Bai! Come join us."

Bai Ju was practising with her shuriken, little metal stars that she could throw accurately into a tiny target from twenty paces. She smiled, collected them from the target, and came to meet the girls, walking in the shadow of the mast without thinking. "What's up, Princess? You seem pleased with yourself, are you planning some fun?"

"Yes! We're going shopping? Want to come?"

"Oh, good idea. Just girls or do we want a man to carry things?"

"I think just girls, don't you? And do you know how we could change silver for local money?"

"There will be a money lender in the docks, probably lots of them. They will change for us, or indeed any merchant will but a money lender should be cheaper."

"I think we should bring a man," said Suzanne.

"We're going shopping, not dancing. They will be bored silly and try to speed us up. No, if it is just girls we'll be better off."

"No, we should bring a man. Not only can he carry goods, but look over there. That merchant has bodyguard. I think we should have one, or we will get silly trouble. And he can always carry what we buy. Not Pat though, he's started getting difficult when we tell him what to do. All your fault, Ju, you are too easy on him."

"Fine, let's take Maciu then," said Sara before Ju could reply.

"No," said Bai Ju, "better to take Mara. He is the same size, looks impressive as well, but he has learnt the night stalker lessons well and will see more than Maciu. And he is scared of each of us, so will do what we say. Maciu will complain like Pat. You are too easy on him, Princess." Her eyes twinkled.

Hinatea wasn't pleased at being left behind, but accepted that she would need more in the way of clothing before wandering around the streets of Kalikut. Both Pat and Maciu tried to come, and sulked when ordered to stay behind. Wiwik managed to talk himself into the group on the grounds that two hands to carry shopping was better, but nearly changed his mind when Bai Ju insisted they wore shoes. Bai Ju collected two staffs for the men to carry, commenting that they hadn't had enough training with them, but were at least able to hit somebody without dropping them.

They came down the gangplank, guarded by the two Spakka warriors, with Sara in the lead and the men trailing along behind. Stiphleek grinned ingratiatingly, while Boersma turned away. Esbech was there, looking surreptitious. Idly, Sara wondered what he was doing and resolved to check with Janis later. She was pretty certain it had been Esbech to smuggle the curry on board, and suspected he might be attempting another illicit feast.

"Andreas, if anybody buys local food without my permission, I will have you locked in the hold for a week, fed on rat. Raw rat. So make sure nobody buys any, won't you?" She smiled sweetly while Esbech digested this, wordlessly seeking a suitable reply.

A few hundred paces down the wharf, the buildings gave way to a street thronging with traffic coming and going. Sara headed straight for it, her eyes flowing over the crowd. Most people were coolies, carrying sacks and boxes, with occasional merchants and sailors.

The coolies didn't meet their eyes, but dropped their heads, while the sailors tended to ogle the girls when they thought they could. The merchants were interesting. Some ignored them totally, looking away occasionally with expressions of disgust. Others smiled and nodded at them. She noted that the ones that ignored them tended to be smartly dressed, all with a head covering, either a hat or a turban, and all with the entire body covered by white or black cloth, monochrome men. Some of the other merchants were freer with their clothing, the occasional bare legs, turbans much bigger and baggier or non-existent. And they had colour! Not just colour, but they happily showed their wealth with ostentatious jewellery, gold chains, brooches and rings.

The road was a short one, leading from a main road, with a steady stream of not just humanity but bullock trucks, heavy wooden wagons each drawn by a single white bull, with a hump on its shoulders, deep dewlap and massive dangling testicles. The drivers all stared at the girls with fascination and no embarrassment, while letting the bulls make their own way. There was a small market on the left of the intersection, and a number of booths beside the road. While most of these sold food and refreshments, others were clearly money lenders.

The girls headed towards them, and hesitated as merchants spotted them coming and called out to them, boiling out of their tents like ants protecting their nest. One fat fellow even laid a hand on Suzanne, trying to drag her towards his booth, by which time the merchants were no longer calling to the girls but insulting each other, screaming away in incomprehensible tongues. Suzanne and Sara shrank back, while Bai Ju stepped forward, but even she wasn't certain what to do, hesitating with her hands inside her sleeves. Which meant on her weapons. A shrill voice cut through the babble as a woman came out of one of the booths and laid into the men, switching to Belada as she did so.

"A fine example of Kalikut hospitality you all are! You do not even speak a language the ladies can understand. Begone! Back to your kennels and stop upsetting the ladies. Ladies, please step this way, I have a cool room inside and some soothing tea. Your servants may rest under the awning here. I am sure you are from the Frank ship that has just arrived, and you will be in need of information as much as anything. Please, come this way." She bowed low and gracefully indicated with her arm.

The girls showed their acceptance by moving quickly through the hanging strings of beads in the doorway, Suzanne still glaring at the fat merchant.

"Welcome to Kalikut," said the woman. "I am Piloo Mulca and I am honoured for your visit to my humble offices."

"Thank you for rescuing us," grinned Sara, liking her. "I am Asmara Starr, my friends Suzanne Delarosa and Sung Bai Ju."

"Forgive me, ladies, if I find your names difficult. I shall try to pronounce them correctly. Now, would you prefer tea or sherbet?"

"What is sherbet? I have never heard of it!"

"Really? It is a sweet, cool drink made from fruits or flowers. I have one of my own family's recipe, made from hibiscus flowers and scented with cardamom."

"That sounds lovely. I will try it."

"Tea for me please, jasmine if you have it," asked Bai Ju.

"Of course." Piloo clapped her hands and spoke in another language. Almost immediately a young girl came through another bead curtain bearing a tray with drinks on it, her head bowed and making sure it was lower than anybody else's. Piloo gracefully took the drinks and distributed them, acknowledging the murmurs of appreciation. Sara studied her curiously. She was a striking woman, with brown skin, but much paler than either Taufik or the Pahippian girls. Her hair was black and straight, without the wave. A long straight nose over a generous mouth and warm black eyes. She smiled as she returned the appraisal.

"I have not seen people like you before. Yellow hair! That is something I have not learnt about, though we have red hair here, if not as bright as yours, Asmara. You are even paler than the Havantine people. Have you journeyed far?"

"We are from Harrhein, which is about six weeks to the North West. We sailed up the island chain and then along the coast of Hind. We have met many peoples and seen many sights on the way, but Kalikut is by far the largest city we have seen."

"Indeed? Yet it is a young city, only a few hundred years old. It was governed by the Saamoothiri for the Eradis after their conquest, and about a hundred years ago they effectively became their own state. It is the wealth of the spice trade which drives the growth and the power of the Saamoothiri." At these innocent words, something clicked in Sara's brain. She had understood the importance of trade, but a new vista now opened up in her mind and she fell silent as she tried to put together a plan on driving the trade to Harrhein.

"We met a Mappila, this morning, one Mohammed Ashrafin." Suzanne took up the conversation, leading it to where she was interested.

"Yes, I saw him go aboard and later leave with some gentlemen."

"He didn't seem to be happy talking to ladies?"

"No, he isn't." She laughed merrily. "The Mappila built the trade with the people of the dhows, the Abbasids, the Sufi and the Umayyads. They have taken their religion, which is very strict. They hide their women away in the zuenna, only allowing them

397

out covered in clothes and veils so you cannot see them. Can you imagine what a dreadful life that must be?"

"What's a zuenna?" Suzanne asked, her eyes wide and horrified. "Some sort of brothel?"

"Oh, no, it is just a building where they keep their wives and daughters, with the servants all castrated."

"Did you say wives? You mean they take more than one wife?"

"Oh yes, I think they take four, and as many concubines as they can afford. It is the same with all the mussulmen."

"But that is just ridiculous," exclaimed Suzanne, annoyed. "One man cannot possibly satisfy four women, let alone more. It would be much more sensible the other way around."

Piloo's laughter pealed around the room. "Oh, I like you! But you must be careful what you say, as many men would be very upset to hear that. Let us keep that conversation amongst us girls. I have to say, that I would be very happy if you decided to trade with us rather than the Mappila, but there are very many of them."

"And who are you, Piloo?" Sara came back into the conversation. "What can you offer us?"

"Ah, Asmara, so direct. I will answer your questions frankly and clearly, with a warning. Nobody else will, and they will not appreciate your directness. In Hind you must go round the subject several times, hint and suggest, never state."

"Just like diplomacy," mused Sara.

"Exactly. I am Parsi, and only recently have I arrived in Kalikut, maybe five years ago. My people are from far to the North West, on the shore of a inland sea. We are Zoroastrians, we believe that God is present wherever there is fire. Many of my people have come to Hind and other countries, driven from our homes by the Umayyads. We are traders and merchants and thrive here far from home. In Kalikut my family has many operations. We are money lenders, of course, which is the branch that I manage. We also own a weaving factory, where we make cotton cloth, and we have a small trade in spices."

"I would like to see your cloth," said Suzanne, looking hard at Piloo's dress. "Is this your own cloth? The weave is very tight."

"Yes, we are proud of this. The count is 500 for this grade." She saw the blank expressions and explained. "There are 500 threads in each angula of cloth, an angula is a measurement like this," she indicated a small square with her fingers." It is hard to get 500 threads into an angula, this is very fine cloth. Also the dye is special, see how the colour is right into the thread."

"I am afraid we would need to show this to our captain - he is the trader rather than us."

"Well, you girls should learn. I won't have you being cheated, not if I am going to be your agent in Kalikut."

"Our agent?" Sara raised an eyebrow.

"Yes, you will need an agent to negotiate the best prices for you and to make sure the quality is high. A good agent will make you very wealthy, and a good client, representing a far country like yourselves, can make agents very wealthy as well. Together we can make much more money. And I am the only lady merchant with the power and ability to help you. I think I can be more beneficial than somebody who considers women to be inferior to his donkey."

Suzanne nodded emphatically at this, happy to be convinced, but still asked, "What's a donkey?"

"Oh," said Piloo in surprise. "You don't know them? They are like small horses, very slow but very strong, can carry lots of things. A Mussulman walks first, followed by his donkey with his goods on its back, followed by his wives."

"Would an agent be able to help us with information?" Sara asked with care, "even if we were not here, but by sending messages?"

"Of course. Information is the lifeblood of trade. How can we trade without knowledge?"

"Piloo, we learnt Belada because we were told it was the language of trade here in Hind. But I have heard nobody speak it, except to us. Have we learnt the wrong language?" All three girls concentrated on the answer to this question. Communication and misunderstandings were a pain.

Piloo looked sadly at them. "The world is not meant for travellers. Belada is a poor language, and it serves for sailors and traders. It is useful as it is spoken from Havant to Sung. But nobody uses it as their everyday language. My own language is Parsi, which is a beautiful tongue much spoken in the courts of Hind. It is used by scholars and poets. The language of much of the coast is Konkani, but here the people speak Malayalam. Inland, the next kingdom speaks Kannada, while to the south they speak Tamil. To the north they speak Marathi, Gujarati and Hindi. We Parsis are required to speak the language of the city where we live, so I speak Malayalam, Parsi and Belada. I can get by in Konkani, Kannada and Tamil, but I am not very good with languages. Most of our traders speak about ten languages."

The girls digested this is silence. Bai Ju spoke emphatically, but it was in Sung, and judging by the way the words spat out, not polite. It was clear nobody was required to answer as she lapsed into a morose silence. Sara knew how she felt. Even with sawblade, learning languages hurt the head and it was easy to mix them up.

Piloo regarded the girls keenly, and recognised their despondency. "I have a sister. I love her very much, but it is very sad. Her husband was killed by bandits last year as he travelled to Kochin. She had no children, and now cannot find a husband that she will accept. She will not be a second wife. She is very good at languages, which is her skill. Employ her as your secretary. She will travel with you, learn your language and be your translator while you are in Hind."

Suzanne thought this a good idea, but left it to Sara to reply. Sara considered for a while. Yes, it was a good idea, but it would also give Piloo's people a big insight and advantage in trading with them. Surely it was too obvious a place for a spy?

Bai Ju broke the contemplative silence as Piloo waited for a reaction. "I not understand. So sorry, not good in Belada. What means employ?"

"She gets paid to travel with us and translate," explained Sara, thinking that she wasn't paying Bai Ju.

"Paid? Ah, you mean with money. I not understand how you trust person who work for money." Bai Ju's eyes were wide and innocent, which instantly made Suzanne think that she was fishing.

Piloo was completely flummoxed, and for the first time was at a loss as to what to say. "Everybody works for money," she said finally, rather lamely. "Don't they?" Her words petered out beneath the stare of all three girls.

"Is that so?" Bai Ju said, who promptly turned to Sara. "How much you pay me? When you pay me?"

"Pay you?" Sara grinned. "I thought you just wanted some food and the chance to kill a few people."

Bai Ju dimpled prettily. "Is true." She started to say more, but stopped herself, thinking that Sara wouldn't find it funny if she said Pat was a pretty good payment. She didn't think Sara knew that she knew about their previous relationship.

"However," Sara continued, coming to a decision. "I think that is an excellent idea Piloo and I would be happy to talk to your sister. When can I meet her?"

Sara went to the court with Mimi Mulca, Captain Larroche and Suzanne, plus her usual guard who stayed outside. They entered with Sung Bai Ju and Sara presented her credentials, laboriously created that morning and translated into Sanskrit, the written court language, by Mimi. An over-dressed court flunky took the papers without a word, but an astonished stare at Suzanne, and indicated for them to wait in a lobby.

They waited a long time.

Finally, another flunky appeared, wearing even more ornate clothing, bowed deeply and invited them to a banquet for that evening. Trade discussions could take place tomorrow, in the cool of the afternoon.

Sara accepted the invitation through Mimi, whose liquid black eyes sparkled as she explained the dress they must wear on the way back to the ship. Suzanne digested this slowly, and disagreed. The girls examined the silk uniforms created for them by the Sung and Mimi declared them perfect.

A procession of palanquins wound its way slowly up the hill to the palace, each one carried by four surprisingly small men. Sara fretted inside hers, while Suzanne luxuriated in her separate palanquin, appreciating the muscles of carriers. Captain Larroche had refused one, as Sara wished. Mimi was surprisingly firm on the subject, insisting she had to be carried to generate respect.

An honour guard of Spakka led the way, commanded by Janis resplendent in armour. Half naked Kai Viti brought up the rear under Maciu's command, while Pat's Scouts flanked each palanquin and the walkers, Captain Larroche, Brian, Taufik and Mimi.

At the gates, the guards were required to wait by the palanquins, but each attendee was permitted a female attendant, so Bai Ju and the Pahippians attended. A flunky led them to a small room where they were asked to wait. After a few minutes, a protocol officer entered and explained to Mimi the correct procedure for greeting the Saamoothiri. Listening to Mimi's translation, Sara shook her head, pointing out that she was a Crown Princess with her own protocol requirements. She instructed Suzanne to handle the negotiation, looked down her nose disdainfully at the protocol officer and went to discuss trade with Captain Larroche.

Suzanne relished the barter, and before long Mimi too entered the spirit of negotiation which took a good half an hour before agreement. The protocol officer left with a smile on his face, shaking his head at the idea of animals in palaces, while Suzanne regretted his firmness on the matter of elephants. She was determined to get Sara on one. She walked over to Bai Ju and whispered in her ear. She nodded and spoke quietly to Hinatea. Sara glared, her frown deepening as Suzanne gave her instructions.

The protocol official returned to smile at Suzanne, who stood, nodding at the others. Bai Ju and Hinatea strode to the door, following the protocol official. With a shrug, Sara followed them, Captain Larroche and Brian just behind her followed by Suzanne and the remaining Pahippian girls. They strode down a marble corridor lined with strange statues of local gods, to empty into an antechamber where Sara was surprised to see Graves standing in full Royal Pathfinder uniform, bugle in hand. He saluted her smartly while Suzanne glowed at her own cleverness. The protocol official met Suzanne's eyes, before opening the door a crack and checking something on the other side. He hesitated a moment, before hissing a guttural instruction.

Immediately there came the loud reverberation of a gong and Graves raised his bugle to blow the Royal Salute. Bai Ju and Hinatea strode through the door in concert, moving to either side, a strange conflicting pair, one in her little girl silks with the tiny jacket and white face. The other barbaric and splendid in her polished leathers and bare skin, standing tall and proud. As Suzanne's restraining hand released her, Sara strode through the door between the pair to find herself in an imposing chamber full of people, with herself the centre of attention.

Head high, looking regal in her immaculate silk uniform, Sara strode forward to stand in front of the throne, her confident demeanour belying her inner turmoil as she wished for her crown, any crown, and some of her jewels. Every person in the palace seemed to be bedecked in jewels and gold. Sara did not realise the powerful contrast she made in her simple yet exquisite uniform, with its martial flavour and Lady Strike nestling on her hip. She came to a halt as the last note of the salute pealed forth, looking at the Saamoothiri with interest, her concerns fading to nothing as the real business began. He was a small man, dwarfed by an enormous turban sprouting massive feathers held in place by a diamond the size of an egg. Lively interested eyes peered at her over a jutting nose and bristling moustache, indicating failing sight. He nodded with fascination as the protocol official proclaimed Sara's titles in a stentorian voice, filling the chamber. Sara was unsure whether he embellished her credentials or Suzanne was to blame, but he went on for an extraordinary length of time.

On completion, Sara saluted crisply, while on either side of her Captain Larroche and Brian also saluted followed by deep bows, while Suzanne performed a deep curtsy. Sara started to turn to walk off to one side when the Saamoothiri raised his hand to stop her. He beckoned her forward, she came hesitantly and he turfed an indignant man from the seat beside him, indicating to Sara that she was to sit. She did so, gesturing to Mimi to sit at her feet. She inclined her head to the others, who melted into the throng of guests, all waiting eagerly to talk with them.

Sara looked around for the first time, while the Saamoothiri watched her avidly. Her eyes were caught by the women, none of whom seemed to be wearing clothes, but instead wrappings of gauze, twisted round their bodies in intricate manner. She had seen this in Kochin and indeed the streets here, but for the first time she saw women of quality wearing them. The gauze was far more revealing here, hardly anything beneath it but jewels which were legion, somehow stuck into belly buttons, which were all exposed, and gleaming from underneath the gauze as frequently as above. The gauze came in multitudes of colours, while the ladies swept their hair up into fantasy sculptures fastened with gold, which dripped down their faces, piercing every single nose in sight. Sara felt the Saamoothiri grasp her hand and turned her attention to the old man, who stroked her hand as he spoke.

"You are magnificent, Princess," Mimi translated, "I can see your breeding at a glance. I admit I was sceptical when I heard about you, but one look at you convinces me. Tell me about your land and your father."

Sara smiled, his words could have come from the mouth of any of the old courtiers at home. She felt a little homesick for the first time as she dived into the diplomatic dance.

Meanwhile, Captain Larroche, Brian and Suzanne were encountering difficulties in communication. Nobody present spoke Belada, but all wished to speak with them and they were individually surrounded, slowly eased away from each other. Their admirers endeavoured to communicate with sign language, rapidly causing Suzanne's eyes to narrow as she suspected she was being repeatedly propositioned.

Sung Bai Ju was uncertain. She recognised Sara as the most important of her charges, but felt the others, especially Suzanne, were in more danger. Vacillation not being in her make up, she whispered to Hinatea, who nodded and manoeuvred herself to a position near Sara without the Saamoothiri's guards noticing and merged into a statue beside her, invisible to most eyes. Sung Bai Ju eased through the crowd, slipping through minute cracks between people with the judicious use of prods from her fan. She arrived beside Suzanne at the same time as an overweight, sweaty man who barged through the men surrounding her. As soon as they saw him, angry expressions wiped from their faces and they backed away, leaving him to the fore where he inspected Suzanne's frontage with indecent concentration. Suzanne bristled, but before she could express herself, Bai Ju broke the man's line of sight with her fan and fluttered between them. He didn't seem to notice as Suzanne stepped back, but grasped her arm and whispered something in his own language. Suzanne growled an earthy reply in Galician. The man frowned and released his grip as Bai Ju's fan struck the tip of his thumb. She turned Suzanne adroitly and manoeuvred her between the men around Captain Larroche while the fat man stared after her, his wet tongue running over his lower lip.

Sung Bai Ju was concerned with her scouts. The feast had proceeded nicely, after a slight commotion in which the Saamoothiri placed

Sara on his left. In the ensuring confusion Bai Ju countered the fat man's expected ploy and managed to seat Suzanne away from him. She noted from his seat that he was an important personage. Now there was dancing and her charges were enthralled. Not just her charges, but her team of Pahippian girls.

The dancers wore dramatic make-up, proclaiming whether they were good or evil, and elaborate gold headdresses which shook to every movement. The dances were slow and languid, with lots of hand gestures and eye movement, while the background music beat rhythmically. A variety of drums and stringed instruments with long necks. The first few dances finished, a fanfare announced the arrival of more dancers, much smaller. Children, no more than eight years old, beautifully made up with wide smiles as they revelled in the dance. This made the girls coo with pleasure, particularly one young boy who pirouetted in front of them.

With blatant disregard for duty and total misuse of their new abilities, the Pahippian girls moved from guarding the backs of their charges to sitting in front of them, closer to the children, eyes only on them. Sung Bai Ju's eyes whirled as she covered as many potential threats as possible. She collected some small pebbles from the bowls of a game left lying unattended, intending to throw them at the guards to recover their attention.

The fat man, whom Bai Ju now decided was oily rather than sweaty, leaned forward and spoke to Suzanne. Mimi, seated close enough, translated.

"He says he sees you like the children, like to watch them dance."

"I love him. I want to take him home," answered Hinatea, speaking for every woman present, even Sara nodding and smiling, every girl's eye on the little boy, who smiled with care not to crack his extensive make-up. His chest puffed with pride as he moved into a complicated sequence, his brow furrowed in concentration. The girls sighed as one.

Not waiting for a translation, the fat man spoke again.

"He says he can make the dance much funnier," said Mimi, who was distracted from the boy and looked with worry at the fat man who leered at Suzanne. The dance ended and the fat man called to the boy, who approached with care, concern written large across his face. The man spoke to him shortly and gave him a bowl to drink.

The boy took the bowl, smelt it and tried to return it, but the man spoke harshly. The boy closed his eyes and gulped the drink down, returning the bowl and wiping a tear from his eye. The girls bristled as he returned to his place, unsure what had happened. It seemed an innocuous gift, a treat, but the joy had gone out of the boy who slunk back to his place.

The music started again and the children resumed their dance. The boy seemed to be going through the motions, his earlier exuberance evaporated. The girls tensed as he swayed with the music and the fat man bit back a laugh. The boy miss-stepped, weaved and fell over. Hinatea and Silmatea were beside him in an instant, lifting him up as the fat man roared with laughter, joined by his cronies. The boy giggled stupidly and vomited over Hinatea's leg.

"He's drunk," snapped Hinatea, venom in her voice. Her glare transfixed the fat man, who began to realise his joke was not appreciated by the girls. The Pahippian warrior girls stood as one, turning on the fat man who sat up on his cushion, snapping his eyes away from Suzanne as he sensed mortal danger, for the girls radiated a dark energy of fury and menace. A number of warriors stepped forward, in front of the fat man, spears still upright and uncertain as to what to do with women, even ones who menaced by their very expressions. Hinatea raised her hand to the collar of her leathers, only to flinch away and shake her numb hand as a stone racked into the back of it.

"Stop!" Bai Ju cried as she shot forward to stand in front of her warriors, her back to the fat man and his guards. "Return to your duty. See, the boy is with his mother. You are guards, not avengers."

To Sara's astonishment, Bai Ju was obeyed instantly, the girls returning to their places where they watched the boy carried away by an older woman, also crying. Except Hinatea, whose eyes never left the fat man. She was the only one to hear Bai Ju's final words, "For now."

Pat smiled at the bird under the fruit tree with incredulity. The colours! It was scarlet, with greens and blues and a virulent orange, hooked beak that it used to rip up a slice of papaya. It sat on a perch with a chain on its leg. Mara and Wiwik beside him were not interested in the bird, but carefully flexing their muscles and stretching for the benefit of the palace girls watching them through a screen. Rat was apparently asleep in the sun, but Pat knew he was watching the guards through his lashes. They were outside the entrance to the Palace reception rooms, where they had been left on refusing to relinquish their weapons. Sara was inside, with Suzanne and the new interpreter. Bai Ju was with her with four Pahippian girls led by Hinatea as guards.

Even so, Pat had a prickle down his spine. Something was wrong. He knew the others felt it and caressed his bow lovingly as he watched the parrot, feeling the oiled wood and the soul of his bow. He kept an eye on Silmatea, who was in position in the doorway where she could relay any messages. He could see her flexing slightly, and knew she was keeping the Kalikut guards attention on herself.

A meeting had been arranged for today to discuss trade and mutual military assistance, the latter somewhat to Sara's surprise. She was meeting with the Varakkal Paranamb. Mimi explained that this was the trade minister.

They waited for them in an airy room, seated on cushions around a low table. The walls of the room were intricate carvings, enabling spies to report their every move.

Suzanne and Sara sat at a table, while Mimi sat at one end of the table to interpret. At the opposite end sat a scribe, also an interpreter, to record the conversation. He stared into space, absently caressing his chest, oblivious of the girls. Sung Bai Ju, in her war costume of doll-like silks and white painted face, placed a Pahippian girl, Trieste, behind Suzanne and Hinatea behind Sara. The Pahippians wore the harness devised by Bai Ju made of leather, which covered them fairly well and was modest, while leaving sufficient areas of bare skin to make them feel comfortable. They had no apparent weapons. Silmatea guarded the doorway, while Bai Ju and Rerata stood half way between, merging into the shadows. There were ten Kalikut guards in the room, smartly dressed in exaggerated puffy orange trousers and blue shirts, while clasping spears that towered above themselves. After half an hour their level of alertness had dropped right down, all looking at Silmatea who was the only girl moving, slowly going through exercises where she tensed muscles one after the other. This created an illusion of dance which gradually mesmerised the guards. Bai Ju watched from behind her fan

For the first fifteen minutes, the girls kept up a desultory conversation, steering clear of meeting subjects. Suspecting they would be kept waiting for some time, Sara decided to speed things up. She flowed into the graceful cross-legged position Takeo taught her, resting her hands on her knees, turned up with thumbs on the second finger. Suzanne followed suit, they turned their eyes up and went into meditative trance. Mimi stared at them. This was only her second day, and while she liked her new masters, she found them a continual mystery.

A slight scuffling noise behind the carved screen wall suggested somebody wanted a better view and Bai Ju and the Pahippian girls, with their trained hearing, heard the footsteps moving rapidly away.

In less than ten minutes a gentle slapping of slippers announced the arrival of a man, a gentle man with greying hair, thin at the top who peered at them over his uncertain smile.

"Good morning, I am Ranjit Pirloo and I have the honour of being the Varakkal Paranamb for Kalikut," he spoke excellent Belada. "Please stay seated, it is my honour to meet such exalted personages." He slipped into a seat opposite Captain Larroche and peered at them, intelligent eyes taking them in quickly. "I believe from your demeanour that you do not share the customs of the Mappila and would be happy to conduct business from the start? Yes? Excellent! I regret I am a busy man and much as I enjoy your company, I need to conclude the business rapidly. However my colleage the Kunjali Marakar wishes to speak with you after this meeting if you would be so kind."

Sara inclined her head and listened while the Varakkal and his assistants dived into a technical discussion with Captain Larroche and Brian, with Suzanne contributing. She struggled to follow it, but berated herself for finding it boring, reminding herself that trade was the true route to power, providing the wealth for the armies to keep her and Harrhein safe. She tried to pick out the highlights, determined to test herself later with the Captain. It was definitely spices that held his interest, though cloth also made a brave show. She noted that Captain Larroche concentrated on the volume of trade, establishing the rarity of each spice rather than the value and use.

A younger man, tall with the piercing eye of a hawk strode into the room, accompanied by four eager young officers, barking something in the local language.

"This is the Kunjali Marakar of Kalikut," introduced the Varakkal. "He asks to speak to you on maritime warfare."

"The Kunjali Marakar is the Admiral of Kalikut," whispered Mimi.

The Kunjali ignored Captain Larroche, instead concentrating on Sara. He made a short bow towards her, then made a snapping gesture with his right arm, first to the front and then across his chest. Sara rose, nodded to him and returned a crisp salute.

"Delighted to see I am correct," he said in accented Belada. "I recognised you as a warrior princess, Highness. Do you fight ships, or just on land?"

"We employ a fleet to protect us from invaders, Kanjali," said Sara, mangling the title.

"Excellent," he replied. "Please, continue to talk shopping, I shall discuss your protection with the Crown Princess." He sat down opposite her as she returned to her seat, his officers arrayed behind him, listening with eager anticipation.

It transpired that Kalikut was, if not at war, not at all happy with Havant, and in the process of building a fleet. The Kunjali Marakar was interested by the Queen Rose and fascinated by Sara's recollections of naval warfare.

A noise came from the door behind the Kalikut ministers, which opened with two more guardsmen coming through and standing to attention. Sara sensed Hinatea tense as a sweaty, overweight man with cruel eyes walked in, their friend from the previous night.

The Varakkal Paranamb and the Kunjali Marakar climbed to their feet and nodded to him, the latter with hooded eyes. The Varakkal Paranamb spoke to Sara.

"This is the Eralppad, who will be our next Saamoothiri," translated Mimi.

"Please tell the Eralppad that it is our pleasure to meet him, and we look forward to our great countries working together over the coming years."

"The Eralppad says that when the Havant come, they speak many words about how wonderful is the Eralppad, the Saamoothiri and

Kalikut. He says that your shortness is rude. And that you should bow down before him." Mimi sounded nervous.

Sara looked the Eralppad straight in the eye, and said, "We are not hypocrites. And remind him that I am the Crown Princess of Harrhein, so of equal rank."

"He, he says he has never heard of Harrhein," whispered Mimi, now plainly scared.

Sara laughed, which lowered the tension slightly. "And I had never heard of Kalikut until I came to Kochin."

The Eralppad turned his attention to Suzanne, who was resplendent in her silk uniform, her yellow hair cascading down the back and her form artfully exaggerated, something she regretted deeply as his eyes dropped. He snapped out an order, which caused Mimi to scream and half a dozen more soldiers marched into the room.

"He told them to take her," cried Mimi, scuttling out of her chair and moving away from the table.

The Varakkal Paranamb and the Kunjali Marakar jumped to their feet, shouting in anger, clearly protesting while their guards dropped their spears to the ready position.

Hinatea and Monata eased to their feet and casually reached over their shoulders, grabbed their leathers and pulled. The leathers fell apart, leaving the girls topless, holding wicked looking multi-lashed whips with metal tips, which they flicked dangerously as they slipped round the table, smiling.

Sara and Suzanne pushed back their chairs and rose to their feet, Sara's rapier in her hand while Suzanne caught the quarterstaff thrown to her by Silmatea. The door behind the Eralppad slammed shut and Rerata pushed a spear through the handles while a soldier whimpered in agony at her feet, blood pumping from his arm where she had relieved him of the weapon.

Bai Ju drifted up to the nearest of the Eralppad's soldiers, the leader with his spear levelled at Hinatea. His eyes drifted to the little girl for a moment before snapping back to the dangerous looking Amazon in front of him. Bai Ju sighed deeply and fluttered her fan. She stepped forward and sliced with the fan, the razor sharp tip slicing neatly through the soldier's carotid artery. She retreated with grace as the blood fountained out, and the soldier slowly slumped to the floor, a look of astonishment on his face. The next soldier cried and tried to turn his long spear towards Bai Ju, whose retreat had taken her inside his spear which she grasped with her left hand while the right snapped the fan shut and propelled it into his Adam's apple. He dropped his spear and fell writhing to the floor, blood pouring from his mouth and choking his screams.

Hinatea's whip snapped at the remaining five soldiers, flaying the skin from the spear hand of the nearest. He jerked his hand back, blood dripping down, just managing to keep hold of the weapon. The rearmost soldier brought back his arm to throw his spear, and Bai Ju's arm flicked, a shuriken sliding into his throat in a welter of blood. Rerata flayed the shirt and skin from the side of the next soldier, having come round the table, and this one did drop his spear.

The other soldiers backed away uncertainly, not having bargained for this. They were there to help their prince take a foreign woman to bed, not to fight hellcats who appeared out of thin air. One of them moved towards Bai Ju and stopped as a monstrous arrow thrummed into the floor in front of him, vibrating. Pat had arrived in the other doorway.

The Eralppad hadn't moved, except for his jaw to drop open.

"Tell him he didn't bring enough soldiers," instructed Sara, "and that it is rude to try and rape diplomats."

Mimi repeated this, her voice wavering and the Kunjali Marakar's eyes gleamed in his grim visage. The Eralppad didn't move. The Kunjali spoke to him heavily, and Mimi whispered a translation in Sara's ear.

"He told him to shut up while he tries to keep him alive and stop the situation getting worse. He also congratulated him on destroying an advantageous treaty."

The Kunjali spoke directly to Sara and Mimi translated.

"I will escort you personally to your ship. And see that you are able to depart on the tide. I am sorry for the collapse of our negotiations, and respectfully request that you spare the Eralppad's life."

One of the soldiers moved and Hinatea's whip lashed, cutting through his shirt and drawing blood, while some strands coiled around the spear and she pulled it from his unresisting fingers as the metal end caps sliced into his hand. There was complete silence as he crumpled to the floor, shocked eyes on Hinatea, who smiled as she looped the whip around her neck and slowly pulled, drawing the lashes up her chest, leaving his blood streaked on her breasts. She took a step towards the Eralppad and slowly pulled her whip hand back, ready to strike. The soldiers stared, transfixed by the barbaric scene while Hinatea spoke slowly in her halting Belada.

"May I skin him for you, Great Princess, Power of Storm, Goddess of Death, Caller of Waves? Very rude man. He poison little children."

It was plain that the Eralppad actually spoke Belada, enough to understand, for he was bowing to Sara and gabbling an apology. Somehow, Hinatea's beauty made her even more terrifying.

"Wait please, Hinatea. Kunjali Marakar, I too am sorry for this outcome. I would have enjoyed sailing with you and defeating your enemies. Will we be able to reach our ship if we leave him here alive?"

The Kunjali's eyes twinkled again at this pretty diplomacy, giving him his own prince's life. His own honesty forced his answer. "Perhaps we could take him with us? We would need to take an escort of his soldiers."

"I walk beside him," announced Hinatea. "He does what I say, true, yes, darling?" She smiled at the Eralppad who was transfixed by her smile, like a rat with a cobra, and nodded mutely. She walked round the back of him, he hunched and then she took his right arm in an iron grip. Sara thought his legs would give way, but he managed to stay shakily erect.

"I think perhaps my soldiers should go first, followed by your guards, then Suzanne and myself with the Varakkal Paranamb and yourself, followed by Hinatea and the Eralppad with his soldiers behind them and Sung Bai Ju will bring up the rear with the other girls."

The Varakkal started to object, but realised he didn't have much choice. Hinatea used her whip to pull the Eralppad's face around to meet her eyes. "Tell soldier what do," she breathed and he whimpered, then shouted hoarsely at his soldiers. They gathered themselves together, including the ones with bleeding arms while Hinatea threw the spear back to the one she had whipped. He dropped it.

"Pat," called Sara, "lead out, slowly at first, till we get organised, then standard pace. Back to the ship. Leave the bodies."

As they moved out, the Kunjali questioned Sara about her military, while a bewildered Mimi continued to translate.

"I knew you understood tactics, but the way you hold your sword, the one we thought was ceremonial, just for show, indicates you can use it."

"The female of the species is much more deadly, didn't you know?" Sara smiled.

"I will never underestimate female soldiers again. There are none in Hind, I did take yours for servants and wondered why you needed so many." He paused, his eyes sorrowful. "You realise that we cannot be friends? It will be hard for me to keep my own position, having seen him humiliated."

"You kept him alive. Remind him of that and you should be fine. Tell him how you were humiliated as well, forced to walk to the ship with me. He is fine, he made that girl take her top off to entertain him. That's what people will think. You complain first."

The Kunjali's eyes twinkled again. "How do I defeat the Havant at sea, when they have ships like yours?"

"Sail with us up the coast, we will leave you at the next port, and we can discuss this. But I think we leave your prince behind. We will tell him we keep you as hostage."

Vijaya

Pat lounged in the crow's nest, naked. His body was baked brown by the sun, while Bai Ju's body was still a creamy white where she lolled under a canvas awning. They were invisible from below, with all the billowing sails interrupting the sight lines. She had a contented little smile on her face and admired her lover through half closed eyes. Pat was looking at the shoreline, dark on the horizon, humped and uneven like the back of a dragon.

"Good to see mountains again," he mused.

"Those dreary baked fields," agreed Bai Ju. "You would love my mountains, high, cool and green, jagged and untamed. I would climb high to talk to the vultures, and not another person for days."

"I don't think these are so high, but they are green. I did not like Kalikut."

"Horrible." Bai Ju shuddered. "And that Eralppad, I wanted to kill him for the way he undressed Suzanne with his eyes. So easy, a little shuriken, a tiny one, and they would think he took sick from a mosquito."

"Untrustworthy bugger," agreed Pat. "The Kunjali was an interesting man though. I think he liked the idea of archers on ships. Bit too fond of Hinatea."

"Maybe, but his ships are too small. They will need to swarm over the Havant."

"There is a headland and some islands in sight." Pat pointed with his chin. "Do you think that is Kadwad?"

"Probably. Tell them."

Pat leaned over the side of the crow's nest and called out. "Headland and islands fine off the starboard bow."

He heard movement on the deck, turned and relaxed. The Queen

Rose sailed on under full sail, the sun beating down brutally on to the sparkling sea. As they neared the headland, Pat breathed out slowly.

"Look honey, the beach. Beautiful." The mountain fell in a sheer rocky drop to a froth of greenery with a sparkling white beach in front, another froth of waves breaking at the bottom.

Bai Ju snaked out from the canvas and slid up beside him. "Aiee! It even looks clean! We haven't seen a village for many a league, so should be safe to swim here. I can't wait."

"Brilliant, there is surf. Hinatea will teach you alaia. So much fun. First chance for you to see her perform."

Taufik conned the ship past the outermost island and turned her due east into a wide bay, then north to the top of the bay where a wide river emptied. Confident, he turned her into the river, the crew having stripped her to a minimum of sails but the tack taking her perfectly up the centre of the river. Once through the entrance, the river widened considerably, giving them more sailing room, and a village was visible on the south bank, with many jetties and small fishing boats tied up. A mile upstream, and the Queen Rose came to a majestic halt off the entrance to a wide body of water, an inland lake to the south of the mountain.

Several boats pushed off from the village and came to them. They were all piled high with fresh fruit and vegetables, and the cook came down to haggle with them. At Captain Larroche's order, Taufik went and spoke to them, returning with a small brown man, sharp eyed, middle aged and wiry.

"This is Subash. He is a senior fisherman from the village. He speaks Belada, not well."

Hulloa Subash," said Captain Larroche with a small polite smile, intended to put him at ease. Subash nodded and eyed Suzanne's hair somewhat apprehensively.

"This is Kadwad?"

Subash nodded.

"And where is the city of Vijaya?"

Subash pointed up the valley behind the village. "There, Sahib, perhaps a day's walk. But much quicker to sail into this river," he pointed at the wide body of water, "and follow the bank round below the mountain. The water is deep, more than enough for your vessel.

Where the mountain ends is an anchorage and the road up to Vijaya."

"Interesting," Captain Larroche stroked his chin in thought, before looking round. Seeing Pat, he called to him. "Pat, take a jolly boat, some of your savages and go and scout the southern river. Don't go more than ten miles, just past the base of the mountain. I want to know the depth, so take a plumb line."

"Sir," said Pat, already moving.

"If it pleases the Captain," offered the fisherman, "Subash can show you the way and the best place to anchor. Subash also knows where there are rivers with sweet water for drinking."

Captain Larroche regarded him for a moment. "Thank you. We will wait for the report of my mate, before we will take you up on your offer. In the meantime, please discuss with my officers," he indicated Taufik and Suzanne, "as to the state of the Kingdom."

"Brian! What is that woman doing?" He turned to his mate in alarm, pointing down to the deck where a young girl had come aboard and was attempting to drag a sailor into the fo'c'sle.

"Damn," said Brian glancing down. "I'll sort it, sir." He didn't stop for the Captain's nod, but headed straight down to the deck, calling for the Bosun who came up hurriedly.

"Bosun, clear these people off the ship. None to come aboard without a letter from the Captain. And get those damn whores off as fast as you can. What the hell were you thinking, you know what the Captain thinks of them!"

"Ah, sorry sir. Blindsided me." The Bosun stormed off, grabbed the girl and threw her overboard, where she went with a piteous wail and a thrashing of legs and skirts, only to surface in short order, climb into a boat and started to scream abuse at the Bosun. She, meanwhile, was screaming in fury at her mates who had missed the girl getting aboard.

Pat took the jolly boat with Maru and Wiwik, while Bai Ju and Hinatea jumped in as they pushed off. Pat gave Hinatea the plumb line and told her to go to the bows. With her entire life spent on the ocean, she was a fantastic judge of depth, so didn't need the plumb line to find the deepest route. Maru and Wiwik pulled up the little sail while Pat took the tiller with Bai Ju perched beside him, watching avidly.

They sailed up the river, close to the south bank and avoiding the main channel and current. Although fields appeared near the village, some miles away, here was virgin forest, right to the edge of the river, a verdant green, silent and empty. On the far side were the ruins of an old fort, crumbling back into the jungle but still prickly with menace. The river was a brilliant blue, sparkling in the sunshine with little wavelets created by the fresh wind. The mountain poured down to the north bank, steep and green, invisible behind its cloth of trees. Pat was watching Hinatea, who indicated a route with her arms, not changing much as the river was uniformly deep. Staying a good 75 yards off the bank, to ensure no problem with depth. Her eyes were fixed on the river, till Wiwik pointed at the bank, "Warrior!"

Standing on a branch of a tree, one arm supporting himself on the trunk, stood a man, dressed in some sort of grey furs. He had a flat face with big eyes and no nose, and was staring fixedly at them. Pat realised the man was tiny and felt the hairs rise on the back of his neck.

"Is it a spirit of the woods? A ghost? Or a child?" Maru wondered, gripping the throwing axe he had come to love.

"Little people," breathed Pat. "Another one behind him. Damn, there's an army! All in the trees. No weapons, but they are watching us."

"Maybe they are gathering to attack the ship," suggested Wiwik.

"We are at a disadvantage," said Hinatea, "I don't like them seeing us first. Should we go back?"

"We need intelligence," said Pat. "We cannot go back and say we ran from some enemies. We need to count them and assess their military capability."

"Yes," said Bai Ju, "let us find their city, it may be built from gold!"

At her tone, the others looked at her sharply. She was shaking with laughter. She punched Pat heavily on the shoulder. "You are so funny! These are animals, monkeys they call them!"

"But they are like men!" Maru objected. "They have hands and can hold things! What sort of witchery is this? Animals like men?"

"It is not witchery," said Bai Ju. "There are many animals here that will surprise you. Coloured birds that can talk. Snakes longer than this boat and able to eat a man. Huge lizards in the rivers more dangerous than sharks. Little snakes at whose bite a man drops dead instantly. A huge pig, nearly as big as an elephant, with a sword on its nose. In the mountains there are even dragons."

"What's a dragon?" Pat said faintly into the deafening silence.

"It's a big lizard, bigger than an elephant, that can fly. It breathes fire and eats people, especially virgins, and gold. Is powerful and can talk."

"You have seen one?" Pat asked slowly.

"No, not myself, but my Sifu is friends with one."

There was silence in the boat as they struggled to digest these wonders. Pat turned the tiller firmly and sailed straight at the monkeys. Immediately, they all shot up to the top of the trees, screaming loudly and showing long teeth at their attackers.

Hinatea burst into laughter. "The one at the back has a baby! She is carrying it on her back! They are animals, they are eating the leaves and fruit!"

Pat and Bai Ju were also laughing at the antics of the monkeys, though Wiwik and Maru were taking a bit longer to come round.

"How will we fight in this land, with all these fearsome beasts in the forests? When we patrol they catch us." Maru asked Pat, concern in his eyes.

Pat considered the question, Bai Ju waiting for his answer. "On your islands you have no big predators, you must think of it as like the sea in which you swim freely despite the big sharks. In my land, there are wild dogs called wolves, which will kill people, and a big thing called a bear, which is like a man but also like a dog, big and heavy, with long claws and teeth. It mainly eats plants, but will eat meat if it can catch it. These dangerous animals are not common, and when you do find them they are usually scared of men, or at least avoid them. They don't take risks. I expect these animals are the same, we have to learn their habits, so we will spend time in the forest studying them and discovering what they do. When we know them, we will not fear them."

This was enough for them, and they went back to their tasks, while Bai Ju considered him thoughtfully.

They sailed on up the river, slowly moving over to the far side as they followed the edge of the deeper channel where the current flowed. In the lee of the mountain the river was much deeper, and they followed the main channel down alongside the shoulder of the mountain, to the point where the river split into three tributaries and became much smaller. Here was the landing place, with a natural quay from the rock and a little further along a small village. Fish traps jutted out of the river, and a well-used road led off through the fields to the East. A haze of dust drifted over the fields, and three stone buildings dominated the village.

They sailed up to the rocks, and tied up to a jutting stone. A troupe of kids came racing down towards them from the village, followed by a number of adults. The kids arranged themselves around them in a circle at a respectful distance, all laughing and smiling. Pat evaluated them - unlike the kids further south, none of them seemed undernourished or sick, though dressed in rags. Bright eyed and cheerful, dark brown skins and jet black hair, all were barefoot. A couple of them leaped into the river with shouts of glee and swam over to inspect the jolly boat, loud shouts indicating they had found something new and wonderful.

The adults now arrived, pushing through the kids, though gentle in doing so. The first man to arrive started talking excitedly. Pat understood not a word.

"Hey guys, do any of you speak Belada?" he asked loudly, which resulted in a huge increase in volume as everyone started talking at once, and an older man was pushed forward, wearing leather sandals and a strange cloth wrapped around his hips, falling to his ankles, something like a skirt. He had a loose white cotton shirt, open to the chest.

"I speak the trade language, I have travelled on a trading ship as far as Kalikut!" he said with pride.

All the other people exclaimed and regarded him with awe. He preened.

"Good, well done," said Pat. "We are from a trading ship, and we are looking for a safe anchorage for our ship as we wish to trade with Kadwad. We are considering this place, and wonder if you have any horses we can hire?"

The man's eyes lit up with excitement and he turned and shouted at the crowd who all cried out in wonder. Pat began to feel decidedly weird. The man turned back to him.

"My name is Ravi Sohal, I am pleased to help you! I am only

person in the village who speaks Belada, I will be your interpreter!" he declared grandly. "Please Sahib, won't you come to my house to discuss what you need?"

"Ah, sure," said Pat. A girl pushed out of the throng and came up beside Ravi, and he stared. She also wore the cloth skirt, but her waist was bare, with a jewel in her belly button, and her torso was wrapped round in a gauzy, sheer sheet. Her long black hair was tied into a rope and hung down her back over one shoulder, while she had a red dot in the middle of her forehead and something yellow on her nose. At first he thought it was mucus, before realising she wore an ornament, a gold shell. Her skin was lighter than Ravi's, more like honey. She was talking to Ravi, who turned back to Pat.

"My friend would like to know your names."

Pat remembered how Suzanne introduced herself. "I am Lieutenant Pat Connorson of the Royal Ship Queen Rose, my colleague Sifu Sung Bai Ju, and my crew Maru, Wiwik and Hinatea. I am from the mainland of Harrhein, Hinatea is from our outer province of Pahipi and Maru and Wiwik are from our province of Vitua where Maru is of royal blood. Bai Ju is from Sung." Pat cursed himself for forgetting all the words, realising he should have given everyone titles and made his own more impressive. He supposed he would have given Ravi and the villagers too much importance if he performed the entire ceremony.

Ravi considered the jolly boat with interest. "Is that the Queen Rose?"

"No," said Pat patiently. "That is a jolly boat from the ship, we needed to make sure the river was big enough for the Queen Rose to sail down. We will return to the ship tonight with a chart of the river."

Ravi was being jostled by the girl and by several other villagers and to Pat's alarm he realised they were all clamouring to be introduced. This didn't happen when Suzanne was in charge.

Pat decided to cut the visit short. "Ravi, I regret we are short of time to report to our ship. We will visit again tomorrow. Can you tell me where we can hire horses, and transport for goods, in the village?"

"There is one horse, sahib, but it is for messages. I will tell the rider, and he will go tonight to Sonda to tell the Rajah you are here.

He will bring horses and transport for you."

"Oh, good. But, uh, what will this cost?"

"I do not know, sahib. The horses belong to the Raja. I do not know what he will do, but I expect he will want to trade with you, it is known the kingdom needs more trade routes. So I am sure it will be a gift for you."

"Right. I shall pass on the message to my Captain. Thanks, Ravi, we will meet you tomorrow." He turned to go to the boat, and Ravi squawked in horror.

"No, no, you must come to the village," he cried, visions of his increased fame and respect in the village crashing to ruins. Sensing the problem, the girl, her friends and the children rushed forward and grabbed his arms, as well as those of Maru, Wiwik and Hinatea. They hesitated at Bai Ju.

Pat found himself being manhandled by a couple of girls and half a dozen children, all laughing, and wondered how to extricate himself. He looked over at Bai Ju, who was laughing at his predicament. His eyes pleaded with her, and she mouthed at him, "The Void!"

He nodded, and relaxed, stopped resisting, cleared his mind and slipped into state. He shook himself and the girls and children slid off. Still in state, he turned to Ravi and spoke calmly and formally.

"Good Ravi, we thank you for your assistance. Now we have our duty and we will return to our ship now. We will be pleased to visit you tomorrow." He bowed slightly, causing Ravi to automatically bow low, turned and made his way to the jolly boat, gently but firmly disentangling the girl's hand from his. He boarded the boat, turned and Bai Ju was slipping the painter rope. Wiwik and Maru quickly unshipped the oars and they pushed clear of the rocks through a crowd of swimming children, who tried to keep up with them.

Next morning the Queen Rose sailed into the harbour and anchored two hundred paces off the quay. The crew were still muttering to themselves, dubious the monkeys they had seen on the way in were really animals and not leprechauns, orcs, pixies, brownies or goblins. At least one person argued for every one of these plus a few more Pat thought invented. Little had come up with at least three monsters on his own and was currently arguing for homunculi which appeared to be something magicians manufactured and caused Perryn to bridle with anger every time he mentioned them. Naturally Little realised this and ensured he mentioned them whenever Perryn was nearby.

Captain Larroche was annoyed at the discussion and called Pat over.

"Pat, they won't believe anything you tell them till they have sent the things close up. Take some of your lads and go and get me one. Shoot it and get back quickly. Leave Bai Ju here, she can point out this Ravi to Suzanne."

For the first time Pat hesitated on receipt of a direct order, then snapped, "Sir," and turned away. With a quick word to Bai Ju, he collected Maru and Wiwik, whistled up Mot and launched the jolly boat, making no objection when Hinatea and Rat jumped in as well.

Once they were away from the ship, he told them the mission.

"No!" Hinatea cried, "They were so sweet! Do we have to kill one? I would never eat one, they look too much like people." She sniffed at Maru and Wiwik who hung their huge heads at her disapproval of their dietary habits.

"I am not happy either," said Pat, wondering at her caring about a monkey while delighting in slaughtering men. "I reckon we can catch one alive, and bring him back. The Captain didn't actually say he wanted a dead one."

"Yes," cried Hinatea in ecstasy, "let's get a little one and I will keep him as a pet!" All the Pahippians loved animals.

"Might be tricky, remember how long that big male's teeth were?"

"I've caught a few cats," mused Rat, absently rubbing a long faint scar on his forearm. Pat looked at him till he flushed. "Um, some of the cheap food stalls would pay well for them."

Pat continued to look at him, then said, "Good, at least you have some experience of catching animals. I expect these ones will have the dangerous ones on the outside and the easier ones in more protection. So what we will do is land there" he pointed to a bit of beach "tie up the boat, and you, Maru and Wiwik will sneak along the coast towards where the monkeys live. Try to get close without them seeing you, get in and grab one. Choose a small one, but not a baby."

Rat interjected. "Take a cloth bag to put them in, they will quieten down in the dark but be careful, they will bite through the cloth."

Maru took the cloth bag shoved at him with a dubious frown.

"What are you going to do?" He asked while checking the drawstring on the bag.

"Hinatea and I will be the reserve. We will sneak in from deeper inland, and if you are spotted we will use you as a distraction to get in closer. Now be careful, this is a real test for all of you as they will be much better at sensing you than a man. Any questions?" Rat shook his head, the others waited without expression. "Right, patrol mode." This meant silence, hand signals only.

The boat glided into the beach, Wiwik landing lightly on the sand holding the painter which he quickly slipped round a tree root. Maru stood on a sloping trunk at the back of the boat and tied up securely. Hinatea and Rat helped Pat select some brush, which he cut quickly with a slash of a machete to be arranged artistically by Hinatea. In moments the boat wasn't visible from ten yards away and Maru, Wiwik and Rat melted into the green without a sound.

Mot was sitting on the ground in the shade watching Pat, who made a last check on the boat before giving a motion with his hand inland and she was gone. He followed her, with Hinatea ten yards behind him. Each moved carefully, but swiftly for the undergrowth was sparse once they were away from the shore and the canopy kept sunlight from the forest floor. They were careful to avoid touching any of the odd bits of foliage and after a couple of hundred yards, Pat motioned with his arm and they swung north, coming slightly back towards the beach. Rat was visible for a moment, ghosting from one tree to the next till he reached a clearing formed by a falling giant tree and the undergrowth thickened with the increased light.

Mot appeared and went into a rigid stance, her nose pointing at thick bush. The monkeys thrashed around in the bush, feeding on small green fruit, and Pat folded into the ground to study them. Outriders guarded the surrounds, and one stiffened and barked. Immediately several big males came up, all barking and the smaller monkeys rushed up into the trees. Pat quickly started moving closer to the back of the troop, Hinatea close behind him while Mot ranged ahead. Maru stood up and confronted the males. With this distraction Wiwik dived out of a bush twenty yards further along and grabbed a small monkey, which screamed in terrified fury and sank its fangs into his wrist. There was an uproar with all the monkeys screaming and the big males left Maru and rushed over towards Wiwik who ran for the beach trying to stuff the monkey into a sack.

The monkeys at the back were ranged through the trees at all heights, standing up and watching. Silently, Pat ran up behind one low down on a branch and flipped his sack over it. The monkey turned its head as he arrived and started to fall off the branch to avoid him, but Hinatea was there, caught it and boosted it into the sack. Quickly they turned and ran back to the boat while the monkey squeaked in the sack and the small ones set up a shrill ululation behind them.

They quickly stripped the camouflage off the boat and pushed off into the water. With no sign of the others, Pat used the oars to row along the beach. Maru came out of the trees, closely followed by Rat. Both dived into the sea and swam to the boat. Maru was laughing uncontrollably. Wiwik appeared, blood pouring down his head, threw his sack towards the boat and dived after it. Hinatea neatly caught the sack, placed it beside the other and helped the men aboard.

Wiwik was swearing. One of the big males had jumped on his shoulders, slammed its upper jaw down on the top of his head so the canines went deep into his skull and jumped away before he could do anything.

The big monkeys appeared on the beach and were jumping up and down shrieking as the kai Viti raised the sail and Pat took the tiller. Mot was sniffing the sacks, her tail wagging. Hinatea picked up the smaller bag and cradled it on her lap, making a cooing noise. The sack quivered and she undid the top, carefully rolling down the sides, exposing a terrified face. She cooed at it, and it chattered quietly at her. Slowly its chittering stopped and the monkey peered at her from big eyes.

The jolly boat was hauled up and Pat took his men up to report to the Captain. By this time the little monkey was out of its bag and clinging to Hinatea for protection, screaming at anyone who came near, which of course half the crew did. Wiwik pulled the larger specimen from his sack and held it high for everyone to see. Blood was all over its head, though dried by now. The monkey sorted that by twisting impossibly inside its skin and sinking its teeth into his wrist. Wiwik cursed, dropped it, and it shot up the rigging, followed by half the crew and the Bosun's bellow as it shat on a sail.

Various sailors took one look at the monkey before demanding their winnings from Little who tried to avoid paying up. He claimed they might still be homunculi, on the basis that nobody had ever seen one.

Captain Larroche wasn't best impressed by the live monkeys but was pleased the crew were placated. He was more interested in Suzanne, Bai Ju and Mimi, who were returning to the boat from meeting with Ravi Sohal. They climbed up the side of the boat and came towards him, casting curious glances at the monkeys.

"Captain, we have a troop of horse sent by the Rajah to escort us to Sonda. There are a dozen horses for us to ride."

"Horses? Damn bloody things, hurt like hell. I am not going. Sara, your show. Who are you taking?"

"Thank you sir. I will take riders, which basically means Harrheinians. I'll take Captain Mactravis and his troop, plus Pat. I suppose you can ride?" She asked Bai Ju.

"Of course. I think you will find these saddles are different to what you are used to. They are different for me, but I can manage."

"Different in what way?"

"Much smaller than ours. Ours are like chairs and fighting saddles hold the warrior on the horse, even if he is injured. They are big and lots of straps to keep you in one place."

"Our heavy horse use similar saddles, essential for a cavalry charge," responded Sara.

"Only if you can't ride," interjected Pat with enthusiasm. "A small light saddle lets you become one with a horse. You need to feel the horse properly and have it respond to you without thinking."

Sara considered him thoughtfully. Of course, he was a plainsman and lived in the saddle. "Do you think the soldiers will have a problem with small saddles?"

"Grey Fox won't. Elves are good horsemen - they taught me to ride."

"We'll manage," said Mactravis dryly. "We practice bareback, although some of us were heavy horse. You will laugh when you see Little on a horse. He looks like a sack of dung but somehow he is always there and has no problem. As usual, ignores all the manuals on the proper conduct."

"Fine," said Sara forcefully and cutting off the conversation.

"Mimi, can you ride and how far is to Sonda?"

"Yes, no problem with small saddles either. Started off on side saddle, after which everything is easy! It's about twenty miles, should take us the morning. I like horses," Mimi volunteered with a smile, reflecting she had had more excitement in a week working for these Harrheinians than in her entire life.

As they came out of the jungle, the city of Sonda rose out of the fields in front of them, about two miles away, looking like a something out of faerie land. A beautiful white wall sparkled in front of them, while gleaming slender spires rose out of rounded roofs. Farmers rested on their tools and stopped their buffalos in the fields, watching them ride past.

Sara flicked her eyes over them, while still listening with half an ear to Suzanne flirting with the escort's Captain. She had elicited a surprising amount of information from him, most of it fascinating. Sara found she was well informed on the political situation and the worry in Sonda as to whether they could withstand invasion. The Rajah's special Kushtu guards were mighty warriors, but not enough of them, the mercenaries being hard to tempt this far south.

Sara caught Pat's eye. "How well do they keep the fields?"

He gave her a scathing look. "I'm a herder, not a bloody farmer. I can't give you an expert opinion, but they look OK. Crops look healthy, whatever they are, not much weed growth, plenty of variation."

"They are good," Bai Ju spoke past him to her. "Plenty of farmers for such an area, the crops are heavy as well. I know most of them. These wet ones are rice." She indicated a series of small fields with water in them, tiered so the water cascaded from one field to another. "They will get at least two crops a year, and it is the staple food of the poor."

Mactravis studied the paddy fields thoughtfully. "I tell you what, Princess, these rice plantations are a highly effective guard on the city."

A labourer, up to his knees in mud, wrestled a plough behind a buffalo. "You would never get cavalry through there," she nodded in agreement. "No wonder they use cows to plough."

"It's a buffalo," said Bai Ju absently, her eyes on the city. "The wall is not high, but it would be hard to get siege equipment up, and with all this water it would be impossible to, how you call it, dig tunnels under and collapse wall?"

"Sap," replied Mactravis. "We call it sapping. You're right. You have to put wood in the tunnels to support them, and set fire to the wood. You could never tunnel there or get the fires to start. It would be tough, storming the walls with ladders and ropes."

"These people have an old culture," said Bai Ju in her best guru voice. "They fight a different way. The armies draw up outside, and the best warriors fight each other, later the armies fight. If the army outside wins, the people let them in."

"Saves on re-building the wall," remarked Sara. "Well, well, we have a reception committee. All those stops on the way up the coast have clearly paved the way. Hope they didn't hear about Kalikut."

Trumpets were sounding from the city as they drew closer, the gates opened wide and half a dozen elephants came out, gorgeously trapped in cloth of gold, with the boxes on top, called howdahs, full of young women who were throwing something out.

The elephants split into two columns and through the middle of them came a troop of cavalry, which also split and formed an outward-facing crescent. As they came closer, the girls threw more flowers, and down the path came a splendid figure on a white horse, moving sedately. Something on his head appeared huge, and sparkled in the sunshine.

The horse came a stop a few paces in front of the crescent, revealing a small rider watching them intently. As they came closer, she realised he was young, and when their eyes met he dug his heels into the horse which bounded forward. She was close enough to see the consternation of the faces of the cavalry, and guessed this wasn't planned.

The rider wasn't just young, he was a boy, and he was laughing out loud as he rode up, shouting in his own language. Sara couldn't help but smile. He stopped in front of her horse, smiling hugely.

"Welcome to my Vijaya," he said in Belada, "I am so happy you have come! And you are young too! Like me! Isn't it boring talking to these old people who rule other places?"

Sara laughed in delight. "Indeed it is! You are a breath of fresh air! I am Princess Asmara, but you are welcome to call me Sara!

"Thank you Sara! You are very pretty! You must call me Rama.

Please come to my palace, you must stay here and talk to me." His eyes sparked. "I want to hear all about how you escaped from the Eralppad.."

An older man arrived on horseback looking horrified. He gabbled quickly at Rama who snapped at him, then spoke in Belada. "Our guests do not speak Konkani, we will speak Belada always in their presence. Do you understand me, Haniph?"

The old man slumped and muttered assent.

Rama turned triumphantly to Sara. "I know you want a trade post. You have spoken to all these greedy people to the south. Now you come to me, and we do not even have a proper harbour! I am very happy, especially because you are so beautiful! I will build a harbour for you and we will help you with all your trade, everything you want I will give you!"

The old man was horrified.

Sara smiled warmly. She was always disarmed when told she was beautiful, knowing she wasn't. She leaned forward and touched Rama gently on the arm. "Thank you. I know I have found what I am looking for. We will stay here, and one of the first things I shall do is teach you all about trade and how to negotiate properly! We shall make both Harrhein and Sunda very rich indeed"

Sara sat cross-legged on a cushion in the position Takeo called the lotus after a flower for some unspecified reason. Her rooms were huge, cool and airy with marble floors and walls. Ornate, intricately carved statues were everywhere, each depicting a local god in some act of divinity. She found it hard to meditate, as she missed Maciu. Unable to ride, he followed on with the marching Spakka, Kai Viti and Pahippians. Hinatea commanded them, confident in her ability to control these hulking brutes. Not misplaced, for the Spakka lived in mortal terror of her, knowing full well she had despatched several of their comrades. Esbech and Boersma still discussed revenge, out of earshot of Stiphleek who would report such indiscretions to Janis.

Glass beads hung in the doorway, and they chimed gently as Suzanne breezed into the room, followed by Mimi. She sat on a cushion opposite Sara, nodding Mimi to another beside her and waited for Sara to come back. Sara opened her eyes, blinked a few times and smiled.

"I'm having difficulty in finding peace, for some reason," she said.

"Probably that wretched statue," said Suzanne, glaring at a large one by the bed.

Sara had not actually realised what the couple were doing and now she turned crimson. It hadn't occurred to her people could do that.

"Mimi, get them to remove it, please," said Sara, desperately trying to remember who had been into her room and would have seen the revolting thing. Beside the bed too. "Everything OK, Suzanne?"

"I wanted to talk to you about sleeping arrangements," Suzanne began. "Mimi is explaining to me the customs and morals of these people, which are a little different to Harrhein."

"I am sure we will need to keep a close rein on the Pahippians," said Sara.

"Hinatea will," said Suzanne. "It is you I am worried about. I have already spoken to Pat and Ju. They have separate rooms sorted."

"What are you talking about? Me? Why, what could I - wait! You can't mean Maciu! He's my consort, damn it."

"No he isn't, he's an island prince with no court manners who you intend to make your consort back in Harrhein because you are revelling in what he does to you in bed," said Suzanne with such brutal honesty that Sara was lost for words. Suzanne carried on, transfixing Sara with a knowing eye.

"Darling, I know he's lots of fun and you are having a wonderful time with him, but I promise you two things. First the Vijayans look down on all the islanders as barbarians - they are racist enough to their own people, let alone foreigners. At the moment they respect you and Harrhein, you look the part and act correctly. In their eyes Crown Princesses do not go around sleeping with anyone, let alone barbarian islanders. If you sleep with him we lose the trading outpost and treaty."

Sara pushed her chin forward in obstinate mode, her lips a thin line.

"The second thing I promise you is if you deny yourself his body for a while, abstain completely, then when he gets the opportunity to ravish you again, he will be a veritable stallion and you won't stop screaming all night." She smiled as Sara digested this, deflating in the process.

"You bitch," she whispered. "You know how much I love him. I need him beside me at night, he gives me strength."

"You will manage. I am sure you can arrange trips to visit waterfalls and beaches with only him as guard. And we can put him as a night guard on your room. The important thing is the locals don't find out."

Sara followed the drop of sweat which trickled down from the tight curls at the back of Maciu's head. It slid down his rich brown skin, disappearing into his shirt collar and she wished she could rub it away, aching to kiss the nape of his neck, her heart beating hot and heavy through her veins.

They were shopping, without Sung Bai Ju this time, Sara with Suzanne and Mimi, Rerata and Maciu as token protection in this safe and lovely city. Maciu was bored as he led them into a square lined with stalls. The constant press of people unnerved him with their constant chatter and filthy clothing. His eyes flicked over the different stalls, wondering which ones would appeal to the girls this time. Rerata found herself distracted by a stall selling jewellery made from sea-shells, remarkably similar to ones she made herself and became enchanted with some carved nautilus shell.

Suzanne spotted some silks she wanted to try and drifted towards them with a slight smile having seen Sara mooning at Maciu's back. Sara wondered if she could see the play of muscle through the shirt, or whether she imagined it. She saw sweat stain the back of his shirt and smiled. The smile turned to puzzlement as he bent forward slightly and his back pushed out against the shirt, staining more of it with sweat. He staggered and fell to one side, revealing a gap-toothed, olive-skinned man in boiled leather armour grinning at her. He held a wicked short sword, Maciu's heart blood dripping from the point.

Sara gaped, a low moan of horror escaping from her as she dropped without thinking to Maciu's side, only for her arm to be roughly grasped by another man in boiled leather armour, smelling unpleasantly of sweat. He held her up, speaking in rough Belada.

"Come, girl, Captain want you." He started to drag her away towards three men standing by the opposite entrance to the square, some hundred paces away, not even bothering to disarm the little girl.

The Captain spoke to his sergeant in Havantine. "Good work, Baptista. Your man is well trained. Perfect heart stroke, the savage didn't even notice him coming. Stupid to use one as a guard. Now, collect the women."

Rerata reacted as Maciu slumped, catching the movement from the corner of her eye. The crowd surged, some away from the body and others towards it as they tried to find out what was happening. Rerata flowed with these people, stepping out from the crowd, dropping her short spear point and lancing the soldier holding Sara cleanly through the laces holding his armour together. She stood in front of Sara, glaring at the soldiers, reached back and pulled off her leathers, making herself naked from the waist up, her fighting uniform, whiop in hand. Sara came out of her shock, drew Lady Strike with a savage hiss, took one step towards Maciu's killer and feinted at his throat, The startled soldier brought his short sword up to block and Lady Strike swerved in the air, sinking deep into his solar plexus, causing him to scream in mortal agony. Sara twisted Lady Strike as she pulled her out, lacerating the bowel and filling the air with a foul smell. The soldier's weak slash at her arm missed and he dropped his sword.

"Die in agony, bastard," she hissed, turning to face two more onrushing soldiers who skidded to a wary halt. The soldier collapsed, clasping both hands to the gaping wound and moaning in despair at the mortal wound.

Suzanne was slower on the uptake, but realised her danger soon enough to twist her staff up between the legs of the soldier detailed to catch her. He collapsed with a pained grunt, and her tap on his head put him to sleep.

Within a minute of giving the command to collect the women, the Havantine captain, on the verge of turning away, found he had three men down, two dying. He blinked in astonishment. Where earlier there were three girls tripping through the market, laughing innocently at everything, now they were transformed.

His remaining men were facing three angry girls, armed with a thin sword, a staff and a short spear. He prepared to shout an angry order, but lapsed into silence as Sara launched a blistering attack.

She came in the high line, her sword held high forcing their heads and eyes up. Suzanne and Rerata swung in to protect her sides. The first soldiers raised their swords to protect themselves, and Suzanne broke one's kneecap while Rerata cut through the calf of another. As they fell, the centre soldier made the mistake of checking what happened and paid for it with his throat sliced out, Sara's extra length proving lethal to the short swords made for fighting in a shield wall.

Sergeant Baptista reacted before his amazed officers, "Form a shield wall you motherless idiots! Quick now, Ferreira, take the corner file, Porto move your bloody ass!"

The soldiers fell into line, shaking at this unexpected resistance but drawing strength from the numbers and discipline of the shield wall, even though they did not carry shields. Sara's first exploratory attack was met by three swords in a defensive parry, while more swords came down to stop the spear and staff.

"Oh my," breathed the captain, "she can fence! Here, Sebastien, take my cloak. I shall run her through her paces." He stepped forward with a gleam in his eye, throwing his cloak at his lieutenant as he went. The captain enjoyed his reputation as the best swordsman in Havant's eastern empire and thrilled in combat.

"Sir," cried Sebastien in some alarm, "don't forget we must take her alive. She is to be tried and crucified in Hua by order of the Viceroy."

"Don't worry, lad, I'll just pink her a few times. Watch a master at work." He raised his voice to his soldiers, "Fall back, lads, I'll take this doxy."

His long sword personified the high arts of the Soledo blade makers, gleaming steel inlaid with silver and gold, jewels gleaming in the basket protecting his hand. He raised his left hand behind his head, bending his knees as he approached Sara looking like a crab scuttling across the beach.

The crowds had long departed as Sara considered his approach from hooded eyes. This resembled Galician court fencing and she wondered if he followed those forms. She moved into a similar stance, but graceful rather than crabbed and the captain purred with pleasure, an almost orgasmic moan coming from his lips which lasted until the blades touched for the first time. Sara flowed through a ritual court form, faster than he had anticipated.

The captain took a step back, with his men arrayed behind him.

"Doxy," he said in Belada, "you sure can fence. I shall enjoy this, then take you to the Viceroy. If you are good, and I enjoy the bout, I shall fuck you myself tonight, otherwise I shall give you to the men. So fight well, slut."

Sara's eyes narrowed. "You are the leader of these men, I presume. You gave the order to kill my man without warning."

"He was but a savage, a barbarian." The captain started a new form, moving into the complicated pattern with pleasure, hoping she would not know it. "There is no honour is being fair with such creatures, though you probably let him fuck you, depraved bitch that you are."

Sara was silent, not allowing the insults to reach her, and recognising the form. She wondered if he knew the wrinkle Takeo had taught her.

He didn't and she pinked his left arm.

The captain cursed and considered her.

Sara stepped back and took a breath. She decided to change her plan. Instead of simply killing him, she would humiliate him first. She slowed her blood, took a deep breath and went into the void, gliding forward in a new form only to switch within a minute to another, then again to a further form, the last being one unknown to the captain who resorted to the defence of the novice, an exhausting cross being drawn in front of his body with his sword, repeatedly, while Sara stood back and regarded him with no emotion.

"Haysus fucks," moaned Baptista behind Sebastien, "the captain's a dead man. We've no chance against this bitch. Keep her busy, Lieutenant, I might have an answer." He turned, leaving Sebastien gaping as the captain's defence slowed and he stood gasping for air in front of Sara.

Sara flowed into a strange, pirouetting stance, her blade resting on her left forearm, which she held in front of her face with just her eyes visible through her fringe of red hair. She high stepped sideways towards the mesmerised captain, who flinched as Lady Strike shot forward and pinked his right wrist. He tried to gather his wits and attack to meet empty air and agony in his side as she raked him. A sudden slash, and his beautiful sword rolled in the dust, his arm dripping blood as his hand flapped uselessly, the tendon cut through. The captain started to cry in pain and despair, oblivious of the dumbstruck eyes as Lady Strike sank through his stomach and scraped against his spine. He almost wrenched her from Sara's grasp as he fell screaming to the ground.

She raised her eyes from his writhing form to glare at the soldiers behind him. They were transfixed by the sight of their illustrious captain so soundly beaten and took a group pace backwards, followed by another. A moment before they turned and ran, their lowly second lieutenant, the toy soldier sneered at by men and superior officers alike, stepped through them to the front, raising his regulation sabre at the towering fury in front of them.

"Stand firm, lads," he cried, his voice quavering only slightly and with just a little crack at the end. "Don't let them turn us. Defend as you've been taught. The sergeant has the answer."

He stood determinedly in the front rank, a slight figure with lank black hair and the hunched forward figure of the slightly short sighted. His left arm grabbed the man beside him, turning him to face the enemy. "Guard my flank, soldier."

The line steadied, and considered the girls opposing them. Twenty five soldiers remained, banked four deep and six across, short in the last file. They ignored the sobs of their dying comrades and concentrated on the women in front of them.

In the centre was the girl, tall and hair dripping like heart blood framing a furious face, prominent beaked nose pointing straight at him like an eagle about to stoop. A silver sword, breath-taking in its simple beauty and savage purpose, grew from her arm with a life of its own. To one side a beautiful bare-chested heathen brown girl, long hair swirling around her, short spear in one hand, dripping with the blood of Havantine soldiers and the right clasping a long barbed lash which she snapped at the front rank. On the other side a buxom girl with long blonde hair, unusual in Havant, and her long skirts tucked up into her underwear, revealing long lissom legs balanced for action, a staff held loosely in the manner of one who knows how to use it.

It did not occur to any of the soldiers that the girls were beautiful - they exuded menace, death and blood. The girls inched forward.

The sword rose and dipped, the soldier second from left followed the tip and screamed as he failed to block the whip which slashed across his face, bursting his right eye and drenching his other in blood. The man behind him grabbed his shoulder and threw him backwards, leaping into the gap before the girls could take advantage. The wall stepped back.

"Steady boys."

Suzanne's long staff swung at heads, before dipping and shooting forward to crunch the toes of the right hand soldier. He grunted and swayed forward, just enough for the tip of Lady Strike to slice through his carotid under his ear. He slumped forward and Suzanne leapt forward, her staff taking the next soldier smack in the belly before swinging sideways into the ribs of the man in the front rank. He died as his reaction exposed him to Sara, while the other three swayed back from the lash cracking in their faces.

Sara struck at Sebastien and somehow he parried, goggling internally at the speed of her strike, wondering how he managed to get his sword down in time. He felt the warmth run down his leg, for a moment believing he was cut before realising his bladder had cut loose. The shame of his body letting him down concentrated his mind and he evaded the next three cuts, not knowing enough about swordcraft to recognise the form. The shield wall staggered back, and Sebastien wondered if the rear ranks were still there or had fled. Sergeant Baptista's voice rose over the pants of his men.

"Steady boys, we're here to save your hide."

The end man glanced back and desperately swung his sword to try and cut the lash wrapped round his ankle, but it jerked his leg forward and he howled as he hacked into his own calf. Sara and Suzanne pressed, the wall fell back and Rerata eased her spear head into the man's throat and up into his brain. She was getting fed up with all the men moaning and screaming as they died. In a moment the wall broke, and Sebastien turned to run, the lash catching him on his buttock as he went and he screamed.

Sergeant Baptista was by the entrance to the square, catching the men and re-forming them. He has three men with him and Sebastien's heart leapt as he recognised slingers. They were whirling the slings and he turned to find the heathen girl fixed on him as she slunk forward. He diverted the first thrust of the spear with an ungainly slash of his sword, which opened him up for the lash which flamed across his cheek and made him drop his sword as the barbed end flicked through the ball of this thumb. Helpless, he stood with his mouth open as her arm went back and tensed as she began the thrust into his guts.

The lead projectile hurled by the first slinger smashed into Rerata a finger's width behind her eye, breaking through the bone and caving in the entire side of her head. She dropped like a stone. The other two girls stopped in shock, staring uncomprehendingly at Rerata, whose prone body convulsed once, bending back on herself, before going still, the one remaining eye protruding horribly, her spear dropping at Sebastien's feet.

A second missile whisked past Sara's ear and a third cannoned into Suzanne's stomach, flinging her back and to the ground. She cried fat tears of agony as she circled herself around the roaring pain in her solar plexus, kicking as her abused muscles convulsed.

Sara turned back as the slingers scrabbled to get more missiles into their pouches and she grasped the weapon's method. She ran at the shield wall, rewarded by three soldiers breaking rank and running, the rest backing up, faces drawn. They hadn't realised two of the fearsome girls were out of action. The front rank braced itself for her arrival - this was more like it, enemies should run singly on to a wall to be easily slaughtered. The first slinger sent his missile towards Sara, who anticipated and turned left, seeking the flight of the stone through the void. Leaping over a stall, she ran up the rough bricks of the wall on the house to the side of the slingers, her body at right angles to the wall and only her speed giving her the momentum to make the move, before dropping down behind the slingers as the third dropped his missile and the second smacked the stall with his. Two fast slashes and two slingers were kicking on the floor, while the last ran to hide behind Sergeant Baptista. This worthy held a short spear pointed directly at Sara with one hand, while grasping a short sword ready for her to come round the side.

The shield wall was in disarray, falling about and trying to come round to face Sara in her new position. Sebastien leaped from amongst them to stand in front of Sara, between her and his sergeant, his sword pointed ineptly at her midriff. She batted it away and kept coming, Sebastien surprising her by stepping forward inside her sword arm and blocking her run. Lady Strike arced down into his thigh and he gasped in agony, grabbing her around the waist with his left arm. She retaliated by ramming her knee into his groin and he staggered backwards, flailing at her with his sword. She blocked the slash and dodged a spear thrust from the sergeant, only to sense a missile coming from the remaining slinger, right at her head. She twisted to one side, throwing herself forward at the same time to avoid another spear thrust. Sebastien jabbed despairingly forward in her general direction. She felt his sword slice through her dress and bisect her nipple as it plunged into her left breast, then the missile caromed into the side of her head and darkness fell.

Pat, Bai Ju and Hinatea sat in a triangle, deep in the void and reaching for each other. Bai Ju wanted to find out if they could feel each other grasp a weapon, but it wasn't happening. Legend said it would, in time, she claimed. All three felt a disturbance from the entrance to their area of the palace and rose as one, gliding fast to the front door where Mimi cried in the arms of a perplexed Grey Fox. The soldiers came around as they arrived, Pat recovering first.

"Mimi! Where is the Princess?"

"She's, she's dead! The Havantines came. They are all dead. I only escaped because I am Parsi, they did not think I was with her."

"What happened?"

"A soldier, he came from nowhere, and he put his sword in Maciu who was not expecting it. The Princess became very angry and she attacked them, so many of them. Maybe a hundred, maybe more. All Havantine, with big swords and axes. She killed them, the ones who killed Maciu. Then they make a row of men, and she, Suzanne and Rerata drive them back, killing so many of them." Mimi bawled loudly, unable to carry on. Lieutenant Mactravis, unable to contain his impatience, shook her.

"Carry on, damn you. Then what happened?"

"They had three wizards. The wizards twirled things in the air and Rerata fell dead, her head smashed in. Then they struck Suzanne dead. Sara attacked the wizards, she kill two when the soldier try to hit her with his sword. She started to kill him when the last wizard hit her and made her run into the sword. Right through the heart." Mimi screamed into the room.

"Where?" Pat asked.

"The, the market square by the southern gate," sobbed Mimi.

Pat ran out of the room, his scouts falling in behind him, grabbing their weapons as they went. Lieutenant Mactravis followed them also without needing to instruct his soldiers. Janis translated rapidly for those Spakka still poor in Harrhienian, keeping up with the soldiers.

They arrived in the square to find a few locals starting to strip the bodies of the dead, and chased them off. Maru claimed Maciu's body, fury in his eyes.

"My brother died to a coward's stroke," he said. "A blade is pushed into his stomach, here. I think this one," he kicked at the short sword under the body of the nearest soldier, turning him over and revealing the wound in the stomach recognisable as Sara's work. The soldier's eyes flashed open, blinking in pain. Maru grabbed him by the throat, pulling him painfully erect so his torn guts fell out.

"You kill my brother when he not looks," he grated in Belada. "Now I eat your liver while you alive and watching."

The soldier had thought his pain could not get worse, but screamed as he realised how wrong he was. Maru plunged his hand into the wound and lived up to his word, the soldier's eyes radiating horror as he died.

Hinatea cradled Rerata's head in her lap, her face flat and empty. "How she die? What this thing in her head?" She asked Pat as she pulled out a knife, and delicately levered out the lead missile, passing it to him while stoically levering up bone and pushing Rerata's mangled head back into place.

Pat considered the missile and showed it to Lieutenant Mactravis, who shook his head. Bai Ju leaned forward and picked up the bullet.

"I think I know this weapon. Not know name in Harrhein. Put this in cloth, whirl it round the head and you can throw it very fast and accurate. If long cloth, can kill people a hundred paces away."

"Never heard of it," said Mactravis. "We need to find out what happened. I will secure the perimeter, Pat, you and Grey Fox go over the scene and work out the battle." He turned to Janis, hovering behind him, telling him to secure the west and north side while sending Russell to the East, his face set in stone.

The Spakka made short work of dispersing the crowds, inching into the square. Their departure revealed more bodies by the gate, including two near the wall. Sung Bai Ju went to these and picked up a sling.

"Here is the weapon," she said. "Sara managed to kill two of them, as Mimi said."

Pat glanced at her briefly, before returning to his discussion with Grey Fox. They spoke in Elvish, to Little's annoyance as he tried to help. They put together the battle with painstaking care from the marks in the ground and the bodies before reporting to Lieutenant Mactravis, as Captain Larroche arrived, Brian at his back, concern written large on their faces. They had arrived from the coast by cart that morning.

"Sir, we have worked it out," began Pat, with Grey Fox nodding beside him. "This one Maru is dismembering struck and killed Maciu before he knew what was happening. Sara cut him and left him to die a slow death with a punctured stomach."

They looked over to where Maru and Wiwik continued their farewell to Maciu, both men daubed in the blood of the Havantine with dust running out of their hair. They washed Maciu's feet in the blood and Pat continued.

"We think there were nearly thirty men in the ambush, and the girls responded by killing nine of them. Most of the bodies are here, but the one killed in the middle of the square is gone. We think he was the leader and Sara killed him in single combat. He died badly, again with a stomach wound. She did so deliberately. We are convinced he is dead because there is so much blood on the ground, even though no body. We think they took his body away with them, the only one of theirs they took. Suzanne took a sling missile here. You can still see the scratches in the dust where her feet scuffed as she kicked, although the area is walked over. Her body is gone, we don't know where she was struck, but if she kicked so much the strike was not the head like Rerata. They have her body, so she may be alive."

"And the Princess, man, what about her?"

"She bled. She did not kick. She fell there and her body is gone. There is quite a lot of blood, we cannot tell if it is a mortal blow or not. The area where she fell has many other footprints over it since she fell. I think she was struck by a sling, Grey Fox is not sure."

"Is she dead?"

"I think so. Mimi says she is, and if she is not, they will mistreat her for killing so many men. The wound she has taken will kill her in this climate if she survives."

"What have they done with her and Suzanne?"

"They will take her body to Hua and crucify it as an example to others, the penalty for those who come to their waters." Sung Bai Ju spoke.

"I won't let it happen," said Lieutenant Mactravis, tightly. The others, except for the Captain, nodded. Pat moved away from the group, his report done, and spoke gently to Maru, who nodded. All three stood beside Maciu, while the Pahippian girls brought Rerata's body and laid it beside him. For a moment there was quiet in the square, as the Scouts put their hands forward above the bodies and touched fists. The Scouts moved off towards the south gate, while Sung Bai Ju turned towards the palace.

Pat turned to the Captain. "Please take our comrades to the ship and consign them to the sea when you are away from land. The great shark god will take them home."

"Where do you think you are going?" Captain Larroche asked, his voice breaking.

Pat showed his surprise. "We get horses and our supplies, then we follow them and soon catch up. We will recover the bodies. "

"You know I cannot wait for your return?" The Captain didn't waste his breath denying their purpose.

"We know. We will see you on your return." Sung Bai Ju did not turn her head as they left at a fast, loping run.

Boersma called out to Janis, in Spakka, and on his response all the Spakka turned and followed Pat. Janis saluted the Captain.

"Hold on there," said Captain Larroche, "you can't follow them."

"We follow the Princess, not you," snarled Stiphleek and they were gone.

Sergeant Russell left the East entrance and returned, speaking to Lieutenant Mactravis.

"By your leave, sir, I shall prepare our stores and the horses. Thirty minutes, I will take three men."

He turned without waiting for a reply, touched Little, Graves and Grey Fox and left at a run.

"Husk," said Lieutenant Mactravis, "please prepare two biers and bring our comrades to the palace." Husk nodded and picked up discarded spears, unwanted by the populace in their looting.

"Captain," continued Mactravis, "the Rajah will mount us and we may be back in less than a week, but I would advise you to sail straight away. Without doubt the Havant will have ships waiting for your departure and the longer you wait the more danger you will be in. We will manage."

"What about my protection from pirates?"

"With your skill at sailing, we are superfluous. She is our Fighting Princess. I cannot leave her body to be defiled by foreigners and if I tried my men would not follow me." He held out his hand. "Good luck, Captain. It has been a pleasure."

Epilogue

The small skiff pushed out from the headland, up went the sail and went running down the wind in the dusk. The girl at the tiller prayed no watchers could see her; with the driving rain they should seek shelter.

Her wait on the headland, camped out, already stretched to forty five days. Her stores of food might last her another three days, her body thin and her face bleak from the meagre rations. Finally the ship she awaited appeared on the horizon and she put to sea on intercept.

As she closed on the huge ship, she realised she had been seen and waved madly. A man come to join the sailor looking at her, holding a crossbow. She waved again, coming in fast towards the ship and started to pull the sail down awkwardly - she possessed little knowledge on how to sail a boat.

A man shouted at her from on board, gesticulating with abrupt hand movements and she realised with horror the ship would run down her small skiff. She dived into the sea.

Coming up, she turned and looked with despair at the bulk of the ship gliding past her, the bows driving over her skiff and crunching it up, seeing all her hopes and dreams go with it. A shout made her look up. A dark face looking down at her.

"Grab this quick, before you get sucked under!"

She didn't understand but the rope he threw landed in front of her and she pounced, holding tight as the sea started to pull her. Her arms nearly went out of their sockets as she took the strain and found herself rushing along the surface of the water, spluttering as waves hit her face. She ducked her head, holding her breath, and struggled to get her foot up and into the loop at the end of the rope.

The rope started to become more perpendicular, before pulling her out of the water and to thud painfully against the side of the ship, almost making her lose her grasp on the rope.

She shot up the side of the ship, where strong hands grabbed her and pulled her aboard. She gasped her thanks, staring open mouthed as she realised the dark face belonged to a huge, dark man. Except for his teeth, which shone out of his smile.

Another man came up, clearly an officer.

"Who the hell are you and what do you think you are playing at?" he asked with heat. "Don't you realise these ships can't stop like your little skiff? You are lucky to be alive!"

"No choice," she gasped, "please, I must speak to the Captain."

"You certainly will. Bring her along, Wiru."

Wiru helped her up the ladder to the poop deck where she found herself in front of a tall man, greying at the temples.

"Yes, I am Captain Larroche," he looked at her levelly from his weather-beaten face. "I trust there is a good reason for forcing yourself aboard."

"Sir, I am here to give warning to one of your crew who may be in danger. A girl who joined you before you sailed, dark hair, called Sara. A mercenary."

"There is nobody aboard by that name."

Her shoulders slumped. "Did you leave her somewhere? Too early to return, perhaps?"

"I think you should explain yourself further, what sort of message is so important to get across."

She pulled herself together and thought. Maybe the Princess had revealed herself, and the Captain protected her.

"The situation in the country changed radically in the time since your departure, sir. It is dangerous for her here." Did a flash gleam in his eyes? No, he was too much a trader.

"In what way did the country change?" His voice stayed level and gave nothing away.

"We have no king," she said, simply.

"Oh, hell," said the Captain and the officer who brought her to the cabin swore behind her.

"What happened? He was my friend," this last said softly.

"Assassinated. Crossbow bolt from nowhere. Parliament cannot find the perpetrator. Indeed the King may have survived, but Count Rotherstone insisted on using his own doctor."

The Captain passed his hand over his face. "Don't tell me, Count Rotherstone is in charge. How has the country reacted?"

"The people are not happy. But he is not in charge. Parliament took over and the country is being run by a minister. The army to the north is undecided and not making patrols while arguing in the barracks. In Harrhein itself Count Rotherstone assumed control, but Parliament revealed its own army, called the New Model Army, supposed to be very advanced. No nobles amongst the officers. They ignored him and rule. Fearaigh seceded. They gathered around a general called Connor who swears allegiance to the Starrs."

"Ha! Good man, Connor. What about Rikklaw's Port? And the Priesthood?"

"Rikklaw's Port is under martial law. There is a new Archbishop, Lord Auterns ate something that disagreed with him. The new one is not recognised by the bishops, imposed on them by Parliament, a puritan. All ships coming in are being searched, and the crew interviewed."

"Looking for the Princess," breathed the Captain.

"I noticed you didn't ask about her," the girl smiled for the first time, and the Captain frowned. She breathed in deeply. "What will you do now?"

The Captain glanced at the other officer. "We can't go to Rikklaw's Port. We'll head for Westport and see if we can speak to Connor. Feel the situation from there." He turned back to the girl and frowned. "So who are you, girl? You must know my loyalty to the Starrs or you wouldn't speak this way."

"My name is Luce. I am the Princess' spy. I need to speak to her."

"Thought as much. Well, I spoke the truth, she is not on board. She is also dead. Killed by a Havantine ambush. The country is in a bad way."

--oo0oo--

Harrhein

More information on Harrhein can be found at www.harrhein.com and at https://www.facebook.com/harrhein

There are short stories available that tell the early life of some of the heroes of In Search of Spice.

Thief in the Night has an insight into Sergeant Russell
Feeding the Dragon tells of Bai Ju as a little girl.
Wagon Master mentions the Princess briefly.

The Making of Suzanne is due for publication in 2015.

More information on these stories is available on the websites where you can also sign up for advance information.

About the Author

Rex is English, but was born in Java, Indonesia and has spent many years in the Far East. He speaks Indonesian and Malay, sadly he has forgotten his Javanese, Dutch, Thai, Hokkien and Teow Chu.

He has had an interesting life - as a youngster worked his passage on a container ship to Australia where he worked as a cowboy, gold-miner, door-to-door salesman and fruit-picker, before switching from Zoology to the Army to study at Sandhurst.

He saw active service in Northern Ireland and was Logistics Officer for Operation Drake in Indonesia. A country manager for an international tobacco trader at 25, he spent two years during the Cold War with MI6 before returning to the UK where he and his wife raised his two sons while working in marketing and publishing, with forays into NLP and personal development. Now they are adult, he and his wife have moved back to the Far East where he travels, writes and researches.

He has always had a passion for writing and this was rekindled by telling stories he made up on the spot to his sons.

His hobbies are angling, reptiles, orchids, reading and hockey, though he fears that in his late 50's he is now a little old to keep playing the latter.

His wide experience and knowledge are interwoven into the tapestry of his writing.

If you have any questions for Rex, please feel free to use his Facebook page.

Lightning Source UK Ltd.
Milton Keynes UK
UKOW06f1359060715

254681UK00018B/533/P